MILLENNIAL GLORY I

HIDDEN LIGHT

A novel about the earth's last days.

WENDIE L. EDWARDS

Cover and book design

Ronn Raymond

Published by Seventh Seal Publishing, Inc.

Cedar Hills, Utah

Library of Congress Catalog Card Number: 2001118288

ISBN-10: 0-9712228-5-1
ISBN-13: 978-0-9712228-5-4

First Printing 2001
Second Printing 2007

Printed in the United States of America

Millennial Glory

Wars of Light,
Millennial Glory II

Bo is the father of the Rogers family. He learns that he and his eldest son, 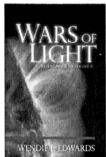 Braun, share a gift of dreams and are able to see mysterious things that often tell of the future. Through his dreams he realizes two of his children will soon fall prey to the mysterious Antichrist that is growing in power. Bo is painfully admonished by the Spirit not to interfere but to allow his children to face the evil man alone in fulfillment of agreements they made before their life on earth. How can he do this? Through his trials he learns that an unseen war comprising all of God's children, both good and evil, continues on the world from when it began in heaven. Bo comes to understand that there are greater powers than his own in charge of his life. He is expected to exercise true faith in God's power and to lean not unto his own understanding. Can he be brave enough to just sit back and trust in Heavenly Father's promises to save his children? It's a request almost too hard to bear.

Apocalypse, the Unveiling,
Millennial Glory III

Chaos hits Utah as a large earthquake rips the land apart. The Rogers family  must escape its fury. It's their struggle to see God's wisdom in the trial of the Saints. Dane Rogers lies in a coma induced by the deadly bacteria unleashed in his hand by the chip. In his deep sleep he is introduced to the Spirit World and the reality of God's existence is unveiled. In the world of light he learns of the eternal nature of God, the importance of the plan of salvation, and preparations of the world by both the living and the dead for the second coming of Christ. He also learns that this life is only a moment in time but it is in that moment that we define ourselves and our futures. Through the Rogers family's difficulties they become stronger, realizing their true blessings on earth lie in each other.

The Ascension,
Millennial Glory IV

Braun, the eldest son of the Rogers family, is directed by the Spirit to fulfill an internship as an aide to the Secretary General of the United Nations. Through his dreams and visions of beasts and monsters he is able to act as Daniel of old, to Secretary Klump to warn him of things to come. Together they uncover an ancient secret design as it unfolds. The man who is one of the richest on the earth plots to take control of the world through manipulating its leaders. Braun feels a great responsibility to stop his ascension to total and complete power, but what can he, a lowly aide do? Conrad, the second oldest in the Rogers family, is on a mission in Israel. At first, he has limited success among the Jews, but as time moves on, the Spirit of truth rests heavily upon him. He's able to be instrumental in the conversion of a group of Rabbis which bring Jews to the church in droves as they begin to believe in Christ.

Hanging by a Thread,
Millennial Glory V

Braun Rogers travels to America and takes on a position at the White House in an effort to warn the President of the danger that awaits the nation. He finds the country in a political disarray as the constitution hangs by a thread. Through his visions, he sees the outcome of the present chaos as it spirals toward destruction. The country must return to the values that inspired its beginnings if it hopes to be protected from the secret combinations that are designing its downfall. Brea Rogers, the eldest sister of the family is trapped in an unholy web of deceit as she unravels the truth about Matt's family. The facts are too horrible to believe and too deadly to ignore. She must make some difficult decisions to protect her unborn children. Just what will that do to her love for Matt and the marriage they share? Elder Conrad Rogers becomes a hostage to the country of Israel but his burden is made light through participating in prophesy. The long awaited Jewish temple rises. The Jews know their Messiah is coming. Do you?

It is the end of days and all is in commotion!

ACKNOWLEDGEMENTS

It is with great indebtedness that I thank Dr. Terie Wiederhold, who was unfailing in her support, expert advice and direction. She has been an inspiration and a role model to me for over ten years. I also would like to thank Dr. Paul Wiederhold, Kathryn Packer, Rosanna Hunter, and Kate Maryon for their amazing editing talents.

What would the world be without family and their support? I have eternal love and thankfulness for the mother that gave me life, Bonnie Thomas. You always believed in me. Thank you, Dad, for giving me your talent. Thank you Ted and Julie Edwards, Darren Carter and Melynda Williams, for unwavering smiles and continual "thumbs up".

I would be amiss in not acknowledging my wonderful husband's genius, in whose eye I was able to catch the vision of a miracle. This book is proof that in the efforts of a team, simple people can work amazing wonders.

DEDICATION

This series is based on a real family. It was written originally to be a gift to my children, to help them find their place in the future and to personalize inspired direction and scripture in their lives. Literary license was used to extrapolate their places in this series' fictional future based on personality traits, birth order, and both spiritual and physical talents. To them it is dedicated.

AN AUTHOR'S NOTE TO YOU

Dear Reader:

This book and all the books that follow this one in this series are an exercise in futuristic extrapolation. Scriptures, statements of the prophets, combined with modern scientific advancements, and political world events, are woven together to project a potential outcome in our world as we come closer to the Second Coming of Christ.

Although all the references cited are explored as accurately as possible, this work is fictional. Research references were added to this book in an effort to help the reader in their own research. In the storyline development it was necessary to project possible outcomes and they are to be regarded as theoretical.

Internet sources were identified whenever possible to allow the reader easy access to research material. All the scriptures and most of the quotes by General Authorities and Prophets found in the text can also be found on The Church of Jesus Christ of Latter-day Saints official Web site at www.lds.org by doing a keyword search.

It is acknowledged that Internet sites are not enduring and may change without any notice. However, the sites that were chosen are reliable sources and are expected to exist well into the future. If the site is not available during a search, other similar information can be retrieved on other sites through a search of the chosen topic. The Web site for this book, and others that follow it, can be found at www.millennialglory.com. This site can also be accessed for any communication with the author and publisher.

In respect to this book, it is an introduction. The exciting adventure that lies ahead of you will roll out like a scroll in front of your mind's eye as you travel through the other books in this series. It is my invitation to you to explore all of them.

Now, sit back, fluff your pillow and allow your thoughts to be carried away into realms foretold by ancient prophets and soon to be experienced by us, the valiant latter-day warriors of both the spirit and the mortal world.

Sincerely,

Wendie L. Edwards

CHARACTERS

ROGERS FAMILY

Bo Andrew Rogers	45	Father
Corrynne Rochelle Rogers	42	Mother
Braun Joseph Rogers	21	First Son
Conrad Ryan Rogers	20	Second Son
Brea Nicole Rogers	19	First Daughter
Dane Russell Rogers	17	Third Son
Carea Lorrell Rogers	16	Second Daughter
Jax William Rogers	11	Fourth Son
Ry Benjamin Rogers	9	Fifth Son
Rocwell Joshua Rogers	7	Sixth Son
Striynna Chandelle Rogers	7 mo.	Third Daughter and First Twin
Strykker Adam Rogers	7 mo.	Seventh Son and Second Twin

TABLE OF CONTENTS

CHAPTER ONE—PROLOGUE

TIMELESS WITNESS

*"Be not thou therefore ashamed of the testimony of our Lord,
nor of me his prisoner: but be thou partaker of the afflictions of the
gospel according to the power of God" (2 Timothy 1:8).*

95 AD
City of Ephesus

John

"Stop!" yelled the large centurion. His voice boomed across the gathering people.

John the Beloved, a Son of Thunder, the brother of James, a son of Zebedee, and soon, the Revelator, stood straight and as tall as his moderate height could manage. Despite his worn and tattered robes, thinning sandals and dust-laden skin, he looked vibrant, young and full of life. His countenance glowed as he taught the people of Ephesus, a city boasted to be one of the greatest cities of the Roman world.

John turned to look at the soldier that commanded him. "Stop the word of God? It is something that has a life of its own and will not stop. He that is of God heareth God's words: ye therefore hear them not, because ye are not of God."[1]

The centurion pushed forward through the crowd to John, who was standing a few steps above the soldier. Even with this extra advantage John was still smaller. The sword- and javelin-armed fighter spoke disrespectfully into John's face. "It is unlawful to preach anything but the divinity of Domitian!"[2]

John stood boldly and without fear upon the very steps of a shrine dedicated to Domitian. It was not the ideal spot to be teaching of Christ, near a pagan god's figure, but in this city there were so many self-figures erected by the rogue Emperor of Rome, there seemed no escape.

John rebutted, "We are children of the God of heaven. We were made in his image. Any other god but the creator of heaven and earth, is of the devil. He who has ears to hear, let him hear."[3]

The soldier looked John up and down, seeming to take note of his humble but lighted appearance. Ignoring John's statements he asked, "Don't you know that preaching Christianity in public could cost you your life? Christians have been covered in pitch and lit on fire for Nero's parties[4] for less offense. Your preaching here against the 'Lord and God' of Rome is treasonous."

"Christians do not fear death," John replied calmly.

"How about a run in the arena with a starved tiger?"

"It mattereth not to me." John's expression communicated the truth of his words.

The soldier looked at John with a steely unwavering stare. Suddenly he asked loudly, "Who are you?"

Without blinking John answered, "I am called many things, but most know me as John."

The centurion's lips parted slightly as he seemed to remember something. He took a breath and exhaled slowly as he considered his thoughts. Finally he asked, "Are you one of the original twelve apostles to that man called Christ?"

A soft reflectiveness appeared in John's features that wasn't there before. "Yes, I was and I *am* his beloved disciple."

The soldier frowned, "How could this be…for that would make you nearly eighty-five years in age." The soldier again looked down to John's sandals and up to his face. "You do not appear to be older than thirty. How old are you?"

John did not answer but lifted his eyebrows as if to consider an appropriate response.

Someone in the crowd yelled out, "He has no age."

Another shrill voice answered, "He has been touched by the hand of God. He cannot be harmed by time or man."

The soldier turned to the group, unsheathed his sword and pointed it at them, "I think this is a hoax, and you are fools. I'm going to take this man. You Christians remember this example and keep your tongues."

John continued to remain silent.

The soldier then put his sword to John's neck and unnecessarily jabbed the point into the skin. When he took it away there was not even a slight mark to tell of it. The soldier then smiled for the first time and said, "Move, Christian!" The centurion then stepped behind John and thrust the point of the sword into the small of his back.

John's weight moved forward with the sudden force. He began to walk without resistance as the soldier took him into custody.

Graven images

The chariot rumbled to a stop in front of the large stone pillars that marked the opening in the great walls that surrounded Domitian's palace.

"Get out, Christian," commanded the soldier loudly.

Slowly John rose from his seated position on the floor of the chariot, shifting the heavy chains that the soldier had securely shackled around his hands and feet. As he attempted to step down from the chariot, the centurion gave him a firm shove that sent him sprawling onto the dusty ground.

The Roman soldier vaulted the space between the chariot and John, landing inches from his legs. With clenched teeth the centurion growled, "Get up!"

John silently got to his feet and hobbled in the direction of the palace with the soldier close behind him. They approached two stone-faced guards, clad in full armor, who blocked the entrance with their long heavy spears crossed over the entry.

The soldier behind John spoke in a loud voice, which bounced off the structures within the gates, causing a quick echo, "I am Claudius, soldier of the royal Roman army. I am here to report to the Lord and God. He will be interested in what I found in Ephesus."

The guard made no attempt to look at the soldier, nor did his face flinch from the frozen state it held.

"I have the password for entry," the centurion continued as he came from behind John to whisper the secret code. Codes were important to ensure the safety of Domitian, who had internal as well as external threats to his life within his dominion.

With a quick contraction, the guard flexed his arm, which was followed by the second guard doing likewise. With their spears erect, a path was made allowing a clear access. The large soldier stepped behind the chain-bound apostle, and they both entered through the gate. Again at the palace doors the password was given to another set of guards before they were allowed to cross the threshold into the massive stone edifice.

In the palace the centurion walked solidly on the rock floor through the great domed rooms, while John took rapid steps in an attempt to stay ahead of the soldier's sharp sword pointed unyieldingly at his back. The soldier would forcefully nudge John if his pace slowed.

At the entrance to the large council room, there was a small elderly man clad in a simple white robe over a light-green floor-length toga, rushing from the Emperor's presence. Nervously he looked at the huge guard, his eyes bulging and wet; he turned and pulled the mammoth, creaking wooden doors closed with great effort. "The emperor is not in good spirits today," he warned speaking over his shoulder. "Two more senators have been accused of treason. Trials are to commence forthwith." He turned and blocked the entrance with his little body.

The guard was unimpressed with the old man's words and said, "I am on an errand for the Lord and God. The person I am bringing to him demands consideration. Please announce me."

The little man gasped. "I am only the sculptor. It is not my duty to announce you. Anyway, it would be better if you come back later." The aged sculptor increased the intensity of his eye contact by leaning forward slightly towards the looming guard.

"You will announce me now. I do not have time to wait for another," the soldier demanded gruffly as he stood to his full height over the small sculptor.

The small man seemed to cower. Frowning, he turned, and with shaking hands he smoothed the white tufts of hair that stuck out on both sides of his head. He stood staring at the mammoth wood doors once again as if to gain courage, then with a sigh he placed both of his hands on the doors and threw his slight body weight against them. The doors complained loudly once more as the hinges grated.

"Who dares to interrupt me yet again?" yelled an angry voice from within.

The sculptor's body jolted and shook at the sound of the angry words. As if kicked from behind by a mule, he skidded into the huge room and fell immediately on his knees. "Please, L-Lord and God, g-g-great being over life and d-d-death. A soldier is here to see you. He says that his m-matter is important to you."

There was silence. Then the sound of something heavy crashed against the floor. The pieces could be heard scuttling across the room.

"Important? I'll tell you what is important! **Loyalty!** *The senators will pay! I will smash their secret plans, just like these inadequate figures that slander my image!"* There was another crash, and then the Emperor's volume increased even more. *"Don't they see that I watch? Don't they understand that I am god? I will not be removed!* **No one can kill a god!"**

"No, Lord. You are great and mighty. You make all other gods bow down before you…."

"Get out before I smash you to pieces, too!" yelled the Emperor. *"I have no interest in what you have to say!"*

"Yes, lord and master!"

"It's **Lord** *and* **God***! Pay attention, you fool, or you will be dog meat by the end of the day!"*

The little man rushed out of the room with frantic speed and turned the corner and ran down the other hallway, leaving John and the soldier standing in the open doorway.

The two men stepped across the threshold of the room and stood motionless at the entryway. Domitian continued to throw clay figures down on the floor, smashing them to pieces. It was obvious that he had been doing this for some time by the pile of broken clay that lay scattered in a chaotic mess starting at the Emperor's feet.

Domitian continued his conversation to some unknown audience. "Yes, loyalty! A perception that these images fail to inspire! That old sculptor made me look weak! The people need strength! How can anyone worship a weak god?" The angry ruler kicked a half-intact head of himself across the floor and watched it shatter against the far wall. "*I have an empire full of deceivers and murderers!*"

Hearing this, the soldier firmly spoke out, causing the Emperor to look up suddenly as if startled. "I have one that is real. I have the last Christian apostle, whom I arrested preaching today."

The Emperor looked at John, who did not return his gaze. Domitian shook his head. "I am tired of Christians. They are unpatriotic troublemakers. They think that it is noble to die rather than to follow laws." The Emperor flicked his hand and callously said, "Put him in the dungeon. I will not fulfill his death wish."

The soldier stepped forward and said, "Lord and God, this Christian is different from the rest. The people at Ephesus claim he is the one who cannot die. He is John, Christ's favorite apostle. Legend is that he will live forever."

The Emperor, losing interest, began looking about the floor for large pieces of pottery to crush with his heel as he said, "There is no such thing. All Christians claim eternal life, but I have killed many Christians and their breath leaves their bodies easily."

The soldier realized that the Emperor was not going to listen to words, so he took John into the middle of the room and walked twenty paces away from him. Placing his sword in its sheath, he took his javelin, positioned it in his right hand, turned and then with one quick thrust he threw the javelin across the room into the abdomen of the apostle. With the momentum of the object John's body was lifted off the floor and landed in a pile of pottery at Domitian's feet.

Shocked, the Emperor looked down at the pierced man and then back up at the soldier. "What are you doing in my chamber? *I said to lock him up, **not** kill him! I do not desire dead men in my palace! Remove him at once!*" The Emperor Domitian turned swiftly and moved to leave.

"Forgive me, Lord and God." The soldier immediately knelt on one knee and bowed his head. "The man is not dead."

Domitian whipped back around and yelled, "*What? **He is dead!** You ran him through with your javelin. Do you **dare** to contradict me?*"

The soldier rose and walked over to the figure on the floor and put his left foot on John's thigh and pulled hard on the javelin. It came out cleanly without blood. John attempted to sit up but couldn't, due to the bindings around his hands. The centurion stepped behind him and lifted him to his feet by the back of his robe.

The wide-eyed Emperor walked around the slight figure of John, as he stood motionless with his head bowed. He inspected John's robe, in which he found a hole in both the front and correspondingly in the back. He lifted the garment to inspect the abdomen and did not find a scratch, let alone a mortal gash. Then he flipped down the robe and inspected the front of the cloth. In the fabric were multiple unraveling rips telling of other deadly encounters.[5]

The Emperor, still studying John said, "I see that you are a hunted man by the holes in your robe. Christians die young under Roman rule, except for you. ...Do you have anything to say for yourself?"

"I testify of Christ," John said unflinchingly, looking straight into Domitian's eyes. "He is the truth, the way and the life. No man cometh unto the Father but by him."[6]

The Emperor stepped back a few paces, as if John had other secret powers that he might strike him with. "Take him away. He obviously has not seen the error of his ways. By his own actions he has made himself our interest. It might be amusing to see how immortal he really is." Domitian smiled thoughtfully.

The soldier smiled back and bowed his head. "Yes, I knew my Lord and God would enjoy this challenge."

The Emperor flicked his hand toward the corridors leading to the dungeons. The soldier responded and turned John around and pushed him forcefully causing John to scramble to keep his balance as the chains on his ankles pulled. Both Domitian and the soldier laughed low, harsh laughs. John submitted and hobbled out of the great room, prodded repeatedly in the back by the soldier.

The Emperor, once left alone, looked around at the many shattered images. Suddenly the sight was unnerving. A shiver coursed his body. He quickly left the room.

ϚϚϚϚϚϚ

It was on the tiny rocky volcanic island called Patmos,[7] spanning only five by ten miles, where John was eventually taken for banishment. It was only after the Emperor had attempted to kill John with boiling oil,[8] starvation and other deadly mechanisms that he realized that words from John could not be stopped. The banishment to the punitive colony was the only solution he could think of to contain John, at least for a while. Christianity was not to be a religious option to Domitian's people. They were to worship only him. He was a selfish, cruel and evil god.

Vision

It was the Sabbath. The sparkling blue waters of the Aegean Sea met the eyes of John, the apostle, as he meditated deeply. He sometimes considered the trials and the blessings that attended a translated body. It was true that although he was a political target, he did not feel pain, neither could he be wounded. Food and drink were not necessary for his body to exist and he never became ill. Physical discomforts were nonexistent for John; however he did suffer.

John often felt overwhelming sadness for mankind and the sins of the world.[9] Any time he was arrested and had to stop preaching, his pain increased. It was difficult to allow the wicked precepts of man to infiltrate the Church when he was in prison. He constantly mourned as the darkness of the apostasy crept over the earth and covered the glorious light that had touched its face for a short time. Even though he knew that the apostasy would eventually fill the earth for more than a millennium, his pain caused him to continually search out the Lord for solace.

The Sabbath day was one such time. Deep in thought he sat on the rock with a soft breeze blowing through his hair and causing the hem of his thin gray prison robe to flap gently. His left knee was drawn up onto the rock so that he could rest his chin on it, his left arm lightly holding it in place. His right leg rested on the next ridge just below his perch on the rock. He traced the pocked black texture with his finger as he searched for the Lord silently. He needed communication. He needed to know the reasons behind man's existence.

Suddenly John heard a great deep voice that shook the very fibers of his body.[10] *"I am Alpha and Omega, the first and the last: and, what thou seest, write in a book."* The voice was loud like a trumpet. *"Send it to the seven churches which are in Asia...."*[11] John turned to see the author of the voice and witnessed Christ standing bright like the sun, robed in white with a gold breastplate upon his chest. His eyes were bright like fire and his hair as white as snow. John immediately fell at his Savior's feet as if he were dead.

Christ reached out and touched John, reviving him, and continued, *"I am he that liveth and was dead; and, behold, I am alive forevermore. Write the things which thou hast seen, and the things which are, and the things which shall be hereafter."*[12]

...And John did write a mighty book, a testimony that made the wicked quake and the righteous wonder. He gave the book of Revelation to all the inhabitants of the earth in the past, present, and future. Its role was to be a comfort to the righteous and a warning to the wicked.

To those who have ears to hear and eyes to see, *all* shall come to pass....

It is the end of days and the world is in commotion![13]

Notes to "Timeless Witness"

John

[1] John 8:47.

[2] Domitian, Emperor of Rome, 81-96 A.D., sought to be an absolute ruler through "Emperor worship." He offended the Senate and the rest of the Roman upper class by demanding that he be referred to as "Lord and God" and by erecting multiple statues of himself. There were

many plots against his life by the Senate, thus there were treason trials held under his reign that took the life of numerous Senators. Domitian surrounded himself with guards to protect himself from assassinations. Despite this, he was murdered in his bath (see "The Throne of the Caesars: Domitian," San Jose State University: College of Education, available online: http://myron.sjsu.edu/romeweb/empcont/e061.htm).

[3] "He who has ears to hear, let him hear." This phrase is said 12 times in the New Testament, encouraging those listening to search for the true meanings of the message being delivered. Often there were multiple meanings to the messages that came before the phrase.

[4] Nero, an Emperor of Rome, was famous for his treatment of the Christians. He sent many to their deaths by cruel means (see "Tacitus: Nero's Persecution of Christians," *Washington State University Department of English*, available online: http://www.wsu.edu:8080/~wldciv/world_civ_reader/world_civ_reader_1/tacitus.html).

Graven Images

[5] The spear assault is a theoretical happening used to demonstrate some of the characteristics of a translated being. A translated body cannot be hurt or suffer physical pain. It does not have the seeds of death, thus cannot die; however all translated beings will die and be changed in a twinkling of an eye from translated to immortal at Christ's coming. A translated person does have pains of the heart and can interact with mortals as normally as any man, as seen in the administrations of the three Nephites and John the Beloved (see 3 Nephi 28).

[6] See John 14:6.

[7] John was banished to Patmos by Domitian for testifying of Christ (search the Internet for John the Beloved, or see the Bible dictionary). Patmos was the place that John received the glorious vision that became the book of Revelation. See Revelation, Chapter 1, for similarities in this section.

[8] Tertullian, a 2nd Century North African theologian, who was born around 155 and died after 220, reports that John was plunged into boiling hot oil and escaped unscathed (see Rev. Henry Chadwick, "John the Apostle, Saint," *Encyclopedia Britannica,* available online: http://www.britannica.com/search?query=john+the+beloved).

Vision

[9] See 3 Nephi 28:9.

[10] This account of Christ appearing to John on the island of Patmos is taken directly from Revelation Chapter 1.

[11] Revelation 1:11.

[12] Revelation 1:18-19.

[13] See D&C 45:26 or Bible Topical guide, "World, End of," 589-590.

CHAPTER TWO

THE MARK

"And the first went, and poured out his vial upon the earth; and there fell a noisome and grievous sore upon the men which had the mark of the beast, and upon them which worshipped his image" (Revelation 16:2).

Sometime in the 21st century
Saturday
September 16th
1:46 a.m.
Provo, Utah

Code Blue

"Code blue, room 527. Code blue, room 527. Code blue, room 527," came the steely voice over the intercom. The code words for cardiopulmonary arrest[1] caused Corrynne to drop her hand-held medical digital display in her effort to answer the desperate call. As the charge nurse in the ICU, she was head of the code team. They would answer any arrests that night, anywhere in the hospital.

Corrynne's chair went rolling across the nurses' station to slam against the narcotic drawers as she instantly left it. She catapulted into the hall along with two or three others that were on the team that night and headed down to the elevators leading to the fifth floor.

Adrenaline hit Corrynne's blood stream and she began to sense the familiar, painful, electrifying feelings of fear, excitement, and the odd numbness that flowed over her like a warm wave of water. With every step she could hear her own breath inhaling and exhaling in cadence with her footsteps as she and the code team ran at full speed toward the stranger who depended on them for a second chance at living. As she ran, time seemed to slow down, and moments became eternities. A myriad of memories played in her mind. She reviewed possible scenarios and strategies aimed at delaying death and prolonging life.

Corrynne and the team rounded the corner near the elevator. Pressing her thumb to an emergency pad on one of the button columns identified her and her authority with lightning speed. Instantaneously, the nearest elevator to the ICU was called. Luckily, one had been sitting on her floor and the mirror-like reflective doors opened to one of the five available. The team quickly stepped in.

"Fifth floor—code blue override!" came her breathy command. The elevator responded to her verbal orders and the doors closed with a loud escape of air from somewhere behind the walls. The elevator rose rapidly, quicker than it would have without the code blue command. The rise through the tower floors made Corrynne feel heavy and then suddenly light as the elevator came to an abrupt stop.

The doors opened without the normal hesitation and an automated female voice intoned, "Fifth floor—code blue override complete." The team exited the elevator and headed down the corridor toward the crowd of medical personnel that filled the hall.

Despite Corrynne's forty-two years and five foot one inch frame, she was quick and powerful. She and a respiratory therapist were the first to meet the group of medical personnel outside room 527. "Code team! Please make room! Back up everybody! Everyone step out except for those directly involved with the code team!" Magically a path was made, and Corrynne and her team slid through the pack of people.

Corrynne instinctively surveyed the situation. She noted the crash cart by the bedside and that a male nurse was performing chest compressions. Oxygen was being administered by a bag and mask by another floor nurse. From the foot of the bed she couldn't see the patient amidst the thrown sheets and people, so she strode to the bed to assess the patient's responsiveness to the cardiopulmonary resuscitation.

Corrynne suddenly became aware of a gut-wrenching stench that was similar to the smell of putrid, liquefying potatoes left in the pantry too long. The smell of it was so thick it seemed to coat her open mouth and tongue with its offensiveness. Gagging, Corrynne covered her mouth with her hand and reached for a washcloth in the linen closet to blunt the smell. It was so unusual for a patient to stink this severely. She had only smelled this scent in the hospital once before when a man had been admitted who was harboring a blackened, necrotic and severely infected foot from complications of unmanaged diabetes. It was unbearable.

Composing herself, Corrynne looked around her at the medical personnel. Everyone had masks on and moisture-proof gowns over their scrubs. Corrynne grabbed a mask, two pairs of gloves, and a gown for protection. After donning the protective wear, she pulled the sheets completely off the patient for better visualization and to assess the origin of the stench. The sight she met was one she was not prepared for.

The unconscious patient was barely a man; he looked about twenty or twenty-one years old. She could tell in a moment that he was an example of worldly physical perfection. Laying in the bed bare-chested and with only hospital briefs as a covering, Corrynne noticed he was chiseled like marble. His body was perfectly proportioned, yet there were huge gaping sores all over his torso that blasphemed the beauty, marring its surface. The wounds were a dusky purple and weeping a pink-tinged, watery fluid.

Corrynne demanded through her mask, "Who's the primary care nurse for this patient?"

A small mouse-like nurse in the corner of the room squeaked out, "I-I am."

As Corrynne broke open the lock on the crash cart she firmly gave the command, "Give me a report! What does this patient have?"

Standing in front of the bedside computer with her hand on the mouse, the little nurse's eyes widened. She looked like she was going to topple over from Corrynne's bold words. Quickly she hid her surprise behind strings of hair that fell forward as she reflexively surfed the screens of the small bedside computer as if looking for answers. She stuttered, initially speaking with difficulty. "Ah, no...no one knows yet."

"Tell me what you do know," said Corrynne as she pulled open the drawers on the cart.

"The patient thought he had the flu because he had a high fever. But he...he decided to come to the hospital because of pain; a burning pain around his torso. By the time he got to the emergency room these sores began to appear. We collected cultures and were in the process of taking vital signs when he started having shortness of breath. From there he crashed. We were trying to get ahold of his doctor when he coded."

"So his assigned doctor hasn't seen him yet?"

The nurse shook her head. "No, not yet. I don't even have orders."

"Great," said Corrynne. "Call the ER and have them send up a doc. Stat!" she said as she motioned for the code team to take over compressions.

The male nurse stepped back from the patient as an ICU nurse from the code team took over. A respiratory therapist placed a breathing tube down the patient's throat as Corrynne attached leads to the patient's chest on the sparse normal skin she could find. She studied the electrocardiogram and found that the patient's heart wasn't beating. It was only fibrillating like jello might in a glass bowl when jiggled.

Immediately Corrynne pulled the paddles off the crash cart and set the machine for 150 joules of energy for the first shock from the biphasic machine. The nurse performing compressions stepped back from the bed as Corrynne pressed the paddles down on the patient's chest.

"Clear!" she called as she administered a powerful jolt that made the young man's body shudder. There was a loud sizzle of wet flesh and white smoke and a few beats, but then the heart's EKG returned to its erratic pattern.

Corrynne called for one milligram of Epinephrine be given intravenously to try to stimulate the heart to beat on its own. Automatically, the ICU nurse stepped back and resumed chest compressions to circulate the medication and give oxygen to the patient's body.

After a minute, Corrynne held up her hand to indicate the compressions should stop.

The patient lay motionless as Corrynne and the other nurses felt for a pulse. But there wasn't any there. The heart stubbornly refused to start. Corrynne delivered another shock, dialing up the joules to 200, but despite her efforts the heart would not respond and instead digressed from a fibrillation to a flat-lined asystole.

Again the ICU nurse resumed compressions and another dose of Epinephrine was given while Corrynne opened pacer pads. Since the heart refused to contract she would force it to beat using a pacing mode on the crash cart. Through pads that were placed on the front and back of the patient, it would deliver jolts of energy through the body in a regular rhythm mimicking the beat of a normal heart.

Corrynne attempted to apply the pacer pads to a semi-dry area of the torso. With her gloved hands she ran her fingers along the ravaged tissue. As she did, sections bubbled and slipped off to expose yet another wounded area. Finally, without options, she just slapped on the pacer pads despite the wounds and began the external pacing. The pacing was brutal and shocks racked the patient's front and back, but the code team was rewarded with a rhythm that corresponded to the metered shocks. The monitor demonstrated capture of the heart muscle. A beat began without compressions. Pulses were felt at the neck and the hip, and the patient began to breathe on his own.

Suddenly the man wakened. In one quick motion, his hand ripped the tube from his throat. The code team was surprised and tried to stop him, but it was too late. The tube was out, and they could hear a blood-curdling growl deep in his chest that sounded like a cat crying in the night. With every shock, his scream became more hideous.

Corrynne's stomach turned. She knew the shocks were painful, but she didn't have any other choices. It was clear that he had to be paced or he would die. She was just happy that this man still had brain function.

Corrynne called to the other personnel gawking in the doorway. "Give me Fentanyl and Versed! Stat!" Sedation medications would induce calmness to help the team continue to prolong this man's life.

While the other nurses rushed to find the medications, Corrynne and her team members lay on the man's torso and held down his flailing hands and feet, wrestling him for control. The man fought like a cornered animal and in the struggle the pacing pads were ripped from his body removing seared flesh and leaving bleeding craters where the pads used to be. Now face to face with the patient, Corrynne looked into the huge pupils of his searching eyes as his heart began to fibrillate with an erratic rhythm again.

"Why are you doing this to me?" his words demanded accountability from Corrynne.

Corrynne wanted to answer the despairing question but she had to concentrate on the tasks at hand. She waited to see if his heart would resume without further intervention, but when it returned to asystole she began chest compressions once again as the staff applied restraints to hold the man's limbs down.

In a matter-of-fact tone Corrynne addressed the young stranger's question. "Your heart has stopped and you are very sick. I'm sure this is very difficult and painful for you, but we are in the process of saving your life. We have to make your heart beat to keep your organs alive."

The patient cringed at her words and closed his eyes hard as if to block her out.

"You need to hang in there and let us put these pads on your body to keep your heart going," encouraged Corrynne, "otherwise you will die."

The patient's expression was one of endurance as he looked at her with tear-filled eyes. He managed to say in a voice halting from the chest compressions, "I can't… stand it…anymore. …Let the fire…consume me. …It's not…worth it. Stop. …I said…stop. …*Stop now!*"

Corrynne wondered at his words. What fire? Maybe he was referring to the shocks of energy from the crash cart. Corrynne felt a rib pop under her weight. The man, still awake, yelled something unintelligible and continued to struggle unsuccessfully. Finally, the sedation arrived and the appropriate amounts were given.

Soon the patient stopped struggling and fell into an induced, unconscious state. Corrynne called out for someone to clean off the pads and get them ready to attach once again. The patient's nurse quickly obeyed. Corrynne reattached the pacer pads to the previously seared spots, since they seemed now to be the driest places on his chest. With the pacer delivering shocks, the heart once again began to beat without compressions.

Corrynne, exhausted from the intense physical and emotional work, stepped back from the patient. In her mind she reviewed his request to stop. The sad thing was she couldn't stop unless she had an order from a doctor. She was obligated to continue until there weren't any other options. She wondered at that responsibility and marveled at the ironic nature of the situation. After all, wasn't she giving this man a second chance to live? Suddenly Corrynne grew irritated with her role. She continued to allow her thoughts to evolve. She asked herself if she really had the right to save this man's life against his will. Maybe she should let his heart fail. Maybe that was how it was supposed to be. Maybe she wasn't the hero, after all, but the torturer. By whose authority did she continue to inflict pain?

Just then Dr. Quaid, a doctor from the emergency room, came around the corner in full garb. "What have we got?" The doctor directed his question to Corrynne.

Corrynne succinctly explained what had taken place before his arrival but as she was talking, the patient's blood pressure plummeted.

Dr. Quaid took over and began barking out orders: "Reintubate! Infuse saline under pressure and get me a Dopamine drip!" Efforts were renewed to save the man's life.

Corrynne however, did not contribute. She was torn. Frozen, she wondered what she should do next. She looked down at the bleeding and broken human being who just hours before, had been whole. Suddenly, she knew what she would do. She would be this man's advocate. She would speak for him because now, he could not speak for himself.

With a bold voice Corrynne spoke to the doctor. "This man has made it clear that he does not want us to continue to try and save his life. He has asked us to stop and considering the futility of our efforts so far, I believe we should honor his request."

Dr. Quaid turned and looked at Corrynne with cool gray eyes. He had a look of confusion. "What are you saying?"

Corrynne straightened her back and hanging on to her confidence repeated herself, "I said, we should stop this code. This man doesn't want us to do this."

"Oh really?" asked Dr. Quaid with a slight laugh.

The Code team paused for a moment looking back and forth between Dr. Quaid and Corrynne.

Corrynne nodded. "Yes, really. He was very clear in his request for us to stop."

The doctor shook his head. "Well if someone was pounding on my chest and shocking me without sedation, I'd tell you to stop too," said the doctor. "It's not exactly a comfortable experience."

"I know that," said Corrynne, "but…"

"No!" exclaimed the doctor cutting off Corrynne. "We continue!"

The code team went into motion and continued to carry out the doctor's previous orders.

"Dr. Quaid!" said Corrynne in a shocked voice as the Dopamine drip was started by the primary care nurse. "It's not our place to act against a patient's will."

With anger in his eyes, the doctor swung around and faced Corrynne as he pointed at the patient. "Tell me Corrynne, does this man have a living will?"

Corrynne was caught off guard. "Ahh…" she began, searching for the answer by looking at the patient's nurse who might give her a clue to the answer but the nurse obviously avoided her stare.

The doctor continued. "Where's his family? How do we know he was in his right mind to ask such a thing?" Then with a slow cadence the doctor asked, "And who are we to *end* this man's life?"

Fury rose in Corrynne as she exclaimed, "We wouldn't be ending this man's life! We would be allowing nature to take its course. There's no crime in that. Death is the natural end of life. It's we who are interfering by forcing our will on him! Stop making this into something it's not. He asked us to stop and we should stop!"

"No. That's not how things are going to be today," said Dr. Quaid defiantly. "I'm the doctor and I decide when we stop."

Corrynne stared angrily at the physician but didn't respond.

Dr. Quaid continued. "You can look at this situation through whatever glasses you choose to justify your actions, but as for me, I won't stop until I've exhausted every avenue. That's my job." The doctor turned back to the patient and his nurse. With the voice of authority he said, "Keep turning that Dopamine up until his systolic is over 100."

The primary nurse nodded and dialed up the rate as the doctor had ordered.

Corrynne stepped back and allowed the patient's original nurse to take her place next to Dr. Quaid at the bedside. She would let her carry out his orders. As for Corrynne, she wouldn't be a party to flogging a man endlessly. Enough was enough. If Dr. Quaid wanted to continue until there was nothing left to save, then she wouldn't stand in his way. He was right. He was the doctor and that was his choice.

Eventually it was obvious to everyone in the room that this patient could not be saved. Finally, with a quick look in Corrynne's direction, Dr. Quaid took a deep breath and said, "OK everyone, step back from the patient. Time of death 0352." It was over.

With gloved hands, Corrynne stepped close to the bed. In sadness she touched the young, expressionless face, searching for the man who had resided inside, but she felt nothing. He was gone. As for his body, it remained, completely lifeless. To Corrynne, it was amazing that just a short time before she had communicated with him. However, never again would this form speak or interact with another. His essence was gone, his spirit unable to live in this body.

Corrynne shook her head. Suddenly she had an overwhelming desire to gather this stranger in her arms and rock him. It wasn't fair that he was alone in his last moments of life. Where were his family members? Who were the people that loved this man? Were there any?

Corrynne cleared her throat as she tried to hold back her emotions. She was becoming too involved in this situation. She needed to maintain a professional attitude. Despite this thought, she knew it would be a while before this event could be cleansed from her system.

As if Burned by Fire

Corrynne turned off the monitor on the crash cart as the primary care nurse turned off the intravenous pumps. The silence in the room compared with the voices and fervor from moments before was deafening. It was always like this when someone died young.

Dr. Quaid shook his head as all eyes remained on the lifeless form. "We're seeing too much of this lately," said Dr. Quaid. "These are the most aggressive cases of tissue necrosis and septic shock that we've ever seen in the ER."

Corrynne was surprised. "This kind of thing has happened before?"

The room remained quiet. Ears and eyes shifted their focus to the doctor. He changed his weight from his right foot to his left and paused. It was obvious that he was willing to discuss this case but not with so many people listening.

Corrynne took the initiative and looked at the other nurses and respiratory therapists and said, "Thank you for doing such a great job here, but there is nothing else to do. I'll stay and help clean up. You guys can all go."

One by one the other staff left the room. The only remaining nurse besides Corrynne was the patient's nurse, who began busily disconnecting the patient from the medical paraphernalia.

Corrynne grabbed a thick blanket from inside the linen closet and covered the body to block out the offensive smell still lingering in the room as well as contain the infection risk. Then with a jerk she ripped the ties for her mask and allowed it to fall off her face and hang from her neck.

Dr. Quaid also pulled off his mask. With a sigh and a look of frustration he said, "We have seen five cases in the last week, and more before that."

That answer didn't make sense to Corrynne. There hadn't been any cases that she knew of in the ICU. "Then why haven't I seen it in my department?" she asked in a controlled voice.

"Because all the cases we've had have died within three hours of arriving here." Dr. Quaid's mouth curved slightly in the corners. "And you know as well as I do that it takes that long just to get into the ER." The doctor was being facetious.

Corrynne scowled. "It seems like after a couple of cases, someone should have been able to identify them earlier and put these patients in the ICU before they crashed. Why else do we have a triage nurse?"

"You have a point. But this infection is so new that our nurses, and the doctors for that matter, haven't been deciphering the immediacy the symptoms demanded. It presents just as a skin infection,[2] which is easily treated. Skin infections wait in the lobby while heart attacks and breathing difficulties get immediate care. It's a matter of protocol."

Corrynne nodded as she listened intently.

Dr. Quaid pointed to the still figure on the bed. "This gentleman was lucky to get an experienced triage nurse so he was whisked up here...." Dr. Quaid seemed to be rethinking his conclusions. "I don't know, he seemed so stable...maybe I should have sent him to the ICU." He kicked the bed wheel in frustration. "We're still learning."

"I wouldn't call this lucky," Corrynne scoffed, gesturing to the bed.

"Maybe not," said the doctor as he shook his head.

Corrynne nodded thoughtfully. "Maybe bringing these patients into the ICU early isn't a good idea, anyway. We just would have more time to torture them with our tubes and procedures with the same outcome. I know that is not how I want to spend my last hours on earth."

Dr. Quaid looked at Corrynne for a moment and nodded. "I know. Neither do I."

His statement spoke volumes to Corrynne. It was a subtle way to tell her that she had been right about the decision to stop the code earlier without declaring it aloud. Corrynne accepted the statement without further comment. Their professional relationship was more important than who was right or wrong. The issue would be dropped and never discussed again.

Corrynne and Dr. Quaid allowed the silence to continue as each was immersed in their thoughts.

Finally, Corrynne licked her lips then asked, "Have you thought of going to the media to educate the public?"

"Yes, I've thought of that...." said Dr. Quaid slowly.

"That way when the earliest signs are discovered they can come here in time," continued Corrynne. "We could set up a separate triage station to be looking for those patients."

Dr. Quaid took a breath and rubbed the back of his neck. "Like I said, I have thought of that but I just don't know enough about how this group is contracting this infection. I have some ideas, and I think I'm getting closer, but I don't feel comfortable going that far. I feel I need to know more before I do anything on a public scale."

"Well, something has to be done now," Corrynne said. "People have to know what to do when they first start having these symptoms. This is an awful way to die!"

Dr. Quaid nodded. "Yes, I agree. I've already sent my preliminary findings to the Center for Disease Control and they have started the tracking process. So something is being done. We just have to be patient and do the best we can until a formal plan is created."

"What is the organism responsible for these awful sores, sepsis, and heart failure?"

The doctor took a wide stance and folded his arms. "Streptococcus type A has been consistently cultured out of all the wounds of the patients who have died a similar death. It's a bacteria that we've had around ever since we could spy into their microscopic world to say 'hello'."

Corrynne pointed at the covered body, her torso straightening to its full height. "Strep…this is Strep, as in Strep throat?" she asked.

"Well, yes. We have seen Streptococcus manifest itself in tissue necrosis before. You know, Necrotizing Faciitis? It's been referred to as the 'flesh-eating disease.'[3]"

Corrynne nodded. "I've dealt with it before but not from Strep—at least I didn't remember it being caused from Strep."

"Other organisms can cause Necrotizing Faciitis but Streptococcus type A is the most common."

"I didn't realize Strep could be so deadly."

"Ordinarily it isn't. This strain of Strep seems to be more aggressive than normal. We estimate that it progresses four inches in an hour rather than the normal 3/4 of an inch in Necrotizing Faciitis. It makes a protein that destroys human tissue but also paralyzes the natural conduction of the heart when it gets into the bloodstream. In six hours from the first symptom of the infection the victim is dead. So in one moment you're feeling like you have the flu; the next, your skin is falling off—and then suddenly your heart stops from buildup of the microbial toxins."

Corrynne shook her head and turned away slightly from Dr. Quaid, refusing the reality of what he was saying. "This is horrible!"

Dr. Quaid nodded in agreement. "Absolutely. That is why we need to continue to gather information, just in case we're missing something."

Corrynne turned back and looked up at Dr. Quaid. "What else do you know about this?"

"In order for the bacteria to be deadly, it somehow has to get into a wound where it dissolves the connective tissue and cuts off the blood supply to the skin. The tissue then dies; once that happens, amputation of the affected area is only the cure, if they live that long. Antibiotics are useless in this situation, unless they're administered when the patient first feels sick."

Corrynne felt helpless and sighed, "This situation feels overwhelming, almost as if these patients have no options. There really isn't anything we can do, is there?"

"Not really, not yet."

"If that's the case, I don't want anything to do with this sickness. No offense, but you can keep all of them in the ER," Corrynne joked.

"Thanks a lot!" the doctor returned.

Becoming serious again, Corrynne asked, "Is this happening anywhere else?"

Dr. Quaid nodded. "At first I thought it must be a condition particular to a pocket here in town because I hadn't heard anything on the news, but in talking to a colleague I have in a New York ER, I guess they have been seeing this manifestation of Strep for the last couple of weeks."

"In New York, huh? That's interesting that their ERs are seeing the same thing we are. I wonder what they have in common." Corrynne bit her lower lip as she thought.

"I think we've found some sort of link, although it seems a little weak," said Dr. Quaid squinting.

"What is it?" asked Corrynne.

"The affected population both here in Utah and in New York is between the ages of fourteen and thirty years; more on the younger side than the older. There have only been a few that weren't in that age range. My colleague mentioned to me that one of his patients had been at a Rave the night before and that got me thinking...."

"What's a Rave?"[4] asked Corrynne, interrupting.

"It's a secret massive party, famous for high-risk behavior. They've become very popular. Here in the Provo-Salt Lake area, they're taking place up in the mountains in secret locations so as to not attract police attention."

Corrynne nodded thoughtfully. "Ahh—yes. I think I've heard of them after all." She remembered a special on 20/20 once about Raves, now that she thought about it. The details were coming back to her.

The doctor continued. "I began to ask the victims here if they had attended a Rave in the last 24 hours, and four out of the five that we've had this week admitted that they had."

"What happened to the fifth person?"

"Well, he just wouldn't say. I think that he did too."

"How could you make that assumption?"

"He just fit the mold."

"I see."

"Another thing each person had in common was a fresh body piercing and a tattoo somewhere on their skin. And when I studied the pattern of the sores they seemed to originate from the piercing and tattooing and spread from there."

"So breaking the protective skin barrier allowed the Strep to get into the wounds?" asked Corrynne, seeing the connection.

"We believe so."

"Strep is normally found in the nose and throat. How is it getting into the wounds on the body?" asked Corrynne. "I can see it getting into a tongue wound or a nose piercing, but on the chest like this patient?"

Dr. Quaid made an expression of contemplation. "We're not sure. Sometimes Strep can just start tissue necrosis without portal of entry, but not in these numbers. Something must be happening during the tattooing process that has encouraged the infection."

Oddly, Corrynne was struck by the idea. Who'd have thought that one could die from a pierced belly button or a harmless tattoo? It seemed impossible, yet here it was happening. Suddenly she felt new-found thankfulness for a living prophet who had counseled against body piercings.[5] Of course the Lord knew what was around the corner and had given instructions to those that would listen so they could escape the coming devastating scourge. Those who had listened were safe from this illness.

"Well, I'm just glad my kids aren't going to those Raves," said Corrynne. "The world's becoming a dangerous place."

"You *hope* your kids aren't going to those Raves," said Dr. Quaid mockingly.

Corrynne shook her head and laughed. "No, I *know* my kids aren't going to those Raves."

"Yeah, right," said Dr. Quaid with a smirk. "I hope you're right."

Dr. Quaid's comments shook Corrynne as she thought about her children. Quickly she went through each one. Could any of them be sneaking out without her knowledge? After contemplating each child she decided that she was right.

"No, Dr. Quaid. My kids are good kids. They don't go to parties," said Corrynne, now feeling she had to go home and question all of her teenagers just to make sure.

"Well, you'd know I think, by the tattoos. They do them at the parties," said Dr. Quaid.

"What?" asked Corrynne, amazed.

"Yes, great party activity, huh?"

"That is so stupid!" exclaimed Corrynne. "No wonder these kids are suffering from tissue necrosis! The tattoo needles obviously aren't sterile!"

"Nope. Listen to this. It gets worse. There was a seventeen-year-old girl who came in at the beginning of the week. We were able to gather information from her before she became unstable. She said that the whole purpose of the party was to perform some sort of ceremony that included the tattooing and piercings."

Corrynne looked at Dr. Quaid for a moment in confusion. "A ceremony? I thought we were talking about a party?"

"I guess it's both. They still have the party; in fact, the use of drugs and alcohol is a big part of the ceremony."[6]

"Did she mention why they did this?"

"She said the tattoo 'showed who she belonged to.' So I guess it's like body graffiti. I wonder if she meant that they declare their loyalty through these practices."

"Sounds like more gang-related activities," said Corrynne nodding and folding her arms.

"Yes, my thoughts exactly." Dr. Quaid walked over to the bed and with a strangled voice from trying to hold his breath, pulled back the blanket to expose the body and said, "See, on this flap of skin, you can still make out the tattoo."

Corrynne also held her breath but drew close to study the pale skin. She saw the letters "B," "A," and something else she couldn't decipher. With a gloved hand she pushed on the blanket to cover the body back up.

After the blanket was back in place, Corrynne asked, "What does that tattoo say? I couldn't quite make it out."

"It said B-A-T," spelled out the doctor.

"Bat? That doesn't make sense."

"It could be an acronym for something. It marked all of the victims. Maybe it stands for their gang name."

"No, it doesn't," said a small timid voice from the head of the bed. Both the doctor and Corrynne turned their attention to the nurse who had been practically invisible. "It stands for 'Beasts Acting Together,'" the patient's little nurse piped up again. Suddenly she seemed uncomfortably aware of their attention and cowered, looking down at the floor.

"Do you know anything about this?" asked Dr. Quaid.

The little nurse fidgeted and looked up nervously. "Some."

"How do you know?" continued Dr. Quaid.

"That girl you talked about was my cousin," said the nurse with a shaky voice. She looked down again and covered her masked face with her gloved hand.

Corrynne took off her gloves and threw them into the nearest redlined "biohazard" trashcan meant for contaminated materials. As she took a couple of steps towards the young nurse, Corrynne looked for a nametag but she was still clad in waterproof multi-layered gowns that hid it from view.

Deciding she didn't need to know the young girl's name to comfort her, Corrynne placed her right arm around her small shoulders and said, "I'm so sorry. We didn't know. It must be terrible to have to deal with something at work that hits so close to home."

The anonymous nurse turned and went to put her face in Corrynne's chest as her tears began to flow. Corrynne restrained her until she could remove her own protective coverings. Then she took the young woman tentatively in her arms in a sideways fashion, careful not to be contaminated by the nurse's gowns.

The little nurse began to lament, "I knew that she went to those parties. She was so committed to their cause. She was always sneaking out. She would call and try to convince me to come to the parties too and tell me not to tell anyone else. I just thought she was being rebellious. I didn't know it was going to kill her!" The nurse continued to cry.

"No one knew. You weren't at fault," said Dr. Quaid attempting a soothing tone. For a few moments there was silence in the room except for the soft noises coming from the tearful nurse. Dr. Quaid walked forward and laid his hand on her shoulder. "When you feel better though, we would really like to hear more about what happens at these Raves. We need to do what we can to stop the needless suffering."

"It's all on the computer," squeaked the nurse.

Dr. Quaid and Corrynne looked up at each other and then at the nurse. "What computer?"

"On the…you know…the Web," the nurse said between sobs.

"Can you show me?" asked the doctor as he approached the bedside computer and accessed the Internet by putting in his password.

The nurse nodded. "I don't know much but I'll show you what I can."

"What do I type in?"

"B-A-T," spoke the nurse with a muffled voice. "Only it's dot-scape, not dot-com, in the address." Her head was still buried in Corrynne's scrubs.

The doctor typed in www.bat.scape[7] and up popped a swastika.[8] The doctor recoiled from the screen. Then the symbol began to morph into all the religious symbols that the doctor could identify and then some others that he could not. He glanced at the little nurse. In almost a strangled voice he asked, *"Is this a religion?"*

"Kind of," said the nurse, now looking back at the doctor.

The doctor scrolled down the screen and clicked on the word "mission." Up came a statement that froze him in place.

> *"We are unified by the mark and blood. We are not separate, but one. We have one world, one government, one religion, one God. We will stand together and inherit the world, or we will die with failed hearts and burn with fire."*[9]

"Corrynne, you need to see this," said Dr. Quaid with a flick of a single finger in the air.

Corrynne left the nurse and came over to the screen. She read to herself what the doctor indicated on the screen. Corrynne shook her head in disbelief as her eyes continued down the page. A statement caught her eye, and she read it out loud.

"'Build Everything After Striking Terror Systematically.' Those first letters spell BEASTS. Oh, great. This is a good one. What do you think that means?"

The little nurse wiped her nose on her sleeve and came over to the computer. "My cousin had been talking lately about some guy that glows who appears out of nowhere. He teaches them that they should fight against society to break it down, so that it could be replaced by the one true society. After that he disappears into thin air."

"A glowing guy who appears and disappears?" asked Corrynne.

"Yes, that's what she said."

"What else did she tell you?" asked the doctor.

"Terror was the tool that they would use to drive the world to be unified. I never understood what she meant, though. I know it had something to do with her markings."

"I don't even want to consider the ramifications of that one," said the doctor.

"She was telling me that I had no choice but to come and join that organization to be protected, because anyone who didn't belong would suffer plagues and famines until they were burned at the end. She said all impurities would be purged by fire."

"Well, it sure didn't save her," retorted the doctor.

"Well, I think I know why," said the nurse.

"Why what? Why she wasn't protected?" asked Dr. Quaid as he looked away from the screen to focus on the mouse-like nurse. "Do you believe this stuff?"

"No, not really. I just know why she thought she wasn't being protected anymore. Before she went into the hospital she called me. She said that she was having so much pain that she felt like she was being burned from the inside out. She was afraid that she was impure and being punished."

"Punished?"

"That's what she said."

"That's crazy. The pain originated from the bacteria destroying her tissues," said the doctor with a frustrated but reflective look in his eye. "What made her think that she was impure?"

"She said that she had 'divulged the secrets' to someone she shouldn't have."

"What secrets?"[10] asked the doctor.

"I don't know which things she told me were secrets and which weren't. She didn't tell me what she specifically told the doctor at the clinic."

"Oh, she told something to a doctor? Are doctors not supposed to know anything about this group?"

The young nurse shrugged. "I guess not."

"You know, I don't like what I'm hearing," grumbled Corrynne. "It sounds too much like pagan ideas and superstition—I believe, despite appearances, that it's these young people, not America that are being broken down by terror. This glowing guy, *or whoever he is*, is being successful in spreading terror to gain control. These horrible and devastating deaths will only increase the people's fear and thus increase his strength over these people."

Dr. Quaid nodded. "I agree."

"Which leads me to another thought," said Corrynne turning to speak to the doctor. "You know, the young man tonight said something before he died that's making more sense to me now. He was begging me to let him die, and then he said, 'Let the fire consume me.' I thought it was strange at the time, but now I think I understand. He thought he was being consumed with fire, too." Corrynne's mouth dropped open as understanding washed over her and her gaze met the doctor's. "This is terrible!"

"It is," said the doctor as he turned his attention back to the screen. "That's why this has to stop."

"Yes, but how?" asked Corrynne.

The doctor didn't answer but instead asked the nurse, "What's the mark on these people and also, where does the blood come in?"[11]

The little nurse responded, "I think the mark is the tattoo. It signifies their membership, just like you thought. Later, though, everyone is supposed to get a special chip that will be imbedded in their palm to actually protect them somehow."

"And the blood?" asked Corrynne.

"I know that they cause bleeding when they do the markings. They tattoo deep into the skin. I remember my cousin saying that if they didn't draw blood, the ritual wasn't true. I asked her what that meant and she said that dedication demanded some sort of sacrifice from the member. When they were unselfish with their blood and allowed it to flow, that would make them truly one with the group."

"I see," said the doctor, thinking out loud. "What about the piercings? What do they represent?"

The nurse scuffed the floor with her foot. "The piercing is to represent obedience."

"How is that?" Corrynne asked incredulously.

"Well, a bull, even though it's huge and powerful, must obey its master because of the ring in its nose. It's the same idea. If you notice, the piercings are all rings."

"Yes, you're right," said the doctor, reflecting on his patients. "They were all rings, or circles. I didn't notice that before."

"Receiving the ring says that you submit to be led. A promise of obedience is given."

"That's very interesting," said Corrynne. She allowed her eyes to scan the Internet screen as she reviewed her new understanding. Suddenly she felt a pang of sadness. With anger in her voice she added, "All the followers of this cult are being tricked! Obviously many are committed. I wish they could see what happened here today. I doubt they would think their 'glowing guy' was that great anymore."

"I think you're right, Corrynne," said Dr. Quaid. "It's too bad that people are being deceived into giving up not only their freedom, but potentially their life. It's time to get busy and see what we can do to stop this." The doctor let out a deep sigh as he headed for the door of the room. Looking back at the last second before exiting he said, "Buckle your safety belts. It's going to get bumpy."

Notes to "The Mark"

Code Blue

[1] A glossary is included at the end of the book for medical terms.

As if Burned by Fire

[2] Compare the following four scriptures to understand the nature of plagues in the last days:

> I. Exodus 9:9: "And it shall become small dust in all the land of Egypt, and shall be a boil breaking forth with blains (blisters or pustules) upon man, and upon beast, throughout all the land of Egypt" (see Bible footnotes for definitions).
>
> II. Deuteronomy 28:27: "The Lord shall smite thee with the botch (blisters) of Egypt, and with the emerods (tumors), and with the scab, and with the itch, whereof thou canst not be healed" (see Bible footnotes for definitions).
>
> III. D&C 29:18-19: "Wherefore, I the Lord God will send forth flies upon the face of the earth, which shall take hold of the inhabitants thereof, and shall eat their flesh, and shall cause maggots to come in upon them; And their tongues shall be stayed that they shall not utter against me; and their flesh shall fall from off their bones, and their eyes from their sockets."

Notice that in Egypt the plagues affected the skin. They were meant to be a noticeable indication of punishment. In the Doctrine and Covenants the plagues describing the last days are more severe. The plague affects the flesh, which falls off their bones. The eyes and tongue are mentioned also. While it is a plague that is visual and noticeable, it is not clear if the internal organs are affected. The description is meant to be gruesome and cause a reaction in the reader. The Lord wishes to cause fear to the wicked concerning potential penalties of their actions and cause them to turn away from their practices. In turning away from wickedness, they can escape if they choose.

[3] The author selected Streptococcus A to be the source of this plague because of the potential similarities to the skin plagues mentioned in the scriptures above, combined with its mysterious history. The "Flesh Eating Disease" is a real occurrence, but it is relatively rare. The mechanisms of attack and treatment are consistent with reality with small changes to enhance the story line. It attacks approximately 3-7 people per million worldwide. Strep A is contracted by direct contact with secretions from the nose and throat of infected persons (search the Internet for "flesh eating disease"). For more information see Troy A. Callender, MD., "Necrotizing Fasciitis of the Head and Neck," December 1992, The Bobby R. Alford Department of Otorhinolaryngology and Communicative Sciences, available online:

http://www.bcm.tmc.edu/oto/grand/123192.html, or see "Necrotizing Fasciitis/Myositis ('flesh-eating disease')," Canada, Population and Public Health Branch, April 1999, available online: http://www.hc-sc.gc.ca/hpb/lcdc/bid/respdis/necro_e.html.

[4] Raves are a worldwide occurrence. Multiple Web sites advertise organizers and places of parties all over the world. The parties are famous for being secret, having techno music, being held in large open spaces, and using the drug Ecstasy. "Researchers have reported the drug can cause brain damage by destroying neurons that produce the neurotransmitter serotonin, responsible for controlling mood, sleep, pain, sexual activity and violent behavior" (Jack Date, "Rave Party Organizers Indicted Under Federal Drug Law," *Cnn.com_law center.news,* January 2001, available online:
 http://www.cnn.com/2001/LAW/01/12/operation.rave/index.html).

President Gordon B. Hinckley addressed Raves in the October Conference in 2000. He quoted from the Deseret News September 17, 2000 issue that described Raves to be large parties that involve teens to young adults that run all night. They have loud music and rampant drug use. He stated that the gathering was "representative of the foulest aspects of life" ("Your Greatest Challenge Mother," *Ensign,* November 2000, 98).

[5] "We—the First Presidency and the Council of the Twelve—have taken the position, and I quote, that 'the Church discourages tattoos. It also discourages the piercing of the body...'" (Gordon B. Hinckley, "Your Greatest Challenge Mother," *Ensign*, November 2000, 99).

[6] Ever since the beginning of cult behavior, pharmaceutical agents have been used to enhance or add to the spiritual experience. We see it in Greek mythology and in the rituals of the god of wine who represents features of the mysterious religion described in the text. "Ecstasy, personal delivery from the daily world, through physical or spiritual intoxication and initiation into secret rites," are prevalent in these environments (see Rachel Gross & Dale Grote, "Dionysus," *The Encyclopedia Mythica,* available online: http://www.pantheon.org/articles/d/dionysus.html).

People who use pharmaceutical agents in relation to evil cults of the last days are identified as one of the wicked who will suffer from the plagues. In Revelation 9:20-21, it uses the word "sorcery." The Greek word that comes from the original text is *pharmakeia*, which is the root word of pharmacy. This word "indicates the use of drugs, elixirs, and contraceptive potions associated with the occult." This same reference is used also in Revelation 18:21, indicating "through the use of drugs is one of the ways that the Mother of Abominations is able to deceive the nations" (Richard D. Draper, *Opening the Seven Seals*, 109).

[7] www.bat.scape is a fictional Internet site address.

[8] The swastika historically has been used by both ancient and modern cultures to symbolize positive religious attributes; the most commonly quoted is "prosperity or good fortune." The swastika still continues today to be an extensively used sign in Buddhism, Jainism, and Hinduism. The German use of the symbol came from their intention to communicate to the world that they were a pure race, stealing the symbol from a factual ancient Aryan people (see www search for "swastika" for more information).

The swastika has been used in this text to symbolically point to an evil organization taking upon themselves outward appearances of good in order to deceive. This has been a tactic used by Satan ever since the beginning of the history of this world.

"One of the major techniques of the devil is to cause human beings to think they are following God's ways, when in reality they are deceived by the devil to follow other paths" (see Bible Dictionary, "Devil," 656).

[9] Satan will imitate God's true language, church, miracles, and whatever else to deceive 'even the elect.' Deception is the main goal of the adversary (see Joseph Smith Matthew 1:21-23). The language chosen in the text to represent the evil organization's statement to the world is meant to imitate the sound and feel of scripture with just enough twists to not be true.

[10] Secrecy has always been a tool of Satan (see 2 Nephi 10:15; 2 Nephi 28:9; Helaman 2:8; for other references, see Bible Topical Guide, "Secret Combinations," 456-57).

[11] See Revelation 13:16; Revelation 14:9.

CHAPTER THREE

IN SEARCH OF SOLACE

"Peace I leave with you, my peace I give unto you: not as the world giveth, give I unto you. Let not your heart be troubled, neither let it be afraid" (John 14:27).

Saturday
September 16th
6:45 a.m.
Provo, Utah

Morning After

Mentally and emotionally exhausted from her shift, Corrynne dragged her body up the stairs of the hospital garage. The revelation of the hours before was very difficult to bear. She felt a deep mourning for all those young people who were giving themselves to such devastating circumstances. She wondered what they thought as they made choices to mark and pierce their bodies. "They're making deals with the devil," she thought. Ironically, she did not mean this symbolically. She wondered if Satan himself wasn't at the helm of such a destructive organization.

Corrynne stood for a moment before the glass door leading outside. She barely had enough energy to open it. She slowly pushed the door open and she stepped through. As she did her face was hit with a blast of cool September air. A few raindrops fell on her forehead and her nose. She didn't even bother to wipe them off but stood in one spot and reveled in their presence. It had been raining in the outside world, away from "stats" and computers and carnage. "Ah," she thought as she filled her lungs with the delicious, cool, fresh oxygen and closed her eyes to just bask in the freshness of the outside environment.

Corrynne loved this transition after work. She needed to be alone, to rest her mind, to just "be," without anyone demanding a single thing from her. She tried to cleanse her mind and erase the new knowledge that she had acquired of secret plans and destructive powers. She desired to return to the unburdened person she was at the beginning of her shift. She took another deep breath; but unsolicited, a vision of the young man with his body broken and torn came to her mind. Suddenly she felt as if her skin were crawling. She could imagine the bacteria from the young fellow all over her. Unconsciously, she rubbed her arms hard as if to remove the imaginary threat. Corrynne shivered, rationalizing to herself that she must be tired.

Shifting her weight forward, her body began to move. Slowly she scuffed her feet on the pavement as she walked toward her car. Beside her large white Suburban, Corrynne touched the numbers on the door panel to disengage the car alarm and unlock the doors.

Once in the car, she pressed her thumb to the identification pad and immediately the car came alive. "Welcome, Corrynne. Where would you like to go?" said the extremely friendly female voice. Corrynne made an irritated face. She wondered to herself why all the cars these days had female voices. And why were they so friendly? What if you had had a bad day and you didn't want the voice to be so chipper?

In one move she flipped the silence button. "Fixed her," Corrynne growled out loud. After a second, she conceded to talk to her car, which always made her feel silly. "Home…car." The car's engine immediately engaged and she laid the seat back and relaxed while the car took her safely home. "Home…." The wonderful thought lingered. "Yes, I want to go home."

Home Is Where the Heart Is

Corrynne heard banging and wondered who was rude enough to be so loud when people were sleeping. It was a fleeting thought and then she was heavily back asleep. Again the banging came, and someone was calling her name.

"Corrynne, wake up, you've been sleeping in the garage again!"

Somewhere far away she heard a door latch click. Suddenly she felt her body falling, falling, falling, and then hanging. She opened one sleepy eye to see her husband, Bo, upside down, with a grin from ear to ear. "Good thing this car has automatic seatbelts as well as driving ability, or else you would be face to face with the cement," he teased.

"Bo, do you think you're funny? Because I don't see anyone laughing but you," Corrynne returned in a sleepy but sarcastic tone.

"Corrynne, I'm hysterical. I've told you that for twenty-three years. As soon as you admit it, you'll be much happier." Bo reached down and unlatched her seatbelt, and Corrynne rolled out of her car like a slinky. Now flat on the floor of the garage Corrynne stuck her tongue out at her snickering husband.

Bo smiled and said, "Good thing I keep this garage floor clean. Get up slacker and come inside."

"You're so rude to just let me fall onto the cement."

"You didn't fall, you rolled gracefully."

"Same difference."

"Hey, I got you out of the car, didn't I?" asked Bo.

Bo held out his thick, muscled hand and in one motion, pulled Corrynne to her feet. Oh, how she loved the feel of his skin and the strength of his arms—but that was beside the point. She was still slightly irritated that he had unbuckled her seat belt.

Bo stepped behind her and guided her into the door of the house.

Inside there was a high-pitched squeal of "Moooommmmmyyyyy!" and then a careening seven-year-old hit Corrynne. Little Rocwell Joshua took hold of her waist with a vise-like grip and dug his face into her abdomen, lifting his legs off the floor. She staggered heavily back into Bo's frame with the impact.

"Hi, sweetheart! Be careful—don't knock me over!" Corrynne said, laughing a little as she hugged his head and then tousled his hair. "So, why are you up so early?"

"Daddy is making pancakes!" came the excited voice. "Then I get to go shopping with him."

Corrynne smiled to herself as she anticipated his answers. Saturday was always a pancake-and-shopping day at the Rogers' home.

Bo poked Corrynne in the ribs, and she turned and looked up at him. "Corrynne, I made you breakfast. Why don't you sit for a minute and eat something?"

Corrynne faced back towards the kitchen as she smiled and said, "I think I will."

"Good! Because it's hot right now."

Corrynne moved to sit at the kitchen counter while Rocwell continued to hold her around the waist, matching step for step. He wore an obviously silly plastic grin, lifting his chin high so she could see his face. She took her place at the corner chair, and he let go of her just long enough to climb into his customary place, squatting behind her so that she had to sit forward on her chair to let him have room. He hugged her around her neck, breathing loudly in her ear. He always did this when she sat down at the kitchen counter and she let him. Sometimes he would play with her ears lovingly, and Corrynne yearned for his innocent, loving touch. It was such a stress reliever.

"So how was work last night?" asked Bo as he took his place around the counter to finish breakfast.

"It was hard," said Corrynne in an exhausted voice.

"Why was it hard?"

"We had a sad situation in which a young man about Braun's age died."

"I'm sorry," said Bo with genuine concern. "But you've taken care of people that have died before. What was so difficult about the patient last night?" he asked.

"Well, the whole experience was downright frightening. I can't shake it out of my head."

"What? Did the patient sit up in the bed and say 'Boo'?" asked Bo, obviously attempting to lighten the mood.

Corrynne frowned, giving her husband a disapproving look. "No, and it's not even something I can kid about."

Bo shrugged. "Well I don't know what you mean by 'frightening.' Give me more details."

Corrynne looked down at the counter and shook her head. Then with a sigh she asked, "Have you heard the term 'Rave' before?"

"You mean as in stark, *raving* mad?" asked Bo, again cracking a smile.

"No, I mean as in a secret party up in the mountains for teenagers and young adults."

Bo nodded. "Ah, yes, I believe I have."

"Well, I guess they've been happening here in our own mountains."

With a flat expression Bo said, "That's not surprising."

"It should be," said Corrynne with sternness.

"Why? Because we live in Utah?" asked Bo. "You and I both know that Utah is quickly becoming like every other place in America. Provo is no exception. Raves happen in Los Angeles, New York, Las Vegas, good old Salt Lake City and now Provo. It's a fact of a decadent society. Welcome to the 21st century."

Corrynne was pained to hear Bo's words, but she knew they were right on the mark. Raves *were* happening in Provo. She didn't like it but she couldn't deny it. She saw the evidence at the hospital and on the Internet.

Corrynne gave one nod and said, "OK, I see what you're saying but I think a Rave isn't just where kids get together to have a party any more. I think the Rave is being used as a tool for recruitment and it's causing people to die."

"You mean more people are dying than expected?" asked Bo. "Because I know kids die from overdoses every day, making the drug dealers rich. It's tragic and wrong and at epidemic levels, but I don't have to tell you that."

"No Bo, you don't. I see it with my own two eyes. I have to tell the mothers and fathers about their children's needless deaths all the time."

"So this is different than that," said Bo with a solemn stare.

"Yes, Bo. It's different. I've seen a lot of death but I've never seen someone die like I did last night."

Bo studied his wife's face for a moment and then said, "So what's going on?"

Corrynne shook her head. "I don't want to go into the details here, but suffice it to say, a young man received an infected tattoo at Rave and the infection practically ate him alive."

"A tattoo?" asked Bo.

"Yes, a tattoo."

"That's strange."

"Even stranger is the reason behind the tattoo."

"Explain it to me."

"There is an organization that feeds off kids at Raves. They encourage drinking and drugs and when the kids are good and plastered, they, whoever they are that run the Raves, have the letters B.A.T. tattooed on the willing."

"What?"

"Yes, and it doesn't stop there. Next the members give each other some sort of piercing with loop-like shapes, and then get this..."

"I'm listening," said Bo.

"They do it all in the name of *world domination*."

"What?" asked Bo with a sound of shock coming to his voice.

Corrynne nodded. "It's true."

Bo let out a loud laugh and crossed his arms. "Come on, Corrynne. That sounds like some dark 'B' movie theme."

Corrynne sat up and patted the counter with her open hand. "I know how it sounds. But I had a young man who died in a bed at the hospital because of this very thing!" With a finger she pointed in the air. "Because of the rituals done under the influence, a young 21-year-old man is dead. His wounds became infected with a flesh-eating Strep. His skin and muscle literally fell off his bones while he was alive."

Bo lifted up both hands and said, "OK, OK, I believe you. Don't say any more. I'm getting queasy."

"What's Strep, Mommy?" asked Roc from behind her.

Corrynne cringed. She had said too much in front of her little guy.

"It's not important," said Bo with a firm expression.

Corrynne looked at Bo and said, "He can know what Strep is."

Bo held out a hand for her to go ahead and explain the details to their son.

"Strep is a bacteria that is in almost everyone's throat in small amounts. Normally it doesn't hurt us. Sometimes it makes us sick and we have to go to the doctor to get medicine, but then we're OK."

"Oh," said Roc, who resumed playing with his mother's ears.

Corrynne folded her arms and said, "Dr. Quaid and I found an Internet site that organizes these Raves. It looks very, very dangerous. You should look at it."

"Where?" asked Bo.

"www.bat.scape," said Corrynne.

"What does the B.A.T. stand for?"

"Beasts Acting Together."

"Cute," said Bo facetiously.

"Not cute! Not cute at all," said Corrynne with a frown. "Look for a man that glows white. He's the main guy in charge."

"A *glowing man*?" asked Bo with amusement returning.

"Yes, now don't give me that look," said Corrynne with a warning finger. "I'm serious."

Bo held out his hands and said, "Hey, I'm trying here." He made a straight face. "OK, I'll try harder."

"Good," said Corrynne.

"Tell me about this—guy."

"A man who seems to have supernatural powers appears out of thin air and teaches these kids to break down society by terror."

"Great," said Bo.

"He also tells them they can't talk to anyone about what happens in the mountains, or they will immediately be burned by fire."

"Hmmm," said Bo as he studied his wife.

"Someone has to stop this," said Corrynne with a serious look.

"Yes, someone should," said Bo as he nodded once. "Tell you what, Corrynne—you eat something, you go to sleep, and I'll look it up…deal?"

Corrynne nodded. "That would be good."

"I think last night was quite enough for you. You need some real shut-eye," said Bo.

"Yes, you're right." Corrynne put her head on her arms, folded on the counter. "I'm sorry. I don't even know what can be done. I guess I just want another person's opinion."

"No problem. That's what I'm here for," Bo said reassuringly.

Bo served Corrynne some pancakes and eggs as Jax and Ry, their eleven and nine-year-old sons, came around the corner, bumping into every wall and each other as they walked, still half asleep. Their sandy blonde hair, despite being closely cropped, stuck out in every direction above swollen eyelids that had huge dark circles underneath them.

"Boy, you guys look like I feel," Corrynne said weakly, managing a smile.

"Hi, Mom," Jax hoarsely whispered as he squinted to see her at the bar.

"Why do you look so tired?" Corrynne asked.

"Mom, we have only had four hours of sleep," Ry piped, beginning a playful smile and obviously very proud of himself for some reason.

Jax suddenly lit up. His eyes opened. "Yeah, Mom, Dane got a real great role-playing game for his Dream Cast III. It's a virtual reality game called Dragon Masters. We got to wear the helmet with the glasses and sit in his surround-sound chair! The game came with a laser. It was like we were in the game fighting the dragons ourselves! Dad let us stay up as long as we wanted to play with him."

"Oh, wow, sounds like Dane spent a mint. I bet Dane wasn't happy that he couldn't have his game all to himself."

"No, he was fine," said Ry. "He said that he wanted to play us because he needed someone to beat."

"That's nice. Remind me to tell Dane that he's a great big brother for beating his poor defenseless little brothers," said Corrynne as she rolled her eyes.

"OK," said Ry, not quite understanding what she was meaning.

"So what deal did you make with Dad to let you stay up so late?" Corrynne asked the boys as she looked up at Bo with a raised eyebrow.

"He said that since there wasn't any school today, he'd let us stay up if we would put the twins to sleep last night," said Ry.

"So, how did that go?" Corrynne asked with amused interest.

"It was no problem," said Ry. "We just let them crawl around on the floor for a while and then we bounced them to sleep on the corner of our beds! I got Striynna, and Jax got Strykker."

Despite Corrynne's lack of energy, she smiled. Bo was smart to let them have time with the twins. It gave them an opportunity to be responsible caretakers. "Aren't you guys tired?" Corrynne asked her sons.

"No way! We're going to do our chores and then play again!" Jax said emphatically.

Bo jumped into the conversation. "We'll see what happens this morning. I think there are some other things we're going to have to do before you get back to your game. I'm having wood delivered."

Both the boys gave a horrified groan.

"Wood?" asked Jax with a look of distain.

"No, Dad, please! We hate to stack wood!" said Ry, just as disappointed.

"Well, good thing you're not chopping down the tree, splitting it, and carrying it here then," Bo chided them.

Right then tiny little baby voices cried in unison from upstairs.

Corrynne took a couple of big bites of her eggs and one of her pancakes and got up, mustering her last bit of energy. She kissed Bo on the neck, leaving a shiny butter kiss mark. As she left, she could hear behind her all three of her sons saying how sick kissing was.

Striynna and Strykker were both crying at the top of their lungs as beautiful nineteen-year-old Brea lay still sleeping on the California king waterbed between them. She still had her arms around their waists, but they were wiggling free.

As Corrynne appeared in the doorway, both the babies stopped crying and smiled happy smiles. They both started breathing fast and hard and squirmed free of Brea's grasp to crawl across the bed in high speed to their mom's open arms.

Corrynne at once hugged them both and buried her face in their little chests as they grabbed her hair and laughed. What a sweet sound, Corrynne thought. I could just disappear in those laughs and be happy forever. Things would be so simple.

"I love you guys!" Corrynne said out loud to her seven-month-old twins. She took in their round faces and perfectly shaped mouths. She kissed them over and over all over their faces and tickled them, absorbing every little baby sound and movement. After playing with them, her body began to shake slightly, and it seemed as if the room had cooled down. She began to chill.

Corrynne called out to her daughter still sleeping on her bed. "Brea, wake up. ...Brea...Brea, I need you to take the babies quickly downstairs. I'm getting very tired."

Brea stirred and opened her eyes. She rolled over and slipped off the bed, still unsteady. Brea stretched tall, exposing a beautiful, thin, strong body. Even with her hair messed from sleeping, she managed to defy all reasoning for natural perfection.

"Hi, Mom," her voice husky from sleep. "How was last night?"

"Don't ask," was Corrynne's response. "It was hard, too hard to talk about right now."

"Oh, I'm sorry."

"No, that's fine. Just promise me that you'll never tattoo or pierce your body up in the mountains."

Brea gave her mother a sleepy, sideways glance. "What did you say?"

"Nothing. I think I'm getting delirious. I'm just melting fast, like the Wicked Witch of the West. Can you take these babies? I'm afraid I might just fall on them any second."

"Sure." Brea reached down and took a baby in each arm. "Come here, you cute, cute babies. Mommy has to sleep." Brea and the twins left the room, Brea hooking the door closed with her foot.

Corrynne fell over on the adjacent pillow and peeled off her scrubs right there in bed and kicked them off onto the floor. She crawled under the covers and pulled the down comforter up around her chin. There was something about an intense night, sleep deprivation and her down comforter that made her feel so humble.

"Thank you, Father, for all that I have, for I have been given so much. ...Please, please help all those people have the courage to see the truth. They don't deserve to die...." She never finished her prayer because deep sleep claimed her tired soul.

CHAPTER FOUR

DEADLY CONSEQUENCES

"And fear not them which kill the body, but are not able to kill the soul: but rather fear him which is able to destroy both soul and body in hell" (Matthew 10:28).

Saturday
September 16th
8:40 a.m.
Provo, Utah

Streptococcus

It was still drizzling lightly when Brea backed around the side of the house and honked the horn long and hard. She flipped down the scarred mirror of the old pickup truck that the driving-age children of the Rogers' family lovingly called "a hunk of junk" and applied some lip gloss. She smacked her heart-shaped lips together and then gave herself a trial smile to see how she looked.

Braun bounded out of his adjacent apartment alongside the Rogers' home and pulled himself into the cab next to his younger sister. Noticing Brea glancing at herself he quickly said, "Watch out, or you'll break the mirror!"

"About time you showed up," Brea chortled flippantly, ignoring his comment. "I was about to leave you behind. It would have been fun to walk to school in this rain."

"Well, it's nice to see you, too!" Braun replied. "It's always nice to know you're loved and looked after."

"Keep up or stay behind, that's what I always say!" Brea pulled out of the driveway, shifting the old manual pickup truck into gear and drove south for a Saturday class.

Classes all over the nation were being held on Saturday. It was part of a new solution to a growing problem in the country. President MacEntire, the first female president of the United States, needed to come up with creative solutions to a huge retiring community and a waning workforce. Economically, it was becoming more and more difficult for industry to keep up with the growing worldwide demand for products because the retiring "baby boomers" left a huge hole in the workforce. To fill that void quickly, an accelerated academic agenda was one aspect of her plans. Undergraduate and advanced degrees were combined in return for increased college federal support. This caused most educational institutions to develop advanced degrees that could be completed in two to four years in an attempt to meet the increasing need for highly educated people in the technologically advanced workforce. Braun and Brea were scheduled to receive advanced degrees in the medical field within a year, but that made Saturday and summer attendance a must.

Brea drove into the student parking lot at BYU and both she and Braun checked their digital displays that they used to take notes. Brea had also brought her new toy that she received as a graduation present from high school. It was a small camera-like audio/visual recording device that transmitted the class to their home TV and DVD recorder. It proved to be a perfect way to store a copy of the lecture at home, just in case she and Braun had a question about the material.

In the class at the Eyring Science Center, there were approximately 700 students milling around the large auditorium, trying to find the best seat for their circumstances. This class was very popular due to the large number of students who were going into health fields, but also because the professor was enjoyable to listen to. Brea and Braun took their seats right in the middle, so that Brea's AV recording device would have clear access to the popular and animated professor.

The class was microbiology, or the study of germs, viruses, and parasites. On the syllabus for that day it identified the topic as "Conjugation and Transformation: Means for Adaptation in Microbes."

Braun leaned over to Brea and spoke in a low tone. "Did you see what the lecture is about today?"

"Yeah, can you say boring?" said Brea as she studied which buttons to push to power up her video camera.

"No, this stuff isn't boring Brea, it's amazing. I think this is going to be a great lecture," said Braun with anticipation. "Especially in light of what happened last night at the hospital."

"What happened at the hospital?" asked Brea, now pushing random buttons.

"Didn't you hear what happened to Mom last night?" asked Braun.

"No. What happened to Mom?" Brea asked, looking up from her camera.

"Dad told me that she and the hospital code team tried to save a guy who had a deadly bacteria attack him. It destroyed his muscles and skin. They couldn't save him."

"Really?" Brea asked without expecting an answer. Her face took on a sullen appearance. "That is so sad—and gross."

"I guess it's killed five people in the last week and a couple more before that," said Braun. "This is serious stuff."

"What kind of bacteria was it?"

"Strep."

"No…" Brea's eyes grew wide.

"Yes."

Brea's forehead wrinkled as she frowned. "I hate to hear about things like that. It makes me worry about the future. I would like to have children without them being threatened by every little thing under the sun."

Just then, Professor Green came into the class and attached his microphone. A hush settled on the auditorium. After a few moments of silence, he looked up at the class that halfway encircled him and began his lecture. "Genetic engineering is a miracle," he started and then paused. "It has allowed us to create pest-resistant crops and increase their yield, giving us adequate food. It has allowed us to create super toxin-eating microbes that clean up our oil spills and our toxic messes. It has virtually revolutionized the face of medicine. We can now cause microbes to manufacture human insulin, or make substances to dissolve blood clots and save heart tissue. We can even make growth hormone to help children with stunted growth grow again."

Professor Green paused and then gave a toothy smile. "For you weekend skiers, microbes have done something for you, too. I bet you never thought you'd be thankful for germs, did you? Well, we can encode a bacterial deoxyribonucleic acid, or DNA, to make a protein that makes snow freeze at a higher temperature so the skiing season can be prolonged."

Brea and Braun heard a confirming rumble roll around the room as the audience responded favorably to his statement. Skiing was one subject that students in Utah related to.

After the auditorium quieted, the professor continued. "The discovery that microbes' DNA could be manipulated, or rewritten by inserting coding that the cell reads and follows, allows us to do the seemingly impossible. However, the bacteria's amazing ability to adapt has turned out to be dangerous as well as useful. We have found out that bacteria can learn from other live—and surprisingly, dead—bacteria. So when you hear the common phrase, 'Dead men tell no tales,' you'll know that they weren't talking about the 'Ladies and Germs' kind of germs."

Again the audience responded audibly. Dr. Green continued, gaining verbal speed in his lecture. "Indeed, it was found that when a successful strain of *Strep pneumonia* that had a gel covering to protect it from our immune system was heat-killed and mixed with a live strain of *Streptococci* that did not have that gel covering, the live bacteria suddenly made a gel covering and took on the characteristics of the dead bacteria. How did this happen? Did they communicate? …No, one form was dead, mind you. What happened was that when the virulent form of bacteria was heat-killed, it released its DNA into the solution, allowing the non-virulent form of bacteria to take up the strands through its cell wall and incorporate it into its own DNA! Now that is intelligence! So next time someone tells you that you are 'slime mold,' I want you to smile a wide grin and say, 'Thank you, you're so kind!' because microbes are smarter than we ever thought possible for a one-celled organism."

The professor waited a few moments with his finger high in the air, obviously ready to make another point. He began again with a raised voice, standing on his toes and shaking his finger at the audience as he continued. "Isn't that amazing that microbes can learn from other dead microbes? To me that is amazing, really. I'd like to see *you* come upon a deceased person and say, 'Hey, I really like his nose. It really shouldn't go to waste,' and slap it on your own face and have everyone believe that it was 'natural.' For us it just doesn't work that way!"

The room erupted as the group laughed once again. Finally, Dr. Green resumed. "This process of bacteria trading DNA to increase their abilities is known as 'trans-for-mation.'" The word thickly rolled off the professor's tongue as he emphasized it for the lecture. "In other words, the bacteria actually changed from one form of bacteria to another form, and thus the name of 'transformation.'

"Bacteria can trade DNA through another method known as 'conjugation.' This method is much friendlier since the bacteria are at least alive! This is where two bacteria come close to each other and one forms a special 'pili,' or a tiny tube-like object that actually enters the cell wall of the other bacteria, in which a selected segment of DNA is replicated and sent in the tube into the other bacteria. The second bacterium then incorporates that new portion into its own DNA to again become a new bacterium with new characteristics.[1] Since bacteria have this ability to change their nature so efficiently, we are beginning to see an epidemic in our hospitals.[2] We have wonderful antibiotics that have saved more than a few generations from the ravages of bacterial attack, but now we are seeing the bacteria learn from their environment and teach other bacteria by *trading* small segments of DNA."

The professor then contorted his face, flipped his glasses down on his nose and pretended to be holding cards and talking with another individual. "Yes, I have resistance to Penicillin, Claforan, and Gentamicin. What do you have?" Then the professor pretended to look at the other imaginary person's cards to trade. "I like that resistance to Rifampin. Do you want to share?" The professor then looked up at the crowd with an innocent stare as if he were just becoming aware of their presence, who were by then in uncontrolled laughter at his sudden change.

The professor then straightened to his full height, adjusted his tie, and cleared his throat, readying himself for the next round of information. "What has happened in the past is the use and abuse of antibiotics. We had little old grandmas and grandpas who came down with chest colds, or frequent urinary tract infections, that had a standing order for an antibiotic from their physician that allowed them to obtain the medicine anytime they felt they needed it. They would take it until they felt better and then 'save' the rest for another day since it was expensive.

"Another scenario that contributed to mutating microbes was the struggling young family. With young families come babies with ear infections. After a trip to the doctor's office, an antibiotic would be given— the child would seemingly recover from the infection and the symptoms would disappear. Instead of continuing with the treatment until all the medicine was gone, the well-meaning mother would save the rest for another time that the baby wakes in the night holding his ear. This saves money, sleep, and time, doesn't it? However, the problem that grew to epidemic levels stemmed from failure to destroy all the bacteria due to inadequate length of dosing time. The few surviving bacteria learned methods of survival against their enemy and incorporated it into their DNA and reproduced. Later, when the antibiotic did not work anymore, the mother had to get another kind for her baby. Then the cycle started over again with a new kind of antibiotic.[3]

"The resistant bacteria are then spread through human interaction. Once a child was colonized with resistant bacteria, he could then share the new strains of bacteria in the day-care center by tasting all the toys and then letting the others taste them, too." The professor then pulled his hair up straight and raised his eyebrows, opening his eyes wide to expose an innocent look, and in a rough baby voice said, "I have yummy germs. Here, want a taste? I slobbered so it would be nice and juicy...." The professor handed an imaginary toy to another imaginary child. Predictably, another round of laughter filled the auditorium.

Professor Green laid his hair down with a quick rake of his fingers, took a deep breath, and waited until there was complete silence before he proceeded. "Really, the bottom line is not a humorous one. We are having difficulty keeping up with the bacteria. We superior humans are finding ourselves prey to the tiny and insignificant. Hospitals all over the world are telling families that their loved one will not be saved because there are simply no more antibiotics that are effective. In addition, the bacteria are becoming more violent in their attack of our tissues."

Braun leaned over to Brea, whispering quietly. "Here we go. He read our minds."

"...Their tactics are changing and we are seeing bacteria attack the body in many ways, expressing their presence with different clinical presentations. For example, *Strep* has become very tricky. It can present itself as a sore throat, an open sore on the skin, or by flushing the skin pink and causing a high fever. It can cause the body's own immune system to attack the valves of the heart or the tubules of the kidneys by having similar identifications on its cell wall. It can cause an inflammation around the heart in the protective sack called the pericardium so that it inhibits efficient pumping of its host. In the most serious cases, it can cause a blood infection that dilates all the vessels and causes system-wide organ death from too low blood pressure.

"The most dramatic manifestation of *Streptococcus* is when it enters a wound and causes the tissue to die from the inside out, causing gross necrosis and gangrene on a living patient. There are cases in which people die within 18 hours from this situation.[4] Now, in the past decade, we rarely saw any of these manifestations because of our antibiotics and our healthy lifestyles. But today, they are beginning to resurface. We are still able to keep them at bay but we are nearing the end of our rope.... Heaven help us."

Suddenly the bell rang loud through the room. Despite jumping with the unexpected sound, the class remained riveted on the professor.

"Class dismissed." Dr. Green looked around the room for a moment as if to communicate the importance of his message, then turned off his microphone and left the room.

Deadly Knowledge

"Listen to this!" exclaimed Bo as he sat at the computer screen.

"What, Dad?" asked Roc, who had been playing with his Legos at the foot of his dad's chair.

"Will you go get someone big I can talk to?"

"I'm big, Dad."

"I know you are, but I need to talk to someone who can read."

"I can read. I'm in second grade."

"OK. I need to talk to someone who can do calculus!"

"Calkumus? What's calkumus?"

"Exactly, go get one of your older brothers or sisters."

Roc frowned and then trudged off as instructed to find either Braun or Brea, walking heavily to communicate that he was not happy with his dad's instruction.

"I bet I could do calkumus," he murmured.

Right then, Braun and Brea came in the door from their class.

"Hi Braun and Brea, Dad wants to talk to someone big who can do calkumus."

"What's calkumus?" asked Brea.

"I don't know, but Dad thinks big people can do it better."

Braun and Brea walked into the family room, where they found their father reading something on the computer screen.

"Look at this, guys," Bo said to his grown children as he pointed to his computer's display, which showed the world news.

"What is it?" asked Braun.

"Have you been listening to the news today?"

"No, we've been at school," said Brea.

"It's plastered all over the news about those people dying at the hospital from the flesh-eating bacteria. I guess Dr. Quaid went straight to the media with what he knew. Your mom didn't tell me that he was going to do that. Boy, he must have been very upset because he pulled out all the stops and even contacted CNN. They did some research and confirmed the story from the doctor's contact in New York. They've found that only within the last three to four weeks, across the nation and in other countries, there has been a rash of deaths of young people, all with the same characteristics of the one that your mom tried to help last night. All of the young people frequented Raves, and all of them had the same tattoos and body piercings that were seen here."

"Oh, my goodness!" said Brea. "I can't believe this is really so widespread! It sounds like an episode from The Twilight Zone."

A rhythmic padding sound came from the next room. They all turned to see Corrynne come around the corner looking pale and very tired.

"Hi, you guys," Corrynne said with a weak voice. She stood behind her husband and looked at the screen. "What are you doing?"

"Talking about Dr. Quaid and that disease you uncovered last night."

"Isn't that so sad?" Corrynne asked her children.

"That's too strange, Mom," said Brea as Braun nodded.

"I know. I wouldn't have believed it if I hadn't been there last night." Pointing to the computer screen Corrynne asked, "Have you had a chance to look up that address I gave you this morning?" she asked Bo.

Bo nodded. "Yes, I have. You'll be happy to know that the media are all over this story."

"What story?" Corrynne asked, her voice still slightly scratchy from sleeping.

"The flesh-eating bacteria story."

"How did they find out about it? Did you call them?" she asked Bo.

Bo shook his head. "Dr. Quaid evidently decided that it was time to tell someone about what he knew."

"I can't believe it." Corrynne said as she started to smile, losing some of her grogginess. "I thought he didn't want to do that, but I have a new-found respect for him because he put everything on the line and went through with it."

"The media were impressed, by the looks of it. It's getting worldwide coverage," said Bo as he flipped through news Internet sites.

"Really?" asked Corrynne as she eagerly watched from behind.

"And there's been a run on all the hospitals everywhere," added Bo.

Corrynne's smile turned into a frown. "Oh, shoot," she said as she glanced at the floor and then back again. "I'm sure that's what Dr. Quaid wanted to avoid. Did they inform the public that not everyone is in danger? And that only people who attended the Raves and received tattoos need to worry?"

"Yes, but I guess there were a lot of those people. All of them want antibiotics prophylactically."

"Hmmmm," said Corrynne as she nodded. "They won't give it to them. They're pretty tight-fisted with those antibiotics now. You'd think they were gold."

"You're right, they didn't. The news said that with the epidemic of resistant bacteria filling up the hospitals, no antibiotics are allowed to be given out. They were just told to come back if they had any sore spot near or around their wounds."

"That's what I thought would happen," said Corrynne.

"I'm sure that was frustrating," said Brea.

"Obviously it was," Bo confirmed. "There are throngs of people picketing the hospitals claiming that they are being discriminated against."

"What?" asked Corrynne, surprised. "That's ridiculous!"

"Whatever," said Braun. "People will say they're being discriminated against for almost any reason. That's just a ploy to try and strong-arm the hospital and the government."

"I agree," said Brea nodding.

"According to CNN, the people from the Raves feel their religion is being targeted by the police and society in general," said Bo. "They're claiming that they are being blocked from protection because they're perceived as a threat to society."

"Well, that perception is their own fault!" said Corrynne. "Maybe they should change their slogan of using 'terror to break down society' if they didn't want to be perceived as a threat," she suggested sarcastically. "Think of it, if you're going to publicly threaten the government, you might expect some kind of retaliation."

"But that's not why those people aren't getting the antibiotics," said Braun.

"No, but it could be in the future," suggested Brea.

"No, that's not true. They can't legally withhold treatment because of someone's affiliation," said Braun shaking his head.

"Are you kidding?" Corrynne asked her son. "We withhold treatment to those who demonstrate high risk behavior all the time. An alcoholic doesn't receive a new liver just because he's destroyed the one he has. For the same reason I don't think the people who choose to go to those Raves should receive prophylactic antibiotics. If they choose to go to those parties they are choosing to put themselves at risk for this disease. Period!"

"But they didn't know about the possibility of infection before," Braun responded.

"Maybe not, but if you're drinking and taking drugs, you have to know you're in danger of death in some way."

"Sure, but I was talking about affiliation," said Braun, "not high-risk behavior. The hospitals can't withhold treatment because of religion."

"Oh, I know," said Corrynne, "but it's all semantics. They say 'discrimination' because it fits their purposes and we say we'll withhold treatment because of 'high-risk behavior.' Either way, the end result is the same. Those people will not receive a controlled resource just because they demand it. In medicine, it's a whole different world. It's all about who decides and in medicine, availability of resources is the ultimate morality. It trumps everything."

"To me, it sounds a little like you're looking for reasons not to service those people, Mom."

"Not me, Braun. You forget it was me who was at the bedside of that young man last night. I'm talking about the powers-that-be who control the medical resources. There's going to come a day in which medicine must decide who receives treatment and who does not. It's unavoidable. As society continues to act in ways that are self-destructive we will not be able to fix everyone. There's going to come a day when medicine will simply say, 'enough is enough' and allow people to deal with the consequences of their choices. Look around, it's almost like that now. Try and get insurance if you have cancer or Lupus."

"That's frightening," said Brea. "When you need medical treatment the most, you can't get it."

"And you're talking about illnesses that are random in nature," said Braun. "Those aren't even associated with high risk behavior. I say there's too much power in someone's hands. I say medical care is a human right and everyone should have access to it."

Corrynne chuckled as she looked at her son. "Said like a true idealist. It'd be nice if that was the reality, but it's not. Maybe as you get older you'll become jaded like me and see reality as it really is."

Bo, who was still studying various Web pages, interrupted the debate. "OK you guys. I know you like your pet opinions but listen to this."

"What?" asked Corrynne, returning her attention to the computer.

"Did you know that the victims' families are protecting their children's involvement in that cult you were talking about?" asked Bo.

"What do you mean?" asked Corrynne.

"The families are defending their children's behavior and demanding privacy from the media."

"Are you saying the families support their children's attendance at the Raves?"

Bo nodded. "That's what it sounds like to me. Look at this headline: 'Despite the violent deaths, the families are not pressing charges against the leader of the Rave meetings but instead are demanding privacy from the hospitals.'"

"No way," said Brea with a look of amazement.

"Yes. I've read a bunch of articles and in each it says that no one from any family of the victims will talk to the media. The only witnesses they have are at the hospitals from nurses and doctors who treated the patients."

"Then I bet it's hard to put the pieces together because of confidentiality issues," said Corrynne.

"Right," said Bo. "The families are refusing to release the medical records or the results of autopsies."

"Good thing that doctor decided to go to the media himself," said Brea.

"Otherwise this stuff would have continued to happen without anyone knowing about it," added Braun.

Corrynne ran her fingers through her hair and said, "I think that proves that the families are scared. They see what's happening to their children and now they're afraid for their own lives."

"Or that they're embarrassed," added Brea.

"No, I don't think embarrassment would cause every family to refuse to talk to the media. Especially in this attention-hungry society we live in, where anyone will air their dirty laundry to be on a talk show," returned Corrynne.

"Yes, that's true," agreed Brea.

"I think the man in charge of this cult has all his followers scared to death."

"Do you know who that man is?" asked Brea. "He's the one who should be under investigation."

"Right. Someone has to stop him," interjected Braun, "rather than punishing the people who are suffering. They and their families have been through enough."

"No one's punishing anyone Braun," said Corrynne.

"Hey!" said Brea with a look of determination. "Back to the topic! Who's the guy responsible for all of this?"

"Spoil sport," whispered Corrynne to her daughter with a sarcastic smirk and then a wink.

"Yeah, back to the topic," said Bo, chiding his wife.

"OK, OK," said Corrynne with a sigh. "One of the nurses at the hospital showed us this Internet site that explains a lot. Take us to that site, Bo…and brace yourselves. I think this is unbelievable."

Bo typed in the Internet address, and the group was met with the swastika and the morphing religious symbols. Braun and Brea's eyes widened.

"*What—is—this?*" asked Braun obviously surprised by what he was seeing.

"This is the site that all those people who are dying are connected with," said Corrynne. "I'm sure that it says something about that man who keeps appearing at the Raves. Bo, let's look. Do you see any headings that talk about him?"

Bo scrolled down until he saw the words *"Imam Mahdi."* He double-clicked on the name and a screen came up with a picture of a man surrounded by a bluish-white hue.

"There he is," said Bo as he sat back and folded his arms. In bolded letters under his picture it said:

> *"I am he that has been foretold for centuries. I am Jehovah, I am Krishna, I am Mitreya, I am Imam Mahdi, I am the Messiah.[5] Come to me, ye who are cast out, and I will make you whole. Take upon you my mark and ye shall be saved in the last day, for fire shall come down from heaven and consume the unbelievers. Through me ye shall find shelter, protection and manna. Come near unto me and I will come near unto you. Pray unto me often for purity so as to not be burned yourselves, for in that day, your heart shall surely fail.*
>
> *"I come to unify the world, to feed the hungry, to clothe the naked. I come to bring the prideful low and raise up the obedient. Be watching always, for I will come to you soon. In the sealing you shall find me.*
>
> *"In me ye will be blessed, for in division ye will find unity. In pain ye will find joy. Through war ye will obtain peace. Through death ye will find life. Through exclusion ye will find inclusion. Give all, and you will receive the world.*
>
> *"I bring terror to the unbelievers, and in this we will establish our world, the perfect society."* [6]

"OK. I've got the chills," said Brea after she finished reading. "I'm getting a stomach ache just reading those words. This is totally crazy!"

Corrynne cocked her head slightly. "Those words might sound good to people in a chaotic world like ours. I can imagine hearing these words from a man who claimed to be Jehovah and I would want to believe them too."

"I can't believe how similar his speech is to the scriptures," added Braun.

"You're right," said Bo. "His words do sound like the symbolic language found in the scriptures. I wonder what he means by those statements," thought Bo out loud as he absently rubbed his chin with his hand.

"Can you believe that this guy claims to be the Messiah?" asked Brea in a disgusted tone.

"He claims to be all the expected religious figures from every major religion!"[7] noted Corrynne. "All those things he says—peace, feeding the hungry and clothing the naked—probably sound inviting. I can see how this message could be accepted by a world that is looking for relief from war and hunger. Mix that with his liberal view on partying found in his ceremonies, and I bet there are some who are begging to label this man as a 'Savior'."

"It sounds cryptic and deceptive to me," stated Brea.

"What do you mean?" sneered Braun. "He has the perfect religion. He has every ingredient to appeal to the world. He has mystical powers to appear out of thin air, the promise to end world problems himself, and he promises destruction to all the bullies who dispute his teachings. Plus it sounds like he gives everyone permission to belt their neighbors to create terror and break down society. I think that appeals to many worldly desires: hunger, entertainment, laziness, violence, and intimidation. Wow, I think I'll go join."

"Well, they do have to do one thing," said Corrynne. "They have to keep his secrets, or stay 'pure'."

"Purity? This guy is not interested in purity, at least not how we understand it," said Bo.

"I bet you it means pure to his cause, or pure support without questioning," said Braun.

"Well, the piercings are to remind the followers to follow without question. That correlates with your idea, Braun. I bet you're right." Corrynne sighed. "With all these deaths from the Strep A looking like Imam Mahdi's promised burnings, I bet it has everyone scared to even think about talking or not supporting his cause."

"Does it say anywhere on his site where this Imam Mahdi came from?" asked Brea.

"Ah, let's see," Bo hit the back arrow key to go back to the main page. "There is a phrase here: *'Origins of Imam Mahdi'*."

"Yes, I bet that's it. Click on it," said Brea.

Bo clicked, and a screen came up with multiple pictures of Imam Mahdi performing healings.

"Now I'm getting sick. They say he heals the sick?" asked Braun.

"Looks like it," said Bo.

"Doesn't that take things a little too far?"

"I guess it fills the whole 'god' identity. It says here that 'Imam Mahdi creates healing springs of water in the areas near his appearances. The healing waters in Mexico, Germany, and India have drawn millions of visitors'."

"What does it say about where he came from?" asked Brea.

Corrynne thought for a moment, "Let's see here. I think I saw the answer to that question." She scanned the screen, "Oh yes, here it is." Corrynne began to read:

"'Imam Mahdi is a resurrected being who descended in July 1988 from his ancient retreat in the Himalayas and took up residence in the Indian-Pakistani community of London. He has been living and working there, seemingly as an ordinary man. Few

people in his community know his true identity. However, Imam Mahdi has been miraculously appearing before gatherings of orthodox religious groups and to select chosen young people worldwide. He addresses them briefly in their own language and teaches the message of world unity in religion, obedience, and government'."[8]

"Europe, huh?" asked Bo.

"I guess so, why?" returned Corrynne.

"There's just a lot in the scriptures that seem to identify Europe and its surrounding areas as being the center for the government of the 'Beast' and the Antichrist found in the scriptures."[9]

"Well, this stuff is scary enough to make me wonder if he isn't the Antichrist. He sure has all the details right. And look, all of his identifying marks have the word 'beast' in them," said Corrynne.

"Wouldn't that be too obvious?" asked Brea.

"I guess not, because people are thinking he is someone they should follow rather than run from," said Bo.

"Look, he even addresses that idea in his own site." Brea pointed to a statement on the screen. "He states that 'the unbelievers will label him as the Antichrist.' Now that's a hoot! Of course we'll say that, because it's true! This is unbelievable! How have so many been deceived?"

"I think there will be a whole lot more deceived by the time Imam Mahdi is done with humanity," remarked Braun.

"That's true. The scriptures are clear about that," agreed Bo. "There are about four different places that say that the Antichrist will sound so inviting and real that, if possible, the very elect will be deceived."

"Let's hope that *this* is not the beginning of *that*,"[10] said Corrynne.

Brea bit her lip in contemplation. "Other than the glowing description, what else does he look like?"

"It says here that he is a man who mostly dresses in white but that he can appear any way he wants to. He will appear to whomever he is addressing how they expect him to appear. Sometimes he even manifests himself as Mary, the mother of Jesus. He has no particular look," continued Corrynne.

"Wow, that's convenient. That means this person can take credit for every spiritual sighting or experience all over the planet," pointed out Braun.

"It looks like from his Internet site that he does exactly that. Look at this list of 'miracles associated with Imam Mahdi'," Bo began to list miracles named on the Internet site. "Weeping and bleeding statues, healing crosses of light and springs of water, divine messages inscribed by the seeds within fruits and vegetables, bronze and stone sacred statues that appear to drink milk. He even takes credit for the end of the Cold War between Russia and the USA, the breaking down of the Berlin Wall, and the end of apartheid in South Africa."[11]

"Oh, yeah, as if that were true!" spat Brea.

"According to him, he will reveal himself to the world through the media on the 'Day of Revealing' in which he will 'declare his true identity to the world.' It says we will see his face on television, but he will not actually speak." Bo continued reading:

> "'*Each of us will hear his words telepathically in our own language, as he simultaneously impresses the minds of all humanity. At the same time, hundreds of thousands of spontaneous healings will take place throughout the world. In this way we will know that Imam Mahdi is truly the only one all humanity should worship and follow, creating a one-world religion'*."[12]

"To me it sounds like he's catering to those who want to identify Christ through a sign. We know that repeatedly the Lord refuses that kind of mentality by saying that faith precedes the miracle,"[13] stated Brea.

"Did you notice that he doesn't once address the plan of salvation, or our eternal life? His focus is the same focus that the Jews expected Christ to fulfill at his first coming.[14] They thought he had come to free them from bondage and answer their mortal needs when he was sent specifically there to save them spiritually. That's the main reason the Jews rejected him. He didn't live up to their expectations of what Jehovah would be like," commented Corrynne.

"I agree. But the people of the world will not know these things that we are reviewing here," said Bo. "They will wonder, and many will believe."

Brea covered her face with her hands and shook her head vigorously. "I can't believe this is starting already!"

"Well, we don't know for sure, but we should prepare for it. I think we are witnessing just the beginning," said Bo.

Abruptly, all the voices went silent as the four stared at the computer screen.

Brea suddenly spoke. "Hey Mom, look at this," she said as she pointed to a statement on the screen. "'*Zulu-fire and blood. To all that turn away or uttereth, a burning.*' Do you think that has reference to the Strep A?"

Corrynne nodded. "Yep. But my question is, how is this man controlling who breaks out in the infection and who does not."

"Do you think he's controlling that?" asked Braun.

"What other answer is there? It seems pretty controlled to me. The dramatic deaths of the people indicate that the infection by Streptococcus A is not small, it's huge. By the look of how many followers this guy has, there should be thousands of people ill, but there's not."

Braun nodded thoughtfully but didn't respond.

"Now look at this," said Brea pointing at another place on the screen. "This other display looks like some sort of time reference. There are two sets of numbers. One set seems to be going backwards. What do you think that is?"

"Hmmm, 01:03:14, 06:45:10," said Bo as he read the numbers right off the screen. "It looks like some sort of clock.".

"Except the second set of numbers are running backwards like a countdown, see?" Brea pointed to the second set of changing numbers.

"But a countdown to what?" asked Corrynne.

"You got me," said Braun, shaking his head.

"Well, if it is a countdown, it looks like there is at least 6 hours 44 minutes and 30 seconds now," said Corrynne.

"Yes, that makes sense that the second set of numbers represents hours, minutes and seconds," said Bo. "I bet that's what it is. We'll have to watch this and see if it correlates with time."

"What do you think the first set of numbers represents? Could it be a date?" asked Brea.

"I guess it could be," said Bo as he pushed back his chair.

"Do you think the 3 represents March, and the 14 for the.... No that doesn't make sense," stated Brea.

"I don't know. We'll have to keep watching it to know for sure," said Braun.

"So I guess we should be looking for something to happen in relation to this countdown. Maybe it will be the 'Day of Revealing'." said Brea.

"Maybe. Whatever it might be, let's keep our eye on it," said Corrynne. "I think we'll find that the significance is something we shouldn't overlook."

"I think you're right," stated Bo.

"This whole thing gives me the willies," said Brea with an involuntary shiver.

Corrynne put one arm around her daughter and then one around her son. She took a deep breath and then said in a quiet voice, "I believe that if we stay close to the Lord, he will guide us through this whole mess. We know that the last days are here, and things will continue to gather speed until Christ himself comes. Together," she said with a whimsical smile, "together we'll fight this, at least in our little corner of the world. Somehow we'll make a difference."

Notes to "Deadly Consequences"

Streptococcus

[1] For details of the discussion presented in the text, see Christine L. Case, Berdell R. Funke & Gerard J. Tortora, *Microbiology, An Introduction*, 227-236.

[2] See Nicole Dyer, "Bacteria Bite Back. (Bacteria That Resists Antibiotics)," *Science World*, February 1999, available online:

http://www.findarticles.com/cf_0/m1590/10_55/55183072/p1/article.jhtml?term=resistant+bacteria.

[3] Mari Edlin, "What Does Not Kill Them Makes Them Stronger. (Development of Drug-Resistance Bacteria)," *Science World*, August 2000, available online:

http://www.findarticles.com/cf_0/m0HNF/8_10/65357554/p1/article.jhtml?term=resistant+bacteria.

[4] Troy A. Callender MD., "Necrotizing Fasciitis of the Head and Neck, or see "Necrotizing Fasciitis/Myositis ('flesh-eating disease')," Canada, Population and Public Health Branch. April 1999, available online: http://www.hc-sc.gc.ca/hpb/lcdc/bid/respdis/necro_e.html.

Deadly Knowledge

[5] "The followers of all religions and traditions maintain such a belief and are awaiting the appearance of such a commanding figure under the divine protection. Each tradition recognizes this figure with a different name and specific title. The Zoroastrians call him Saoshyant (meaning the 'savior of the world'); the Jews know him as the Messiah, whereas the Christians regard him as the Savior Messiah" ("Al-Imam al-Mahdi, The Just Leader of Humanity," "The Messianic Leader, Mahdi, in Other Religions," Chapter 3, available online: http://www.al-islam.org/mahdi/nontl/Chap-3.htm#two).

[6] Messages like this one from groups that claim that the Messiah has already returned exist even now on the Internet.

[7] Many of the ideas for the modern day Antichrist came from a real character that claims to be the world's Messiah (see http://www.shareintl.org/index.htm). This site is mentioned in conjunction with a modern day Antichrist in the book, *"As A Thief In The Night,"* (Roger K. Young, 46).

[8] This paragraph closely resembles the description of the person described in endnote #7 and can be found on that Internet site.

[9] See Revelation 17:3-7, 9; "And here *is* the mind which hath wisdom. The seven heads are seven mountains, on which the woman sitteth."

Comparing Revelation 17: 9, Rome is known through all ancient Latin literature as the city of seven hills or *usbs septicollis*, the number seven represents the complete political power this center will have, as Rome had back in John's day (R. H. Mounce, *The Book of Revelation*, 315).

[10] See Matthew 24:24; Joseph Smith Matthew 1:22; Mark 13:22; D&C 45:57.

[11] This list of miracles corresponds to those listed on the Internet site referred to in endnote #7.

[12] The following verses show that there will be one government that will combine forces with an Antichrist that can work miracles through evil powers. Because the Antichrist is presented as a false Christ to lead the people from the truth, this could be construed as the influence of a one-world religion.

"And I saw three unclean spirits like frogs *come* out of the mouth of the dragon, and out of the mouth of the beast, and out of the mouth of the false prophet. For they are the spirits of devils, working miracles, *which* go forth unto the kings of the earth and of the whole world, to gather them to the battle of that great day of God Almighty" (Revelation 16:13-14).

"…And the beast was taken, and with him the false prophet that wrought miracles before him, with which he deceived them that had received the mark of the beast, and them that worshipped his image. These both were cast alive into a lake of fire burning with brimstone" (Revelation 19:20).

[13] See Matthew 12:39; Matthew 16:4; Mark 8:12; Luke 11:29.

[14] "The Jews were looking for a redeemer quite different from the Christ. It was a temporal salvation that they desired. It was an earthly kingdom for which they longed. It was not faith, repentance, and baptism for which they sought, but national vindication, the destruction of gentile oppressors, and the establishment of a kingdom of peace and justice" (Joseph McConkie, "Messianic Expectations among the Jews," *A Symposium on the New Testament*, Salt Lake City: The Church of Jesus Christ of Latter-day Saints, 128).

CHAPTER FIVE

INNER UNDERSTANDING

"For my soul delighteth in plainness; for after this manner doth the Lord God work among the children of men. For the Lord God giveth light unto the understanding; for he speaketh unto men according to their language, unto their understanding" (2 Nephi 31:3).

Saturday
September 16th
4:30 p.m.
Provo, Utah

Left Behind

"Hey, Dane, wake up!" Carea called right into the ear of her snoring brother, who was crashed on the living room couch.

Dane uncoiled out of his fetal position and came up to his knees fighting. One swing, two swings.

Carea, who was very familiar with his reflexes when he woke from deep sleep, ducked each swing and then pushed him off the couch.

Dane landed with a thud, his huge muscular body vibrating with sudden adrenaline. Above him stood his gorgeous, blond-haired, brown-eyed 16-year-old little sister. She was in her full cheerleading uniform. Dane had fallen asleep after he had rototilled the garden to get it ready for winter.

"Sorry to have to do that to you," Carea crooned, "but aren't you about to sleep through something you don't want to miss?"

Dane's face turned red with anger as he looked at her through fogged eyes. He stood up to his full 6'0" height and towered over her tiny, twiggy frame. He pumped up his chest and leaned into her and whispered in a very threatening growl, "I've told you never to do that to me! Carea, you wouldn't look very good cheering with a *big, fat, broken nose!*"

Carea cocked her head and looked at Dane out of the corner of her eye and said with her arms folded, "You're not that lucky. You can't connect when you just wake up. Plus I'm too good at ducking. I'm your best friend right now. I wanted to make sure that you remembered the game. You need to get ready. I'm leaving and everyone else is gone, so it's now or never, *Bud*! I'm leaving in 30 seconds. If you're not outside by then, you'll have to call someone else for a ride."

A light suddenly went on inside Dane's head. "What day is it today?"

"Saturday…game day…remember?"

"What time is it?"

"It's 4:30…hellllloooo! The school's best linebacker better get his hiney in gear."

"I can't believe I fell asleep! I was just resting for a moment."

"Well, you looked pretty comfortable. Believe it or not, I was worried that if I didn't wake you good and hard, you would've stayed there until midnight and enjoyed it!"

"I've got to get going. Thanks for waking me up, but next time you don't have to push me off the couch, OK?" Dane's eyebrows rose dramatically as he waited for his sister to agree.

Carea gave him a sarcastic smile then turned quickly, causing her skirt to fly out around her. The door slammed as she left, punctuating her lack of agreement and her exit.

All the football games were held on Saturday in the new District Stadium, complete with metal detectors and a security force. Due to increased gang and youth violence, federal law demanded that sports events occur only in a protected environment like the Provo Sports Center Stadium. School rivalries were the perfect fuel to ignite hot tempers into raging infernos all over the country.[1]

Dane bounded up the stairs to his room. Frantically, he searched for his shoes. Seeing one white shoe sticking out from under his bed, he scooped the athletic trainer forcefully out into the open with his right foot and jammed his toes into the gaping hole. As he hunted for the other shoe, his eye caught sight of a corner of his blue football bag tangled in his bed covers. With a yank, Dane ripped it out. Despite the force of his motion, dirty socks still clung to the zipper. Scowling, he threw them back onto the bed.

Dane quickly scanned the room again for his missing shoe. Not seeing it, he fell to his abdomen to look under the bed. Flipping back the covers that hung loosely across the bed in wrinkles, he searched the debris that had magically accumulated underneath the box springs in vain. Surprised, he found a pair of sandals that had long been lost, with dirt from the summer still clinging to the tread. With a quick, snake-like snap, he reached out and grabbed them as if worried they would get away. He would wear these instead, since time was such an issue.

In another second, Dane was on his feet and flipping off the athletic shoe that was hanging on the toes of his right foot. He ran out of the room barefoot, with the sandals and his football bag in hand. He leaped downstairs, bridging five stairs at once in his frantic pace.

Dane ran out the front door to "the hunk of junk." To his great dismay, it wasn't in the driveway. Carea had already left. He ran back into the house and began yelling the Rogers' family names. "Brea! Braun! Mom! Dad! …Anyone!" Of course no one was home to answer his panicked calls. Carea had just told him he was the last one left.

Dane was angry. "Carea's going to die…" he said through clenched teeth. "What was she thinking?" He wondered why she even bothered waking him up if she was just going to leave him behind?

Dane went into the living room and threw himself on the couch, slapping the sandals on his huge feet. Continuing to murmur he said, "I can't run to the school because the game's at the District Stadium, and I'll never get there in time…." Next, he found his cell phone sitting on the table near where he had been sleeping and began dialing numbers of his friends but no one answered their phones. All his buddies were probably suiting up.

Again he sat down on the couch in the living room and dejectedly looked at the pattern in the carpet as he worried about his position on the team. He had worked so hard to get where he was. The whole school was going to be at that game tonight. He could just imagine the flack he was going to reap from being late, or even absent.

Dane's eyes wandered down to his big white toes sticking out of his sandals. He wiggled them as if to prove that they belonged to him. For some reason his toes made him remember a Primary song that he had learned years ago. The tune came into his head and began to bounce around in his mind. "What were those words? Da, da, da, da, da, hm, hm, hm, hm, hm," he began to himself. "Oh, I remember," he said audibly. "Heavenly Father, are you really there? And do you hear and answer every child's prayer?"[2] Suddenly he stopped and looked out the window and made a disgusted face. "What am I doing? I have to figure out how to get to my game, or I'm dead!"

Dane got up from the couch and began to pace. He dialed everyone in his family who had a phone this time. Again, no one answered. "Where's everybody?" he asked aloud. Dane looked at the clock. It was 4:50 p.m. He was late for the locker room, but he still had time. He mindlessly searched the counters in the kitchen and into the deserted family room for a clue as to what to do. Again, the Primary song came back into his head. "…Some say that heaven is far away, but I feel it close around me as I pray…."

Dane sat once again on the couch. As he reviewed his lack of options he looked at his hands. He noted their massiveness compared to when he was little. He remembered comparing his hands with his father's and thinking that his hands were wimpy. Now they were huge. Dane wondered how that happened. When did he grow up?

Dane interlocked his fingers as a scripture came to his mind: "Trust in the Lord with all thine heart and lean not unto thine own understanding."[3] He again wondered at his thoughts. "Why am I quoting scriptures and singing songs at a time like this?" he muttered to himself as he lay back into the cushions of the couch.

Then a thought came clearly to his mind. Maybe he should pray about this situation. Would being left at home with no transportation to a football game be a reason to pray? He couldn't help but feel silly about this thought but then knew that prayer leads to answers to any problem.[4]

Dane slowly moved from the couch onto a kneeling position on the floor. He interwove his fingers once again and closed his eyes and began to pray a simple prayer. "Dear Heavenly Father, please help me. I know that this is only a game, but it's very important. My whole family's coming, and I need to get to the stadium.

"Thou hast told us to pray constantly. Well, I haven't been that good at praying that much, but I do pray when I should, unless I forget.

"When I was a kid, I knew thou answered my parents' prayers all the time, and I saw that power. Because of that, I know that thou canst help me even with this insignificant problem. After all, isn't this why we have prayer...to ask for help?

"OK, I know I am nothing without thee, even though I'm finally big. I am really small inside. Please help me....I love thee. In the name of Jesus Christ, amen."

Dane knelt in his position for a few moments before he opened his eyes. A part of him was thankful that no one was home to see him at that moment, but he then chastised himself for his hypocrisy. Dane whispered a quick repentance for that moment of pride and got up from his place on the floor.

Ten more minutes went by without any hint of aid. Then all of a sudden, he heard the familiar "chinka, chinka, chinka" of the hunk of junk's loose hubcaps, and he craned his neck and saw the wonderfully ugly truck come around the corner with Brea, his oldest sister at the helm.

Dane grabbed his stuff and ran out full bore to the truck.

Brea looked at him with a disgusted look through the opened window. "Do you know what time it is?"

"Yes, I do! Let's go!" said Dane as he opened the door and jumped in.

Brea shook her head as she put her foot on the gas and accelerated. "I had a strong feeling to come home. I didn't know what I was looking for. I thought you were already at the game so I didn't think it was you."

Dane was quiet for a moment and then said, "Thank you for listening. I owe you one."

"Yes, you do," said Brea smiling.

"Believe it or not, I prayed for you to come," said Dane quietly, maybe exposing too much but still feeling like he wanted to. After all, he had just had a small miracle happen to him. It was important he acknowledged it so the Lord knew he was grateful.

Brea's eyes opened wide. "No problem," she said but offered nothing more.

Dane could tell she was trying not to embarrass him. That was nice. She could have tried to rub this situation in, but she didn't. He liked her a lot—for a big sister.

At the stadium Brea drove Dane as close to the locker room as she could. Dane opened the door and jumped out.

Dane turned and looked Brea in the eyes, "Thanks again. Like I said, I owe you one."

Brea smiled and said, "Don't worry, I won't let you forget."

Fleeting Moments

Bo gave the command to their Suburban to drive to Pizza Hut on University Parkway. Corrynne, Bo, and their youngest five children were looking for dinner before they headed to the football game. Pizza was the traditional Saturday pre-game meal. Corrynne was wedged on the back bench between the twin's car seats as they howled loudly. They hated their car seats and always cried when they were strapped in.

Bo rolled his eyes and wondered how many times he had seen this scenario. Crying children strapped into safety devices—his wife not sitting with him, but with them. It happened with every child they had. It didn't seem to bother Corrynne as much as it bothered him. She'd just assume her place in the back to keep them happy. As for him, he hated crying. That was his biggest weakness in life. Crying grated on his nerves more than anything else, especially in an enclosed space like the car. If he could have his way, he'd just have his wife sit up with him and install a sound proof glass window between him and the family to give him peace while he drove. Was that unreasonable?

Bo was amused by his thoughts as he looked back again at his family. He noticed how good-looking his sons were. Jax was growing into quite a strong young man. Ry was coming along too. It wouldn't be long until they would play high school football just like Dane. But then the realization hit him. It was astounding how fast time flew. As soon as the boys played football, he knew the next minute they'd be grown just like his older children. It was a sobering thought. Life moved by too fast.

Bo glanced at his young twins once again who were now laughing with their mother. Their little laughs gave him an unexpected itch to laugh too. A pang of love swelled up in his chest. He was a lucky man. Taking in all the little faces in the back he realized life was giving him another chance to take time to enjoy the moments, almost like an instant replay. With this set of children he could make the decision to savor the rest of his life. He could slow down and grab hold of every moment of every day and not let go until the moment was absolutely past so that he had no regrets of lost opportunities like he had with his first few children. The plan sounded good. It sounded right. He decided right then and there he would watch as many sunsets as possible, give long snuggles at bed time, go to each game and concert and maybe—eat more desserts before dinner. Life was too short to be irritated. Life was too short for anything negative. Life was just too short, period.

The car stopped at a red light and Bo pulled out two pieces of caramel he had hidden in his pocket. He threw both back, one for each baby.

Corrynne caught one but the other landed square in front of Striynna. "What are these?" asked Corrynne snatching the stray caramel from her daughter.

"Caramel to help keep Striynna and Strykker happy till we get to the restaurant."

"Before dinner?" asked Corrynne with a smile.

"I'll have it!" said Jax from behind Corrynne; his hand flinging over her shoulder.

"I want one, Dad!" said Ry.

"Can I have one, too?" asked Roc.

Corrynne looked back. "Hey guys, we're going to dinner. I'm sure Dad has more in his pocket for the game, right?" asked Corrynne giving Bo that look that said, "You better agree with me."

Bo, in response, pulled four more from his pocket and threw them back. "Yep. I've definitely got more where that came from."

"Yeah!" yelled Roc as all the pieces of candy showered down around him. He quickly snatched one and pulled off the wrapper.

The other boys did the same with equal noises of excitement.

Corrynne looked like she was trying to stifle a smile as she closed her eyes and shook her head. She knew she had been overruled but it wasn't a bad thing. It was a good stray from the usual and Corrynne sensed it.

When Corrynne opened her eyes again Bo winked at her in the mirror and she winked back. With a smile she picked up a nearby caramel and looked at it. "We're eating caramels before dinner now?" she asked. "Does this have anything to do with a mid-life crisis?"

"It's only 30 calories," said Bo smiling and nodding. "So much happiness in 30 calories. I thought we could afford it. Life's short."

Then with a sly look, Corrynne carefully unwrapped one piece of candy and put it in her mouth. A smile spread upon her face as the sweetness hit her tongue. Next she unwrapped one for each baby and they smiled happily as they tried to stuff the whole thing in their mouths.

"That's it," said Bo, feeling very satisfied. It took so little for everyone to feel so happy. "Enjoy the moment. It's too sweet to let it get away," he said to his family.

For the next few minutes the car was silent.

Yes, life was good. Bo smiled again with contentment as they rolled up to Pizza Hut.

Let's Give It a Cheer

Carea stood in front of the full-length mirror in the locker room. She made sure that her hair and makeup were flawless. They were. She knew, however, that halfway through the game it would be as if she had never even prepared herself for the event because her hair would be wet and straight and her face naked and shiny with sweat. The makeup would end up on her towel, and her hair would hang in strings. But that was fine. You weren't a good cheerleader unless you got good and sweaty. It showed your spirit. Despite the futility, she wanted to look perfect at the beginning of the game, if only to prove that she could. Carea smirked as she thought how silly the whole 'beautiful-cheerleader' thing was.

Carea reached tall and then bent in half, stretching over her right thigh. While she was down nose-to-shin, she noticed how the new nylon-like thermal stockings looked on her legs. They were almost transparent. Their support made her legs look sculptured. She stretched high again and then repeated the process on the other side. Pleased, she took both hands and started at the right ankle and pulled the stockings inch by inch higher to take the slack from her ankle. Again she repeated the motion on the left. She was impressed with their resilience as well as their insulation. They were a new invention for anyone who was ignorant enough to wear outfits that defied the winter. The new stockings kept in the body heat without compromising the look. "The woman is a genius," she said out loud, referring to the inventor.

"What did you say?" asked Kessa, her best friend on the cheerleading squad. She was tall with endless, gorgeous legs. She had ebony black, thick hair and supernaturally clear, olive skin. Her reflection popped into the mirror as she moved next to Carea to talk while she also stretched.

"I was just saying that these new nylons meant to keep us warm on game day are awesome! Last game day I didn't even think about my legs. Normally they're frozen numb."

"Oh, yeah. I noticed that, too." Kessa slid her hands up her legs to pull the nylons tight, feeling the smooth silkiness of them. When she reached her left upper thigh, Carea caught sight of something black on her leg in the mirror.

"Kessa, you have something on your leg."

"What?"

"Let me show you," Carea lifted up the edge of Kessa's skirt to expose something that looked like black ink.

Suddenly Kessa hit Carea's hand away violently.

"What is wrong with you?" Carea asked, shocked by the sudden painful slap.

"Nothing's wrong. I just don't want you lifting up my skirt."

"What? I was just trying to help you!"

"I don't need your help," said Kessa.

"Kessa, you're trying to hide something."

"If I am, that's my business."

"Well, you had better go get makeup on whatever you're trying to hide, or wash it off, because it's obviously black. Everyone will notice," said Carea.

Kessa's face flushed. She whipped around and left the room faster than Carea had ever seen before.

"Wow, she's really bugged about something." Carea adjusted her sweater and smoothed her skirt. She shook off the conflict. She would back off and give Kessa space. If she wanted privacy, she would give it to her. No big deal. Everything would be fine. It always was.

Carea turned, grabbed her gloves and ran out the door for the game. She pushed her way through the thronging crowd migrating toward the bleachers. She knew her family would be up in the stands. She would look for them later. Now it was time to pull the squad together and get the crowd going.

In front of her she saw a group of kids. Many of them were clad in leather and Levis. Most were wealthy. They were a part of the new and rapidly growing "Bat" group. Essentially, they were the popular, tough and rough crowd. They liked to congregate and cause havoc everywhere they went.[5]

As Carea approached the group, she heard one of the guys yell out something at her. She made it a habit not to notice that kind of behavior. Suddenly, she realized that four guys she had grown up with from her old neighborhood had broken away from the group and were heading her off. Her heart leaped within her to see them, but then it fell hard when she realized that they were Bats. Being a member of that group meant that their association was dangerous, and she couldn't afford that kind of risk, not to herself, her beliefs, or her family.[6] She desperately tried to control her face and her emotions as she approached. The four guys positioned themselves directly between her and the stadium fence. She did not slow her pace but continued confidently.

As she got nearer, Jack, the ringleader and her closest childhood friend of the bunch, called out her name. "Carea...yo, Carea!"

Carea continued to walk toward them with a blank face, ignoring his hail.

"Carea...you have become...one *hot tamale*....Strut a little faster and you'll have to give us mouth-to-mouth."

"Yeah, to cool us down," added one of the other boys.

The rest of the guys hooted in response.

Carea stopped about four feet in front of the group. "Jack, Nick, Ray, Ken." She calmly acknowledged the old acquaintances then continued. "I'm afraid if it were left up to me, you'd suffocate because nothing defiled shall ever touch these lips!"

"Ooooo, low one. Why are you so mean after so long?" asked Jack, smiling.

Carea smoothly caught her full blond hair and flipped it over her shoulder. "Looks like you're still bad, bad boys. I remember when you were good boys and went to church."

"What, Carea? You break our hearts! We still go to church. It's just the true church now. The church of party-hardy until you can hardly party!" The boys laughed boisterously at their own joke.

Carea just stood there with her hands on her hips and waited until they were done. When it seemed like they were semi-composed she said, "Stand aside. I have to get out on the field. You guys need to go do something productive. Go watch the news or something."

"Go watch the news?" asked Ray, looking at the others.

"What's on the news that we'd be interested in?" asked Jack with his hands spread.

"Haven't you heard?" asked Carea. "Your Bat friends have been falling like flies."

"Yeah right," said Jack.

"What do you mean?" asked Ken.

"I mean that you better be more careful who you hang out with or it might kill you."

"Oh, that. That is not going to happen to us," said Jack flatly.

"Why is that?" asked Carea with raised eyebrows.

"It just won't."

"Jack, you and I both know that faith without works is dead.[7] You got to put your money where your mouth is or else it's just talk."

"Do I know that? Gee, I must have missed that Sunday School lesson," Jack joked.

"OK, stop the sarcasm. Be serious for once in your life," said Carea as she looked unblinkingly into Jack's eyes. "Do what's right, and get away from those people. At least think about it."

Jack mistook her serious eye contact to mean interest, despite her negative comments. A smile slowly spread on Jack's face. "I'd rather think about you, Carea." Jack moved closer as if to take Carea into his arms.

Carea held up her hands, stopping Jack's progress. "Sorry, off limits. I know it's hard for you to understand, but you're not my type anymore. ...And you know what? I think that's too bad."

Jack stood there without expression at first.

Carea watched understanding flow over him. It was painful to her to see his confidence dissolve in front of his friends. She saw he couldn't reply and the difficulty he had in swallowing. She moved past him quickly so she wouldn't have any remorse for her words. She knew her attitude towards him hurt him but she told the truth. She had no apologies.

As Carea moved on she heard on of the boys say, "There's nothing worse than a self-righteous, self-proclaimed saint. It looks like she's grown up to be one of the worst of them."[8]

Then Jack piped in, "Someday she's going to be sorry that she crossed the Bats. There will be hellfire to pay."

The other boys laughed uproariously as they patted each other on the back.

Carea did her best to ignore all of them as she continued to walk quickly to the front of the stadium but the smell of Jack's cologne still wafted in her memory. Unconsciously, she breathed deeply as if to take in his essence without his knowledge. She noticed that she had a sick feeling in the pit of her stomach. She sincerely regretted that Jack and his friends had continued in their wild ways and she didn't want them to think that their behavior was acceptable to her. She knew they knew better. She reflected on all the good times they had had together when they were younger. Since they lived so close, they swam and played together almost every summer day. She remembered when they had started to change. It had felt as if they had died and were replaced by mean, raunchy imposters. She had cried then. For some reason, she wished she could cry now, but she knew that it would do no good. "Goodbye, Jack," she whispered to herself, and ran into the stadium.

ξξξξξξξ

"Where's Kessa?" Carea asked the other cheerleaders when she arrived. No one had seen her yet. Carea began to get worried, but she would give Kessa more time to get out onto the field. She probably was just trying to wash that black stuff off her legs. Carea was sure she'd be around in a few minutes.

Carea looked up into the stands for her mom and her little brothers. They always sat approximately in the same spot every game, right in the middle. After looking for a few seconds, she saw her mom and dad. She waved and signed that she loved them. It was another one of the Rogers' strict traditions. She loved the look on her mom's face when she did that and thought she would always remember it.

Right then, Dane ran by. "Hi, Carea!" he yelled over the crowd's deafening noise. "Thanks for leaving me home!"

"No problem!" she yelled back, teasing him. He needed a little teasing. "Play hard!"

Dane waved above his head in response and kept on running with his team.

The game started, and still there was no sign of Kessa. The cheerleaders had to do all their routines with a hole in the center of every formation because the tall cheerleader always had the middle position. Carea was sure that everyone noticed the void. With every dance routine, the squad became more frustrated. Finally Carea told the others that she had seen her in the locker room and was going to go back to find her. The squad decided to just do chants until Carea came back with the missing squad member.

Carea ran out of the stadium and back into the locker room.

"Kessa!" Carea yelled loudly. Her voice echoed off the walls of the empty room and rang through the lockers. "Kessa!" Still there was no answer. Carea decided to search the corners and the showers. When she was about to give up, she noticed a sports shoe sticking out from one of the shower corners that had a wall about chest high. She ran over and peered around the wall to find Kessa sitting in the corner of the shower.

Kessa looked up at Carea revealing mascara running down her face in obvious tear tracks and bright red, irritated eyes.

"Kessa! Why are you hiding from me?" asked Carea.

Kessa looked up at Carea and mumbled, "I wasn't hiding. I just wasn't answering."

"OK, why weren't you answering?"

"Because I look terrible and can't cheer. If I go out there, everyone will ask me what's wrong, and I'll have to deal with that. I would much rather just sit here and think."

Carea moved to face Kessa. With her right hand, Carea tucked Kessa's long, shiny black hair behind her ear and then hugged her. Over her shoulder she said, "Sweet Kessa, why are you crying? I know that you don't want to deal with all the attention, but tell me. I'm you're friend."

"You probably wouldn't be my friend if you knew me better," mumbled Kessa.

"What? We've been buds ever since I moved here. We were twins in the spirit world, remember?"

"No, Carea, we are not twins. We're so different. You just think we're the same. I am not like you."

Carea was taken back. She had never seen Kessa this upset. Something must be very wrong to bother her so much. She was talking in riddles. "Can you give me a clue why you're saying things like this?"

Kessa just sat motionless, staring down at her hands.

"Kessa…Kessa, please talk to me."

Suddenly Kessa looked into Carea's eyes. Tears flowed down her cheeks as she pulled her skirt from her leg. The black letters B.A.T. were thickly tattooed into her skin on her upper left thigh.

Carea gasped and fell backwards to land on her haunches, while trying to cover her gaping mouth with her hand. "Not you!" Carea said loudly. "Why, Kessa? Why?" Now Carea was crying.

"See, I told you that you wouldn't be my friend if you knew me better."

Carea sat on the cold tile and fumbled for words. "No, Kessa, it's not that. I just don't know what to say. I'm still your friend. I just don't understand. You're not like those other partiers. You're like me. We don't need what they have. Remember us talking into the night about this?"

"I remember, but things change," said Kessa.

"What do you mean? How can something like that change?"

"I couldn't deny the void that I've had inside for a long time. I had to pay attention to it. I made my choices."

"What void?" asked Carea, still with tears streaming down her face.

"I was pretending when I tried to be like you. I carried a lie with me all the time. I always knew that I was not 'good' like you. I knew that someday I would fail and everyone would notice. Now at least I don't have to be a hypocrite anymore. I can be me. I'm really relieved."

"Kessa, why are you talking like this?"

"Like what? I'm just telling you how it is."

"Like you were some evil person at heart! You're not bad. You've never been bad."

"See how you really don't know me? You don't, Carea. You don't know what I think about at night, or what I do when you're not around."

"Well, it can't be that bad," said Carea.

"Can't it? According to you, I bet I'd be going to hell."

"You're letting Satan win, you know. He wants you to believe that malarkey! He wants you to think that you're a lost cause. There is no sin that is too bad for the atonement except for cold-blooded murder. Have you killed anyone lately?"

"No."

"Well, then, what are you talking about?"

"I'm just saying that I'm tired of falling below the mark. I want to rest. I can't run that fast."

"To be a Latter-day Saint, you don't have to be perfect, just trying to be your best. The Lord accepts what we can give him. He understands our limits and our abilities. That is why we have the Sacrament every week, so that we can repent of our sins and be given another week to learn and to grow!"

"I just don't believe it. To me it's just words—it doesn't mean anything," said Kessa shaking her head.

"What are you saying? Are you saying that you don't believe in the Church any more? Kessa, remember Girl's Camp? Remember the testimony meetings? Don't you remember feeling good? You told me that you were gaining a testimony of the gospel."

"Carea, we were hungry, tired, silly and emotional girls. You can feel many things under those circumstances."

"I can't believe that you're saying these things."

"Well, believe it, because it's true," said Kessa.

Carea sat dumbfounded, not knowing what else to say. Finally in a tiny voice she asked, "When did this all happen? When did you go to a Rave?"

"I've been going for a while."

"You have?"

"Yes, I just didn't want to tell you, because I didn't want you to hate me."

Carea quickly came up to her knees and lunged for Kessa, hugging her tight. "I could never hate you. Never, ever! Do you understand me? I'll love you forever. You're my pal. My bosom buddy." They sat there, both crying and rocking, for a few minutes. Finally, "Kessa?" Carea pulled back and sat by her friend.

"Yes?" Kessa's voice was shaking.

"Why are you so sad?"

"I don't know..." Large tears continued to fill Kessa's big dark eyes. "Well, that's not true. I think I know..."

Trying to help Kessa talk about her feelings Carea said, "I know why I'm sad. I love you, and I feel you're hurting. But you...you must have thought that you would be happier if you made the choice to go to the Rave. Did it make you happier?" Carea tried to look into Kessa's eyes.

Kessa, turning slightly away from Carea said, "Yes, for a while. I was very happy. At least it seemed like I was happy. I'm just sad now because I was told that I would have to give you up as a friend."

"Why would you give me up?"

"No...not me...it would be you. You're going to reject me because of my beliefs."

"Who told you that?"

"People at the Rave."

"How would they know?" asked Carea.

"They know. They've been through it and I knew it was true today when you saw my tattoo."

"That's not fair. I didn't even know what it was."

"I don't care. You'll still reject me. I just know it. It's how you are."

Carea fidgeted with her fingers as she thought about what Kessa was saying. Was it how she was? Was Kessa right or was she just baiting her into becoming a Bat? Was it safe to be Kessa's friend? Would she want her to go to the Raves with her? Carea didn't know. She looked at Kessa and asked, "So, you're serious about this thing?"

"Yes, I have to be," said Kessa.

"Why? I don't understand. What do they have that our religion doesn't have?"

"Carea, they don't judge you. You don't have to be perfect there. Everyone is just everyone, and that's OK. It's like one huge, happy get-together. Everyone belongs."

"Kessa, we don't judge in our Church. Our whole religion is based on Christ-like acceptance and love."

"Sure, that's what everyone says, but it really isn't true."

"Yes, it is. Kessa! Why? Do you think that we don't love you?"

"Yes, that's part of it. Everyone is pretending—fake smiles, fake caring. I can feel it the whole time I'm there. Everyone watches everything. Everyone judges everything. Heaven help you if you *commit a sin*!"

"Then 'everyone' is wrong. That's not how we're supposed to live our religion, and you know it! We are to have boundless love for each other and carry each other's burdens."

"I know. I've heard it all. The bottom line is, I just don't like myself when I go to your church. I don't care what you say. Reality is reality."

"*Our church*, Kessa! It's not just mine. It's yours, too."

"No, not anymore."

"Why?" Carea stopped and tried to imagine what Kessa had been through that would cause her to feel so differently. It seemed she was emotionally running away from something. "Has anything happened to you that has made you feel this way? Have you been taken advantage of or something?"

"Not without it being my choice."

"What?"

"Yes, Carea, all your conclusions are right about me."

"You mean you fully participate in all the things that go on up in those mountains?"

"Yes, Carea, everything."

"How? …Why?"

Kessa suddenly took Carea's arms in both her hands and drew her close. "Carea, prove them wrong. Prove that you won't reject me. You should come up there, too. Come next time and be with me. We can do everything together and become true blood sisters."

Carea pulled away from Kessa's grasp and had to blink hard and refocus on her to see if she was serious. Here was the answer she was looking for and she hated it. "You want me to come up there?"

"Yes, I want you to be with me always, and if you don't, this will come between us just as they say. We will always be different."[9]

"Kessa, do you know what you're asking?"

"Yes, I know it sounds off-the-wall, and at first it's hard to partake of the prescribed sacrament—you feel immense guilt—but after a while it truly makes you feel wonderful! You have no cares in the world!"

"Are you talking about alcohol and drugs?"

"Don't say it like that, Carea. It makes it sound so dirty."

"Isn't that what it is? After all, the partiers at school brag about how plastered they get when they go to the 'Bat church'."

"Well, yes, I guess they are drugs and alcohol to you, but they're used to help us commune with God himself."[10]

"Kessa, what you say doesn't make sense! First of all, to feel good, Heavenly Father has never said that we have to take controlled substances!"

"Well, they weren't controlled when Jesus was on the earth. Don't you remember that he gave his apostles wine? That was real wine, Carea."

"What, are you going to say that the bread was a loaf of cocaine?"

"Yes, a loaf or a batch of some substance that took you to another spiritual level. Maybe it was a bundle of leaves or something. All I know is that the truth has been revealed to us. You don't have it because your scriptures have been changed to meet your ideals. Why else were our bodies made to be able to experience such a higher spirituality with them?"[11]

"Kessa, you're talking crazy!"

"No, Carea, through that process I have met The Holy One. The actual Son of God."

"Come on! You don't believe that bunch of hocus pocus, do you?"

"Yes Carea, I've seen him and felt him! At his feet I have learned that there is no good and bad. That was a big relief. It set me free."[12]

"No good or bad? This is getting riper by the second. Kessa, truth sets you free, not lack of responsibility for your actions. That just causes more chaos and more chains around your neck."

"Actually, I learned that society invented the idea of good and bad to control the masses. It makes sense."

Carea gasped, "What?"

Nodding, Kessa said, "Yeah. Guilt that comes from going against society's beliefs is developed and nurtured by role models like teachers, politicians and police, until we are totally brainwashed. It's destructive, and it confuses us. Eventually we develop hate for the natural tendencies that make us who we are."

Carea had an irresistible urge to cover her ears, but with sheer will, she refused it. She knew that such an action would alienate Kessa. "You're talking out of both sides of your mouth! Why would you have the sacrament but not believe in right and wrong? That would mean that there was no need for the atonement."

"There wasn't. You're right—there wasn't a need for it. The blood in our sacrament represents our physical unity, and our 'bread of life' takes us to spiritual elevations that make us one with God."

"Boy, that is so skewed! This is absolutely amazing!" Carea looked long and hard at Kessa.

Kessa dropped her head and sat quietly for a moment.

Carea began pleading, "Kessa, please don't be tricked. Don't listen to these people! Look at the scriptures to identify Christ. He prophesied himself that there would be those that would come and profess to be him. Remember? He told us specifically how he would come and how we would identify him. How many times does it say in the scriptures that Christ will be seen 'coming in the clouds in great glory'?"[13]

Kessa's head rose quickly. Unblinkingly she said, "He did come from the clouds."

"He did?" Carea was shocked.

"Yes. He told us that he came down in that manner in the year 2000, at the beginning of the millennium. Doesn't that sound right? Where is your Christ? He hasn't come yet. Do you know why? It's because he doesn't exist!"[14]

Carea felt her head spinning. She got up from her place on the floor and began to retreat.

Kessa continued, "Where are you going, Carea? I thought you were my friend. Why are you leaving? Is what I'm saying too hard for you? Does it make you uncomfortable? That's the spirit of God, Carea! He's telling you that what you believe is wrong!"

"No, Kessa! You've got it so upside down! I can't believe that you accept what that imposter has been telling you! Kessa! Can't you see? They get you to drink and take drugs so that you would be open to their false teachings. Then you're filled with guilt for participating in *whatever*…. I guess only you know. Then psychologically you run to this false teaching that there is no good or bad. That makes it so you have no accountability. You then lie to yourself for your own sanity! He has taken you and made you his slave. He has bound you in chains and is slowly leading you down to hell![15] Can't you see that, Kessa? Are you so blind as not to see that you already have one foot in the grave? He has taken away all your choices! Now you feel bound, as if there are no other ways."

Kessa looked at Carea for a long time. "I see that you will be leaving me now," she said, suddenly callous.

Carea broke down and started bawling into her gloves, leaving two watery black marks in her palms. "I don't know what to do, Kessa. …I can't go with you." Suddenly Carea lifted her head and began to speak, "I know my Father lives! He has a body of flesh and bone. He loves me, and I love him very much. I want to be like him. He helps me daily. I talk to him all the time, and he talks back. He helps me with the tiniest problems, and I love him for it. …I might not have touched him with my hands in this life yet, but I know someday I will. I also know that Jesus Christ lived and died for us! He is real. We can become heirs in that heaven above because of the atonement. …I know these truths! I know with every fiber of my being. I promise you, Kessa, that the same Jesus Christ who died and was resurrected will come again. He will come soon. I also promise you that he loves *you*. It is never too late to come back. Please try. Please?"

Kessa was unmoved. "I don't know that God. I don't know if what you say is true. I wish I did. …In a way, you're very right, Carea—I am a slave to my religion, just as you are to yours. I cannot leave my beliefs, just as you cannot leave yours. If I leave, I will die. You believe that if you leave, you will die spiritually. So maybe you're right. In our opposites we are alike. Maybe we are twins, but in opposite ways. Maybe we're negatives of each other. Yes, that makes sense. I guess that's how it's always been.... Why don't you go now? I think the time is right."

Carea turned and ran out of the locker room. She ran to her car and quickly sped from the stadium parking lot and went home. She needed safety at that moment, and there was no other place she could find it.

Notes to "Inner Understanding"

Left Behind

[1] Gang violence can be one symptom of evil influences permeating society predicted in the scriptures. It fulfills the edict that the "wicked shall slay the wicked, and fear shall come upon every man" (D&C 63:33), "for where envying and strife is, there is confusion and every evil work" (James 3:16). This kind of mentality will eventually cause that "among the wicked, that every man that will not take his sword against his neighbor must needs flee unto Zion for safety" (D&C 45:68).

[2] Janet Kapp Perry, "A Child's Prayer," *Children's Songbook*, 12.

[3] Proverbs 3:5.

[4] "And all things, whatsoever ye shall ask in prayer, believing, ye shall receive" (Matthew 21:22).

Let's Give it a Cheer

[5] In Alma there is a clear description of worldly behavior exhibited by the Bats in the text. "For those who did not belong to their church did indulge themselves in sorceries, and in idolatry or idleness, and in babblings, and in envyings and strife; wearing costly apparel; being lifted up in the pride of their own eyes; persecuting, lying, thieving, robbing..." (Alma 1:32).

[6] President Hinckley said this about teaching children to choose friendships that would influence them for the good: "Teach them to seek for good friends. They are going to have friends, good or bad. Those friends will make a vast difference in their lives. It is important that they cultivate an attitude of tolerance toward all people, but it is more important that they gather around them those of their own kind who will bring out the best they have within them. Otherwise they may be infected with the ways of their associates" ("Your Greatest Challenge Mother," *Ensign*, November 2000, 97).

[7] James 2:20.

[8] Historically, others have misconstrued adherence to standards by Saints as a type of conceit. Saints have always been persecuted because of this misconception. See the lives of apostles in the early church, Christ's life, or the history of the early Church of Jesus Christ of Latter-day Saints. This perception has long been attached to the Jews and has been a source of persecution for hundreds of years.

"As a Latter-day Saint, your high standards are well known, so you become a target. Also, some people automatically think that if you profess high standards, you are looking down on them, so they strike back. For example, someone who drinks may feel you condemn them just because it is contrary to your personal ideals" ("Q&A: Questions and Answers," *New Era*, May 1990, 17).

[9] The ideas for this conversation were compiled from consensual interviews of actual people who have fallen away from the church. Motivations and perceptions were explored to understand in a generic way how once faithful members change their beliefs and practices.

[10] Elder Boyd K. Packer stated: "I have come to know...that a fundamental purpose of the Word of Wisdom has to do with revelation...If someone 'under the influence' [of harmful substances] can hardly listen to plain talk, how can they respond to spiritual promptings that

touch their most delicate feelings? As valuable as the Word of Wisdom is as a law of health, it may be much more valuable to you spiritually than it is physically" (Ensign, November 1979, 20).

[11] Substances ingested to alter perceptions of the mind and body in relation to religious experiences are common historically. See previous discussion in the chapter "The Mark," endnote #7.

[12] Absence of laws and accountability are common teachings of Antichrists found in the Book of Mormon. "And many more such things did he say unto them, telling them that there could be no atonement made for the sins of men, but every man fared in this life according to the management of the creature; therefore every man prospered according to his genius, and that every man conquered according to his strength; and whatsoever a man did was no crime. And thus he did preach unto them, leading away the hearts of many, causing them to lift up their heads in their wickedness, yea, leading away many women, and also men, to commit whoredoms—telling them that when a man was dead, that was the end thereof" (Alma 30:17-18).

[13] See Matthew 24:30; Mark 13:26; Luke 21:27; D&C 34:7; D&C 45:44; Joseph Smith Matthew 1:36.

[14] This is another teaching of Antichrists: "O ye that are bound down under a foolish and a vain hope, why do ye yoke yourselves with such foolish things? Why do ye look for a Christ? For no man can know of anything which is to come. Behold, these things which ye call prophecies, which ye say are handed down by holy prophets, behold, they are foolish traditions of your fathers. How do ye know of their surety? Behold, ye cannot know of things which ye do not see; therefore ye cannot know that there shall be a Christ" (Alma 30:13-15).

[15] "And that great pit, which hath been digged for them by that great and abominable church, which was founded by the devil and his children, that he might lead away the souls of men down to hell—yea, that great pit which hath been digged for the destruction of men shall be filled by those who digged it, unto their utter destruction, saith the Lamb of God; not the destruction of the soul, save it be the casting of it into that hell which hath no end" (1 Nephi 14:3).

CHAPTER SIX

SIGNS OF THE TIMES

"And unto you it shall be given to know the signs of the times, and the signs of the coming of the Son of Man" (D&C 68:11).

Sunday
September 17th
7:39 a.m.
Provo Utah

Earthquakes

Jax opened his eyes to see a ray of golden sun streaming through the blinds in his bedroom. He lifted his head off his pillow to see if his two little brothers were still sleeping. They were snoring in their adjacent single beds, with blank expressions and their mouths wide open. Jax quietly pulled back his covers and sat up. Slowly he eased out of bed to decrease the squeaking of the old coils in his box springs.

Jax tiptoed, slipped out of the bedroom, and headed for the video games. He surveyed the living room, kitchen, and family room for any other family members awake. He was alone. Controlled excitement began to fill him as he realized that he was the first one up and would have the video systems all to himself. He flipped on the TV to channel four. Immediately a voice filled the room. Jax turned down the sound so as not to wake anyone and mess up his opportunity, but as he did, he couldn't help but listen to the news broadcast that was in progress.

"An earthquake hit Chile with a magnitude of 9.8. Numerous cities were heavily damaged. The earthquake created a deadly tsunami more than thirty feet in height along the Chilean coast, eliminating entire villages. The tsunami from the earthquake continued across the Pacific, striking Hawaii, where it killed sixty-one people, despite the warning that had been issued five hours earlier. Later, the tsunami killed hundreds more in Japan, more than 8,000 miles from the earthquake source."

Jax's eyes widened as he continued to listen.

"Hundreds of large landslides were triggered, including several that have blocked Rinihue Lake. It has increased the water level over eighty feet in the surrounding areas, submerging homes and whole villages deep under water. The earthquake may also have been related to the eruption of Puyehue Volcano, which happened hours after the earthquake. Sections of the Chilean coast were raised or submerged more than ten feet."

"That's awesome," Jax breathed quietly. He liked to watch shows about earthquakes. His eyes continued to stare at the images on the liquid-plasma display.

"Recounting the rash of natural disasters that have hit the world, on the border near Arkansas and Missouri, there was another set of four earthquakes estimated to be magnitude 7.0 or larger that have occurred in the last two weeks. These earthquakes changed the course of the Mississippi River and caused it to flow backwards for several hours.[1]

"Japan, Alaska and Hawaii are also experiencing an increase in seismic activity. Alaskan earthquakes have become so numerous that the inmates who live in the prison cities have voiced strong concern. The vast cities set up in the frigid northern Alaskan tundra for violent criminals have had a difficult time maintaining utilities due to the constant shaking. Their representatives are appealing to the penal system to obtain a special audience with Congress to consider moving their cities to another area of the U.S. So far all requests have been denied...."[2]

"No big deal, those things happen all the time," Jax said as he flipped on his game. Within seconds his interest was consumed with a pseudo-world where he was the sole hero and in control of the disasters.

Chaos

Bo woke from a deep sleep. Rarely was he able to sleep past 6:00; however, this morning he had needed extra rest for some reason.

He peered with one eye toward the pillow where his wife should have been sleeping, but the bed held only his twin babies, who were lying perpendicular to each other up near the headboard. He looked lazily around the room and found Corrynne sitting on the recliner with her computer in her lap.

"What are you doing?" Bo asked in a whisper.

"I'm checking my e-mail, reading the news...normal things." Corrynne threw a smirk in her husband's direction. "If there was such a thing...."

"In that case, maybe I'll lie here a few minutes. If I'm lucky, I might fall asleep again," said Bo.

"Yes, get your rest. I'm sure Carea will need some of your energy today after last night's shocker with Kessa." Corrynne smiled without looking at Bo as she reflected on the great relationship that Carea had with her father.

"She'll need to talk over her feelings with you. You are always such a good sounding board."

"OK," Bo said casually as he fluffed his pillow, flipped it over and laid his head down again.

Corrynne bit her lip and then said, "I figure that I should be receiving an e-mail from Conrad soon. I hope it comes today." She returned her attention to her computer screen.

Conrad was Bo and Corrynne's second oldest son. He was beginning a full-time mission for the Church of Jesus Christ of Latter-day Saints in Jerusalem, of all places in the world. When the call came, it seemed like a miracle. Who would have thought that there could possibly be missionaries in the Holy City?

Ironically, missionary work became possible when all peace talks between warring Palestine and Israel failed. The United Nations stepped in, after years of patience and negotiations and strong-armed peace.

Under UN control, the old and new cities of Jerusalem still remained a central focus to both Palestine and Israel nations.[3] The UN's solution to encourage peace between the warring factions was to take Jerusalem from both of the fighting factions and make the city neutral, being owned by neither and secured by UN troops. In an effort to cater to the Christians, Jews, and Muslims, the UN opened access to the city to all religions. Suddenly, access to the tribe of Judah in Israel by the children of Ephraim, descendants of the tribe of Joseph, was possible. In fulfillment of prophecy,[4] the Latter-day Saint Prophet immediately sent the sons of Ephraim out as bearers of the "good news" in a last effort to bring the lost sheep home.

Corrynne perused the CNN Web site looking specifically for information about violence in the Middle East. They always had great coverage. Clicking on the title *"Violence Continues, Despite UN Efforts,"* she began to read silently.

"Anxiety continues to be poignant in the Middle East. Israel threatens retaliation and demands their city even at the expense of their extinction. 'Jerusalem or die' has become the widespread cry from the Jewish people...."

Corrynne took in a sharp breath. She hated having Conrad in continuous danger so far away. It was obvious that Israel would continue to fight everyone until they retrieved their beloved city, Jerusalem.

"Bo?"

"Huh?" A sleepy Bo opened one eye again to look at Corrynne.

"There is still fighting all around Jerusalem. I worry about Conrad," answered Corrynne.

Bo yawned his response. "Missionaries are protected unless the Lord has need of them on the other side."

"I know. Still, I'm a mother, and I worry about my son. I'm not ready to lose any of my children."

"We won't lose anyone. I'm sure all will be fine. Is the e-mail there?"

"No," Corrynne said with a disappointed tone. "Maybe it will be here after church."

"I'm sure it will be." Bo flipped back his side of the covers with a grunt and slowly got out of bed. His index finger hooked the sweats that were lying across the chair next to the bed, and he put them on with great effort. His body still felt heavy. "I'm going downstairs to make breakfast. Is there anything that you want?"

"Eggs are fine," said Corrynne thoughtfully, as she read something on her screen.

"Omelets?" Bo questioned.

"No, that's too much work. Normal eggs are fine."

"Oh, you mean hard eggs. That's enough to make a grown chef cry," Bo teased.

"You'll get over it, I'm sure. I'll be down in a few minutes."

"OK." Bo sauntered down the stairs to the kitchen. Except for a quiet video game being played in the family room, it appeared that most of the children were asleep. He poked his head into the family room to see who was up.

"Hi, Jax."

"Hi, Dad."

"Do you want some eggs?"

"Yeah," Jax returned without taking his eyes off the screen.

"Will you go and wake up everyone? Breakfast will be done real quick."

"Sure…"

Bo waited a moment but Jax didn't move. "Right now?"

"OK Dad, I will in a minute."

Bo waited a few more moments but Jax continued to play. "Jax! Hit the pause button. Go! Now!"

"OK, I'm almost there," said Jax with gritted teeth.

Bo, losing his patience, said, "Alright, here's the deal. I believe it's Sunday and you shouldn't be playing videogames, so either you save, quit, and do as I ask or the video game lock will go back on so you can't play for a week. The choice is yours."

Jax immediately accessed the save screen and then quit the game. With a big sigh he got up from his place on the floor and trudged into the various bedrooms to summon everyone to the kitchen.

Soon the sound of frying eggs could be heard throughout the house, and the bacon smell helped Jax coax everyone out of warm beds. Lethargic bodies dressed in flannel, scrubs, pajamas, and bathrobes began to appear from all corners of the house. The sleepy trek continued from the halls to the large oak family table in the dining area of the kitchen.

"Hello, my royal subjects, peasants and paupers all of you," Bo began in a deep Shakespearean voice, feeling in a lighter mood now that the food was cooking. "Methinks that I rule you, but I am but a fool. The truth is a sad one but as real as the sun that shines on this roof. I am but the servant and you the kings and queens. Rise and shine, for the kingdom is yours!" Bo teased his children.

None of the children acknowledged his performance but continued to walk emotionless to their seats at the table.

"Boy, lots of smiling faces! The happiness is killing me!" said Bo as he flipped some perfectly shaped eggs and jabbed at the frying bacon.

"You're in a good mood today," commented Dane as he sat at the table, slumped in his chair and then closed his eyes.

"Of course. It's a beautiful day in the neighborhood! The sun is shining, the birds are chirping and I'm making breakfast!" said Bo as he pulled paper plates that were clinging to each other. "What could be better?" Turning to his eleven-year-old son, Bo called, "Hey, Jax."

"Yeah?" asked Jax, just pulling out his chair to sit at the table.

"Call Braun and see if he wants some eggs, too."

With an audible sigh, Jax pushed back in his chair and then walked across the room to the intercom. He pushed a button that allowed him to call over into the adjacent apartment where his oldest brother lived. "Braun! Hey, get up, sleepyhead! Dad wants to feed you again! Eggs and bacon! Can't you smell it? Hurry or it will all be gone!"

A voice came over the intercom, "Coming. Thanks!"

After a few moments the garage door in the mudroom opened and shut. Braun appeared around the corner looking fresh and clean. Since his mission to South America, he was always an early riser. He sat at the table with a smile that looked like it belonged to the Cheshire cat. Braun surveyed the scene at the table. He reached over and lifted Brea's limp arm off the table and let it drop with a thud. "Looks like a bomb site with all these bodies lying around." No one responded to his joke. Suddenly Braun's look changed from relaxed to tense. He sat up straight and yelled out "Dad?"

"Yes, my eldest?" answered Bo, continuing the Shakespearean theme.

"Talk about apocalyptic happenings—have you been watching the news?"

"No, all I've done today was what you're seeing me do now," Bo said as he flipped another row of eggs.

Just then Corrynne came down the stairs with a baby on each hip. "Hi, Braun!" Then she looked at the table full of sleepy eyed children. "Impressive. Everyone's at the table already. There must have been an earthquake or something."

"Yes, actually, there has been. It was a 9.8 quake." responded Braun.

"Where?" asked Corrynne, who stopped walking and focused her attention on Braun.

"Oh, yeah! I saw the earthquake on the TV when I turned it on! There was a huge one!" exclaimed Jax. "Floods everywhere."

"Chile," said Braun. "It caused the ground to fall ten feet in some areas and submerged whole villages. The whole area was devastated."

"A volcano erupted too!" added Jax.

"A volcano?" asked Corrynne as she strapped her twins into their highchairs.

"Yep." said Jax.

Corrynne shook her head and sighed as she sat in a chair between her twins. A faraway look came over her face. "Upstairs I was just contemplating the many changes that are happening around us. Evil is lurking in every corner[5]—violence in the Middle East, huge earthquakes and volcanoes. It definitely feels like the world is a threatening place no matter where you live."

"Not here," said Ry. "We live in a safe place, huh mom?" Ry waited patiently for an answer from his mother.

Corrynne cringed and then smiled. "Well, luckily, in our house it's safe, Ry, but we have our share of dangers outside our house."

"Like what?" asked Roc.

Corrynne thought for a moment. She considered the Raves that were stealing the lives of the youth in the mountains. Should she tell her little sons about them? After a moment she decided she would. It was important to teach and arm her sons against the dangers they would face as they grew. She hoped by doing that she might keep them safe later. This kind of strategy had worked with her older set of children.

"There are evil people who will try and trick you to get you to do and think things that aren't safe because they will say it's fun. They'll say, 'come to our party…'" began Corrynne.

"What's wrong with parties?" asked Ry. "I like them."

"Yes, but when you get older, parties won't be good," said Corrynne.

"They don't have cake and ice cream at the parties once you get about 13," said Dane lifting his head only long enough to make his statement then he returned to his possum sleep attitude.

"No, they don't," said Corrynne nodding. "Instead they'll be a place that kids drink alcohol and take drugs."

"And smoke cigarettes?" asked Ry.

"Cigarettes and things that are much worse. And at those parties they will tell you to do things that are very dangerous."

"Like jump off a cliff?" asked Roc. "I would never do that," he said while shaking his head.

Corrynne smiled. "No Roc, like join a gang, sneak out at night, disobey your parents, get tattoos…"

"Why?" asked Roc, interrupting his mother.

"They'll tell you it's for fun but that will be a lie. People at parties want your money, or they want power, or they want to do bad things to you…"

"Or in the case of the parties that are happening in the mountains," offered Carea, "they want to take control over your life...."

"Why?" asked Roc again.

"Because if you give them money or control, they become rich and strong..."

"Why?" asked Roc yet again.

Carea pounded the table and then exclaimed, "Because they're *evil* and they don't care about *you,* they only care about themselves!"

Carea's outburst surprised everyone and her emotion caused even Roc to be quiet and just stare at her with unblinking eyes.

After a few moments of silence, Brea sat up a little and took a breath. "It's true. I'm lucky because I'm out of school. And because I'm going to BYU, I don't have to deal with the peer pressure that you guys will soon have to deal with."

"Yeah, sometimes my friends swear," said Jax, thinking he was adding something substantial to the conversation. "Ton's of kids swear in the sixth grade."

Corrynne smiled at him and touched his hand. With a serious look she said, "It will get worse, I promise you. And when it does you have to be brave and strong and say 'no' very firmly when someone asks you to do something that's dangerous."

"*No!*" yelled Roc, shocking everyone at the table once again.

Corrynne looked at Roc who had a big smile on his face. She realized he was practicing. "That's great, Roc. Do it again."

"**No!**" yelled Roc even louder and lifting fists above his head.

"No!" exclaimed Ry, joining in but laughing at Rocwell's zeal.

"No!" said little Striynna, with one baby fist in the air too, mimicking her brothers.

Then the whole table began to laugh hysterically. Striynna was just too cute.

"What's everyone laughing about?" asked Bo as he brought steaming plates of food from the kitchen.

"We're just discussing survival skills," offered Braun. "Striynna is getting into it."

Bo nodded as he began at one side of the table and began to serve the food.

"Speaking of survival," said Brea. "Here's a question."

"Go ahead," said Bo as he spooned two eggs onto Ry's plate.

"I wonder how far away the Second Coming is. What do you think, Dad?"

"I believe that we still have some things to go through. It will be a while yet," said Bo.

"But how long is a 'while'? How long can we continue to have earthquakes like the one in Chile? I mean, a 9.8 is about as big as it gets."

"Earthquakes, storms, plagues, violence and famines are to continue until Christ comes,"[6] offered Braun. "We might have large storms and natural disasters now, but they'll continue to increase until the nations have all been destroyed. We are far from that now."

"That's scary, Braun. Why do you say things like that?" said Carea with a frown.

"I don't say those things, the scriptures do. I'm just quoting what they say," said Braun.

"Well don't quote them then. It's bad enough that the world is falling apart. It only makes it worse to talk about it," said Carea.

Braun looked at his sister with surprise.

"Carea. You don't mean that," said Corrynne. "Depression doesn't come from talking about challenging things. Depression comes from not acknowledging your challenges so you aren't adequately prepared when they happen."

"Yes, little sister," agreed Braun. "Whether you like to hear it or not, these are the last days. We have to know what's coming. Anyone who ignores the future will become a victim to it."

Carea looked away from her brother, the reality of his statement hit too close to her heart because of her experience the night before with Kessa.

Bo sat down with the family and salted his eggs. "OK people," he said putting the salt shaker down. "There's something you're missing here."

"What's that, Dad?" asked Braun.

Bo cut his egg and took a bite. Then he said, "The promises. We have great promises concerning the last days."

"What are those, Dad?" asked Jax.

Bo took another bite and then said, "The Lord has promised safety[7] to those who listen to him during the last days and follow his instructions. Those instructions tell us to prepare both physically and spiritually.[8] I believe that your Mom and I have tried hard to teach you guys how to be spiritually prepared all your lives. But you have to apply that spirituality yourselves— that part is up to you.[9] Physically we're prepared with food storage and other necessities, just as the Prophet has commanded.[10] So, Jax, to answer your question, the Lord has given his people the promise of being able to escape the calamities of the last days in one way or another.[11] Now that promise doesn't just have to do with calamities of nature, it has to do with the all calamities of life."

"Such as the sadness that can come from divorce, debt, addiction, sexual abuse, or any other malady that wickedness brings to people," offered Brea. "If we are righteous and live the commandments of God and try to be like Christ, we can avoid or find ways to escape all those calamities in our lives."

"Right," said Corrynne nodding and cutting the food on the twin's trays. "That's exactly right."

"Of course there will be the normal sicknesses and accidents that happen just because we're living," said Braun, "but for the most part the Lord's people will be spared and given the strength to handle their hardships as long as they listen to his warnings."

Reflectively, Carea looked across the table and asked Braun, "Do you think the Lord will warn us individually of danger, or do we just have to roll with the punches?"

"I think it will be a little of both," said Braun. "I think that if something is going to happen that will affect a large group of saints, the prophet will tell those saints how to be prepared, just like he did in the days of Noah, Nephi, Lot, and the Brother of Jared. Individually, however, I believe that we have to be open to the Spirit, as he whispers to us the things we need to do for our own protection. That is why receiving personal revelation is a matter of life and death now, where it used to be that we could look at others around us and do what they did and be safe."

"Yeah, now watching other people might get us killed!" commented Dane.

"What do you mean?" Jax asked his older brother.

"Well, today even people you think are good can be bad. You never know if someone is really good. That's why it's best to listen only to the prophet or the Holy Ghost instead of your best friend, neighbor, or someone at school. When the prophet says to jump, you can bet I'll ask, 'How high?'"

"Yes," said Corrynne, "that's a very important point. Always, always follow the prophet. In him you will find direction[12] and an example to keep you safe."

"Doesn't it say somewhere that the Saints will gather together for safety from evil and violence?"[13] asked Brea.

"Absolutely," said Bo nodding.

"And aren't we told that if nations tried to come up against us they would run away because of the Lord's glory upon his people?"[14]

Bo continued to nod as he took a bite of bacon. "Yes, Brea, you're definitely right. We, the righteous, are going to gather and become very strong. I know from what I've studied that the Lord will become our personal bodyguard and lead us with smoke during the day and fire at night and fight our battles for us, just like he has done for his people at other times in the scriptures."[15]

"That's so cool!" chimed in Ry.

"And it's my opinion that everyone of you will live to see it happen," said Bo.

"How about you?" asked Roc.

Braun, Brea, Dane and Carea all laughed at Roc's question and looked at each other. Roc had no sense of social appropriateness.

Bo lifted his eyebrows and shrugged. "I might see it too. Who knows?"

"You'll be there, Dad," said Braun as he patted his father's shoulder. "You're a bull. No one can stop you."

Bo shook his head. "Don't know about that, but I'll see the last days whether in this body or outside it. It doesn't matter to me."

"What are some of the other signs of the times, Mom?" Ry asked, looking at his mother with an intense focus.

"Well, one of the signs is that the Jews will begin to believe in Christ,[16] and we know through the Church's publications that there are more and more Jews who are beginning to believe in Christ; although I believe that most will not change their minds until they see Christ themselves at his coming."[17]

"Yes, as a part of that same spirit, the gospel is now almost being preached to every nation of the world. Soon it will go to every nation.[18]" said Bo.

"Another thing is that the Church has been growing by leaps and bounds, along with temples being built all over the world," added Braun. "Many people can't believe that we have over 300 temples all over the world.[19] It wasn't very long ago when you could name all of them in 30 seconds."

"We're still looking forward to the continued gathering and the return of the tribes of Israel. The city of Enoch is also supposed to return to the earth and join Zion, but I don't believe those events will happen until after the city of Zion is built,"[20] said Bo.

"What city?" asked Roc. "Will we live in that city?" Roc looked around at the people in his family for the answer.

"Roc, we may live in that city, but we don't know now. The city of Zion will be built in Missouri, and it will be a beautiful and glorious place. We would love to live there, but we can't until it's time," said Corrynne.

"When will it be time?" asked Roc.

"When it won't be safe for us to live here anymore and the Prophet tells us it's OK to go. I think somewhere I read that angels would help us build the city.[21] Won't that be cool?"

"Yep!" said Roc as he smiled big and nodded his head rapidly.

Silence permeated the room as everyone sat in deep thought while they ate. Finally, Carea asked a question that surprised everyone. "Isn't there supposed to be a huge world war?"

Braun looked her in the eyes. Everyone could tell that even he was worried about that event. "Yes. There will be a world war,"[22] he said thoughtfully.

"Will we have to fight in it?" asked Dane, looking a little worried.

"Maybe," said Braun. "There aren't any scriptures that say that the people of Zion will have to fight in a war, so maybe everyone will be at war except us."

"That would be good," said Carea nodding.

"That would be very good," acknowledged Corrynne. "There's one thing that I know for sure. I know that if we continue to look for direction from

Heavenly Father, study the scriptures and strive to obey the prophet, we will be safe no matter what happens."

"No matter what?" asked Jax with a sly questioning look.

"No matter what," said Corrynne nodding and smiling. Her vision changed to her husband who had an amused look. "No matter what," she repeated as she hugged her little twins who were happily eating beside her.

"What if a volcano hit us?" asked Jax. "And covered us with lava?"

"Then it would be over quickly, wouldn't it?" asked Bo as he stood from the table with his plate indicating the discussion had run its course. "Then we'd be safe in the spirit world where nothing could hurt us ever again."

"Yes," said Braun who also got up from the table. "There's more to the word 'safe' than just physical safety. What Mom says is right. If we do as we should we'll always be safe so that if it is the Lord's will that we die, we'll be ready and we'll be safe for eternity."

"That's a cop out," said Jax, following his oldest brother into the kitchen with his own plate. "That's not what I meant."

"But, it's the truth."

"Cop out," said Jax back.

"The truth," said Braun teasing his brother.

"Cop out."

Corrynne rolled her eyes. Well, it was back to normal family life, but the conversation was good for about fifteen minutes. That might have been a record. What more could a mom ask for?

Notes to "Signs of the Times"

Earthquakes

[1] Earthquake accounts found in this text were patterned after real events. See National Earthquake Information Center for more information about the earthquake described in the text, available online: http://wwwneic.cr.usgs.gov/neis/eqlists/WORLD/1960_05_22.html .

[2] The prison cities are a fictitious solution to the predicted rise in crime and violence that is to occur in the last days (see D&C 45:33).

Chaos

[3] "Ground zero in the current intifada is a hill in Jerusalem known to Jews as the Temple Mount and to Muslims as the Noble Sanctuary. That precious piece of real estate contains the ruins of Judaism's holiest temple, on top of which stands the Dome of the Rock and the Al Aqsa mosque, Islam's third-holiest site" ("Jerusalem's Holy Sites," *Cnn.com Mideast Struggle for Peace*, available online: http://www.cnn.com/SPECIALS/2000/mideast/ select the topic: "Issues" under "Fact files").

[4] "Ephraim was given the birthright in Israel (1 Chronicles 5: 1-2; Jeremiah 31: 9), and in the last days it has been the tribe of Ephraim's privilege first to bear the message of the restoration of the gospel to the world and to gather scattered Israel (Deut. 33: 13-17; D&C 133: 26-34; D&C 64: 36). The time will come when, through the operation of the gospel of Jesus Christ, the envy of Judah and Ephraim shall cease (Isaiah 11: 12-13)" (see Bible Dictionary, "Ephraim," 666).

[5] "The Lord speaks of calamity to befall the inhabitants of the earth. Calamities come in different forms. From time to time the forces of nature convulse, and we are wrenched by their destructive powers. Even more devastating, however, are the calamitous forces of evil which surfeit us continually. In accordance with the prophecy of 1831 (see D&C 1:17, 35), peace has now been taken from the earth, and the devil has power over his dominion. His beguiling ways are mesmerizing the people. Temptation is on every hand. Crassness and wrangling have become a way of life. What was once considered awful is now considered tame; what at first titillates, soon captivates and then destroys" (Bishop Keith B. McMullin, "An Invitation With Promise," Ensign, May 2001, 61).

[6] "And thus, with the sword and by bloodshed the inhabitants of the earth shall mourn; and with famine, and plague, and earthquake, and the thunder of heaven, and the fierce and vivid lightning also, shall the inhabitants of the earth be made to feel the wrath, and indignation, and chastening hand of an Almighty God, until the consumption decreed hath made a full end of all nations...Wherefore, stand ye in holy places, and be not moved, until the day of the Lord come; for behold, it cometh quickly, saith the Lord. Amen" (D&C 87: 6, 8).

[7] "Wherefore, he will preserve the righteous by his power, even if it so be that the fullness of his wrath must come, and the righteous be preserved, even unto the destruction of their enemies by fire. Wherefore, the righteous need not fear; for thus saith the prophet, they shall be saved, even if it so be as by fire" (1 Nephi 22:17).

[8] "Wherefore the decree hath gone forth from the Father that they shall be gathered in unto one place upon the face of this land, to prepare their hearts and be prepared in all things against the day when tribulation and desolation are sent forth upon the wicked" (D&C 29:8).

[9] President Gordon B. Hinckley stated: "How do you prepare for the Second Coming? Well, you just do not worry about it. You just live the kind of life that if the Second Coming were to be tomorrow you could be ready. Nobody knows when it is going to happen...Our responsibility is to prepare ourselves, to live worthy of the association of the Savior, to deport ourselves in such a way that we would not be embarrassed if He were to come among us. That is a challenge in this day and age" (Church News, 2 Jan. 1999, 2).

[10] "For over forty years, in a spirit of love, members of the Church have been counseled to be thrifty and self-reliant; to avoid debt; pay tithes and a generous fast offering; be industrious; and have sufficient food, clothing, and fuel on hand to last at least one year" (Ezra Taft Benson, "Prepare for the Days of Tribulation," *Ensign,* November 1980, 32).

[11] "Nevertheless, Zion shall escape if she observe to do all things whatsoever I have commanded her" (D&C 97:25).

[12] Amos 3:7; See also D&C 1:14.

[13] "And it shall come to pass among the wicked, that every man that will not take his sword against his neighbor must needs flee unto Zion for safety" (D&C 45: 68).

[14] The City of Enoch was protected by the Lord. "The fear of the Lord was upon all nations, so great was the glory of the Lord, which was upon his people. And the Lord blessed the land, and they were blessed upon the mountains, and upon the high places, and did flourish" (Moses 7:17).

The same promises will be Zion's in the last days, "And the day shall come when the nations of the earth shall tremble because of her, and shall fear because of her terrible ones. The Lord hath spoken it. Amen" (D&C 64:43).

[15] "And the Lord will create upon every dwelling-place of mount Zion, and upon her assemblies, a cloud and smoke by day and the shining of a flaming fire by night; for upon all the glory of Zion shall be a defense" (2 Nephi 14:5).

[16] "And it shall come to pass that the Jews which are scattered also shall begin to believe in Christ; and they shall begin to gather in upon the face of the land; and as many as shall believe in Christ shall also become a delightsome people" (2 Nephi 30:7).

[17] "And then shall the Lord set his foot upon this mount, and it shall cleave in twain, and the earth shall tremble, and reel to and fro, and the heavens also shall shake. And the Lord shall utter his voice, and all the ends of the earth shall hear it; and the nations of the earth shall mourn, and they that have laughed shall see their folly... And then shall the Jews look upon me and say: What are these wounds in thine hands and in thy feet? Then shall they know that I am the Lord; for I will say unto them: These wounds are the wounds with which I was wounded in the house of my friends. I am he who was lifted up. I am Jesus that was crucified. I am the Son of God. And then shall they weep because of their iniquities; then shall they lament because they persecuted their king" (D&C 45: 48-49, 51-53).

[18] "And this gospel shall be preached unto every nation, and kindred, and tongue, and people" (D&C 133:37). See also Revelation 14:6 and D&C 134:12.

[19] "From Adam to the time of Jesus, ordinances were performed in temples for the living only. After Jesus opened the way for the gospel to be preached in the world of spirits, ceremonial work for the dead, as well as for the living, has been done in temples on the earth by faithful members of the Church. Building and properly using a temple is one of the marks of the true Church in any dispensation, and is especially so in the present day" (Bible Dictionary, "Temples," 781).

[20] The return of the ten tribes: "And they (lost tribes of Israel) who are in the north countries shall come in remembrance before the Lord; and their prophets shall hear his voice, and shall no longer stay themselves; and they shall smite the rocks, and the ice shall flow down at their presence...And the boundaries of the everlasting hills shall tremble at their presence. And there shall they fall down and be crowned with glory, even in Zion, by the hands of the servants of the Lord, even the children of Ephraim" (D&C 133:26, 31-32).

Gathering of the 12 tribes and return of the City of Enoch: "...and righteousness and truth will I cause to sweep the earth as with a flood, *to gather out mine elect from the four quarters of the earth*, unto a place which I shall prepare, an Holy City, that my people may gird up their loins, and be looking forth for the time of my coming; for there shall be my tabernacle, and it shall be called Zion, a New Jerusalem. And the Lord said unto Enoch: Then shalt thou and all thy city meet them there, and we will receive them into our bosom, and they shall see us; and we will fall upon their necks, and they shall fall upon our necks, and we will kiss each other" (Moses 7:62-63, emphasis added).

[21] The following statement about angels aiding in the building of the temple is found in the Journal of Wilford Woodruff. It originated from a dream that John Taylor dictated to Willford Woodruff about the last days. "I then saw a short distance from the river twelve men dressed in the robes of the temple standing in a square or nearly so. I understood it represented the twelve gates of the New Jerusalem and they were with hands uplifted consecrating the ground and laying the corner stones. I saw myriads of angels hovering over them and round about them also an immense pillar of a cloud over them and I heard the singing of the most beautiful music the words: 'Now is established the Kingdom of our God and his Christ and he shall reign for ever and ever, and the Kingdom shall never be thrown down.' And I saw people coming from the river and different places a long way off to help build the temple, and it seemed that the hosts of the angels also helped to get the material to build the temple, and I saw some come who wore their temple robes to help build the temple and the city and all the time I saw the great pillar of cloud hovering over the place" (*Journal of Wilford Woodruff*, December 1877, 183).

[22] "And thou shalt come from thy place out of the north parts, thou, and many people with thee, all of them riding upon horses, a great company, and a mighty army: And thou shalt come up against my people of Israel, as a cloud to cover the land; it shall be in the latter days,

and I will bring thee against my land, that the heathen may know me, when I shall be sanctified in thee, O Gog, before their eyes" (Ezekiel 38:15-16).

This prophecy "points to a time when the heathen nations of the north would set themselves against the people of God and would be defeated, and led to recognize Jehovah as King. All this appears to be at the Second Coming of the Lord" (Bible Dictionary, "Gog," 682).

CHAPTER SEVEN

DEPTH OF THOUGHT

"O LORD, how great are thy works! and thy thoughts are very deep" (Psalms 92:5).

Sunday
September 17th
9:00 a.m.
Provo Utah

Cold Hearts Void of Affection

The Rogers family entered church and sat in the fifth row. Because of their large numbers, they took up the whole pew.

Corrynne gazed down the row at her family. She studied each one of her children. She looked at their profiles, their gestures, how they were interacting with each other. A feeling of love filled her. She loved every part of them. Next she looked up at her husband that sat beside her. She imagined looking into his clear, emerald green eyes like she had done thousands of times before. She had a weakness for his eyes; they haunted her, followed her, and enamored her. They were hers forever. It was a good, satisfying thought.

Before Corrynne was even married she would imagine these moments; good moments of togetherness. They had all worked hard to weave their lives together like a beautiful tapestry. In this day, good relationships were few and far between. She counted her blessings with a silent prayer.

A sudden unwanted memory cut through her peace. A vision of the dying young man, from a couple days before flashed before her eyes. It made her instantly sad but also angry as she remembered the phone call that told her that no family member ever called the hospital to ask about him; thus, no one came to claim the body. Since his identity was unknown, the man would be buried in an anonymous grave. Now that was sad.

Corrynne looked down at her hands lying deceptively peacefully in her lap considering the emotions that were now simmering inside her. She rubbed a knuckle and watched it turn white from the pressure and then released it, allowing the skin to turn pink again. As she did this, she considered the injustice that existed in the world. Life just wasn't fair. It wasn't fair that a young man just beginning to live had to die alone with no family to love him, no one special to support him, shouldering insurmountable pain, loneliness and a desperate sadness that would drive him to join a radical cult to find what he was missing. It wasn't fair that he didn't have the network of family that she enjoyed. She wondered why some people lived a life that ended in abandonment. Where was his family anyway? She would like to know! A family was meant to be a built-in support system for all humanity. *Every human deserved a family so no one would be left alone!*

Corrynne allowed her eyes to move to the wood grain on the pew in front of her. She noted how the long fibers alternated in light and dark patterns. She thought of its solid nature and how it was solid and yet each fiber varied from the next. Corrynne couldn't help but think that humanity could learn a thing or two from a slice of wood. People didn't have to look alike, or even be alike. Each could be unique and different like the varying patterns in wood. Some could curl this way; others could be straight with a knot in the center. But in the end all should stand side by side, bonded as one, solidly together despite differences.

Corrynne's thoughts turned to the ironic isolation of the world's inhabitants, despite the growing number of people who lived on its surface. She marveled at Satan's cunning. What a great way to destroy the souls of mankind! Ruin natural affection. Divide the family, and conquer the souls. Make everyone isolated and defensive. Create so much dishonesty and selfishness that trust is abolished. Cut the bands that bind. This was the recipe for the breakdown of the family worldwide.[1] She shook her head as she saw clearly that it was by the hand of Satan that families were being destroyed and by his hand that the members were being gathered to him. He did it by creating an atmosphere of loneliness. He would break down the natural social patterns found in a family, and then the members came to him in droves for his false promises of acceptance and belonging. Teen pregnancy, gang activity, cult behavior—all seemed to be motivated by the natural desire to be accepted and be a part of a group. But these groups seemed such a shallow substitute for the rock solid foundation that a family could provide, especially when the family was dedicated to serving righteousness.

The family was the one organization that had the power and influence to solve most of the evils of society, but the world denied the traditional family in the name of modernization. Sadly, the number of good families was in short supply. Selfishness and the natural tendencies of mankind had caused the breakdown of the family to be the norm. Yes, the world was ripe for destruction. Corrynne took a deep breath and exhaled. She rubbed her forehead hard, imagining her wrinkles becoming deeper from stress.

Right after the sacrament was passed, Strykker and Striynna began to howl from the laps of their siblings. It was always extremely embarrassing when one began, because it would always set the other off. Corrynne knew that she had better take both twins out of the chapel quickly or else everyone would only be able to hear the Rogers' twins instead of the speakers.

From the mother's lounge she was able to listen to the talks over the sound system wired into the room. They centered on the topic, "Wolves in Sheep's Clothing," or things that appeared good when in actuality they were very dangerous.

"What a perfect topic!" she whispered to herself. "I hope everyone is listening, because the wolves are among us!"[2]

The youth speakers began by talking about safety during dating by making wise choices.

"Excellent ideas!" said Corrynne with a smile, nodding. She was pleased her children were in the audience. As she listened, a poignant memory of her own youth surfaced unsolicited.

Corrynne's thoughts were catapulted back to the time she dated a young man named Tony. He was athletic, smart, and new to her high school. Ordinarily, for safety's sake, she did not date anyone who did not belong to her religion, but he pursued her and after some persuasion, she accepted one date.

One date lead to another and then another. Eventually, Corrynne found herself in a very serious relationship. As she sank deeper into an emotional attachment, Tony began talking about being together after graduation. To her surprise, he eventually asked her to marry him. She was both enthralled and appalled by his request. She knew that a marriage to him would be wrong for her because they would not be able to share a temple marriage or a unified belief system. It was against all that she had hoped for.

Corrynne wanted everything the gospel had to offer her. She wanted her husband to hold the priesthood and to have served a mission. She wanted to have family home evenings and read scriptures with her children. She wanted her husband to be a good example of gospel living. She knew no matter how much she loved Tony that he could not give her those things. Desperately, she decided to introduce the gospel to him in hopes that they could be together without the religious rift between them.

Tony's reaction to the gospel was very surprising. Corrynne remembered watching his eyes change quality as she handed him a Book of Mormon. As if bored, he flipped through the pages carelessly and then without warning threw it across the room to have it slam against the opposite wall. In a loud voice he yelled at Corrynne that she would be damned for being a Latter-day Saint, that Satan tried to be God and he was thrown out of heaven and that she, because she believed that she would be a God someday, would reap the same penalty. Tony claimed that he was sent to her to save her from that awful fiery pit. He claimed that her church was a cult and that their prophet was duping the followers. He then began to do something that totally threw her off guard: Tony began to cry and bear testimony of her eventual state of endless torment. Then he begged her to leave the church.

Corrynne ran out of Tony's home, escaping the pain that his words caused her. They were too hard to bear. She remembered her eyes full of tears and her breathing heavy. She remembered looking up into the large expanse of heaven and in torment yelling, "What is this?" She was familiar with LDS people bearing testimony of things they believed were true. She was accustomed to believing the truth in testimonies, but in this situation, Tony's words couldn't possibly be true. Could Satan mimic testimony-bearing to sway her? Could Tony really have a testimony of such things? She didn't know that other religions did this. His tears and his words confused her. He sounded so convincing. He seemed like he truly feared for her welfare. If she hadn't had a strong testimony of the truthfulness of the gospel, she knew she would have left the church at that moment.

After agonizing thought and prayer, Corrynne decided to talk and end their relationship. Clearly, they were incompatible. However, every time she approached the moment to break it off, she couldn't stand the pain of not being with him. It was all that she thought about. She found herself considering marriage to him, if only to be mortally happy even if it wasn't for eternity.

Deep inside she knew that this kind of thinking was extremely dangerous. Somewhere she began to get the impression that this was a trap. She thought that it was her background whispering to her, but as days went by Tony began to change. After long periods of denial, she began to notice inconsistencies in Tony's attitude versus his words. He would say all the right words, but his actions began to show that he wasn't sincere. Eventually, Corrynne learned that he was living a double life. To her horror, she began to understand that she was the butt of a very cruel joke.

One day, one of her friends let her in on the secret that had surrounded their relationship. He was on a mission, and it wasn't a mission to save her soul. In fact, it was a mission to steal her virtue. As a new guy in school, he was introduced to the school and told, without her being aware, that Corrynne was the kind you wouldn't want to date because there wasn't a payoff at the end. She was the marrying type; they kidded that her innocence was safeguarded with iron. Tony believed that this was the ultimate challenge and decided that Corrynne would be his prize. At first, Corrynne could not believe that the rumor was true, until Tony told her personally in a way that was cruel and eerily evil.

It was a reality that seemed so awful that depression surrounded her so deeply that Corrynne couldn't eat for weeks. As her figure became gaunt, she would gaze at herself in the mirror and wonder how she could have been so gullible. Her hunger seemed a just punishment for her foolishness. How could she have thought that he was seriously in love with her and wanted to marry her? Her disgust surprisingly was not for Tony, but for herself. Inside she still craved his attention and his touch. After all, he knew what to say and what to do to entice her.[3] He had studied her very carefully and came to know what she expected and needed. Luckily her knowledge of the gospel and her standards saved her from the devastating mistake of giving in to Tony's intentions. Thankfully, she would only have a broken heart and a painful understanding of Satan's ways instead of a destruction of her eternal salvation.

Corrynne shook her head as she realized that she was crying. Tears rolled down her cheeks onto the babies' heads and faces as they looked up at her from her lap.

"What am I doing?" she asked herself. "Why am I crying over this?" She had been happily married for so long and had a beautiful life. So she wondered why thinking of Tony still bothered her so much. As she contemplated the possible reasons, she realized that the fact that she could be tricked and manipulated still affected her deeply. She felt vulnerable. In light of her recent findings relating to the teen deaths around the world, she found that she was also crying for them, for millen, for their vulnerability and their tender feelings. Tony was a perfect example of a wolf in sheep's clothing. She had trusted him and had given him her heart only to have him laugh and jeer at his ability to trick her.

It was frightening that Satan knew her well enough to find the chink in her armor. He had used Tony to get to Corrynne. Although he was not successful, it was true that she had considered compromising her standards of marriage.

Corrynne's mind returned to the speaker's words that filled the small lounge. Suddenly, she listened with all her attention.

"Christ is the bridegroom, and the people in his church are his bride. All who are symbolically married to him, or bound by covenants and are faithful to their promises, will experience everlasting happiness by being enfolded in the true love and safety of Christ and Heavenly Father forever. Worlds upon worlds will be ours if we can just endure.[4] However, Satan desires to steal that experience away from the righteous, and he will do everything he can. Satan will send one who looks and feels like Christ. He will be sent to distract the righteous from the real Savior. He will say and do all the right things. He will perform miracles and claim to want only to save mankind.[5] He will promise anything to trick even those who are covenanted with Christ. Sadly, it is prophesied that there will be those who will make covenants with the Antichrist, being loyal with betrayed faith. There will be those who will give their life for him, sacrifice everything for his acceptance. But in the end they will realize that they were only trophies in a war that had beginnings in another sphere. Those poor souls will be left with nothing but that unsatisfied hunger and the bottomless ache of deception."

Corrynne's jaw hung open. "Bravo!" Someone was really in tune! This was the perfect talk and warning. Yes, there is a war between Satan and Christ going on right outside the doors of the church, maybe even within its congregation!

Yes, the Antichrist would trick the elect if they were not aware. Sadly, it wasn't just one individual; there would always be someone who would take his place unknowingly. Satan was always pining for souls, and as long as the hearts of men ran cold, it would continue to happen until Christ himself stopped it.

Corrynne kissed both of her twins and brushed their hair with her hand. Then she stood up with the twins and placed them on the counter near the sink. Blocking their way to the edge of the counter with her body, she stared at her image in the mirror. She recognized her brown eyes. They were the same eyes that were deceived by Tony. The body was no longer gaunt, a sign to her that she was not depressed but very happy.

Corrynne cleaned off the makeup that had smeared with her unexpected tears. She once again turned her attention to the speakers and realized that the meeting was over. Corrynne hugged both of her babies, breathing in their sweet smells, then picked them up and left the lounge.

Corrynne caught up with Bo and their oldest son and daughter just as they were leaving the chapel. "Did the children go to their classes?"

"Of course!" said Bo. "No thanks to you." He gave her a huge smile.

Braun turned to his mother and said, "What do you do in that lounge? Whenever you go, we don't see you till the end of the meeting." Braun and Brea laughed.

"I was meditating with the twins," said Corrynne with a smile.

"Did you learn anything?" asked Brea.

"You'd be surprised," returned Corrynne with a serious reflective glance.

Prophecy Revealed

Brother Anderson was a large, robust man with rosy red cheeks. He taught the Gospel Doctrine class in the adult Sunday School for the Meadowdale Ward. He loved to get into deep discussions and reveled in the intricacies of the gospel. He always smiled contagiously as he taught, flashing a gold front tooth as he spoke in a rapid tempo.

Brother Anderson was busy spreading out his materials on the table in the front of the class. Above his head the board read: "The Seven Seals of the World's Dispensations of Time."

Sister Schole, a well-bred and influential woman sitting on Bo's right, rolled her heavily outlined eyes. "Not again," she huffed in disgust. She then leaned over and spoke quietly as she held up her scriptures to shield her mouth from the other class members' view. "We can't have another 'end of the world' discussion—my Prozac is getting low!"

Bo turned and studied the jewel-garnished woman. Her strong perfume wafted around his head. He didn't comment at first.

Sister Schole continued, "I think Brother Anderson is slightly fanatical about this subject. Don't you agree?"

Attempting to keep his opinions in check, Bo just smiled at her, although he was feeling very irritated at her flippant statements. After considering his words carefully, he whispered back, "Repetition is good. Sometimes there are things we miss. It might be the thing that saves us some day." Bo smiled politely, not revealing his twisting irritation. Silently he reminded himself to be tolerant.

Without a hint of acknowledgement, Sister Schole returned her attention to the front of the classroom. She picked up a Sacrament program and began slowly fanning herself with it.

After the opening prayer Brother Anderson took his position in the front of the class. "The earthquake this morning in Chile was very dramatic. Beaches fell into the ocean from a rupture 525 miles long and 80 miles wide. If this earthquake had occurred off the shore of California, it would have stretched from San Diego to San Francisco. If it had occurred on the East Coast, it would have stretched from New York City to Wilmington, North Carolina. If it had occurred off the coast of Europe, it would have stretched from Amsterdam to the Brittany coast of France.[6]

"We tend to think that these shakings are bad, but in all actuality, it's the Lord pleading with his people to repent and come unto him. He employs whatever tactic it takes to call his children home. He's meaning to get our attention!"

With a broad smile, Brother Anderson opened his mouth and without warning broke out in a rich tenor voice, bellowing loudly, "*Ohhhh, that I were an angel...and could have the wish of mine heart....*" He held his large clasped hands out to the shocked crowd and continued to serenade them as if pleading with them. "*...that I might go forth and speak with the trump of God...With a voice...a voice...TO SHAKE THE EARTH....*" Suddenly his expression changed to longing, and he dropped to one knee and took the hand of an elderly sister on the front row. The class couldn't help but lean forward to see him on the floor. In a soft, whisper-like melody he continued singing, "*...and cry repentance...*"—a crescendo erupted again from the teacher as he stood once again—"*...repentance unto ev-ery people!*"[7] Brother Anderson stood frozen as the room still vibrated from his last long syllable. The room remained absolutely still, waiting for the next explosion.

Instead of singing, the teacher began to speak quickly, "'Keep all the commandments and covenants by which ye are bound; and I will cause the *heavens to shake for your good*, and Satan shall tremble and Zion shall rejoice upon the hills and flourish,' Doctrine and Covenants, section 35, verse 24." Quiet again permeated the room as his voice abruptly stopped.

Brother Anderson took a deep dramatic breath and continued, "Consider another scripture! 'For by doing these things the gates of hell shall not prevail against you; yea, and the Lord God will disperse the powers of darkness from before you, and *cause the heavens to shake for your good, and his name's glory.*' That scripture is found in Doctrine and Covenants, section 21, verse 6. Isn't that interesting?

"These scriptures tell us that one day the shaking of heaven and earth will be a righteous weapon for our protection. As a faithful and righteous people, we will command it to quake through the priesthood power. It will not cause fear, but inspire strength in our bosom! Elder McConkie from his book *Mormon Doctrine* says:

> '*Since the earth has been in its present fallen or telestial state, it has been subject to earthquakes. These are part of the Lord's plan; they come by His power and fulfill His purposes. By them He delivers His servants from perils, destroys the wicked, and leaves a sign that His hand has been in transcendent events.*'[8]

"We see that earthquakes are not chaotic happenings. They are the extension of the mind and will of the Father predicted to come in greater intensity and frequency in the last days.[9]

"I am going to change the wording of some select scriptures to drive home a point. All scriptures should be taken personally and applied to us at this time and place in this season.[10] Alma, chapter 1, verse 4: '...[we] *need not fear nor tremble.* ...*that [we] might lift up [our] heads and rejoice....*' Second Nephi, chapter 31, verse 20: We 'must press forward with a steadfastness in Christ, having a perfect brightness of hope, and a love of God and of all men. Wherefore, if [we] shall press forward, feasting upon the word of Christ, and endure to the end, behold, thus saith the Father: [we] shall have eternal life.' So, everyone, *shake* off that glum countenance!" Brother Anderson laughed. "Pun intended! All of you, rejoice! For...'the end is nigh at hand....'"[11]

The large teacher took his scriptures in both hands and held them up to the class. "It's obvious that in every arena of the world we are seeing the signs of Christ's return. Earthquakes play a significant role in announcing the Second Coming." Brother Anderson began to flip through the pages as he talked. "We are going to study points that are especially timely. I hope to establish a relative timetable and identify aspects of our world that correspond with scripture. The Lord continues to warn us that His coming will be very quick,[12] that there will not be any time left to prepare.[13] Thus, today we search to understand the eminent end of days.

"To begin, I would like to explore the seven seals spoken of in Revelation. Often when people read the Book of Revelation, they are put off by the symbolism and seemingly cryptic messages of those passages. For me this book is exhilarating, a work of art and food for my soul. Why does it hold such delight for me? Because I search and contemplate its meanings. I see its messages of hope for the deserving and understand the warnings for the wicked. I have learned to appreciate its unique flavor by savoring it slowly as a piece of melting chocolate in my mouth. One cannot consume it in one huge bite, or he or she will become overwhelmed with its richness.

"Referring to the title of this lesson, has anyone been able to identify the meaning of the seven seals, which are found in Revelation, chapter 6?"

Bo raised his hand, and Brother Anderson nodded his head to tell Bo to go ahead with his comment.

"In the Doctrine and Covenants, section 77, verse 7, Joseph Smith is asking the Lord specifically what some of the things in Revelation mean. We are told that the seven seals represent the seven dispensations of the world's history."[14]

"Yes, that is true. Until Joseph received that information, there was rampant confusion concerning the text in Revelation. Now we see with new eyes and can apply the messages to our day.

"As we review the seven seals, keep in mind that John was writing of the consequences of evil in every era. Whether it is battle, famine, earthquake or death, it is in response to the evil in the world and not the deeds of the righteous. In every instance, except the time of martyrs in which their blood sealed the condemnation of those who murdered them, the righteous were protected and saved from the plagues of their day. We will begin to see that pattern as we systematically explore this section.

"Open please to Revelation, chapter 6. Sister Cox, will you please read verse 2?"

Sister Cox rifled through the thin pages of her scriptures, paused, cleared her throat, and then began with a shaky voice. "And I saw, and behold a white horse: and he that sat on him had a bow; and a crown was given unto him: and he went forth conquering, and to conquer."

"John the Revelator saw a white horse with someone who had a bow and a crown on his head. The color white is very symbolic in the scriptures. What does it mean?"

Sister Cox answered, "It is the symbol for purity."

"Yes, it is. It also is the symbol for victory. It used to be an Eastern custom for conquerors to ride white horses when they won battles.[15] The rider is carrying a bow, which obviously is a symbol for war, and he is wearing a crown. In the original text of Revelation, the word used here was '*stephanos*,' meaning a crown of victory rather than a political crown.[16] So who do you know who was pure, was very victorious in battle, and who lived during the first thousand years of man's history on this earth?"

"Adam?" said Sister Cox.

"Good guess, he definitely is an important figure in the history of the world, but I don't believe that I have read about Adam fighting in any battles," returned Brother Anderson. "Any other ideas?"

"How about Enoch?" said an elderly man.

"That's my guess. In Moses we learn that Enoch was so faithful that he led the people of God with no weapons but with only the words of his mouth. When their enemies came against them to conquer them, their wickedness made them powerless against the faith of Enoch's city. Enoch would command the earth to tremble, mountains to move, rivers to change their course, and lions to roar from the wilderness. All nations feared them greatly, so powerful was the word of Enoch.[17] As we learned a few minutes ago, we will see this same power performed by the righteous in our day. Our enemies will flee before the people of Zion.[18]

"Continue reading verses 3 through 4, Sister Cox, if you would."

"'And when he had opened the second seal, I heard the second beast say, Come and see. And there went out another horse that was red: and power was given to him that sat thereon to take peace from the earth, and that they should kill one another: and there was given unto him a great sword'."

"Thank you, Sister Cox." Brother Anderson took a breath and exhaled as he continued. "Now, the horse is red. What is the symbolism of the color red?"

Sister Cox suddenly interjected, "Blood is red, and since it is mentioned that people were killing each other during that time with swords, this seems to make sense."

"Oh, Sister Cox, that is excellent. The color red often represents violence in the scriptures. The wickedness of that era brought upon them wars and bloodshed. Their vast wickedness is testified to in multiple scriptural passages dealing with the second thousand years. For example, in Genesis 6:5, 11-13, it says that the wickedness of man was great, that the thoughts of man were evil continually. It also said that the earth was filled with violence. Finally the Lord and the hosts of the heavens wept[19] over the wickedness of the people. Because 'all flesh had corrupted his way upon the earth,'[20] a flood was sent to destroy them.

"So where did the righteous go?" asked Brother Anderson with his hands out to his side. "How was there so much victory, and then in the next moment, suddenly, the world was filled with violence again?"

"Weren't the righteous translated?" asked Sister Cox.

"*Yes, they were*. Excellent, Sister Cox,"[21] commented Brother Anderson. "The Lord knew the world was becoming more and more wicked and he wanted to protect and preserve the righteous as he always does in perilous times. As the flood drew near, the righteous continued to be translated until only Methuselah, the son of Enoch,[22] was left behind.[23] He was ordained under the hand of Adam[24] and it was prophesied that he would be the source of all the kingdoms of the earth,[25] leaving only the wicked to war amongst themselves."[26]

Some heads nodded as the instructor continued to string his logic.

"I have another question for you," continued Brother Anderson. "What about the statement, 'power was given to him that sat thereon to take peace from the earth...'?[27] Who was sitting on the horse...and why was he *given* power...and by whom?" Quiet surrounded the teacher. "Maybe Satan?" asked Brother Anderson. "...Do you think the Lord would give him power to influence the world to the degree of total destruction?" asked the teacher as he looked from person to person.

"What do you think? Brother Jess?"

Brother Jess, who was a WWII veteran and nearing 100 years old, always sat in the very front row to hear Brother Anderson. It was his favorite pastime to contradict the teacher every chance he could. During this particular lesson he had been unusually quiet.

Brother Jess looked up at Brother Anderson with a cocked head and a squinted eye and spoke with a loud, slow, aged voice. "I believe that you are right, Brother Anderson. This time I'm not going to fight ya. Satan is a tricky one. Ya know the word 'chains' is mentioned in the scriptures 68 times?"[28]

"No, I didn't know that," said Brother Anderson. "How did you figure that out? Did you count them?"

"Yes sir! Indeedy I did!" said Brother Jess, stomping his cane into the carpet.

"That's impressive," said Brother Anderson.

"I was just lookin' it up the other day and counted because my genealogy was done and I had nothing better to do," said Brother Jess with a crooked smile.

The class chuckled in response.

Brother Jess continued, "More than three quarters of those times it's used in reference to Satan's power over men on this great earth."[29] Brother Jess pointed a crooked finger at Brother Anderson. "Ya wanna know who gave that awful being power to take peace from the earth?"

Brother Anderson nodded with a large smile. "Yes, I would."

"...We did, Brother, we did," said Brother Jess as he patted his chest with arthritic fingers. "...The people of the world did, and we still do today."

"Explain further," said Brother Anderson.

"The Lord called after his people through Noah for 120 years![30] He gave them lots of time to hear his warnings and repent, just like he's doin' today. Satan can't do diddly without *us* dancing to his tune."

With a firm pat on Brother Jess' shoulder, Brother Anderson addressed the class. "Brother Jess is so right! We are told in Second Nephi, chapter 2, verse 27 that men are 'free to choose liberty and eternal life, through the great Mediator of all men, or to *choose captivity and death*, according to the captivity and power of the devil.' It is through this influence that he has over man and their choices that he receives power over the inhabitants of the earth. Evil nations make evil choices. We see that widespread evil choices cause natural catastrophes.

"Let's move on to the third seal." Brother Anderson looked around the room for another reader. "Sister Corrynne Rogers, would you read verses 5 and 6 in Revelation, chapter 6?"

Corrynne looked up from her twins who were playing at her feet and nodded. She quickly found her spot. "And when he had opened the third seal, I heard the third beast say, come and see. And I beheld, and lo a black horse; and he that sat on him had a pair of balances in his hand. And I heard a voice in the midst of the four beasts say, a measure of wheat for a penny, and three measures of barley for a penny; and *see* thou hurt not the oil and the wine."

Brother Anderson's front tooth caught the light as he smiled at the class. "So, any ideas about this scripture? ...We have a black horse this time with a rider who is holding a balance used to measure out dry produce for sale. We also have an interesting statement at the end. ...Who would like to try?"

Bo hesitated a second, turned his scriptures, and he began to scan the pages. Finding the passages that he was looking for, he spoke out with a slightly raised hand. "The black color is often used to signify the lack of light, or darkness. Most often it represents evil."[31]

"Good," said Brother Anderson nodding.

"The evil of the world during this time period called upon itself terrible famines," said Bo. "The black color could be symbolic of death, both physical and spiritual death, in which they have lost the light of the spirit."

Brother Anderson nodded. "I hadn't thought of it that way, but yes, we know that during this time period many people died. It was a time of wandering people in search of adequate food. Recall that we learn that Abraham had to relocate because of the famine in which his brother, Haran, died of starvation.[32] Another famine caused Jacob to relocate his family to Egypt where Joseph was able to save them from death because of his inspiration to prepare for a seven-year famine.[33]

"But look now to the balance and the reference to the wheat and barley referred to in this same period. I was intrigued to how they were related as I studied for this lesson. How much again did a person pay for a measure of wheat and three measures of barley?"

"A penny," said a couple voices in the audience.

"Right, a penny. To me, a penny for food didn't seem like a large price to pay for food during a famine, so I had to look a little deeper for the meaning of a 'penny.' I found that a 'denarius,' or the equivalent of a penny, was a day's wage for a laborer.[34] Ordinarily, a penny would be able to buy 10 to 16 times the amount of wheat or double the barley that the person on the black horse offered. So because of the famine we find the price of food was actually inflated so that a day's wage would buy only enough to keep one person alive for one day."[35]

Brother Anderson flipped the page of his scriptures. "So now, tell me what's meant by the statement 'see thou hurt not the oil and the wine'?"[36]

There weren't any answers offered, as it seemed the class tried to think of a response.

"I had no idea either," said Brother Anderson after a couple of moments, "but Elder McConkie did. He says that those words are an indication that the Lord has limits to how far the famines extend. The Lord is aware and in control.[37] So although the famines were devastating, there was a planned end and extent to how far they could go.

"The fourth seal continues to demonstrate the toll of wickedness on the earth as famines and death continued. A quarter of the earth died this time. We see that the rider is pale as he is identified as death himself with hell following after him. We read this in Revelation 6, verse 8."

Brother Anderson scanned the room again. "Sister Brea Rogers, would you read?"

Brea began, "And I looked, and behold a pale horse: and his name that sat on him was Death, and hell followed with him. And power was given unto them over the fourth part of the earth, to kill with sword, and with hunger, and with death, and with the beasts of the earth."

"Thank you, Sister.

"The horse in this era is pale. This is death symbolized and personified. He looks like mortality without life's blood coursing through his veins.

"The battlefront is the backdrop, which sends men to their graves. World history is characterized by the successive rise and fall of empires during the fourth seal. The Babylonians, Assyrians, Persians, and Macedonians[38] all went forth to conquer and were in turn conquered. Huge areas were depopulated and wild beasts were able to run free among the ruins.[39] Masses of men fell by the sword, and the spirit world gaped open to receive them. Famine and plague naturally followed after such widespread destruction.

"The fifth seal identifies a time of martyrs. Brother Vandine, would you read Revelation, chapter 6, verse 9."

A middle-aged man peered over his reading glasses to look at the teacher and then down again to read. "'And when he had opened the fifth seal, I saw under the altar the souls of them that were slain for the word of God, and for the testimony which they held.'"

"What do you think that passage is referring to, Brother Vandine?" asked Brother Anderson.

"This scripture is pretty clear. It is referring to the time when the church was set up in the world by Jesus Christ himself, and then Christ and all of his apostles were killed for the sake of the word, except for John, who was granted a translated state until Christ came again."

"Yes, excellent. Brother Vandine, why does John describe the souls of the testifiers as being *under* the altar?"

"I am not quite sure," said Brother Vandine as he perused his scriptures quickly.

"What was the altar used for in the days when this scripture was written?" asked the instructor.

"From Adam up to the time of Christ's own sacrifice, it was used for sacrifices in similitude of the Savior's sacrifice."[40]

"Yes, you're right. Going along with your premise, the altar itself represents the sacrifice that the saints made for their beliefs. Their position under the altar suggests that they were martyrs. During the sacrificial rites the blood of the victim, symbolic of its life,[41] was poured out at the altar's base,[42] seeping beneath it."[43]

"I'm sorry, but the vision that this scripture inspires of blood dripping down an altar gives me the heebie-jeebies," stated Brea, interrupting the study of the class.

Brother Anderson looked up suddenly at her and said, "Well, good."

"What is that supposed to mean?" Brea was smiling, but her eyebrows were raised high, questioning.

"It's supposed to mean that the killing of the Lord's anointed is not a warm-fuzzy occurrence. That feeling of uneasiness is supposed to harrow up the wicked into a remembrance of their sins. It is to define the lines between God's people, whom he will avenge, and those he will punish. It is very clear that the early saints were the Lord's representatives and not the crazed, dangerous people that the Romans and other groups who persecuted them made them seem."

The instructor looked at the clock and fidgeted as he gazed into his scriptures. He then asked slowly as if gathering his thoughts, "Now where are we?" Brother Anderson looked around the class. "Hmmmm, Sister Slater, do you know?"

"Know what?" The startled middle-aged woman looked at Brother Anderson.

"I said, where are we?"

"You mean in the scriptures?"

"Well, yes, in the scriptures and literally."

"Well...we are in Revelation in Provo, Utah, learning revelations about Revelation," said Sister Slater, trying to be funny.

The group snickered politely.

Brother Anderson gave Sister Slater a look of friendly warning and shook his finger at her as he waited for order to return to the room. "OK, I guess that wasn't a fair question. I mean, aren't we now caught up to our day in the scriptures? We are now in the sixth seal. Sister Slater, do you know what the scriptures say about our day?"

"I'm afraid to ask." Sister Slater made a face.

Brother Anderson swiped the air with his fist. "Don't be afraid—ask the questions! Find your place in the last drama before Christ's second coming!"

"Wait a second, Brother Anderson," asked Braun, with a frown on his face.

"Yes, Brother Rogers?"

"You just said that we were in the sixth seal, am I right?"

"Yes?"

"If each seal corresponds with one thousand years, that would place us past the sixth seal, especially if the fifth seal opened with Christ's birth. The year 2001 would have opened the seventh seal."

"You have a good point, and I probably would agree with you. However, the events mentioned in the sixth seal have not taken place."

"No, they haven't," agreed Braun. "Yet we are past the time of both the opening and the ending of the sixth thousand years by your limited definition."

"You mean the Lord's definition," clarified Brother Anderson.

"No, I mean yours," said Braun confidently.

Brother Anderson frowned and smiled at the same time, if that was ever possible and asked, "How is that?"

Braun looked down into his scriptures and then back at Brother Anderson. "I wish to point out that if we look carefully at the scriptures, we can get an expanded point of view that might explain this discrepancy."

"Are you saying that the sixth thousand years and the sixth seal may be referring to two different things?" asked Brother Anderson.

"Yes, and no." Braun looked up at the clock. The time was 11:05, past the time the class should have let out. "But I'm afraid that discussion will have to occur at another time."

"Oh, that statement was quite a tease to our hungry minds," said Brother Anderson with a laugh.

"The feast can come later, when our palates are prepared and our souls are hungering," said Braun, imitating the language of scripture.

"Well, come next week, Brother Rogers. I'll have a block of time just for you to serve us a feast."

"I'll be here with fish and loves of bread, enough for a multitude," said Braun, teasing but being serious at the same time. "If you're serious."

"Of course I'm serious," said Brother Anderson looking about the class at all the nodding heads. "Inquiring minds want to know what you know."

"OK, then," said Braun. "I'll teach next week."

"Good," said Brother Anderson with a nod. "Now, in conclusion to our class, today we see Revelation is a full and prophetic book that holds the keys to both our past and our future. I pray we will search its types and shadows to help guide us though the tumultuous times ahead, in the name of Jesus Christ, amen."

"Amen," said the class in unison.

Names and Numbers

The Gospel Doctrine class members began to gather their things to exit to their next classes. Braun zipped closed the cover over his tattered missionary set of scriptures. As he got up from his seat and turned to go, he felt a tapping on his shoulder. He turned back to see Brother Anderson standing at least six inches taller than he at his eye level. Of course, he was smiling at him with his famous generous smile.

"Brother Rogers, I would like to take a moment of your time, if you don't mind."

Braun's mouth turned up conservatively. "Sure, what is it that you want to discuss?"

Brea, who was standing next to Braun, saw the signs of an involved conversation and excused herself by whispering in his ear, "I'm going to go to Relief Society to get good seats."

"Fine," Braun nodded and returned his attention to the large instructor, just as Bo and Corrynne joined the pair.

The teacher wrinkled his forehead causing his skin to blanch as he began his train of thought. "I have been poring over the scriptures in preparation for future lessons. One topic that intrigues me is the rise of the government entity that will control all the nations before Christ's coming.[44] Are you familiar with that subject?"[45]

Braun nodded.

Bo nodded too.

"I just have one question," said Brother Anderson. "I found some historical information that leads me to believe that the Caesars, Nero, and Domitian fulfilled the verses in Revelation discussing the governments that will control the world and persecute the saints.[46] If that's the case, then those words are already fulfilled. Have you ever heard this line of thought?"

Corrynne gave Brother Anderson a puzzled look. "What chapter are you talking about? Who are Nero and Domitian?"

"I'm talking specifically about Revelation 13."

Corrynne nodded. "OK."

"Nero and Domitian were tyrant leaders of the Roman Empire who killed the saints of the early church, often for sport and leisure,"[47] explained Brother Anderson.

"For sport and leisure?" asked Corrynne.

"Sure," said Bo. "That's during the same time the apostles were all killed.

Corrynne shrugged. "Well, I know that they were all killed. I just didn't know that they were killed for *sport and leisure*. I thought they were killed because they wouldn't deny Christ, or that they preached in the wrong place at the wrong time."

"Some were, Mom, but others were needlessly tortured for the sheer pleasure of the emperors," explained Braun in a matter-of-fact tone.

"The argument that the Romans were the entities pointed to by John is pretty strong," said Brother Anderson, returning to his original topic. "What are your feelings on it?" He looked expectantly at both Bo and Braun as he put his hands in his pockets.

Braun turned his head slightly as he pursed his lips together before he spoke. "I believe John was describing them, but I believe it was only to use them as an example. John wrote Revelation during the time of Domitian and had seen the needless deaths of his friends and close associates. I'm sure their treatment was fresh on his mind, but I believe that their treatment was only a type and a shadow of what will come in the last days. To believe otherwise would confine that interpretation to the Roman period. I know that for sure is wrong."

Corrynne turned toward her son and asked, "Are you saying that we are going to be persecuted to that degree again?" Corrynne turned to her husband. "Do you think that, too?"

Before Bo could answer, Braun turned to meet his mother's gaze and said, "It's not my idea alone. Joseph Smith indicates that the persecution depicted by John is in reference to things that would happen in the future, not in his day. Nero and Domitian lived during John's life, so those passages couldn't apply to them."[48]

Corrynne shook her head and said, "I had no idea." Turning back to Brother Anderson, she asked, "What chapter did you say this was in?"

"Revelation 13," said Brother Anderson.

"...but I remind all of us that the Lord has pronounced that once the gospel was restored, it would never be taken from the earth again,[49] so I believe that not all the saints will be in danger," said Braun.

"I agree," said Bo.

"Whoever that entity will be in the last day that will attempt to rule the earth, I think the saints within his grasp might suffer the kind of persecution that John spoke of, but not those who live in America."

"Why would you say that?" asked Corrynne.

"Because in the Doctrine and Covenants it states clearly that there will be special blessings attached to Zion, the New Jerusalem. The Saints are promised that, if they stay righteous, they will be protected from all manner of threats."[50]

Brother Anderson was listening to the conversation between the family members with a blank stare. He took a breath and tried to understand. "So you're saying that there will be a real threat to some degree in the future and that the historical data is wrong."

Braun shook his head, "No, I didn't say it was wrong. I said that evidence from revealed sources points to other interpretations."

"Close enough." Brother Anderson looked down, then suddenly interjected another thought. "How about this? ...I read somewhere that the number 666 written in its numerical equivalent in Hebrew translated into

'Nero Caesar.'[51] That is pretty coincidental, don't you think, for it not to mean anything?"

Corrynne changed her weight and asked, "How can you write a numerically equivalent name?"

Bo answered this question. "The ancient people didn't have a separate numbering system from their alphabet. Often letters and numbers were interchangeable."[52]

Braun addressed Brother Anderson's statement. "Well, I've also read that if you're creative, you can spell out many things with different combinations."[53]

Braun continued with another thought. "A valid point to this discussion is that some of the early Greek manuscripts name the beast as 616, not 666. That confuses everyone's theories."[54]

"I hadn't heard that." Brother Anderson laughed sarcastically. "I didn't even consider that the numbers could be wrong. Well, that shoots my theories out the window."

Braun reached out and patted Brother Anderson's shoulder. "Don't lose faith, Brother, the Church is still true," he teased.

Brother Anderson and the Rogers family members laughed and moved toward the door and out into the hallway. As they walked, Brother Anderson continued to ask questions. "So, Bo, have you wondered who the government that Revelation refers to, might be?"

"Funny you should ask, because I have some definite opinions," said Bo. "I think a Germanic connection of some sort will be this world's downfall."[55]

"Bo!" said Corrynne with a disapproving look.

"What?" asked Bo, looking at his wife questioningly.

"Why do you attach the downfall of the world to any ethnic group?"

"Because that's what I believe."

"Well, that's exactly how the Saints are going to be persecuted. They'll be labeled and then targeted. We can't label any other people like that. It will only cause bigotry and contention."

Bo shook his head. "No Corrynne. I have a simple opinion. I can say what I think."

"Why do you think that way, Dad?" asked Braun.

"Because the German government fits many of the clues in the scriptures. I can show you when we get home if you'd like."

Braun smiled and shook his head. "Be careful, Dad, that kind of information has not been revealed by the brethren. You would be making leaps of understanding on your own," he warned.

Bo scoffed, "Like it or not, it's what I think." Bo looked at his wife and his son with a puzzled look.

Corrynne shook her head and frowned. "Just don't be so forward about it. I end up defending your opinions for you when people ask me later what you meant, and that is frustrating when I have nothing to do with what you say."

"You should tell them to come ask me. I'll have no problem telling them what I think. I am without shame."

"Well that is a perfect statement, even if I didn't say it!" said Corrynne emphatically.

"OK, Mom and Dad, keep the heated discussions down...at least in church!" said Braun, stepping between his mother and father. Continuing to tease his parents, he said, "I might have to ground you because you can't get along."

"They're getting along," laughed Brother Anderson as he wrapped his large arms around the three adults and two babies. "You guys are my favorite people. You say it as it is. It's so refreshing! We will definitely have to talk more later!"

Notes to "Depths of Thought"

Cold Hearts Void of Affection

[1] The Prophet of the Church of Jesus Christ of Latter-day Saints comments on the family being the strength or weakness of society: "The Church is a constant in a world of change. It is an anchor in a world of shifting values. It emphasizes the importance of the family, and all of us have to know that family life is unraveling across the world. We are holding on to the family. We are trying to strengthen the family. We teach family ideals. We have a great program for the development of family solidarity that is satisfying a human need and offers hope to many, many people who are desperately looking for something as fathers and mothers, as they see their children moving in the direction of drugs and other things. Divorce is rampant across the world, and growing. There is need for stability. The family is the basic organization of society. A nation can be no stronger than the strength of its families" (a quote from Gordon B. Hinckley in an interview with Lawrence Spicer, *London News Service*, 28 Aug. 1995).

[2] "Beware of false prophets, which come to you in sheep's clothing, but inwardly they are ravening wolves" (Matthew 7:15).

[3] "Wherefore, all things which are good cometh of God; and that which is evil cometh of the devil; for the devil is an enemy unto God, and fighteth against him continually, and inviteth and enticeth to sin, and to do that which is evil continually" (Moroni 7:12).

[4] This discussion is reminiscent of Matthew 25:1-13, Parable of the 10 virgins.

[5] "Let no man deceive you by any means: for *that day shall not come,* except there come a falling away first, and that man of sin be revealed, the son of perdition; Who opposeth and exalteth himself above all that is called God, or that is worshipped; so that he as God sitteth in the temple of God, shewing himself that he is God... And then shall that Wicked be revealed, whom the Lord shall consume with the spirit of his mouth, and shall destroy with the brightness of his coming: *Even him,* whose coming is after the working of Satan with all power and signs and lying wonders, And with all deceivableness of unrighteousness in them that perish; because they received not the love of the truth, that they might be saved" (2 Thessalonians 2:3-4, 8-10).

Prophesy Revealed

[6] The earthquake described in the text is taken from a real event. Subtle changes have been made for the storyline. It is assumed that others like it will and already are occurring. For more information about this particular earthquake in Chile, see M. Zirbes "Largest Earthquakes in

the World," *National Earthquake Information Center, World Data Center for Seismology*, 5 April 2001, available online: http://neic.usgs.gov/neis/eqlists/WORLD/1960_05_22.html.

[7] Alma 29:1.

[8] Bruce R. McConkie, "Earthquakes," *Mormon Doctrine*, 211.

[9] "And great earthquakes shall be in divers places, and famines, and pestilences; and fearful sights and great signs shall there be from heaven" (Luke 21:11). See also Matthew 24:7; Mark 13:8; Mormon 8:30; D&C 45:33; Joseph Smith Matthew 1:29.

[10] "Let us ... seek to read and understand and apply the principles and inspired counsel found within the [scriptures]. If we do so, we shall discover that our personal *acts* of righteousness will also bring personal revelation or inspiration when needed into our own lives" (Spencer W. Kimball, *Ensign*, Sept. 1975, 4).

[11] Jacob 5:71.

[12] "For the day of my visitation cometh speedily, in an hour when ye think not of..." (D&C 124:10).

"For yourselves know perfectly that the day of the Lord so cometh as a thief in the night" (1 Thessalonians 5:2).

[13] "And it is like unto a man who is an householder, who, if he watcheth not his goods, the thief cometh in an hour of which he is not aware..."(JST Luke 12: 45, Appendix).

"... but if ye are prepared ye shall not fear" (D&C 38:30).

[14] "Q. What are we to understand by the seven seals with which it was sealed? A. We are to understand that the first seal contains the things of the first thousand years, and the second also of the second thousand years, and so on until the seventh" (D&C 77:7).

[15] R. H. Charles, *A Critical and Exegetical Commentary on the Revelation of St. John*, Vol. 1, 162; Richard D. Draper, *Opening the Seven Seals*, 62.

[16] Richard D. Draper, *Opening the Seven Seals*, 62.

[17] See Moses 7:13.

[18] "And the day shall come when the nations of the earth shall tremble because of her, and shall fear because of her terrible ones. The Lord hath spoken it. Amen" (D&C 64:43).

[19] "And it came to pass that the God of heaven looked upon the residue of the people, and he wept; and Enoch bore record of it, saying: How is it that the heavens weep, and shed forth their tears as the rain upon the mountains?" (Moses 7:28).

[20] "And GOD saw that the wickedness of man *was* great in the earth, and *that* every imagination of the thoughts of his heart *was* only evil continually...The earth also was corrupt before God, and the earth was filled with violence.

And God looked upon the earth, and, behold, it was corrupt; for all flesh had corrupted his way upon the earth. And God said unto Noah, The end of all flesh is come before me; for the earth is filled with violence through them; and, behold, I will destroy them with the earth" (Genesis 6:5, 11-13).

[21] "And Enoch beheld angels descending out of heaven, bearing testimony of the Father and Son; and the Holy Ghost fell on many, and they were caught up by the powers of heaven into Zion" (Moses 7:27).

[22] "And Enoch lived sixty and five years, and begat Methuselah" (Genesis 5:21).

[23] "And it came to pass that Methuselah, the son of Enoch, was not taken, that the covenants of the Lord might be fulfilled, which he made to Enoch; for he truly covenanted with Enoch that Noah should be of the fruit of his loins" (Moses 8:2).

[24] "Methuselah was one hundred years old when he was ordained under the hand of Adam" (D&C 107:50).

[25] "And it came to pass that Methuselah prophesied that from his loins should spring all the kingdoms of the earth (through Noah), and he took glory unto himself" (Moses 8:3).

[26] "But, behold, the judgments of God will overtake the wicked; and it is by the wicked that the wicked are punished; for it is the wicked that stir up the hearts of the children of men unto bloodshed" (Mormon 4:5).

[27] Revelation 6:4.

[28] See Bible Topical Guide, "Chains," 54.

[29] "And he (Enoch) beheld Satan; and he had a great chain in his hand, and it veiled the whole face of the earth with darkness; and he looked up and laughed, and his angels rejoiced" (Moses 7:26).

[30] "And the Lord said unto Noah: My Spirit shall not always strive with man, for he shall know that all flesh shall die; yet his days shall be an hundred and twenty years; and if men do not repent, I will send in the floods upon them" (Moses 8:17).

[31] For example: "Which dark and blackening deeds are enough to make hell itself shudder, and to stand aghast and pale, and the hands of the very devil to tremble and palsy" (D&C 123:10).

[32] See Abraham 1:29-30.

[33] See Genesis Chapters 41-44.

[34] See Matthew 20:2, "And when he had agreed with the labourers for a penny a day, he sent them into his vineyard."

[35] R. H. Charles, *A Critical and Exegetical Commentary on the Revelation of St. John*, Vol. 1, 166-167; Richard D. Draper, *Opening the Seven Seals*, 66.

[36] Revelation 6:6.

[37] Bruce R. McConkie, *Doctrinal New Testament Commentary*, Vol. 3, 480.

[38] See http://www.wilsonmar.com/1history.htm for world dates that correspond to scripture.

[39] Richard D. Draper, *Opening the Seven Seals*, 67.

[40] See Moses 5: 5-7: "And he gave unto them commandments, that they should worship the Lord their God, and should offer the firstlings of their flocks, for an offering unto the Lord. And Adam was obedient unto the commandments of the Lord. And after many days an angel of the Lord appeared unto Adam, saying: Why dost thou offer sacrifices unto the Lord? And Adam said unto him: I know not, save the Lord commanded me, And then the angel spake, saying: This thing is a similitude of the sacrifice of the Only Begotten of the Father, which is full of grace and truth."

[41] "For *the life of the flesh is in the blood*: and I have given it to you upon the altar to make an atonement for your souls: for it *is* the blood *that* maketh an atonement for the soul" (Leviticus 17:11, emphasis added).

[42] "...shall pour all the blood of the bullock at *the bottom of the altar* of the burnt offering..." (Leviticus 4:7, emphasis added).

[43] Richard D. Draper, *Opening the Seven Seals*, 69.

[44] See Revelation 13 for a complete scriptural source of said government in text.

Names and Numbers

[45] A more complete discussion of Revelation will come later. This discussion is to introduce the subject into the storyline.

[46] For a discussion on various theories fulfilling these passages mentioned in the text, see Homer Hailey, *Revelation, An Introduction and Commentary*, 285-86; Richard D. Draper, *Opening the Seven Seals,* 143-144.

[47] See Chapter 1 notes for a review of historical documentation of "Nero" and "Domitian."

[48] "There is a grand difference and distinction between the visions and figures spoken of by the ancient prophets, and those spoken of in the Revelation of John. The things which John saw had no allusion to the scenes of the days of Adam, Enoch, Abraham, or Jesus, only so far as is plainly represented by John, and clearly set forth by him. John saw that only which was lying in futurity and which was shortly to come to pass." (Joseph Smith, "Morning Session of Conference," *Church History*, Vol. 5, April 1843, 341-42.

[49] See D&C 13:1, Joseph Smith History 1:69.

[50] "For, behold, I say unto you that Zion shall flourish, and the glory of the Lord shall be upon her; And she shall be an ensign unto the people, and there shall come unto her out of every nation under heaven. And the day shall come when the nations of the earth shall tremble because of her, and shall fear because of her terrible ones. The Lord hath spoken it. Amen" (D&C 64:41-43).

"And, now, behold, if Zion do these things she shall prosper, and spread herself and become very glorious, very great, and very terrible. And the nations of the earth shall honor her, and shall say: Surely Zion is the city of our God, and surely Zion cannot fall, neither be moved out of her place, for God is there, and the hand of the Lord is there; And he hath sworn by the power of his might to be her salvation and her high tower. Therefore, verily, thus saith the Lord, let Zion rejoice, for this is Zion—THE PURE IN HEART; therefore, let Zion rejoice, while all the wicked shall mourn. For behold, and lo, vengeance cometh speedily upon the ungodly as the whirlwind; and who shall escape it? The Lord's scourge shall pass over by night and by day, and the report thereof shall vex all people; yea, it shall not be stayed until the Lord come; For the indignation of the Lord is kindled against their abominations and all their wicked works. Nevertheless, Zion shall escape if she observe to do all things whatsoever I have commanded her" (D&C 97: 18-25).

[51] Richard D. Draper, *Opening the Seven* Seals, 150-51.

[52] Richard D. Draper, *Opening the Seven Seals*, 149.

[53] R. H. Charles, *A Critical and Exegetical Commentary on the Revelation of St. John*, Vol. 1, 366-68.

[54] Richard D. Draper, *Opening the Seven Seals*, 150.

[55] This statement does not represent any statements of scripture or beliefs of the Church of Jesus Christ of Latter-day Saints. It is purely a fictional storyline extrapolation.

CHAPTER EIGHT

THE SKY IS FALLING

"And all things shall be in commotion; and surely, men's hearts shall fail them; for fear shall come upon all people" (D&C 88:91).

Sunday
September 17th
11:05 a.m.
Provo Utah

Hail

"Look!" said someone loudly as they were standing inside the glass doors of the church building.

Carea was drawn to the door. She looked out the windows to see what the gathering crowd was watching. Across the parking lot and into the lawns of the neighboring houses a thin blanket of white was accumulating. Marble-size hail was beginning to come down fast. Each piece bounced wildly before it came to rest.

"It's beautiful," Carea whispered to herself. She marveled at how fast the landscape was changing, especially since it was September. She loved it when snow covered the surrounding mountains, trees and houses. She thought that heaven would look that way—pure and perfect white. This, however, was not snow. As she watched, she noticed that the pieces were bouncing higher and now she realized that the size of the hail was increasing.

"Wow, Carea, look at those snowballs!" said a young voice beside her.

Carea looked down to see her seven-year-old brother, Roc, standing beside her, nose to glass. Carea patted his head and returned her gaze to the mesmerizing accumulation. "Yes, aren't they fun? That's called *hail*. It's…" But before she even finished her sentence, Carea felt a blast of cold air on her face and legs as she realized that Roc had pushed through the doors and rushed out into the storm.

Carea caught the glass door as it rebounded and yelled into the escalating wind, *"Roc!* What are you doing? Stay in here until the storm passes. *Roc…come back!"*

Roc did not hear her, or if he did, he didn't pay attention.

"Roc! Get back here!" Carea yelled with more authority, wondering if she should go out after him before the hail got any bigger.

With a joyful look in his eyes, Roc was looking steadily into the sky with his tongue held out and his hands open wide when a golf ball-sized hailstone pelted him square in the forehead.

Carea screamed and covered her mouth as blood emerged from the wound and began trickling down his right cheek. ***"Roc! Get out of the hail, NOW!"*** Carea yelled with all the energy she had.

Roc reflexively ducked, covered his head and looked back at Carea momentarily with a terror she hadn't seen in his face before.

Carea thought Roc would come back to the church after being hurt but before he could, another sharp piece of ice slammed into his back and sent him scurrying to the nearest car for shelter. Luckily the door was unlocked, and he pulled on the handle with both of his little hands. Carea held her breath as she watched little Roc wiggle into the back seat through a door that opened only a few inches.

Lightning and raging thunder ripped through the darkened sky as if to warn onlookers of the pain that threatened anyone who dared to leave their shelters.

Carea searched the gathering crowd behind her frantically for her mother and father. Not seeing them, she pushed through the pack of people, dodging the on-coming group. She knew her parents would be coming that way from class.

Finally she caught sight of Braun, Brother Anderson, and her parents with the twins coming towards her. *"Mom, Dad! Come quick!"* called Carea with intensity.

"What's wrong?" asked Corrynne with a sudden worried look on her face.

Carea pointed outside. "Roc just walked out into a hail storm."

"Is he hurt?" asked Bo.

Carea nodded as she started to cry in frustration. "Yes. Some ice cut his face. I yelled for him to come back but he wouldn't."

Corrynne and Bo handed the twins to Carea and pushed past her.

"We'll get him," said Bo with a determined look.

"He's hiding in the small red car right outside the church doors!" yelled Carea after them.

Corrynne and Bo forced their way to the doors through the thick layer of people. As they approached the doors and saw the dark, angry skies and heard the violent thunder, Corrynne asked Bo in astonishment, "Where'd this storm come from?"

Bo shook his head. "I don't know, but this storm is big."

"Look at that hail!" said Corrynne with a gasp. *"I've never seen such hail before!"*

The hail had grown to baseball size and was bouncing at least six feet in the air, hitting the earth and anything else outside with violent energy.

Corrynne searched for the little red car outside the doors. Seeing a car that fit the description, she said while pointing, "Bo, look. There's the red car. Roc's in there."

Right then, a ball of ice hit the windshield of the little red car and the windshield partially caved in with cracks in the glass extending out like tentacles.

Corrynne swallowed hard as her heart beat hard in her chest. *"Did you see what just happened to that car?"*

Bo nodded.

"This storm will kill a little guy like Roc. *Bo! What are we going to do?"* asked Corrynne in a panic.

The car door opened slightly.

"Look! The door! Is Roc opening that door?" asked Corrynne, standing on her tiptoes to try and see clearer but her view was obstructed by the adjacent car. "He can't go back out in that storm! Maybe he's trying to come back in!" she said almost breathless. *"Stop him, Bo!"* urged Corrynne.

Bo pushed through the glass doors and stood right under the eaves to avoid the deadly hail, but even though he was out of the way of a direct pelting, he was still being hit by ricocheting, wild balls as they bounced off other objects.

Corrynne watched in fear as Bo dodged the oncoming missile-like pieces as he tried to motion to Roc to stay in the car. She could see that Roc was watching his father through the fogging window. She just hoped he'd understand and obey.

The hail continued to increase to a softball size. Bo looked around. It looked like he was preparing to run to his son.

Corrynne shook her head and poked her head out the door. "Don't do it, Bo," she said. "He's OK as long as he stays in that car."

"Go back in, Corrynne," yelled Bo over the wind. "Close the door."

"I'm serious, Bo. Don't run out in that hail! He saw you and knows you want him to stay in the car!" said Corrynne.

"I'm not sure about that," said Bo, squinting as he braved the wind blowing in his face. "Go back in the church. I'll be fine."

Corrynne tried one more time, knowing her husband wasn't going to wait for the storm to blow over, "Look, Bo. Look at the cars. All the windshields are cracked and the hoods are dented. You could die if that hail hit you in the head."

"Exactly," said Bo, "and Roc's little. He wouldn't stand a chance in this storm."

"Bo!" called Corrynne with anger in her voice. "He's safe right now. Don't go out there!"

But Bo did not listen. He did ventured out into the storm, only to be hit square in the chest by a large ball of ice that had ricocheted off the bumper of the closest car. The force of the blow knocked Bo off his feet and he landed on his back.

Brother Anderson pushed by Corrynne and took hold of Bo's arms and dragged him back into the church doors. "What are you doing out there?" he asked, chiding Bo.

"I was getting my boy..." said Bo gasping for air.

"Your boy will be fine. Just stay here," he said in a friendly deep tone.

Corrynne knelt down next to Bo and touched his chest. "Is it hard to breathe?"

Bo nodded and winced. "My ribs are cracked. I heard them pop."

Corrynne took in a frustrated breath between her teeth.

"Mom! Rocwell!" yelled someone from behind.

Corrynne looked up. It was Carea, pointing outside. Corrynne stood to see the door of the car open even wider. "What's Roc doing?" she asked, grimacing—afraid to know the truth.

As the door stood open in the storm, the doorframe of the car was pelted into a disfigured form and the glass shattered into thousands of pieces. A moment after, Roc stuck his little arm out the frame and waved for someone to come and rescue him.

"He must be scared," said Corrynne as she shook her head. She pushed on the door and yelled through cupped hands, "We can't come out to get you!" yelled Corrynne. "Stay there and get your arm..." But it was too late. Like the doorframe, hail hit Roc's arm with an angry force, bending it where there wasn't a joint.

Roc withdrew into the car.

"Roc!" Corrynne yelled as she saw his little arm contort. Her hands went up to her mouth as she restrained a scream.

"What happened?" asked Carea.

"Roc's been injured," said Corrynne trying to keep it together. "I don't see him anymore. He must be laying on the bench or even on the floor."

"That's good," said Bo in a pained voice. "That's the best place for him."

"Look, the storm's easing," said Brother Anderson.

Corrynne studied the weather outside. Yes, it was lightening. The hail was slowing and growing smaller.

Another roll of thunder sounded, but it seemed further away. Soon the hail eased to the point that Corrynne slid out the doors.

Small pebble-like hail continued to fall all around Corrynne and the others that emerged with her. Jax, Ry, and Dane, who also had been watching at the windows, came out after Corrynne, anxious to help retrieve their brother.

Braun and Brea who had been caught in the crowd of people, pushed through to help their father to the couch in the foyer.

Carea ventured out but she stayed under the eves to protect Striynna and Strykker while she watched the commotion.

Pulling open what was left of the mangled door of the red car, Corrynne looked into the backseat. To her surprise, Roc was not on the seat or the floor of the car. Corrynne looked in the front seat, under the seats and under the dashboards.

Dane, Jax, and Ry repeated her efforts but it was clear that Roc had disappeared.

"Rocwell! Rocwell Joshua, where are you?" Corrynne yelled as she checked around the outside of the car. Still she couldn't find him. "Dane, do you see him over there?" she asked her son who was on the opposite side of the car.

Dane shook his head as he searched. "No, Mom, I don't."

"This is the car he was in!" said Corrynne. "This is the window that exploded," she said now putting her hand through the open frame where the window used to be.

"You're right," said Brother Anderson, who was now helping in the search.

"Where is he then?" asked Corrynne, grabbing her hair and looking around in frustration.

Dane shrugged as he continued to recheck every part of the red car. "I don't know. It's like he just disappeared."

"Do you think he's back in the church?" Ry asked.

Corrynne shook her head. "Not unless he's a magician."

"Maybe we should check, just to make sure," offered Ry.

"Maybe," said Corrynne, heading back to the church.

Back in the church, Corrynne asked Bo, "Did you see Roc come in here?"

Bo gave her a confused look. "No, he's in that car."

Corrynne shook her head. "No he isn't. We've checked everywhere and he's not out there!"

"What do you mean, he's not out there? ...He has to be out there...." said Bo in breathless gasps. He continued to have a difficult time taking in breaths. "There was no way for him to go anywhere else. Look again."

"I'm going to," said Corrynne. "Come out with me to look."

Painfully, Bo got to his feet and walked out to the car, as did the whole family now. Holding his side, he looked into the car but just like his wife, couldn't find his son. He studied the interior of the car for a few moments and then said, "Here's his blood, Corrynne," he said pointing. "So he was definitely here. Maybe these seats pull down and he crawled into the trunk. See if you can pull on those seats. I can't because I hurt too much."

Corrynne crawled into the car and pulled on the back of the seats. One of them came down, opening a gaping black hole leading into the trunk. She peered into the darkness for her lost child. She couldn't see anything.

"Rocwell, are you in here?" Corrynne called.

There wasn't a response.

Corrynne listened carefully for any noises from the darkness of the trunk. She thought she could hear a faint breathing. "Who owns this car?" Corrynne called out to Bo.

"I do," said Brother Anderson. "It's my car. Would you like the keys?" he asked as he dangled the trunk keys in front of her.

"Oh, that would be great! Thank you!" she said as she took the keys and rushed around the back end of the car. As she turned the corner, her feet slipped on the ice and she went down face first, with a thump. Her black, shiny, high-heeled shoes sprawled into the center of the parking lot.

Seeing her fall, Bo walked cautiously around to help her up. She stood with ice covering her front, hands and face. Despite the cold, Corrynne shook her hands free of the ice and, standing in stocking feet, unlocked the trunk, while Brother Anderson with his large frame walked gingerly into the parking lot to get her shoes.

Inside the trunk, to Corrynne's relief, she found Roc curled up in a corner, lying unconscious in a small collection of blood from the cuts on his head.

Corrynne leaned over the frame to get her hands under his thin, lanky body. As she picked him up, he whimpered and began to cry slightly, although he didn't open his eyes.

Quickly handing Roc to Dane who was standing next to her, she said, "Please take him inside and call 9-1-1. I'll be there in a second."

Her large son obeyed.

Corrynne carefully picked her way through the ice and ran into the church. She came up to the couch where Rocwell was lying. Someone had brought wet paper towels, and Brea was washing the blood off his face.

"Mom, why won't he wake up?" asked Brea with a worried look.

Corrynne opened his lids to see if his pupils were reactive. They both responded the same to the light in the room. "I think he's just sleeping. Kids do that after a stressful event."

"You think that's all?" asked Brea, dabbing his head.

Corrynne studied her little boy. "There's always a chance of an epidural bleed in his head with a knock like he's received. People can be alert one moment and then in a coma the next."

"Aren't you worried?" asked Brea.

Corrynne nodded. "Yes, but what more can we do but call 9-1-1? We have to keep our heads about us. We can't worry about things we don't know." Corrynne patted Brea. "We'll get him to help, just in case."

Just then Rocwell stirred. He whined a high pitch and then called for his mom.

"I'm here, Roc. Sweet baby, it's OK," Corrynne cooed to her son. "He's waking up. That's a good sign," she said to Brea and the others standing around the couch. "He'll be fine," she said with a smile as she gathered Roc up in her arms. She was careful of his obviously broken arm, and held him against her body. Slowly she rocked him.

"Mom, my arm hurts," Roc whined quietly.

Corrynne nodded. "I know, sweetheart. We're going to the doctor to get it fixed."

"Uh, Mom?" said Dane as he jogged up to his mother from down the hall. "The lines are down. I can't get through to 9-1-1."

"Did you try the cell?" asked his mother.

"Yes, but I just get a busy signal."

"I should have thought of that. I'm sure that there are a lot of calls right now for help from that storm." Corrynne considered other options. "Bo, how did our car fare during the storm?"

"The window's cracked, but you can still see out. I just had Jax check for me," said Bo.

"Good," said Corrynne. "Alright, since Roc's awake, this isn't an emergency anymore. We don't need an ambulance. We'll take our own car." Turning to Brea she asked, "Did you drive the truck here?"

"Yes, it's right outside, across the parking lot from the Suburban. I'm afraid it doesn't look quite as pretty as it used to, and the windshield is totally obliterated, but I bet it still runs."

"OK." Corrynne turned to see where all her family members were. Carea still had hold of the twins hands, although they were squirming to get away. Dane and Braun stood next to her. "Dane, go out to the truck and get all the glass off the seats…. Braun, would you help him and then kind of supervise everyone at the house till Dad, Roc, and I get back from the hospital?"

Braun nodded.

"Brea, take Carea, Ry and the twins home in the truck first then come back for everyone else." Turning to Carea she said, "Carea, would you please make sure everyone gets fed. Feed them peanut butter and jelly sandwiches. Have Ry make them for the family."

Carea nodded. "Yes, I can do that."

"Come on, you guys," said Brea first hugging her mother and then motioning to Carea and Ry to follow her.

Dane crouched down to talk to Roc. "Bye," said Dane. "Hey, guy, you're being pretty brave. Your school football team will love ya cause you're tough!"

"…And cute," said Carea, as she tried to keep the twins reigned in. She was able to kiss Roc on the cheek before she left.

Brea also kissed Roc on the forehead. "No more hailstorms, OK, kid?"

"K," said Roc in a weak voice.

Despite his painful ribcage, Bo reached down and gently lifted his little son out of Corrynne's lap into his arms. Bo, Corrynne, and little Roc were escorted out the front door of the church and to their car by some of the ward members. Together they trudged through the ankle deep lake of water created from the melting ice.

Men's Hearts Shall Fail Them

Finding their way along the street shoulders to avoid cars that were strewn across the streets at odd angles, Bo and Corrynne drove slowly, peering through their badly cracked windows. People were still untangling themselves from the glass and metal of their damaged cars in the city.

The sun came out from behind the clouds to shine on the broken glass lying on the wet pavement. It cast a brilliant, jeweled reflection into the shocked faces of the victims of the storm, like water from a pool during the summer heat. It was a surreal sight that didn't fit the circumstance.

Two blocks away from the hospital the road became grid-locked. Bo turned off the engine and looked at Corrynne.

"What are you doing?" asked Corrynne, surprised by his actions.

"We aren't going anywhere," said Bo.

"So what do we do?"

"Get out and walk."

"Aren't we going to park?" asked Corrynne, looking out her side window for an empty placc on the side of the road.

"We are parked," said Bo simply.

"Here?" asked Corrynne, continuing to search for somewhere to park.

"Yes. Here," Bo said as he took his keys out of the ignition and put them in his pocket. "We need to get Roc to the hospital to be looked at."

"Yes, but won't they tow our car if it's just sitting in the middle of the road?"

Bo nodded as he unlatched his door. "Of course. They'll tow ours and all the others out here too. Look around. There's nowhere to go. We're locked in here by stalled cars. Might as well get out."

Corrynne looked. Bo was right. No matter which direction she looked, there were other cars boxing them in. It was time to just walk on foot and deal with the car later.

Corrynne unlatched her car door and, while being careful not to slip on the melting ice, she gingerly stepped out onto the slushy pavement.

Bo came around the car to help her.

"No, I'll carry Roc because of your ribs."

"I can carry him," said Bo. "I don't want you to slip again in those shoes."

Corrynne looked down at her pointy black shoes. They were a dangerous pair for walking in the ice. "How about I carry Roc and you make sure I don't fall."

Bo thought for a moment, rubbed his side where the broken ribs were and then nodded. "Deal."

"Grab the first-aid kit out of the glove box," said Corrynne to Bo, gesturing to the inside of the car with her head. "Just in case."

Bo looked at her with a puzzled stare. "In case of what?"

Corrynne shrugged. "I don't know. I just know I always kick myself when I don't have it. It's good to be prepared when you're a nurse. People expect you to do things."

Bo unlatched the glove box and retrieved the first aid kit. With a disgruntled look he said, "We have our own emergency right now." As he slid it into his suit-jacket pocket he said, "I'm all for helping other people, but there's something to be said for helping ourselves too."

Corrynne nodded and said defensively, "I know. I'll make sure Roc is taken care of."

Bo nodded but didn't reply.

Together, Bo and Corrynne wound their way around the cars and people to the sidewalk. As they picked their way down the sidewalk filled with people and broken things, they began to understand why there was a grid-lock near the hospital. Today, all the roads led there.

"What a mess of people!" gasped Corrynne, looking around her at all the desperate faces. "Have you ever seen such craziness?"

"No, this is pretty unbelievable," returned Bo.

"I bet the doctors and nurses in the hospital are feeling pretty claustrophobic right now," said Corrynne, feeling sorry for them.

"I bet all the victims are feeling that way, too," said Bo with a laugh. "Not too many options for them."

"How are all these people going to be seen?" asked Corrynne as she shook her head. The amount of work these people represented was unmeasurable.

"I don't know, but remember that your family needs you now, too," said Bo with a serious look, reemphasizing his earlier point. "Don't get caught up in civic duty and leave us hanging."

Corrynne considered Bo's words. She knew she'd be asked to help. The hospital had probably already tried to get ahold of her but couldn't because the cell phones weren't working. She looked at Bo. "I can see where you're coming from. You know they'll expect me to do something. What if I just help out while we wait our turn for Roc?"

Bo shook his head with a shrug. "I don't mind that at all. I just want you to come home when I go home."

"OK," Corrynne said as she mentally geared up to refuse what she knew was coming. She had to stop herself from feeling guilt, or the struggle between her family and her duty would rip her up inside. She closed her eyes hard for a second to eliminate the emotional struggle that was already beginning. Opening her eyes, she maintained a blank mind, refusing to contemplate anything having to do with medicine. It would have to be this way while she walked through these people.

After walking for about a half hour, finally,Bo and Corrynne made it to the hospital parking lot. It was wall-to-wall people; mothers with crying children, men with arms in home-made slings, others with blood-soaked towels pressed to bleeding wounds. Corrynne and Bo pushed through the people without stopping. They were almost at the hospital doors when suddenly, a man yelled above the crowd.

"Help! Someone help me! My dad's having a heart attack!"

Corrynne automatically looked for the man in the crowd who was calling for help. He was only four people away from her. Simultaneously she saw his father clutch his chest and fall onto the pavement in a heap.

Corrynne looked at her husband.

Bo reached in his pocket and handed her the first-aid kit and then held out his hands for Roc. "Go," he said with a grin.

Quickly, Corrynne took the kit and handed Roc to her husband. Then she pushed through the crowd to find the young man lying crosswise over his father, crying uncontrollably.

With a gentle touch, Corrynne tapped the younger man. "Sir? I'm a nurse. I might be able to help your father."

The young man looked up at Corrynne and then moved out of the way.

Corrynne knelt beside the elderly man and put her ear to his mouth and nose. She was listening and feeling for breathing sounds while watching for his chest to rise and fall. But to her dismay, there wasn't anything.

Corrynne ripped open her kit and pulled the mouth barrier out of its plastic. Placing it over the old man's face, she forced a large breath into his mouth, but his barrel chest refused to expand. She repositioned his head to open the stubborn airway, and tried again. Finally the air moved into his lungs as she watched his chest rise with her breath. She repeated it with another large breath for the man. Next she felt for a pulse at his neck. She couldn't feel any. She put her head to his chest and confirmed that his heart was not beating. Immediately she began CPR.

"One, two, three, four, five," she whispered to herself as she used her body weight to compress his heart through the chest wall. "Six, seven, eight, nine, ten," she continued, being sure to deliver quick and deep compressions. "Eleven, twelve, thirteen, fourteen, fifteen." She continued compressions this way until she had counted to thirty.

Positioning the man's head so his airway remained open, she gave him two more breaths through the mouth barrier. Then once again she went back to giving quick and deep compressions.

Corrynne looked at a woman in a yellow sweater standing by. "Will you count for me?"

The lady nodded.

"OK count. I'm on five."

"Six, seven, eight, nine…" began the woman.

Next Corrynne turned to the son as she continued compressions. "You, go into the ER and get someone to come out here and help me. All you have to say is that a nurse is doing CPR outside on the cement and they'll rush out. But you have to be firm and get their attention."

The young man nodded and took off towards the door of the ER.

"What number are we on?" asked Corrynne.

"Twenty eight," said the woman.

"Good, thank you," said Corrynne as she delivered two more compressions and then moved to breathe for the victim.

Once again, Corrynne started compressions when the crowd divided and allowed a gurney through. The older gentleman was loaded up and wheeled into the ER as the ER staff took over compressions.

Corrynne motioned to Bo to follow her closely with Roc as the people closed around the stretcher.

Bo pressed in behind the moving gurney, trying to shield his son's arm from so many people who could bump it, and joined Corrynne and the man's son leading them right into the hospital.

Once in the hospital, Corrynne headed for the stairs. "Come this way Bo. Let's go to the ICU. There we don't need to wait in line. I know the intensivists will help us out."

Bo followed.

Corrynne pressed her thumb on the identification pad to let them into the stairwell that led to the ICU. Together they climbed the stairs and then on the second floor, Corrynne once again pressed her thumb on a pad and the door opened automatically.

"OK, I concede," said Bo as they both walked down the hall in the ICU.

"What do you mean?" asked Corrynne with a smile.

"Let's see…" said Bo pretending to think. "I have to admit, you know your stuff. I was impressed back there."

Corrynne looked at her husband and said, "Thanks."

"I don't get to see you in action, so that was fun. You're quite the woman."

"You just remember that," Corrynne said feeling very happy. Looking at Roc, she asked, "How are you feeling?"

Roc nodded. "Fine."

"You don't hurt?" asked Corrynne.

Roc shook his head. "Not unless I move my arm."

"He's tough," said Bo in a proud voice.

"Let Roc walk now. I don't think anyone will bump his arm anymore," Corrynne said as she moved to a computer terminal.

Bo set Roc on the floor.

"How are your ribs, Bo?" Corrynne asked as she pressed the screen with her thumb to log in.

"They're beginning to hurt again, now that you ask," said Bo grimacing. "Nurse, can you give me CPR, too?"

Corrynne jabbed him in the ribs.

"Hey!" exclaimed Bo. "That hurt. Don't cheat."

"Then don't flirt with the nurse," said Corrynne as she turned back to the screen. "I'm on duty, see?" she said pointing to the display.

"What are you doing?" asked Bo, watching Corrynne.

"I'm admitting Roc from here, so we can be billed."

"What? We're being billed for this?" asked Bo with an astonished look on his face but teasing his wife.

"Of course we'll be billed," said Corrynne.

"But aren't you going to be Roc's nurse?"

"Sure," said Corrynne as she began to enter orders into the computer under one of the intensivists names that she knew would be on duty that day.

"So the hospital's going to bill me for your services?"

"Bo, the hospital pays us and pays for our insurance. The least we can do is pay our co-payment for our visit."

Bo looked around. "Now wait. I didn't see you clock in. You're not getting paid today."

Corrynne looked at Bo with an irritated stare. "You're kidding, right?"

"Partially," said Bo. "If you're working, you're working."

"So you want the hospital to pay me to take care of my own son's arm?"

"Sure," said Bo with a shrug. "And for saving that man's life outside."

Corrynne turned back to the screen and said, "Whatever. You've lost your marbles."

"You give your services away too cheaply," said Bo. "We'll never get rich if you keep working for free."

"Sit down, Bo, and just relax," said Corrynne, laughing to herself as she entered orders for an X-ray. Her husband was a goof. "We are rich, honey," said Corrynne in a sing-song voice. "Don't you know we're rich in looove?"

"Yeah but love doesn't pay much," said Bo, sitting down in a chair against the wall and pulling Roc onto his lap.

"Hmmmm," said Corrynne as she looked at her screen.

"What?" asked Bo.

"There isn't an empty room in the ICU so I'll just call the technician to tell them where we're at."

Bo nodded mindlessly.

Corrynne heard the electrical grinding noise of the X-ray machine as it rolled up the hall. She looked just in time to see John, the technician, rolling it into a nearby room. "I'll be right back," said Corrynne as she rushed to catch him.

Within minutes, the portable X-ray machine was hovering over Roc in the hall and Corrynne and Bo were clad in lead.

"Stay still," said John as he snapped the picture from a safe distance as Corrynne and Bo held his arm in the positions necessary to look at the bones.

"I'll put this film on the digital system," John informed Corrynne.

"Thanks, John."

"No problem."

As John rolled the X-ray machine away, Bo asked, "So how long is it going to be until the X-ray is ready?"

"A couple minutes. It doesn't take long anymore. Let's go into the viewing room and wait for it."

Bo, Roc, and Corrynne walked down the hall and entered a dark room with a double-screened computer sitting on one side.

Again, Corrynne touched the screen with her thumb and it came to life. She typed in Roc's name and up came the X-ray she was looking for. "See, it's already here."

"Good," said Bo, coming close to the screen.

Right then Dr. Page, a young doctor right out of medical school, walked in. He eyed Corrynne and Bo.

Roc hid behind his mother for some reason.

"Hi, Corrynne, why are you here on a Sunday. Aren't you a staunch Mormon?" he asked.

Corrynne smiled and said, "The staunchest."

"So what's going on?" asked the doctor but then he saw the X-ray. "Wow, nice fracture. Whose film is this?"

Corrynne stepped aside to reveal her son. "This is Rocwell. The ice storm broke his arm."

Dr. Page squatted down so he was eye to eye with Roc but Roc hid again behind his mother's leg.

"Hey guy. Come out here and talk to me. What happened? Did you fall on the ice?"

Corrynne waited for her son to answer but when he stubbornly refused, she stepped aside again and said, "No, he thought it would be fun to play in the storm until he was hit by a mongo ice ball. He received a laceration on his forehead from that hit. After that he dove into a nearby car for protection."

"Nice cut," said the doctor looking at Roc's face. "That cut can be fixed, no problem. That was smart of you to get into the car. You're pretty smart, huh?"

Roc nodded.

"Then he was waving at us to come and rescue him from the car when another, even larger ball came down on his arm and snapped it."

"Ouch," said Dr. Page. "Does it hurt?"

Roc shook his head.

The doctor looked at Corrynne and smiled. "We can fix that too, can't we?"

"I hope in a good way," said Corrynne nodding, not wanting to reveal the true nature of Dr. Page's joke to Roc. She didn't want to scare him.

"Always," said Dr. Page.

"By the way, I'm glad you said 'we'," said Corrynne. "Because the ER is jammed, I thought I could come up here and solve this problem faster and easier with one of you guys."

"And then here I am," said the doctor with arms out to his sides as if he was going to take a bow.

"Yes, here you are," said Corrynne. "Would you be willing to help me set his arm?"

Dr Page looked back at the X-ray and said, "Yes, I think it would be a nice diversion from what's happening around here. I was good at this kind of stuff in my ER rotations."

"Good!"

"The break looks pretty clean. We can just line up the bone ends and cast. A little traction should stretch those muscles back to their normal length. You can do most of it."

"OK," said Corrynne nodding.

"Get the supplies together and we'll do it in the physicians' sleeping room."

"Perfect. Thank you, doctor."

"See you in a few minutes," said Dr. Page.

After Dr. Page left the room, Bo said, "Who was that guy?"

Corrynne frowned. "What's that supposed to mean?"

"He seemed full of himself," said Bo with a grimace.

"Hey! He's a good man. He's taking time out of his busy schedule for us. Be grateful."

"I don't like that doctor, Mom," said Roc with wide eyes.

Corrynne looked back and forth between her son and husband and said, "What's gotten into you guys? It's not like we have any choices here. Dr. Page is a good doctor and he'll fix Roc's arm. That's what we came here for. End of story. Now let's go into the physician's sleeping room and I'll get things ready."

"I'm not coming," said Bo abruptly.

"What?" asked Corrynne with her hands on her hips.

"I don't like medical things. I'll go out in the lobby till you're done."

"Are you serious, Bo?"

"Yes. I'm serious," said Bo.

"Why? Are you mad?"

Bo shook his head. "No, you know I faint at the sight of blood."

"There won't be any blood here," said Corrynne.

"No but there's going to be stretching muscles, traction, bones being aligned. I think I'm getting a little queasy just talking about it."

"Are you telling the truth?" asked Corrynne, squinting to try and see into Bo's mind.

Bo nodded and headed out the door. "I'll see you later. I think I'll go lay down on the couches out there."

After Bo left, Corrynne looked at Rocwell and shook her head in disgust. "What?" asked Roc.

"Nothing," said Corrynne, feeling it was better not expressing her thoughts to her seven-year-old. "Come on, Roc. Let's go into the other room. It's time to fix your arm."

ξξξξξξ

"That went very well," said Dr. Page. "Don't you think?"

Corrynne looked at her sleeping son. His arm was back to its normal shape in a new white cast and the cut on his forehead was neatly sewn shut. "Yes, Dr. Page. You did a very good job. I see you have many hidden talents."

"More than you know," said the doctor with a laugh almost to himself.

Corrynne smiled as she studied him. He was being kind of odd today.

"I was tempted to take Roc to Dr. Quaid down in the ER, but I'm glad I came up here.

Dr Page put his hands in his jacket pockets and said, "Dr. Quaid doesn't work here anymore."

Corrynne was shocked. "What are you talking about?"

"So I gather you don't know what happened to him."

Corrynne took a breath and held it, afraid to hear the news. "No, I didn't. Was he fired?"

"No, he died last night," said Dr. Page, his tone matter-of-fact.

Corrynne choked and said, *"What?"*

"Yes. He died from that Strep A that we've been seeing in the ER. In six hours he was dead from heart failure, just like all the other patients."

"I can't believe it!" Corrynne suddenly felt lightheaded, as her heart skipped a beat. She sank to the bed her son was sleeping on. "I can't...I can't believe it. I was just talking to him," Corrynne said, now a little breathless.

"Yeah, I know. I was, too," said Dr. Page. "It happened so fast. We think he just contracted the aggressive bacteria from his patients. He was handling all of them, you know."

"There's no way!" Corrynne's mind was still reeling. "There is no way that he would be so reckless! That bacteria had to be almost injected under the skin. ...He was always robed and double gloved. ...At least, when I worked with him the other night, he was very careful."

"All I know is that he went quick," said the doctor.

"Do you know if he had any tattoos or piercings on his body when he died?" asked Corrynne.

"Well, yes, he had a navel piercing." Dr. Page lowered his voice and talked from behind his hand. "He must have lived a double life."

"No," said Corrynne shaking her head. "None of this makes sense."

"I know. It doesn't to me either. Dr. Quaid always seemed so straight arrow." He lifted his head quickly and cleared his throat. "But to each his own. Who am I to judge?"

"This is too much…." Corrynne looked up into Dr. Page's eyes, searching for something. "I—I think he was killed, Dr. Page. There's no other answer that makes sense."

Dr. Page laughed. "Killed?"

Corrynne nodded with a serious look on her face.

"You've been watching too much CSI," said the doctor flippantly. "Of course Dr. Quaid's death was accidental. It was just an unfortunate accident. He just got too close to his patients."

"No," said Corrynne, becoming more confident. "I think it's strange that the day after he went to the media about the Strep A and the outbreak in relation to the Raves that he's dead."

"That's just a coincidence," said the doctor with a shrug.

"I'm going to get to the bottom of this," said Corrynne as she stepped over to the sink and washed her hands in scalding hot water. "We can't just let this tragedy go unanswered."

"Well, Corrynne, you do what you feel you have to, but you'll be wasting your time," said Dr. Page.

"Not if I figure out what's going on around here," said Corrynne with a flash of anger.

Dr. Page approached Corrynne and placed his hands on her shoulders and squeezed.

This made her very uncomfortable. With a quick flick of the wrists to get rid of the extra water on her hands, she turned to face the doctor, breaking his grasp.

With a look of contrived concern he said, "You seem stressed. You need some time off."

Corrynne shook her head. "No I don't."

"Sure you do. If I were you, I'd kick my shoes off, relax in that heated massage chair and give some plasma for some extra money for a great vacation away from this place."

Corrynne was really confused now. With a frown she said, "What chair? Give plasma? What are you talking about?"

"Haven't you received your letter?" asked the doctor.

Corrynne shook her head. "What letter? Who sends letters anymore?"

With a finger in the air the doctor said, "One benefit from being in healthcare in this day is that your blood is worth its weight in gold. I'm sure you have a letter in your box telling you about it."

"Go ahead, explain it to me," said Corrynne. She was becoming angry with Dr. Page's inappropriate comments and attitude. "I don't read mail in my box."

"Because of resistant bacteria that can't be destroyed with antibiotics, we're having a larger and larger group of patients that do not have treatment options. Plasma might hold the key for recovery by offering natural, human antibodies needed to fight those particular infections."

Corrynne nodded. "OK."

The doctor continued, "There's a new procedure that extracts the immunity that healthcare workers achieve naturally by working in the hospital with those who have colonized resistant bacteria. We are able to create an infusion of antibodies from nurses like you, to give passive immunity to compromised patients. Through multiple infusions, theoretically, a patient can recover if used early enough."[1]

"That sounds good," said Corrynne, finding herself impressed.

"For the healthcare workers," Dr. Page continued, "plasma pays handsomely. In return for a nurse's plasma, I bet the pay is better than your wage here."[2]

"There's no way that's possible," said Corrynne, now thinking Dr. Page was pulling her leg.

Dr. Page smiled. "Oh, yes, it's more than possible. It's true and it's happening here in our hospital."

"Here?"

"Yes. Right now you receive four hundred dollars per pint of blood that is spun."

"Four hundred dollars?" asked Corrynne, her jaw went slack out of shock.

"Yep, and the amount's only going higher."

"How high?" questioned Corrynne.

Dr. Page shrugged and said, "Who knows. It depends on the depth of the epidemic and need. I thought you'd be glad to hear about it. You can even hook yourself up in the nurses' core. They have a collecting machine right here." The doctor pointed his thumb over his shoulder toward the nursing classroom. "After it's done, it gives you four crisp one-hundred-dollar bills."

"It pays you immediately?"

"Yes. We thought that would be a good touch to try to encourage donation. Immediate gratification."

"'*We* thought'?" asked Corrynne with a suspicious look. "You're in charge of this project?"

Dr. Page nodded. "I'm one of the instigators."

"How does that happen?"

"I went to a buddy of mine with a project that I worked on in med school that demonstrated successful treatment for those with compromised immune systems. I suggested we try it out in the real world. So, through great sweat, and a lot of political hoops, we finally got a plasma machine in here and venture capital to push it through." The doctor turned and motioned for Corrynne to follow. "Come into the core. I'll show you my baby."

Corrynne picked up Roc and followed Dr. Page into the education classroom, otherwise known as the "core."

As Corrynne entered, she spotted a stainless-steel machine with a deep, soft, leather reclining chair alongside it. "Is that it?" she asked.

Dr. Page nodded. "Isn't she beautiful?"

Corrynne moved to the machine and took a seat, being careful to position Roc so he could continue to sleep in her arms. "I like this recliner."

Dr. Page flipped a button and Corrynne could feel a thousand fingers massaging her back. "Ahh, yes. This is nice," she said.

"We provided the top-of-the-line recliner that has a massager and heater to relax the donor." The doctor pointed to all the aspects as he talked about them, a little like a game-show demonstrator. "Hopefully, nurses on their break will come and press their thumb to the identification pad, and a drawer opens that gives them an IV start. Then they'll puncture their vein and secure it with a Velcro-edged op-site that hugs the appendage. After that the nurse can sit back and read, watch TV or sleep for fifteen minutes."

Corrynne laughed and closed her eyes. "Fifteen minutes?" she asked, feeling a little groggy. "That's only a tease! That's not near enough time."

"That's the idea. However, there's a two pint maximum for every 24 hours," said the doctor.

"That's eight hundred extra dollars."

"Yes, it is."

"All while you sleep."

"All while you sleep," echoed the doctor with a satisfied smile.

Corrynne opened her eyes and said, "So show me how the machine works and where the serum ends up."

"Sure." Dr. Page opened the panel on the front of the machine to reveal a series of tubes, spinners and filters. "The blood goes through this system of micro-filters after being spun a couple times to separate blood products. The antibodies end up in these tubes, and the rest of the blood is returned to the donor, warmed to body temperature."

"Isn't blood type an issue?" asked Corrynne.

Dr. Page nodded. "Yes, the healthcare workers have to be typed. The machine is able to test for 100 different antibodies, including blood-specific antibodies. Then we match the patient's blood tag to the type, including the RH factor, labeled on the vial. See, here at the end, the types are all separated into different compartments."

"I see," said Corrynne.

"We're going to teach all charge nurses how to change these filters to ensure smooth functioning."

Corrynne whistled once and said, "Sounds to me like you're going to be very rich, Dr. Page."

"Hopefully you will be too, Corrynne." Dr. Page winked and smiled.

"So, when do we see the application of the antibodies here in the hospital?" asked Corrynne, laying her head back again in the chair, enjoying every moment of tingling the chair was causing in her skin and muscles.

"Sadly, it's still in trial. We've been trying to get the whole thing through the Food and Drug Administration, but we've been stone-walled." Dr. Page shrugged.

"But that's silly," stated Corrynne. "Why does it have to pass through the Food and Drug Administration? It seems like the same protocols to assure blood was safe would work here too."

"Hey, I don't write the rules. I'm just trying to find a solution to help humanity." Dr. Page smiled broadly again.

"I hate red tape."

"So do I."

"When there's an ingenious idea like this, it calls for emergency action to get it to the people!" Corrynne fidgeted with frustration. "I don't think I can stand to see people suffer and die knowing that this serum is in here."

"I know. Me either. But if anyone ever gave this to a patient they would be fired on the spot, prosecuted and stripped of their license."

"Harsh punishment!" said Corrynne with a frown.

"That's the FDA, my friend. What can I say?"

"Well," Corrynne sighed, "OK. At least I'll be able to make some extra money on my breaks," she said closing her eyes again. "In fact, maybe I'll quit and just donate!"

"I'm afraid that's out of the question," said Dr. Page, suddenly serious. "That's the one stipulation. You have to be employed at least part time to receive the option of donation."

"Well, I was just kidding," responded Corrynne, a little surprised at Dr. Page's change in demeanor but uninterested in figuring out the cause of it.

"I know, I just wanted to make sure that everyone knows that's not an option," Dr. Page continued. "You, being a charge nurse, will hear people talk. Be sure that you emphasize that aspect, OK?"

"Sure, no problem, I'm a good task driver," said Corrynne with a finger in the air.

Just then the steely computer voice was heard overhead. "Code blue, Surgical ICU. Code blue, Surgical ICU. Code blue, Surgical ICU."

Dr. Page looked up at the ceiling and reflexively grabbed the stethoscope that was wrapped around his neck. "Well, duty calls." He took a deep breath. "It seems like it's getting harder and harder to keep hearts in working order around here.[3] Talk to you later." Dr. Page took off down the hall with his white coat flapping behind him.

World Changes, Hidden Danger

At home, Corrynne and Bo were barraged by voices clamoring for something to eat. Bo started some spaghetti while Corrynne sat on the couch and fed the twins. Roc climbed on the couch and sat close to Corrynne's side, still a little sleepy from the medications.

As the twins hungrily consumed the milk from their bottles propped on pillows in Corrynne's lap, she found comfort in her children's presence as they pressed close to her. Laying her head back on the headrest of the couch, she allowed herself to meditate about the events of the past couple of days.

Corrynne reviewed her hospital experience with Roc and what Dr. Page had revealed. She still couldn't comprehend how Dr. Quaid could be dead. …How could it be true?

Corrynne's thoughts took a different turn. No matter what Dr. Page said about Dr. Quaid dying from patient contamination, she still thought that his death seemed very suspicious. To her, it was logical that Dr. Quaid could have been singled out because he went to the media and made himself a clear target of whoever was the power behind the Raves. If that was true, then Dr. Quaid was *murdered*…. If he was murdered, then there was a *murderer*…. If there was a murderer, then anyone associated with Dr. Quaid could be in danger until the murderer was caught…. But if everyone thought his death was an accident, then no one would be looking for a murderer and all who were connected to Dr. Quaid could be in—*mortal danger.*

Corrynne's heart skipped a beat as if a punctuation to her thoughts. She brought a hand to her chest and felt the regular rhythm return. Could it be that who ever killed Dr. Quaid might view *her* as a threat? …Corrynne's thoughts raced through the other night. Could anyone think Dr. Quaid and she were linked in some way? The only connection that they had with each other was the code from the other night and the information they discovered together…. Oh, no! A pit was forming in the center of her stomach….*The information!* Could she be *killed* for what she knew?

With a tremoring hand she lovingly brushed Striynna's strawberry blonde hair back. Striynna looked up at her from her lap but then quickly returned to the business of drinking her bottle.

With a slight shake of her head, Corrynne quieted the fear that was growing inside her. She was just being paranoid. Nothing was going to happen. After all, only Dr. Quaid knew she knew anything, and he was dead. Anyway, she was probably blowing everything out of proportion anyway. Chances are, the doctor really did die from a cross-contamination and she needed to just drop it. She laid her head back into the headrest and took a deep breath. Nothing to worry about, she told herself.

Her thoughts continued to churn. A new consideration emerged. It wasn't one that she was comfortable with but it was one that she couldn't ignore. It had started quietly in the back of her mind but now it was rushing to the forefront. It had to do with *responsibility*. What exactly was her responsibility now that she knew about the cult? She knew it was killing people. It was taking the children of the community and sacrificing their lives needlessly. Could she just look the other way? Would her conscience let her? Because of her religious beliefs, she knew she had an uncontrollable tendency to protect the innocent, even at her own jeopardy. That's why she was in health care. There were risks in helping others, but she was willing to assume those risks to make a difference. Was this one of those times?

Corrynne pursed her lips and sighed deeply. She smirked at herself. What was she thinking? Was she so full of herself that she thought she could do anything about this situation? Who was she but a simple nurse? She wasn't in any position to do *anything*. This situation was too big for one person to even try, and any way you looked at it, by either caring for those patients or interfering with the parties, it was too deadly. No, Dr. Quaid had done what needed to be done by alerting the police and the media, and according to CNN and the local news, steps were being taken worldwide to stop the threat. That was enough. She decided right then that this time her overwhelming morality might just have to take a backseat to herself and her family.

With those justifying thoughts, Corrynne tried once again to relax. She cleared her thoughts and just thought about nothing, but it wasn't good enough. She had a cramp in her back that went all the way up her neck. She lifted her body weight in the couch and attempted to change her position. With her sudden movement, the three children looked up to see if she were going to get up from the couch. She smiled at them and pulled them closer.

Still, Corrynne felt bothered, or irritated. She couldn't decide which it was. She wondered what was wrong with her. She took a deep breath and let it out slowly, closing her eyes once again in an attempt to achieve some sort of peace…. Still, she was bothered.

Corrynne knew on some level that the real reason for her irritation was not the couch, nor her body alignment. She could sense the danger. It was personal. Somehow it affected her and her family. She analyzed where the warning feeling was coming from. …Finally, after considering all the options, she realized that no matter how she looked at it, she had to admit that it was the Spirit warning her to watch and be careful.

Corrynne swallowed a couple of times and looked around the room. Those physical motions helped her somehow focus on what she should do. It was obvious that she needed to take steps at least to protect her family, especially after Carea's experience with Kessa. The threat of the cult, along with the other events of the last few days, were beginning to permeate the very fabric of their daily lives. In an instant, she suddenly understood clearly that everything would get worse before it got better. Silently, she began praying for inspiration. If anyone would know how she could protect her family, the Lord would.

As she sat and meditated, she presented the whole situation to the Lord. She told him the circumstances that she was in and her desire to protect her family and do her duty as a mother and a nurse. She also asked how she could serve all responsibilities safely and fairly. ...After a few moments, a thought clearly came to her head that *in fighting evil, sometimes there were costs.* That message settled deep inside her. What did it mean? Were any of her children going to suffer? Was that possibility acceptable? She didn't think so.

She continued to pray, telling Heavenly Father that it wasn't OK to lose even one of his children to evil. ...She was meaning to death...but another answer came that said that she was exactly right. ...*Not one of his children should be lost to evil.* Suddenly she understood the broader view. He loved all of his children. All of humanity was in jeopardy, not just her family. The Lord was saddened that this kind of thing was going on. He was grieved that people were suffering, that mothers and fathers were losing their children and he was losing souls to Satan. He needed everyone to stand up and fight. Not just her, not just her family, but every righteous person had to become strong and brave and begin to battle Satan.[4] No longer could people let others fight their battles. That kind of thinking had allowed Satan to get a huge start.

Even though she didn't want to believe it, she understood that it was not an option for her to sit back and ignore the happenings around her. She understood. ...*It would be difficult, and it would require her to have a very strong testimony. There would be things that were so difficult to bear that her faith would be the only thing that would save her soul....*

Corrynne suddenly turned her head. It was too much. She couldn't bear any more. Silently she asked for forgiveness for being weak. She promised that she would come back later to hear the rest of his message, but at that time she was too tired and too scared. She didn't want to consider the depth of the required sacrifices before Christ came. And somehow she knew that the rest of the message had to do with allowing the Lord to lead her and not coveting her own life and family more than his will.

Tears welled up in her eyes. It was so hard just to consider losing even one of her children that sometimes she wished that she would die first. But she also knew that was a selfish wish. The Lord needed her, and she knew it. Those who would be left behind would need her, too. She wiped her eyes and kissed her three smallest children's heads once again. At least she had this moment, and she was thankful for it. She ended her prayer with the request that the Lord would guide her in her responsibilities.

Corrynne quietly sat for a few minutes. Calmness filled her, and suddenly her mind became clear. She knew what she had to do first. Antibiotics!

"I have to get some Penicillin or something to safeguard against a Strep infection," she whispered. Just in case Dr. Quaid's death was not an accident. Infection would be an obvious way to get rid of any other threats.

Corrynne closed her eyes and meditated, trying to think of other things she could do. A picture of the back of the little nurse that she met during the code the other night came to her mind. Then she realized she had forgotten she was even in the room! She concentrated to remember her face. She tried to picture her nose, her eyes or her mouth, but her mind was blank. The girl had been so plain that she couldn't remember anything specific. She didn't even know her name. Corrynne cringed. That was very unfeeling of her. The young nurse was very emotional and felt responsible for her cousin's death; the least Corrynne could have done would be to have checked up on her later.

Then Corrynne had a new disturbing thought. What if that nurse had joined the cult? Who knows what she would have done to try to make sense of things? Corrynne was under the impression from the nurse's extensive knowledge that she had been on the edge of accepting the cult's beliefs. It was obvious that she had been doing her own research.

Again, worry filtered through Corrynne. What if this were true? Then Corrynne would not be safe at all. It could be construed that she was a threat because of her position and her knowledge. Plus, she was an easy target. Charge nurses weren't exactly hidden. She would have to find the nurse and talk to her again as soon as possible. She would attempt to pacify the nurse's perception of her role in relation to Dr. Quaid. She remembered that she was on the fifth floor. She would go there on her next shift and try to find her name and phone number.

One thought led to another, and her mind returned to Dr. Quaid. She wondered if his piercing was a new one. If it were new, she wondered how he came to have it. Would he go up to a Rave to research the cult and come back with the infection? Or could the organizers of the Raves go to the hospital to find him because he had notified the media? …How would she find out these answers? She knew she could probably look up his home number on the employee list on the hospital intranet. She was sure they would not take off his number right away. She could then talk to his wife. But that would probably be difficult, since his wife might not want to talk to anyone, at least, not for a while. Ry came down the stairs and interrupted, but she wasn't upset. It was a relief to be distracted.

"Roc, let me see your cast! That is so cool!" cooed Ry.

Jax followed closely. "Yeah, Roc, did it hurt to get it on?"

Roc held up his cast and said simply, "No."

"Hey, you got stitches, too!" said Ry in an envious tone.

"How many did you get?" asked Jax.

Roc looked up at his mother for a prompt to answer him. Corrynne whispered in his ear, "About ten."

"Ten," Roc said, echoing his mother's answer.

"Cool," said Jax and Ry at the same time.

"You're going to be asked a lot of questions at school, Roc," mused Jax, nodding his head knowingly.

"I wish I had a cast and stitches," said Ry wistfully.

"No, you don't," Corrynne corrected her son. "That isn't anything that someone should wish for."

"I just want to know what it feels like," said Ry.

"It feels heavy," said Roc.

Changing the subject, Corrynne said, "Ry, will you find the remote and turn on the TV to CNN?"

"What kind of channel is that, Mom?"

"It's a news channel."

"Yuck, that's so boring. Why do you like to watch that channel?" asked Ry.

"You're so silly! Just do as I ask. I need to know what's going on in the world. You should be interested, too. What happens in the world will affect your life. You don't want to be caught off guard by something important. When you're a dad someday, you'll want to watch CNN."

"OK." Ry shrugged. He seemed to accept that answer and looked around for the remote and found it between the cushions of the couch.

"That's where it was! I knew you'd be able to find it. You're always so good at finding things," said Corrynne. Ry smiled big and flipped on the power. The channel was already on CNN. Someone had been watching this channel before her.

"...new Secretary-General-designate at the UN. The confirmation took place at the new UN center in England in an emergency weekend meeting. The German delegate who will be assuming the position was appointed for a term of five years, beginning September 26. The untimely death of the previous Secretary-General called for an early selection to be held...."

Despite Corrynne's previous solemn attitude, the announcement from the UN struck her as funny. Corrynne couldn't help but let out a stifled, abrupt laugh. She recalled her disapproving remarks to her husband earlier that day when he suggested Germany fulfilled the ambiguous prophecies in Revelation. At the moment he had voiced his opinion in front of Brother Anderson, she had been deeply embarrassed at his overtly shameless finger pointing. Of all things, she didn't want to be associated with the same mentality. She still believed that Bo's comments were ridiculous, but still, it seemed an uncanny coincidence that the UN would announce that Germany's delegate was taking over one of the most influential positions in the world on this day. She wondered if Bo had been watching the news before church.

Corrynne called out, "Bo!" Her outburst made the twins, who were almost asleep, jump. "Bo, come in here. ...The UN has a new Secretary-General from *Germany*! Come see!"

The TV continued its coverage. "...The quick and decisive change made by the two hundred and fifty-three member governments comes after many of the delegates expressed their belief that the affairs of the world could not be left unaddressed for any amount of time. Therefore, a new leader had to be elected quickly...."

"Bo! Come in here quick!"

"What?" Bo poked his head out from the kitchen doorway. "It's time for dinner. Everyone, come and eat!" Immediately, all the children between eleven and seven years vacated the living room and headed for the dining room, where the delicious aroma of spaghetti sauce and meatballs lingered. Hunger had made them unusually obedient.

"I know, but you'll want to see this," contested Corrynne. A girlish giggle bubbled out of her throat. "I might have to say I'm sorry for not agreeing with your opinions about Germany. ...You know it's important if I'm apologizing!"

The reporting continued. "...Some of the complex issues the new Secretary-General will be working on with the UN member governments include: solutions to economic inequality among countries in the open market; a tax request from the UN to all the nations; relief for the Chilean earthquake victims; and the maintenance of peace in the Middle East...."

Bo quickly took a place on the couch next to his wife. "Ha, ha! See, I told you that Germany was getting into the middle of world affairs!"

Corrynne looked at her husband and asked, "When you made those comments today about Germany playing a sinister part in the last-days prophecies, I thought you were being rude, but you were serious, weren't you?"

"Sure! I'm much smarter than I look."

"Were you watching the news earlier? The channel on the TV was already on CNN."

"Always."

"Always what?"

"When you have a worried wife, a son out on a mission in a dangerous place, and six more getting ready or planning to go out, you have to be informed."

Corrynne was impressed, despite herself. She smiled and said, "You're right—you are smarter than you look."

Bo ignored Corrynne's friendly jab. He knew that he deserved the spar. He hid a secret smile that he knew Corrynne sensed was there.

As the report continued both Corrynne and Bo's eyes returned to the screen as the twins, still in Corrynne's arms, wiggled free. Corrynne distractedly put them down, and they crawled out of the room.

"Sarah Taylor from the England center for the UN is standing by with the new Secretary-General, Ray Klump, and his PR committee. Sarah?"

"Yes, Joan."

"We understand that Secretary-General-designate Klump has decided to take an aggressive agenda for the short-term future, in response to the member governments' requests."

"Yes, Joan, I believe he has. There are very important administrative decisions that have to be made immediately, as I understand. I have Secretary-General Klump right here." The commentator then turned to a short, square, balding man with questionable dental hygiene. He smiled broadly as his long fringe of hair flapped around his head in the wind. "Secretary-General Klump, could you elaborate on your priorities at this time? And what are the first steps you will take as Secretary-General?"

"Ah, yes, I would be happy to address the world with our agenda, in return for liberal coverage. We are excited for the support and look for direct response from the people whom the members of our organization represent," spoke the man in English with a thick German accent.

"Yes, Secretary-General, this will be worldwide coverage. Go ahead."

"There are a couple of issues that must be worked out immediately. We have a lot of work ahead of us."

"Tell us what work you are referring to."

"First of all, it is essential that all of us work together to ensure that we have a multilateral trading system that gives benefits to all of our citizens. As an organization, we have been working diligently toward this end. There have been multiple studies that conclude that free trade helps reduce poverty. Trade liberalization helps poor countries to catch up with rich ones, and this faster economic growth helps to alleviate poverty. For example, one hundred years ago, South Korea was as poor as Ghana. Today, thanks to trade-led growth, it is as rich as Japan."[5]

"That is amazing! Mr. Secretary-General, what do we have to do to continue that kind of transformation for the poor countries?"

"Trade liberalization is the key. It is a positive contributor to poverty alleviation—it allows people to exploit their productive potential and assists economic growth. Movements for this cause have already begun. In Africa, whole villages' incomes have doubled and sometimes tripled because factories like Nike or Levi's have moved in and are now employing their workers. Change is rapidly increasing the standard of living. However, a huge disparity still exists due to the vast differences in the currencies among the countries. We need to work on an equitable solution to cause small countries not to become victims of economic rape in the name of growth."

"What could be a solution, Secretary?"

"We believe an international currency that would be traded in business among the countries of the world would eliminate the large differences.[6] Although this would limit the gargantuan profits over time that are sometimes one hundred times what the production costs are, it would allow natural market movements to continue, to encourage worldwide prosperity rather than a situation where only the rich nations profit."

"Would that demand that the countries give up their own currency?"

"Absolutely not. We encourage all countries to maintain their own currency. Only when they do world business will they have to convert their individual currency into the world currency."

"Would they receive equal value for their money as they do now?"

"No, each country's money would be either devalued or inflated by graduated percentages to allow all conversions to reflect a balanced market over time."

"Wouldn't that cause the rich countries not to participate in the world economy?"

"No. We still believe they will participate. We believe that although the rich nations' money will be devalued, the benefit that exists even after that devaluation will outweigh their costs of doing business anywhere else. It will also help eliminate the employee crunch that is happening all over the rich nations due to decreased birth rate in those areas and a decreased working pool. In the poor countries of the world, the work force is full and ready to work. It's a very exciting union, solving problems on many levels."

"Mom," Jax called from the kitchen.

"Not now, honey, we need to listen to this news information," said Corrynne with a curt edge.

The English interviewer continued, "What if a country does not want to be a part of the world economy?"

"Each country has the right to decide to trade on the world market or not. No action will be taken to force countries to be involved. However, we believe that no country would want to be left out of the world economy because of the miraculous changes that it is bringing about already. For a country to refuse this progress would be ludicrous. They would be isolated economically. But according to the support that we are hearing from our member governments, this will not be an issue."

The Secretary-General continued. "As national economies become more and more interdependent through information, trade, investment, and financial ties, the UN is helping to fill a growing need for international cooperation and regulatory consistency to spread the benefits of globalization."

The interviewer seemed to be enthralled with the Secretary-General's answers. Her momentum continued as the pace increased. "What does the UN plan to do about the continued violence in the Middle East? Many thought that giving Palestine their independence and forcing Israel to comply with their peace agreements would solve the violence. But the cry of the Israeli and the Palestinian people over the city of Jerusalem has become almost fanatical. If something isn't done soon, we'll have two nations of martyrs."

"I agree with you. We have a plan that we think will satisfy both parties. Even now, we have talks commencing. We believe that if we can help the

Jews build their temple that they might be willing to allow the Palestinians parts of the neutral city of Jerusalem."[7]

"Mom!" yelled Jax. "Come here!"

Corrynne held up her hand in the universal "stop" signal to her son Jax, who was peeking around the corner of the kitchen.

The interviewer continued. "That sounds like a very creative solution. When will we know of its results?"

"We have given the two nations one week to come up with a compromise. Otherwise they will experience no changes, and things will remain the way they are, martyrs or not."

"One more question, Mr. Secretary-General."

"Yes?" Secretary-General Klump smiled, exposing his gray, crooked teeth.

"With the new roles of the UN, will the UN be involving itself in the rebuilding of areas of the world that are victims of natural disasters, like the earthquake in Chile today?"

"Yes, we would like to be. We would like to function as a fully empowered government entity to the world that acts as a defender to all in the name of world peace and unity. However, we need economic support from all the nations of the world to continue those roles. We are proposing a change in the way the UN is funded."

"And what is that change?"

"Instead of dues given by countries who belong to the UN, a new plan to create a world tax of one percent of world currency for every UN dollar spent on the world market would be given in support of the UN. This money will be used to carry out the business of the world."

"Impressive. That doesn't seem too large a price to pay for a good governing body."

"We are hoping that it is acceptable. From preliminary sources, we feel good about the people's support of such a tax. It doesn't burden any government or people but is from the international trade that we represent."

"Excellent, Secretary-General. Any other words that you wish to convey to the people who are listening to you right now?"

"Yes, one more thing. Governments and parliaments must support our agreements in the UN. We all need to be more accountable. Parliaments and congresses sustain governments. Public opinion sustains governments. Elected representatives are the main expression of civil society. Their support is measured, and they are accountable. This is a real way in which we can counter some of the anxieties about globalization and public alienation. Elected representatives have a responsibility to become more involved. We invite them to scrutinize where the global taxpayer's money is going and ensure that the great international institutions created to manage global affairs have the moral authority that comes from the ownership and participation of member governments. Thus, together we can create the dream of a truly united and functioning world. It is our destiny."

"Thank you, Secretary-General-elect Klump. This is Sarah Taylor, live from the new England center for the UN"

"Thank you, Sarah...."

"Wow," said Corrynne, continuing to stare at the display as the images changed. She muted the sound. "Now, that was very politically inviting," said Corrynne. "Don't you think?"

"Absolutely," said Bo, "who wouldn't like this guy with all his ideas about world unity, increased economy, and did you catch the part about the Jewish temple?"

"Yes, I can't believe it! I think I was swayed today. I can't help but be thankful for all that Klump is trying to do. Maybe he's not the person the scriptures are talking about. What do you think, Bo?"

"Well, although his talk is sweet and it all sounds so wonderful, the jury is still out on whether he is a good guy or a bad guy. I personally am very wary, considering the language in the scriptures. We are told in Revelation that a government will arise that has two horns like a lamb and speaks like a dragon."[8]

"What does that mean?"

"We can only guess, but the symbolic nature of the statement indicates that a government that at one time had two power centers, represented by the two horns, will seem harmless like a lamb and then speak the words that Satan, or the dragon, gives him."

"Oh, and you think Germany fulfills that statement?"

"Think about it. Don't you remember when the Berlin wall segmented Germany? At that time we had an East and a West Germany. Now we have a German UN Secretary-General who says politically acceptable things to create a one-world entity. Sounds like Satan is right on target with his agenda."[9]

Corrynne thought for a second then said, "But the Secretary-General doesn't really have political power over the nations that the UN represents."

"No, maybe not at the moment, but whoever has the gold rules the world. If he's able to pass this one-percent tax on the international world market, the amount of money that it will bring in will be gargantuan! One percent might sound humble, but I'm sure Klump has run his numbers and knows it will be huge. Naturally, he will gain power and influence for his own agendas, especially if the nations of the world like what he's doing."

"Well, he seems like he wants all the countries of the world to be equally successful. ...I have to admit that I would like that, too."

"I'm sure that he does! It will help him out immensely if they are. But see how his words are so inviting?"

"Wow, Bo. I understand how you're coming to your conclusions. But I still think that pegging Germany as the 'whore of the earth'[10] might be a bit much."

"I knew you'd think that. You are kind by nature and slow to see malice. However, whoever those scriptures are pointing to, whether Germany now or someone else we haven't been exposed to, we better be willing to see the similarities written about in the scriptures."

"I agree with that statement." Corrynne nodded.

Again a young voice interrupted. "Mom, Dad, you guys need to come in here!" yelled Ry this time.

"What is it? The sky better be falling, by the way you are interrupting us," said Corrynne.

"We tried to feed ourselves the spaghetti without your help...."

"That's good," said Bo

"And so did the twins."

"The twins? What do you mean?" Corrynne immediately got up from her place on the couch and ran into the dining room. On top of the table sat her twins with the spaghetti bowl turned over and the twins sitting squarely in the mess of sauce and strings of noodles. Spaghetti covered the table, hung off their heads and shoulders, and covered the floor. Bo came around the corner. When the babies saw their parents, they became self-conscious. Strykker got up on his hands and knees and rocked back and forth and smiled big while he stared at the spaghetti mess. Striynna continued to squish spaghetti through her fingers slowly and seriously with her gaze fixed on her father, as if to communicate that she enjoyed her new experience. It was too much for Bo, and he grabbed his right side and began to laugh hysterically, moaning with pain from his injured ribs between gasps of laughter. The sight of the whole situation caused Corrynne to crack a smile, despite her initial shock.

"How did this happen?" asked Corrynne, trying to hide her smile, as Bo continued to laugh loudly.

"We tried to feed them in their chairs, but they wouldn't stay. They crawled onto the table and turned over the bowl before we could stop them. Then they were too gross to touch," said Jax.

"They made a mess!" noted Roc.

"We tried to tell you," said Ry, with lifted eyebrows and his head cocked.

"Yeah, I called you two times," said Jax, in his own defense.

It was a Kodak moment to be sure. Bo had the camera out in a moment, and soon all of them were laughing so hard that it made Dane, Carea and Brea come out to see what was so funny. Then the laughing started all over until all the laughs were spent and muscles were sore.

After the massive cleanup, cold cereal was dinner that night, but it was the best bowl of cereal any of them had ever tasted.

Notes to "The Sky is Falling"

Men's Hearts Shall Fail Them

[1] Passive immunity is a factual medical treatment of many diseases today including Hepatitis A, Hepatitis B, Tetanus, Measles, and RH Hemolytic disease of newborns. The application of this treatment is expanding (for further information, a good online source for this treatment is: http://www.cat.cc.md.us/courses/bio141/lecguide/unit3/u3iide.html).

[2] Payment for blood plasma is a factual detail, although the amount is greatly exaggerated in the text to extrapolate future demand.

[3] The phrase referring to failing hearts in the last days is mentioned four times in the scriptures (see D&C 45:26; D&C 88:91; Luke 21:26; and Moses 7:66).

In three of the four times failing hearts is mentioned in the scriptures, fear is also mentioned. It is proven that stressful events bring on the angina associated with heart disease (see http://www.heartinfo.org/reuters2001/010312elin014.htm for an informative site about heart disease, stress and angina).

Indeed heart disease is becoming more prevalent during the latter-days. "1997 U.S. statistics show that coronary heart disease (CHD), which causes heart attack and angina, is the single leading cause of death in America" ("Heart Attack and Angina Statistics," *American Heart Association*, available online: http://www.americanheart.org/Heart_and_Stroke_A_Z_Guide/has.html; also see: http://www.americanheart.org/statistics/index.html for more recent statistics).

"And all things shall be in commotion; and surely, men's hearts shall fail them; for fear shall come upon all people" (D&C 88:91).

World Changes, Hidden Danger

[4] "…We cannot be indifferent to the great cause of truth and right. We cannot afford to stand on the sidelines and watch the play between the forces of good and evil. Wrote John the Revelator: 'I know thy works, that thou art neither cold nor hot: I would thou wert cold or hot. So then because thou art lukewarm, and neither cold nor hot, I will spew thee out of my mouth' (Revelation 3:15-16)…"John's imagery is vivid. It points to our critical duty to stand strong, even to become leaders in speaking up on behalf of those causes that make our civilization shine. Each of us can be a leader within our sphere of influence. The adversary of all truth would put into our hearts a reluctance to make an effort; we must cast that fear aside and be valiant in the cause of truth, fairness, and right" (Gordon B. Hinckley, *Standing for Something: 10 Neglected Virtues That Will Heal Our Hearts and Homes*, 170-172).

"In a very real sense it is a war—a hot war—a war between right and wrong, between the powers of heaven and the forces of Lucifer…This is not a war for territory or wealth; it is a contest for the eternal souls of men and women, boys and girls, the literal offspring of God, our Heavenly Father…If we *do* know what is right, have we the courage to stand up for it, to defend virtue, to declare the validity of our faith, to oppose false teachings, and to fight the unpopular battle?"(Mark E. Peterson, "Where Do We Stand?" *Ensign*, May 1980, 68).

[5] Talks given by the UN to increase economic globalization can be accessed at the UN Internet site (www.un.org). Ideas for the discussion found in the text were taken from multiple talks given by the recent UN Secretary-General, Kofi Annan. One good example of the UN agenda can be found in an address given at The World Economic Forum in Davos, Switzerland presented on January 28th, 2001. The address is available at: http://www.un.org/News/dh/latest/address_2001.htm.

[6] The resolution of one global currency is a fictitious solution extrapolated from the current world economic environment. However, the occurrence of one in the future is predicted in the scriptures; see Revelation 13:17.

[7] The premise of another Jewish temple in Jerusalem is not a new one. Somehow it will be built. There are multiple scriptures that predict there will be a third temple built in old Jerusalem with water that flows from it to heal the Dead Sea. See Ezekiel 41:1-2; Joel 3:18; Zechariah 14:8; Revelation 22:1.

The temple will be built before Christ's second coming. We know this because it will be built in a day that the Antichrist will be able to sit in it and proclaim himself God (see 2 Thessalonians 2:4).

[8] "And I beheld another beast coming up out of the earth; and he had two horns like a lamb, and he spake as a dragon" (Revelation 13:11).

[9] See Roger K.Young, "...*As A Thief In The Night*," 31-32 for more discussion on this topic.

It is not the intent of this author to predict or identify the government predicted in the scriptures to control the earth. It is the author's intent to offer a plausible, logical scenario of its coming to power that could catch us unaware due to its palatable nature. When the true government does reveal itself, it will be through this method of scriptural recognition and validation from the true and living Prophet that we will recognize it.

The discussions and conclusions concerning the identities of the Antichrist and the government which will control the world made in this text are not those put forth by the General Authorities or the Prophet and are assumed to be fictional.

[10] The term "whore of the earth" is used often in the scriptures to identify an entity that will entice men of the earth away from the truth. Sometimes it is used to indicate a church (1 Nephi 14:10; 1 Nephi 14:12; 2 Nephi 28:18; D&C 29:21) and other times a political entity (Rev 19:12; 1 Nephi 14:11; 2 Nephi 10:16). In the last days it is said that the political entity and the Antichrist will join forces and potentially be the same entity (Revelation 16:13; 19:20).

CHAPTER NINE

FAMILIAR VOICES

"...even according to their faith it was done unto them; and I did remember the words which they said unto me that their mothers had taught them" (Alma 57:21).

Monday
September 18th
7:04 a.m.
Provo Utah

Routine

Corrynne felt like lead as she struggled to sit up in bed. Looking at the clock she squinted to see what it said, but her vision was fuzzy. All she could make out was a seven for the first number.

"Seven? What?" she asked herself aloud, feeling surprised. It couldn't be seven. She squinted again, leaning over to get closer to the clock to see clearer, but she had been right the first time. "Shoot! I slept in!" she said as she threw back the covers and leaped out of bed.

Her twins were still sleeping in adjoining toddler beds, but her husband was gone. Most likely he had left a while ago for his commute to Salt Lake City.

She threw on a robe and ran down the stairs. Carea was in her bedroom getting her books together, and Dane was in the bathroom brushing his teeth. Corrynne stood in the hall between the two rooms. "Thank goodness you guys are up!"

"Of course we're up, Mom," said Dane, with a mouth full of toothpaste.

"I slept in. I'm sorry," lamented Corrynne.

"We wanted you to sleep in. We thought you could use a little extra," stated Carea.

"That was nice of you. Are Jax, Ry, and Roc up?"

"Yep, they're at the table eating breakfast," said Dane.

Corrynne nodded. "Oh, that's great. Have you seen Brea yet?"

Carea came out into the hall. "I just heard her alarm go off."

"Good. I'll meet everyone in the living room in five minutes for family prayer."

"Okey-dokey," Dane smiled and intentionally caused the toothpaste to gush out of his mouth and down his chin for his mother to see.

"You're a goof," Corrynne said shaking her head and headed into the dining room.

"Mom, tell Jax to stop bothering me!" said Ry in a tattling voice.

"Mom, he's bothering *me*!" returned Jax, obviously getting angry.

"What's going on?" asked Corrynne.

"Jax says that his guy on Dragon Masters can kick all over my guy, and he can't," said Ry, with a well-rehearsed grimace of contrived torture.

"I did not! I said that my guy was an ultimate dragon master, which does kick all over a dragon master. I can't help it if your guy hasn't leveled up yet!"

Roc, watching his brothers squabble, sat beside them with his cast on the table. He was eating his cereal like a machine, as he took in every detail of the argument.

Corrynne took a moment to decide what to do. Then with conviction she said, "I will not solve your problems. You are old enough and smart enough to know how to have peace between you two, so this is your choice. You can both kiss and make up, or you can't play Dragon Masters. I'm fine with either choice."

"What?" both her sons said at the same time.

"I will not kiss him," said Jax, as his face began to turn red.

"I won't kiss him, either!" said Ry, as he squished up his nose.

"Well, look at that. You guys are already agreeing on something. That's a good start.

"Come on, Roc, it's time for family prayer," Corrynne said, holding her hand out to him.

"I'm almost done," said Roc as he took another bite.

"Come on. You can finish in a minute."

Roc put down his spoon and joined his mother.

Jax and Ry still held their angry stares.

Corrynne called over her shoulder, "Come on, a prayer will be extra good for you guys."

Everyone who was available congregated in the living room and knelt down in the center. Ry and Jax were still breathing hard and throwing deadly glances to let everyone know there was a conflict.

"What's wrong with them?" asked Dane.

"You know, a normal 'who's better than who' fight," said Corrynne, rolling her eyes.

"Oh, yeah, I understand now," snickered Dane. "It's important to figure that out, Mom."

"I guess."

"Jax just likes to say things to make me angry," whined Ry.

"Well, you're in control of whether you get angry or not. Sounds to me like you guys cooperate pretty well in deciding to fight. Who says you don't get along?"

"Mooom!" complained Ry.

"If you don't like what Jax says to you, ignore him, and Jax, stop trying to cause contention. Who cares who's better?"

"I wasn't saying anything that was wrong. I was just saying...," Jax started defensively.

"I know what you were saying. Just don't say it if you don't need to, OK?"

There was a moment as Jax considered his options. Finally he looked down and conceded, "OK."

"Ry, pray please. Ask Heavenly Father to help us all get along."

"And to help me with my test today!" added Carea.

Ry thought for a moment, and then began. "Dear Heavenly Father, thank you for this day. Thank you for our world. Please help us to be happy. Please help us to be nice to each other. Please help Carea with her test. Bless her to do well. Please help us to obey and do what is right. We love you. In the name of Jesus Christ, amen."

"Amen," said the group in unison.

After everyone got to their feet, Corrynne started with her list. "Let's see, Dane, you have a football game this week, don't you?"

"Yes, Mom, it's Saturday at the district field. Are you guys coming?"

"Sure!" answered Corrynne. She turned to Carea. "Is there anything you need?"

"Nope, I have it all under control. But thanks, Mom," said Carea as she and Dane walked out the front door.

"Oh, wait you guys!" called Corrynne in an afterthought when her teens were halfway down the porch steps. "I forgot to tell you—I have to work tonight and Friday night at the hospital. Carea, you're in charge of dinner tonight, and Dane, you've got Friday."

Both of them stopped to consider their plans. Dane looked up at the sky. "I think that'll be fine. Do you mind if I make macaroni and cheese?"

"Whatever you want. You're the culinary boss when you cook. Just remember to include some vegetables or fruits."

"No problem," returned Dane. "I love you, Mom."

"I love you too, Mom," said Carea.

"I love you both too. Have a good day!" said Corrynne as she waved and closed the front door.

Corrynne turned back to the three younger sons. "Let's see where we are."

They turned to her to wait for the checklist she always gave at this time in the morning. "It looks like you're dressed. Good job. Roc, you need to get your hair wet and comb it."

Roc licked his hand and tried to smooth his hair with his free hand.

"Are you done eating?"

All three of the boys nodded.

"Is your room cleaned?"

All three nodded again.

"Then go put your dishes in the sink and brush your teeth. After you're done Jax, I'll meet you in the laundry room to do your chore, and then Ry, I'll come into the kitchen to help you rinse the dishes. Until then, you can unload the dishwasher. Roc, the living room and the family room don't look too bad, so you can straighten them yourself with one hand."

Corrynne moved to the oven and set the timer for twenty minutes. "On your mark, get set, GO!"

The three boys peeled out of their places and headed off to complete the same routine they did every day. It was always a race to see how fast they could get everything done so they could play either the computer or the video games. Their computer time was very limited so they were always trying to capture more. With these three boys, it was Corrynne's most powerful tool for compliance.

Out of the corner of her eye, Corrynne saw Brea go from her room to the bathroom. "Brea?" she called.

"Yes?" echoed Brea's voice in the bathroom, behind the closed door.

"What's your schedule this week?"

"Ah," said Brea, "I have class at the 'Y' Monday, Wednesday, and Friday like normal. I want to spend some time with Matt, my fiancé. Remember him? I barely do, since I've been too busy lately even to take a breath. Why?"

"Dane and Carea's football game is Saturday. Are you going?"

"Yep, I'll be there." Brea opened the door so she and her mother could talk.

"Do you know if Braun is going?"

"Yes, I know he is, because he asked me to give him a ride in the truck."

"OK, I'll see you guys there."

"Do you have tickets?" asked Brea.

"Yes, right smack in the center. Fifty yard line."

"Matt can't go—he has to work on his dissertation."

"Fine," answered Corrynne, mentally logging the calendar information. She would have to write it down soon, or she knew she would forget. "I didn't buy Matt a ticket anyway. Normally he's busy."

"Don't remind me," said Brea with a sigh.

Corrynne went into the living room to check on Roc. She found him sitting in the middle of the room, despondently looking around.

"What's wrong?"

"I can't do it."

"What can't you do?"

"I can't clean without my hand." Roc held up his broken arm.

"Sure you can. You just throw everything in the middle, separate it, and then put it away."

"I'm used to using my other hand," said Roc.

"I know. Hey, I know what. You throw the things into the center of the room, I'll separate them, and you take the piles to their rooms."

Roc thought about his mother's offer and then said, "OK." He stood and said, "I'm putting on the super-sonic power."

"OK," said Corrynne with a smile.

Roc then ran from corner to corner, tossing toys, socks, shoes, etc. into the center of the room.

Corrynne had to dodge the flying objects. "Hey, bud, watch where you're throwing those things."

"Sorry, Mom, I can't throw good with my wrong hand."

"It's your left hand, sweetheart, not your wrong hand."

"It's wrong to me!" smiled Roc, as he threw a dirty sock in her face.

"Yes," Corrynne said, as she pulled it off quickly and threw it into the pile in the middle, "maybe you're right."

Roc laughed hysterically.

E-mail

The house was still. Corrynne sat on the edge of her bed and just listened. Life had been so hectic lately. A moment of quiet calm like this was delicious. She took in a deep breath, filling her nose with the humid air from the recent baths of her twins and a lingering smell of baby lotion. She loved that smell; it brought back such wonderful memories of her other children when they were little.

Corrynne sighed as she said aloud, "Little ones grow up so fast." It made her sad to imagine her twins grown and walking out the door like her older children had that morning.

Striynna and Strykker, who were crawling on the floor at her feet, looked up at the sound of her voice.

"Yes, they do. …Yes, they do," Corrynne prattled with a high, cooing lilt. She reached down and tickled each one. Striynna let out a muffled baby giggle, while Strykker just held his breath with a big smile. "You are cute, cute babies!" She sat on the floor, and Strykker climbed into her lap. She rubbed the top of his fuzzy head and then kissed his baby face.

Little Striynna continued to search for treasure on the carpet, crawling with her little bottom moving back and forth, like a windup doll. Just then, she stopped crawling. Obviously, she had spotted something that caught her interest. Striynna looked back at her mother with a mischievous glance. She gave Corrynne a single-toothed smile, as she raised something to her mouth.

Corrynne put Strykker down and crawled over to Striynna to see what her tiny daughter was trying to taste. It was an Israeli coin, a shekel that Grandma Bonnie had given Corrynne's son Conrad after hearing he had been called to the Holy Land for his mission.

"No, no, no, little girl!" Corrynne said in a loving voice. "You don't eat those! I wonder how that got on the floor." She gently removed the coin from her daughter's chubby hand.

The coin reminded Corrynne that today was the day she should receive an e-mail from Conrad. Even though she had put him out on his mission four months ago, he had just barely arrived in Jerusalem due to Visa and passport problems. So she was anxious to hear how the Holy Land was and if he was settled in.

Corrynne stood and went to the computer to check. After she logged into her e-mail account, she saw her son's name in black. He had sent is letter! "Yes, it's here, guys," she called out, as if her twins understood her words.

The e-mail was titled, "Hello from the other side of the world where pigs are free." Corrynne laughed. Conrad was so wonderfully strange. The mission hadn't changed that part of him yet.

As the twins continued to crawl on the floor, Corrynne began to read.

> *"Dear everyone--Can I tell you that being out here in Israel, especially the holy city of Jerusalem on a mission for the Lord, is definitely cool? Talking about Jerusalem and reading about it in books is one thing, but being here in person is absolutely unreal. Wish you could be here with me so you could see all the sights...NOT! OK, just kidding. No, I really would, it just seemed natural to pretend that I didn't. (You know, a throwback from when we were kids--huh, Braun?)*
>
> *"Anyway, all the missionaries have to live at the Jerusalem Center.[1] To me, that's surreal. Instead of living in some mildewed apartment, we are treated like kings, living in the nicest place here. The reason for the posh surroundings is because the violence between the Palestinians and the Israelis is unpredictable. The Church leaders want to keep missionaries far from the Gaza Strip and the West Bank for that reason. The security here is extremely high. We feel like we're secret agents with all the passwords, cameras, laser beams, etc., but I'm thankful for it.[2] It really is freaky out there. We have to follow mission rules perfectly and stay in the neutral area, which of course is the old and new cities of Jerusalem itself, or we'll be transferred.*

"Actually there is only one area where we are allowed to be unless someone invites us to their home. It's a town square of sorts. There is a large pad of cement right next to the pool of Bethesda where Christ told the crippled man to take up his bed and walk on the Sabbath, in Matthew 5.[3] You can look that up if you want. Anyway, this is where all religions are allowed to be represented, hand out pamphlets, preach, or do anything that pertains to their religion. We spend a lot of time there, or at least we have so far. I like to think of myself healing these people from their spiritual infirmities and teaching them to take up their faith and walk, like Christ did over 2,000 years ago in this same place. Being by the pool gives me courage to declare the truth loudly.

"Talk about religion, people around here are pretty jumpy about religions other than Judaism or Islam. They look at you like you're trying to steal their soul or something. I hope it gets better.

"I wanted to give you some excerpts out of my journal that tell about my impressions out here. I think I do my best writing there; plus I can just transfer the files, and you have more to read! Instant letters! Cool? OK, here goes.

"Tuesday, 9:10 p.m.

"Israel, in this part at least, isn't as barren as I imagined it. I guess from pictures it appears to be a desert land, but up close, there are evergreen trees and bushes all over. I understand that in the spring there are wildflowers everywhere that make this place colorful. As I rode in on the bus I couldn't believe that I was actually here. I mean, this is the HOLY LAND! What an amazing experience this is going to be! It's a lot larger than I pictured and actually majestic in a way. I don't know what makes me say that. Maybe it's the Dome of the Rock, or the holy sites, or just that Christ, the future and looked-for King of this world, walked here and will again.

"The Jerusalem Center, the place that we will call home for awhile, is a cool building. It's built like an indoor, outdoor building. When you are inside, you still feel the wind blowing around you since the walls are only arches to the outside in some places. Sometimes when I'm walking in a hall I have the impression that I'm indoors, but then I look up to see not a ceiling but the sky.

"We were given the history of this place, and it's a miracle that it's even built. There was a lot of politics that the Church had to overcome. It took forty men two years to chisel every block of Italian marble for this building. They use a lot of French teakwood for decoration and accents that we don't have in Utah. It gives the building a foreign smell that I'm still not used to.[4]

"An Israeli genius helped design this building so that it blends in with the other buildings here. The Center is built on a hill so that from every window you can see the 180-degree view of the city. Our address here is actually the 'Mount of Olives.' Now that's cool!

"Right now I'm looking at the inner city of Jerusalem itself, which has four different quarters, each representing four different religions: Armenian, Christian, Jewish and Muslim. I see The Dome of the Rock clearly from this vantage point...and there's the Golden Gate, the old entrance to the city. It's been sealed off from use.

"My companion's name is Elder Martin, of Little Rock, Arkansas. He's an OK guy. At first, when I met him, I wasn't sure if we were going to get along very well, because he didn't talk much. But now, after we've been together, I've found that we have a lot in common. He comes from a big family (six kids) although not as big as mine. He's the second oldest boy, and he loves computers as I do. He has a great testimony of missionary work and of our job here. He will be a great senior companion. I like him because he's not stuck on himself. He's humble and easy to work with. The only thing he won't share is the beef jerky that he gets from home. That, he says, is off limits. I've got to get my own supply of beef jerky because it drives me crazy when he eats his! Beef jerky is impossible to find here, because it's not kosher.

"Tuesday, 11:30 p.m.
"It's in the middle of the night now. I couldn't sleep.

"I have a garden patio outside my room. I like to go outside to write in my journal. It's so different here from where I've ever been before. It feels like I have been thrown back in time. I listen for cars. I don't hear any right now. I know that there are many during the day, but right now they're silent. I also listen for anything electronic, and there's no evidence that it exists here by the absence of the sounds. I hear crickets, and dogs barking. Down the hill and across the street, in the Palestinian neighborhood, there was a Muslim chanting a song by himself. His voice made me homesick for a moment. I realized that I was very far from home in a different place with different people who do not think as I do. I have to shake my thoughts, to not let myself think like that.

"I think I'm going through technology withdrawals. I've been so busy up to this point that I haven't have had time even to want to surf the net or play games. Of course, mission rules say that I can't do either. Writing my journal on a computer and sending it is actually a relief to me. It's familiar. Of course, I miss my family, but that was expected. I think nights are hard because they are so quiet. I can think way too much.

"*I was reviewing my Patriarchal Blessing. It says that answers to my questions will come loud to my ears, and that communication will be as an instant between Heaven and myself. What does that mean? I hope that I will begin to have this gift soon. I really need it now. I hope it means that I'll be able to pray about things and get answers I will understand. If that is what it means, I'm grateful.*

"*Another thing it talks about in my Patriarchal Blessing is my deep association with Israel. I have often wondered what that meant, too. I got the blessing way before I was called here. I wondered if it meant that I would come here. Since I did, it probably was just talking about my mission. But the wording is kind of funny. It says that I will be a protection and a guide to the Jews. It says I will spend my life unselfishly in the service of my brethren. There's a final line that gives me comfort. It says, in the day that the Lord appears in all his glory, I will be a witness as all the world will see. It also says that I'll be caught up in the last day. Interesting language, huh? I wonder what it means. I know that every righteous person will be caught up,[5] but how will the world see? And will I be caught up when Christ comes, or later? Lots of questions. I think I will get working on that gift of hearing answers loud in my ears. I sure need it. I'll be sure to stay out of the crossfire that happens all around this place.*

"*Wednesday, 6:20 a.m.*

"*OK, I have to repent for my selfish thoughts last night. I think it's natural to have feelings of missing what is familiar. Sometimes people can even wonder who they are without the things they used to do. It's just a matter of finding new things in this place to help define me. Actually, I'm grateful for this opportunity. It came at a time when my soul needed teaching. Here I will find the strength to dedicate myself to the pursuit of the Lord's service without distraction. It will be very good for me.... 'Radical!' (I have to include a little of my old self to feel halfway normal.)*

"*OK, Mom, don't worry about me. My journal gets kind of deep and really honest. I just wanted to send you some thoughts from me.*

"*Love you all, Elder Rogers, the one who speaks three languages now. (That trumps Spanish, Braun! He, he.)*

"*P.S. Please send teriyaki and peppercorn beef jerky. White chocolate wouldn't be bad, either.*"

Corrynne immediately got out a sticky note and wrote "beef jerky and white chocolate." She stuck it onto her digital planner. She looked at her note and smiled.

Family Ties

The phone rang.

Corrynne picked it up, and a familiar happy face appeared on her computer screen. "Hello, Corrynne!"

"Hello, Mom!" Corrynne returned. "How are you doing?"

"I'm doing great! How are the children?" asked her mother with a big smile.

"Everyone's doing well. Going a million miles an hour, but doing well."

"Are you sure there's nothing to tell me about?" asked Corrynne's mother.

Corrynne half grimaced and half smiled. "Oh, there's always lots to tell you Mom. Got a couple of hours?"

"Well, I have one hour. My student canceled and so I have one hour till my next one comes."

Corrynne nodded. "That should be enough if I talk fast. Where do you want me to start?"

"Tell me about that hail storm that hit Utah. I was watching it on the weather channel. It looked like a big one."

"Well, I was going to call you actually but you beat me to the punch."

"Did something happen?" asked Corrynne's mother, her expression changed to a serious one.

"Well, yes. Little Roc's arm was broken…."

"What?" Grandma looked shocked.

"And Bo probably has fractured ribs…."

"Huh?" Grandma Bonnie gasped as a hand came to her mouth.

"Our Suburban has cracks that stretch across the front window, and it's still stranded in the middle of the street, not to mention our truck window, which was obliterated into millions of pieces. The Neon, thank goodness, was protected in the garage, so it's fine. At least we have one car to drive."

"Oh, my goodness, I feel like my breath was knocked out of me!" said Grandma. "My heart is beating so fast! How did little Roc break his arm?"

"He thought it would be fun to play in the hail, and he was caught in it after church. I'm sorry I didn't tell you last night, but I was too tired and too much was going on. Otherwise, you would have been the first I would've called."

"So everything is all right now?" asked Grandma with a hopeful look. "Is his arm in a cast?"

"Yes."

"Good."

"We're all fine," said Corrynne.

"Is little Roc in pain?"

"He doesn't seem to be. He left for school like normal today, anxious to show off his cast to his friends. He thinks for some reason that it's going to make him popular or something."

Grandma Bonnie laughed.

"So, Mom, when are you going to move here with us and away from Seattle, where I hear there's a drought?"[6] Corrynne let out a muffled snicker and continued chiding her mother. "I really can't believe Washington, the rain capital of the world, is having a drought." She laughed again. "I'm sorry, Mom." Corrynne tried to compose herself.

Grandma Bonnie replied without a tiny bit of negativity, "I love the rain, but without the clouds in the way, I love to look up into the clear blue sky. Maybe a drought every so often isn't bad."

"There you go, always calling a dandelion a daisy."

"I've found that counting your blessings makes everything more beautiful. I'm much happier that way."

"You win. I consider myself taught." Corrynne changed the subject. "You know, we have an apartment that Braun would give up in a second for you."

"Oh, sweetheart, you know that I can't leave this area. I have my piano students, and your dad loves it here. He wouldn't leave if wild horses dragged him."

Corrynne shrugged. "OK, just checking. We have a lot of water here. Isn't that funny? In the desert mountains there's a lot of water? It seems ironic."

"Well, that makes me feel good that at least you have what you need and everyone is fine. As for me, a little sacrifice didn't hurt anyone. We have what we need, when we ration."

"What about that earthquake in Chile yesterday? Wasn't that a huge one?" asked Corrynne. "You heard about that one, right?"

"Oh, yes. I'm afraid that I can't take my eyes off the news lately, since there's always something dramatic going on somewhere."

"Don't you live on a fault, Mother?"

"Yes, but don't we all?" asked Grandma Bonnie with a smile.

"Yes, I guess we do, too. But I hope that because the church is centered here, we'll be given an extra dose of protection, or so I hope," said Corrynne.

"Saints are gathered all over the world, sweetheart. The Lord protects them all," said Grandma Bonnie.

"Yes, again, you're right. True saints have the Lord's protection."

"Is there such a thing as a false saint?" Grandma Bonnie asked.

Corrynne nodded. "Yes, of course there is. We all have to look into our hearts everyday to see how authentic we are. I think the hail storm yesterday was a friendly warning to all of us to wake up and get serious."

"Do you think it worked?"

"No, it was just a tease. The real scary stuff is yet to come," said Corrynne.

"Oh, Corrynne, I don't like it when you talk like that, as if you already know and it's around the corner."

"Well, Mom, in some ways I do know. We all do. And around the corner? We'll soon find out just what's out there."

Notes to Familiar Voices

E-mail

[1] Missionaries are not allowed to serve in Israel at this time due to the violence and laws concerning religion.

[2] The high security at the Jerusalem Center for Near Eastern Studies is a reality today. All the details found in the text are current.

[3] Also see John 5:2-9.

[4] Factual descriptions of the Jerusalem Center were taken from the personal journals of Darren Carter, accounting his experience as a student in Jerusalem studying the Old Testament. He participated in the Brigham Young University Study Abroad program in 1992.

[5] "And he who is faithful shall overcome all things, and shall be lifted up at the last day" (D&C 75:16).

[6] Drought is often described in relation to wickedness of the world (see Ether 9; Helaman 11) and will be felt in the last days "...These have power to shut heaven, that it rain not in the days of their prophecy: and have power over waters to turn them to blood, and to smite the earth with all plagues, as often as they will" (Revelation 11:6).

CHAPTER TEN

STRANGE WHISPERINGS

"Yea, thus saith the still small voice, which whispereth through and pierceth all things, and often times it maketh my bones to quake while it maketh manifest" (D&C 85:6).

Monday
September 18th
5:30 p.m.
Provo, Utah

A Soft Word

"Bo, the police called."

"About what?" asked Bo, who was preparing dinner in the kitchen.

"The Suburban's been towed to the side of the road. I need you to take me to work so you can drive it home."

"Take one of the kids," said Bo as he poured frozen corn into a bowl, salted it, and put it in the microwave.

"No, I want you to come," said Corrynne as she slipped her hospital ID over her head. "Whoever claims the car has to prove ownership. I was told that police are patrolling the area since some of the cars have been robbed. I think you need to come."

"Can't you stop, show the police ownership, and then have Dane drive it home?" asked Bo with a look. "I have some hamburgers on the barbecue."

Corrynne made a frown and folded her arms. "Come on, Bo. Anyone can flip a burger. Have Dane do *that*."

Bo looked at Corrynne with shock in his eyes. "Dane flip my burgers? Are you kidding? I don't want the house to go up in flames."

"What? Dane's been cooking since he was little. He'd do fine."

"Not with these gourmet burgers. If you don't flip them just right, the meat will fall into the coals and start a fire."

"Yeah, yeah, excuses, excuses," said Corrynne, shaking her head. "Whatever."

Bo gave Corrynne a smirk and said, "Get Dane to help you. Make him useful. He's in the living room. Tell him his break is over."

With a sigh, Corrynne poked her head around the corner to see her son sprawled out on the couch in a diagonal, semi-recumbent position, with freshly washed wet hair. He was in a T-shirt and sweats, obviously resting from football practice.

"Hey, Dane, I need you to help me," Corrynne said in a loud voice, trying to compete with a McDonald's commercial in surround sound.

There was no response. Dane's stare continued unblinkingly straight forward as the commercial's crescendo signaled the end.

"Dane!" Corrynne spoke quickly and loudly to catch the silence between programs.

But still there was no response.

Finally, Corrynne moved to Dane's side, leaned down and whispered in his ear, "Dane Russell!" It was a trick she found worked with him when he was a small child.

"Yeah, what Mom?" Dane looked at her with surprise, as if she had yelled at him.

Corrynne smiled. "Oh, good, you are in there. I wondered who had snatched you without taking your body."

"Sorry, did you say something to me?"

"Yes, I need you to come with me to work and drive the Suburban home. It's on the side of the road by the hospital."

"OK," Dane said with a concerned look on his face.

"What's wrong?" asked Corrynne.

"Do I have to put my shoes on?"

"Well," said Corrynne. "You will have to get out of the Neon to get into the Suburban. Your feet might get cold."

Dane beat his fist on his chest. "I'll brave it. I'm a real man," he said in a pseudo-deep voice with a grunt.

Corrynne chuckled and said, "OK, 'He-man.' Come with me."

Dane gave another primal grunt of agreement and they headed out the door.

Harsh Truth

Corrynne rushed around the corner of the ICU hall into the classroom where the charge report was held. She put down her duffel bag and threw off her coat. She would take them to the staff locker room later.

Chris, the day charge nurse, was typing in the night shift's patient assignments. She looked back at the sound of Corrynne's hurried entrance. "I'm so glad you're here." Chris' voice had a hint of exhaustion.

"Why? ...Or should I ask?" Corrynne took steps backward to peer down the hall of the ICU, as if it would give her clues to what had happened that day. Seeing hallways filled with people, Corrynne returned into the room. "Who are all those people out there?"

Chris made a tired attempt to smile and said, "I'll get to that. Come sit down. This report is going to be complex."

Corrynne took a seat next to Chris and looked at the patient assignments. Her eyes scanned the patients, their diagnoses and the physicians that attended them. It occurred to her that there were too many patients slotted for how many rooms were in the ICU. "Why are there so many patients?" she asked.

"I'll get to that, too."

Corrynne swallowed and nodded. She could feel stress creeping into her.

Chris took a breath and sat for a moment as if she was collecting her thoughts. Then she looked at Corrynne and said, "My day was as hectic as it comes." said Chris as she pulled her own hand-held, medical digital display's record of admissions from the oversized pocket in her scrubs. "I don't want to frighten you, but we are in the middle of something scary."

"What do you mean?"

"The sky is falling," said Chris.

"What?"

"Codes, life flights, multiple admissions, triages…. You name it—it happened to us. We're doubled and tripled in some cases."

Corrynne studied Chris and nodded, waiting for the details. "OK."

"No, seriously, I think I'm ready for the nuthouse. Administration has gone over the edge and they're driving me crazy!"

"OK, tell me the story," said Corrynne getting a little impatient as she took Chris's hand-held display and scanned it for the answers.

Chris tapped Corrynne's knee which made her look up. Chris had a serious stare. "You know, last week if someone needed to be admitted here and there were no beds, we would triage a stable patient to another floor and then admit the person, right?"

Corrynne nodded. "What? Has that changed?"

"Oh, yes, it's changed! We don't have stable patients to triage—but the admissions keep on coming."

"Why aren't we on divert?" asked Corrynne. "We can't handle this amount of patients."

"Administration won't let us. They say we have to take whoever comes and just deal with the demand. I understand the whole valley is like this."

"What? That's crazy!"

"I know. It's dangerous, crazy, and out of control, but that's what we're dealing with here."

Corrynne suddenly felt hot as she anticipated the stresses ahead. "So where do we start? What kind of staff do I have to work with?"

"Well, we've called in everyone we could find. We're having to team care using the staff ICU nurses as the team leads."

"Team nurse? What do you mean?"

"Use teams of registered nurses coupled with licensed practical nurses and medical technicians to handle groups of patients."

"Are you serious?" asked Corrynne, wondering how she was going to handle all of this.

"Very serious. It's the only way to do what we need to do."

Corrynne nodded. "OK."

"Believe me. We've called in every cluster, on-call, and staff nurse from the house to support the teams. Our pickings were sparse, since all the hospitals everywhere are going crazy with a sky-high census, but I think you're staffed enough to get through tonight."

Corrynne shook her head. "I don't know about this."

Chris patted her on the shoulder and said, "I know it sounds hard but you can do it, kiddo."

"Is it too late to call in sick?" asked Corrynne, kidding but feeling like she was getting a little nauseous.

Chris laughed and said, "Way too late."

Corrynne studied the patient list and asked, "Have all the extra staff been oriented to what's expected?"

Chris shook her head. "No. We're just having them go to their assigned rooms, and the staff going off shift is teaching them. Giving them the crash course of their lives."

Corrynne covered her face and said, "I am *not* excited for tonight."

"Chin up! All the hard work has been done for you! We've been scampering all day so you would have these resources for your shift."

Corrynne nodded. "I know. I'm sorry for my pessimism, but I'm feeling uncomfortable about this situation. I'm sure it will be better once I get out there and see what's been done and who needs help."

"It will. Do your best," said Chris.

Corrynne chewed the inside of her cheek and then asked, "How are we monitoring all these people? There's only one monitor per room."

"We have the mobile monitors used for transfers from all over the hospital in the rooms," Chris said matter-of-factly. "Still, there are some rooms missing one. In those cases we're switching from patient to patient and spot-checking heart rate and rhythms and blood pressure. That means the vital signs are not being downloaded automatically into the computers. We have the digital displays switched to voice recording to take care of patient records. Charting will be done by voice command, because there isn't enough time to do anything else."

"OK, this is a nightmare."

"No. We'll get through this," assured Chris.

"Easy for you to say, you're going home," said Corrynne smiling nervously.

"I've done my job, now it's your turn."

Swallowing, Corrynne said, "I don't know how you did it, but thanks for all the work that you've done."

"No problem. Now, let's go over the patients."

Corrynne refocused her mind. She needed to understand what kind of patients were on the floor and where she would be needed. "OK, I'm ready."

"I've tried to keep the patients clustered by diagnosis, at the same time matching heavy loads with lighter ones, but to be honest, if they're here, they're sick. Sick puppies, all of them...."

"What diagnosis are we talking about?"

"Neuro patients and traumas in the west end and cardiac patients in the east end..."

"We're taking traumas?" asked Corrynne, shocked. "Why aren't they going to the trauma center?"

"No room at the inn."

"We can't take those patients. We don't have the specialists."

"We have to, honey," said Chris with a nod. "There's no one else who can."

"No one?"

"Nope. The canyons are sending out more motor-vehicle accidents than ever. I don't know what the deal is, but every weekend we have teenagers come in with massive head trauma. We've filled up from this last weekend. We have to get them out before next weekend."

"Now, that's a bad commentary. You make it sound like these kids are inventory."

"Aren't they?"

"No, they're people," said Corrynne.

"Well, if they act like a potato head, they are a potato head and after a car accident they become a true potato head."

Corrynne nodded. "I guess that's true."

"And we have to deal with them. We have to try and save them, for what? To go back and do it again?" asked Chris.

Corrynne nodded "I know."

"I get tired of it."

"Well, I know why that's happening," said Corrynne.

"Why?" asked Chris.

"There are Raves being held in the mountains."

"Well, I don't know anything about Raves, but you would think people would get a clue that drinking and curvy, dark, mountain roads don't mix."

"That's sad," said Corrynne, feeling her emotions beginning to churn.

"It's more than sad. It's tragic," said Chris. "It's a tragic waste of a human life."

"OK," said Corrynne, changing the subject. "Now tell me about my cardiac beds. Do we really have enough cardiac patients to take up the whole east end?"

"Are you kidding?" asked Chris. "Heart attacks are dropping from the sky! And I don't mean chest pain. I mean everyone is diaphoretic, with huge ST changes on their EKGs and cardiac damage." Chris rubbed her forehead with the back of her hand, and then flicked some stray hair out of her eyes. "Yes, honey, we've got cardiac patients."

Corrynne nodded. "OK. What else?"

Chris poked at her digital display with a miniature stylus to scroll down as she spoke. "Then you have your end-of-stage sepsis from all the bugs we can't treat on the south side. I don't know why they keep sending them here. There's really nothing we can do for them either, but prolong their suffering with vasoactive drugs.

"Oh, and get this," said Chris as she poked Corrynne in the shoulder.

"What?"

"We're telling all the surgeons we can't handle their elective procedures, including heart surgeries!"

"Really?" asked Corrynne with wide eyes.

"Dr. Waldemount, the cardiac surgeon, has been ranting and raving all day about how her patients will die if they don't get bypasses. I guess she went all the way to the top of the corporate ladder, but they told her to manage them medically until after this rush."

"I bet she liked that. What about the other surgeons?"

"They didn't have a choice either. There are no beds. I mean none, zilcho, nada." Chris formed a zero with her hand, a frantic, wide-eyed look on her face.

"So what's going to happen?" asked Corrynne with a worried look. "How can we control this? How long can this go on?"

Chris shook her head and looked down at her display. With a sigh she said, "I think we need to come up with a system to rank patients the way they did in the war, a kind of hierarchy for care. We need to identify those who have real, immediate emergencies who have a potential to be saved. We just can't help everyone anymore."

Corrynne nodded. "I see what you mean. We can do only so much. We need to stay productive and manage the inflow, as well as the outflow."

"Oh, I forgot to tell you…"

Corrynne didn't like the sound of that statement. "What?"

"There are children being admitted here."

Corrynne shook her head. "We're not supposed to take care of children in the adult ICU."

"I know, but the Primary Children's Medical Center's overflowing, and our pediatric unit cannot take care of unstable children on vasoactive drips. So guess who's elected."

"Does the administration know about this?"

"Yes, they're the ones who told us to accept them."

Corrynne threw her head back and hit her leg. "I can't believe this! How do they expect us to care for all these patients safely?"

"I don't know, but some of these juvenile cases are going to just break your heart. One little girl is deathly ill with Methicillin-resistant *Staph aureus* in her blood. I don't know if she'll make it through the night. Her mother's beside herself."

Corrynne looked down at the floor and shook her head. She didn't have any more words that could describe how she was feeling.

"So is that it?" Corrynne asked Chris after a pause of silence.

"It'll have to be," said Chris who stood up. "You'll find the details and anything else you're wondering about on the report screen. I'll wish you luck."

"Thanks," said Corrynne half-heartedly. "Can I call you if I need help?"

"No. I'm accidentally losing my phone on the way home," said Chris as she pulled on a sweater with a smirk.

"Ha, ha, that's funny," said Corrynne. "I know where you live. I could come get you."

"I'll call the police and report you as an invader."

Corrynne hung her head. "OK. I won't bug you. Have a good night."

"I'll try," said Chris as she headed for the door. "You too."

Corrynne nodded as Chris left the room.

Inquiry

Corrynne cruised the hall, making her first sweep. Surprisingly, at the moment, in all the areas of the ICU everything seemed to be under control. She was grateful and took the opportunity to get her bearings.

Next, Corrynne reviewed her medical digital display repeatedly to assess the nursing coverage and where there might be deficiencies. The west unit would need extra support for how many patients they were handling. She would go there next.

Exhaling slowly, Corrynne headed down the west hall. At the nurses' station she scanned the oversized plasma screens listing the initials of the patients and the associated nursing teams. A renewed pang of worry hit her stomach as she looked over the list. She didn't recognize most of the names of the medical staff working with her tonight. That was a problem. Untried nurses in ICU always spelled trouble. ICU was too complicated, emotion-charged, and unpredictable for just any nurse to walk in off the street and work. She knew that mistakes were easy to make in unfamiliar surroundings. She would need to be extra alert tonight to head off any disasters.

Corrynne closed her eyes for a moment and said a silent prayer. She would need heavenly help. There was no way she could be in every room in every moment to assure proper care was being given. She prayed that her regular ICU nursing staff would be alert and prioritize adequately. She prayed for the safety of the patients. She prayed for the ability to let go of the anxiety inside her that threatened her thinking abilities and to deal with problems appropriately. Finally, she prayed for trust. She needed to know which nurses to trust and which ones needed extra support. That was the key to success this night.

Holding those thoughts in her mind, Corrynne opened her eyes and turned sharply to her left. As she walked, her thoughts cleared and immediately she knew what she needed to do. She would go from room to room and assess each team personally. If she could understand each group of nurses and their patients' situations, she would be given the insight she needed for her prayers to be answered.

Corrynne started with room W225. It housed two patients. She studied the master list of patients logged in on her medical digital display. The first patient had cranial surgery. It was a woman of thirty-five years. She had had a brain tumor removed.

Corrynne stepped forward to peek into the room for a better view of the second patient, a man of fifty-six years who had been involved in a motor-vehicle accident. His car had crashed into an embankment during the ice storm the day before, and he had multiple facial and cranial fractures. He was in a coma from brain swelling. His car's air bags failed to deploy.

Corrynne continued to study the patient from the doorway. She assumed he had broken ribs by the presence of chest tubes that snaked from under his gown, even though her display didn't mention any. She knew that in car accidents, broken ribs could puncture the lungs, collapsing one or both of them. The treatment was to insert chest tubes hooked to a suction container. The suction would reestablish the negative pressure on the outside of the lung, reinflating them. She studied the patient's monitor. Luckily, he seemed physiologically stable at the moment.

Entering the room, the nursing team looked up at Corrynne from their various tasks.

"How are you guys doing in here?" she asked.

Her ICU staff nurse, Carillon, responded, "Things are good in here. Both of these patients are pretty stable. We're watching for bleeding and more brain swelling for Mr. Thorpe, but I think we'll be fine."

"Good," said Corrynne nodding. "How about your other two in the next room?" she said with a thumb over her shoulder.

Carillon nodded. "I have a question concerning them."

"Then let's go see," said Corrynne. She and Carillon went into the next room together.

The first patient in room W224 was a twenty-four year old man. His face looked like an eggplant topped with beige bandages. He had a history of drug abuse and had been found unconscious in his living room by a neighbor.

Corrynne made a twisted face. "Why do people have to bash each other around like this? What good does it do?"

Carillon shook her head. "We should make the guy that beat this person up take care of him. That's my vote."

Corrynne cocked her head as she smiled and tapped her chin. "You know, that's a great idea."

"I was kidding," said Carillon as she turned to check her alarms on her monitor.

"I'm not," said Corrynne. "It would be an interesting human experiment to require violent offenders serve those they harm, don't you think?"

"Interesting would be the key word," said Carillon.

"I bet if criminals could look at the human damage they caused day after day their lives might change. 'You break people, you fix them,' could be the new motto."

Carillon laughed, "Yeah, right."

"I've had a theory about these things for a while," said Corrynne as she pulled on the sheet that covered the young man, straightening a stray wrinkle.

"What's that?"

"I think if society would stop hiding their sick, wounded, and dying, mankind might have a real chance at being a kinder and gentler people."

"Hide them?" asked Carillon with a look of interest.

"Yes, think about it. When someone is hurt, like this man, we whisk him away and hide him in a hospital, so he magically gets better or quietly passes away. Isn't that convenient?"

"What are you getting at?"

"There aren't any consequences. There should be consequences. Society needs to recognize the human price that's being paid in here. Society is disconnected and I think it's jading our perception of reality."

"There's a cost; a *huge* cost. Have you seen the ICU bill lately?" asked Carillon.

Corrynne shook her head. "No, that's not enough. There's no connection between cause and effect. As it is today, healthcare is like a video game; for example, this man, he'll receive another chance to live life given to him by the medical profession. Because of a concussion and being in a coma, he won't remember this time. The men who did this to him won't see the work we have to do to help heal him because he's in here, thus when he's returned to his previous health, both he and those that assaulted him are free to continue their destructive ways without really comprehending the price paid by others because of their choices."

Carillon nodded slowly. "Now I understand what you're getting at."

"By fixing this guy," continued Corrynne, "we're not only supporting his lifestyle, enabling him to return to it but also, by fixing this guy, the cold-hearted animals who did this to him won't be charged with murder."

"Hmmm," said Carillon with a thoughtful look. "I never thought of our work that way, but you're right. It's like we're diverting fate. We're interfering with the natural outcome so the full penalty can't be applied for the crime and the proper lesson can't be learned by the victim."

"Exactly. So how is that right? How are we ethically expected to do something so socially irresponsible as to remove consequences of such terrible actions?" asked Corrynne.

Carillon looked at the patient and then said, "Because this man's a human being and we have an obligation to save him?"

"Right. So, we're caught in the middle," said Corrynne. "We're expected to do our job even if it isn't necessarily the right thing for society."

"I guess you could say that."

"So, I have a thought."

"What?"

"What if we made these patients more accessible to the public? Put a little more accountability back into the social system?"

"How?"

"We can't have the perpetrators care for the patients they create, and we can't pick and choose who we save, but we can expose their actions and the consequences to society."

"Isn't that what the news is for?"

Corrynne shook her head. "No. The news is still too displaced."

"What then?"

"What do you think about giving elementary school children the opportunity to come to the hospital and see these patients?"

Carillon shook her head. "No way!"

"Sure, I think something like that could change the course of many irresponsible choices in many little people."

Carillon shook her head again and said, "Oh, I don't think so. It'd be too hard for children."

Corrynne shrugged. "I don't think so. If you think about it, children are the only ones left our society who are impressionable. Everyone else is too hardhearted.[1] That's how this kind of violence happens." Corrynne gestured to the devastatingly beat-up man. "I bet children would remember something like that for the rest of their lives, don't you think?"

"Maybe." Carillon shrugged. "But would you let your kids see this stuff?"

Corrynne nodded. "Absolutely! I think the shock of the experience would be great for them. Then they would know that mom was telling the truth about life and long term consequences of momentary choices. Don't you have something that happened when you were a child that affected you when you grew up?"

"Yes, once I stole a pack of gum in front of a policeman when I was seven."

"Really? What happened?"

"He put his handcuffs on me and threatened to take me to jail. It scared me to death."

Corrynne laughed at the thought of a little seven-year-old girl with huge handcuffs on. "Have you stolen anything since?"

"No, are you kidding? I don't think I could if I tried. I'm still traumatized."

"Exactly my point. I think injury by crimes should be a matter of public record, and everyone should be able to stop by and see the effects in person."

"Well good luck on that one. I think you're fighting a lost cause. Confidentiality is the law right now."[2]

Corrynne nodded and frowned. "I know and I don't think it's going away anytime soon. So I guess society.'s values will continue to spiral and we'll have no choice but to continue as the clean-up crew."

"Guess so."

Both nurses were quiet for a few moments as they considered the human cost of violence and destruction that they were privy to.

Looking at her watch, Corrynne's mind returned to her tasks at hand. She walked around the bed and peered at the victim's monitor up close. "How is this patient doing anyway?"

"He's not doing very well," Carillon returned. "His pupils are not responding to light. They are completely dilated, and he has no responses even to deep pain."

"None?" Corrynne asked.

"No. I guess earlier he would move, but we haven't seen it on our shift."

Corrynne frowned and went over to the intercranial pressure monitor and read it. The monitor read thirty-one, far beyond normal measurements healthy for a human brain. "Is the surgeon aware of this pressure and his unresponsiveness?"

"Yes, he was just in. He doesn't think this man is going to make it."

"Hmmm," said Corrynne. "I guess the consequences will be felt in this situation after all."

"Maybe."

"Has the family been notified?"

"We couldn't locate his family. His neighbors were just here. They said he had lots of company, but none looked like the family type."

Corrynne studied his arms. They were covered with small marks, telling of a history of intravenous drug use. "Has this patient been tested for HIV and hepatitis?"

"Yes, and he is positive for both."

"Well, just double glove, my friend."

"I know. We are. But we have a question about when he dies."

"Yes?"

"Since his injury was the result of a crime, what do we do? Isn't there a different protocol for crimes?"

"Yes, you do not remove any IV lines or anything. Just call the coroner's office, and they'll come and pick him up as he is. Be sure to write on the death form the drips you were using and the lines you had placed. They need to know the difference between what we did and what was done at the scene of the crime."

"OK, will do."

"Good, now what about this other patient?"

On the next bed lay a large gentleman of sixty-eight who had a history of smoking, diabetes, renal insufficiency, and anxiety disorder. He was having difficulty recovering from a bypass heart surgery, the second one in ten years. It was way past time for him to be weaned off the ventilator, but because of his chronic obstructive pulmonary disease caused by smoking, his lungs were just not resilient enough for him to breathe on his own. The family had been very worried.

"How's the family of this patient doing?"

"They're doing better today. At least they're not in here every moment. They're beginning to trust us, I think."

"I'm glad."

"But this patient has developed an arrhythmia. I want you to look at it. What do you think?"

Corrynne looked at a recording strip of the electrical conduction of the heart from the monitor. It definitely was not normal. This kind of rhythm always reminded her of a lacy border around a dress. It was quite beautiful in its repeating pattern.

"This is atrial flutter. The atrium is contracting three times faster than the ventricle. Call the doctor. She would want to know about this change."

"OK."

"Any other problems?"

"No, I don't think so."

"Are you comfortable with your team?"

"Yes, my group is great. I think we'll be fine."

"Good. Sorry about going off on society and ethical dilemmas," said Corrynne with a smile.

"No problem," said Carillon. "It was fun. It made me think."

"Good. Talk to you later."

"OK."

Corrynne left the room just as her beeper went off at her waist. The sound caused a shock wave to go through her. A voice came over the small box: "Corrynne, come to room E208, stat!" Fresh adrenaline hit her system as she automatically began to run.

On her way to the Cardiac Care Unit, she took mental note as she passed by the multiple bursting ICU rooms. Everything still seemed under control. Maybe team nursing wasn't such a bad idea.

Corrynne found herself looking into the various rooms as she passed by, as if to look for further evidence of her unit's stability. But unfamiliar faces looking back at her caused her uneasy feelings to return. As she ran, it didn't get better. Strange eyes turned to look at her as she passed. Vacant, unemotional eyes acting as a shield to hide the erratic feelings always present under stress. The air was electrified with heightened emotion.

As she ran, Corrynne noted something else. Were nurses pointing and whispering to each other? She looked again to see if she was right. Yes, she did see some focusing on her and whispering. Were they whispering about her? How could that be right? She felt very strange and self-conscious. Insecurity welled up inside of her, which was irritating. What right did these nurses have to come to her unit and then be so insubordinate and rude? She had an impulse to stop and confront the visiting nurses right then but she knew that wasn't a choice right now. Any discussion would have to wait.

Corrynne turned away her gaze. But, at the last second before she averted her eyes, she noted someone familiar. ...She didn't even see the face, but somehow she knew the person working slowly.... It was a girl. Where did she recognize her from? She racked her brain for an answer, but it escaped her. Whoever it was, she felt it was important to find out. But again, at the moment she couldn't stop to investigate; she had to keep going.

Corrynne finally rounded the corner of the east unit. As if in slow motion she looked up at the monitor. The patient, who was an older man, had a blood pressure that was too low. She also noticed his heart rate was slowing and he had tombstone-shaped T-waves on the EKG. Her stomach dropped. Death was near. She pushed the button on her emergency pager—it was directly linked to the cardiologist on call—and began furiously working with the staff to hang potentially life-saving medicines, Nitro, Neo, and fluids.

Minutes passed that seemed like hours as they frantically adjusted the concentration of the drips but there was no response. A quick response would not save this patient this time. The heart rhythm changed to fibrillation and the nurses performed the first principles of life saving. CPR was always tried as a last hope to prolong life, but death quickly claimed its victory. The cardiologist appeared only to call the code.

Corrynne suddenly felt cold. There was something about losing a patient that clawed at her soul. It ate a piece of her every time it happened. She began to disconnect the patient from the lines when she realized the man who had just died was the same man she had saved outside the ER the day before.... It wasn't fair....

She stared at the man and brooded like a wounded child. It was the first death of the night. Would she have to endure more? Suddenly Corrynne had a deep, sharp pain that originated in the poignant desire for this night to be over.

Painful Epiphany

It was 1:00 in the morning, and Corrynne was ragged. The night had been filled with problem solving, answering questions, and calling doctors. With the later hour, however, it seemed like things were slowing down.

Corrynne reflected on the night. Despite the tenuous environment, her teams had surprised her with their capacity. Corrynne had to admit she was very pleased. They had done well.

Now, it was time for a break. She decided to take it in the nursing core on the new recliner next to the blood-titer machine where she could be alone for a few minutes.

Corrynne walked into the room, dragging her feet. She stared longingly at the inviting chair. Her body was yearning to rest. Automatically, her eyes were drawn to the stainless-steel machine and a sign that read,

"Donate the gift of life."

Corrynne couldn't help but draw a sarcastic smile. The statement struck her as funny. She wondered how giving blood could be *donating* if you were receiving money? She shrugged as she took a seat in the gorgeous, soft leather recliner. She decided the statement was just a marketing ploy. It didn't matter to her. She'd sit in the chair despite the corny phrase.

The recliner fit Corrynne's tired body like a glove. Every curve of her back was filled with luxurious support. She laid the chair back and turned on the heated massage. The chair came alive. As she settled her head back, she could feel the tension draining away. It was glorious. She yearned to stay in the chair for the rest of the early morning, but she knew it would not be her lot. She would eventually have to leave again to face the ravaged world; yet for now, she settled deeper into the warmed vibrations. She would at least take her break here. She deserved that much.

As she relaxed in the chair, Corrynne resolved to go ahead and give her plasma. It would justify her semi-comatose state. She sat up slightly to pull down the arm adjacent to the machine that was meant to draw the blood. She deliberately snapped her left arm in, and then she put her thumb to the identification pad. The machine welcomed her by name and scanned her arm. A light came on highlighting the ideal veins for puncture according to proximity and diameter. She followed the simple mechanized directions spoken in soft silky tones and successfully hooked herself up.

Automatically, the stainless-steel machine came to life like a huge mosquito, humming quietly as it drew the blood out of her arm. She watched the red, thick liquid fill the transparent tubing and disappear into the guts of the machine. After ensuring it was functioning appropriately, Corrynne laid her head back into the chair once again. Now she was completely justified in her inactivity.

Corrynne closed her eyes, but then opened one again. She remembered she had seen a blanket warmer underneath this machine. Blindly, she felt around with her right arm under the chair where she pictured the door of the warmer. Finding the door handle she pulled open the door, reached in, and pulled out a soft, perfectly warmed blanket. With a shake the blanket opened up and she tucked it around her. Warmth enveloped her. The feeling of relaxation was delicious to a sore, tired body. Despite her intentions of resting only for her break, soon Corrynne was fast asleep.

ξξξξξξξ

"So, I see you like my chair," came a loud, intruding voice. The shock of it broke the mesmerizing hum of the machine.

Corrynne's senses went on alert as she jumped. A sharp sting at the site of the puncture in her arm reminded her not to move. She felt like a hostage as she was forced to stay put. An overwhelming feeling of claustrophobia filled her as her heart beat in her throat.

Looking up, Corrynne saw the satisfied, smiling face of Dr. Page. She gathered her wits about her and managed to say calmly, "Oh, hi, doctor. I'm afraid you caught me in a moment of weakness." A false smile crossed her face.

"No, it's perfect. I love to see someone relaxing in my chair. I was depending on you to donate to my cause."

"Donate? I'm expecting hard cash for my work here. Sleeping is hard work!" Corrynne teased, her heartbeat starting to return to normal.

"Well, 'donate' is only a term we're all familiar with when it comes to blood. You know, it's synonymous with the thought of allowing someone to poke holes in you and drain your life's essence because it's worth it."

"Ah, yes, I see."

"It wouldn't be good to say, 'Give us your blood so we can make a bloody fortune.'" Dr. Page laughed loudly.

His laugh grated on Corrynne's already oversensitive nerves. There was something about his demeanor that made her feel she had been suckered.

"No, I'm just kidding. Sit there as long as you want. I thank you, my children thank you, my dog thanks you...." Dr. Page was still smiling as he walked over and looked at the glowing digital display.

His statement took Corrynne back. She thought for a second. "Do you have children?"

The doctor laughed and turned around. "Heck, no! I live too fast and hard right now for kids. I was referring to my future children, if there will be any."

"Oh," said Corrynne, as she noticed that he was acting strange.

The doctor reached into his pocket for keys. "Corrynne, you did very well," he said as he opened a side door and reached in to pull out two small one-hundred-milliliter bags of yellow fluid. "You've just spun some gold. This is better than the goose that laid the golden egg!"

"Oh, that's good," said Corrynne, now wishing she could just get out of the chair. The doctor was freaking her out. He was too excited about this whole thing.

"When you're done, just push this button and you'll receive your money,"

"OK," said Corrynne.

"Look," said the doctor as he studied the label that the machine had imprinted on the bag. "You're the universal donor. Your plasma can go to anyone." The doctor smiled even more broadly if it were possible. "We need a lot of this kind of serum. You've really done some good today."

Despite Dr. Page's positive words, Corrynne felt only deep blackness. Something was not right. "I thought no one can use it yet because of the FDA."

"Right," said the doctor, nodding. "You're right, no one can, but we're closer to pushing it through. If we can prove these samples are filtered, virus-free, and safe to use for patient care, it won't be long." With that, Dr. Page kissed both bags.

Corrynne again felt her stomach turn a little. Dr. Page liked this situation just a little too much. He seemed giddy. She had never seen him so happy. It was eerie in a strange sort of way. He reminded her of a mad Frankenstein who had just created a monster.

"Well, I've got to get back to work. Got lives to save," Corrynne said as she unhooked herself from the machine.

"No, that is *my* job. *You*...just follow orders," the doctor said with a sterile voice.

Stunned, Corrynne looked up at Dr. Page to see if he were kidding. He was still smiling. Corrynne decided to return the chide, feeling guilty but satisfied at the opportunity. "Yes, if we could *read* your orders!" Corrynne's voice was jagged; unconsciously, she meant to inflict pain. "The secretaries and I have to translate your orders from a foreign scratching. If you are saving lives, no one knows it because we can't figure out what you are saying."

"Oooo, ouch." Dr. Page made a resigned face. "I better watch you more closely."

Corrynne smiled in defense. "Hey, I'm just kidding." Corrynne realized that her inner feeling of threat had caused her words to come out too harsh. She sought immediate forgiveness. She felt an intense need to smooth things over. "I'm just kidding."

"Kidding, *right*. You nurses are all collusive. I've got to watch my back!" Dr. Page looked at his watch and started for the door.

Seeing Dr. Page leave caused Corrynne to remember she needed antibiotics for her family. She wondered if he would give it to her, since he knew she had been working with Dr. Quaid the day before he died.

"Ah, Dr. Page?"

"*Yeeesss?*" Dr. Page slowly turned back around.

"I have a personal concern."

"It's against my religion to get personal," Dr. Page continued to tease.

"I don't think you have to worry about me in that respect."

"Darn." Dr. Page smiled wickedly.

Corrynne ignored his insinuation. "Seriously, the other night when I went on the code with Dr. Quaid, I was exposed to the Strep A through the man who died. I was wondering if I could have some antibiotics for my family and myself prophylactically in case I have another exposure. The bacterium is so devastating and quick, I would like to protect all of us. You know—just in case."

Dr. Page stiffened. His smile disappeared. With a serious voice he said, "Antibiotics won't help you now. If you had contracted the Strep, you would be dead by now."

Corrynne nodded. "I know. I am talking about future exposures. I'm sure it's going to get worse, and it's logical to protect myself and my family since I'm in a position of risk."

"Well, even if you did have antibiotics, you wouldn't know to take them until it was too late."

Corrynne frowned. Her hair on the back of her neck was beginning to stand up, but she maintained a calm demeanor. "Dr. Quaid told me if you take antibiotics right after contamination, the bacteria would be killed before it could necrotize tissue. That would be my goal."

"Yes, but how would you know?"

"Dr. Page, I would know if I had been contaminated. Give me some credit." Corrynne was losing patience.

"No, I don't believe you would. The medical staff is contaminated all the time. Our gloving and gowning are only mental crutches to relieve our own minds. How do you think we all became colonized by resistant bacteria in the first place?"

Corrynne shook her head. "Come on, Dr. Page. Don't you think you're going a bit too far? Barrier protection works. I shouldn't have to prove that to you."

The doctor didn't respond.

Corrynne continued, "So what am I supposed to do? Just pretend I'm safe? ...Quit? ...What?"

The doctor was silent.

Corrynne cocked her head and looked at Dr. Page with a sideward glance. "It seems like you're not saying what you're thinking. What's going on?"

"Corrynne, doctors who give out antibiotics should be shot for murder. It is they who have caused the bacteria to evolve and become resistant. It is they we have to thank for millions of needless deaths all over the world."

"Your perception seems to be a little bit skewed," Corrynne returned vigorously.

"Well, you ICU nurses think all you have to do is sweet talk a doctor and you can get anything you want, and most of the time you're right. In the past, we as a profession have been irresponsible with our privileges and we've given out medications but now it has to stop—and it will stop with me. It's my moral duty to deny your request. We have to start limiting antibiotic use for when it's appropriate and not whenever it's requested."

Corrynne couldn't believe what she was hearing. Dr. Page had become uncharacteristically angry, and about what? Now she was sure there was something else going on. "Fine, I didn't think I was being immoral."

"*That* I wouldn't have minded." Dr. Page suddenly smiled again.

"Not funny and totally inappropriate." Corrynne looked piercingly into Dr. Page's eyes.

Dr. Page held up his hands. "Sorry, thought it was getting rough in here. Just a joke to lighten the mood."

"You don't make sense."

"Well, just keep on donating. It's a worthy cause." Dr. Page changed the subject abruptly to end the conversation and held up the two gold bags as he sauntered out the door of the room.

Corrynne felt dirty and taken advantage of. She pushed a button to unhook the machine from her arm. Finally the cycle was finished. She looked down at the puncture wound in her arm where a small dot of blood was emerging. She turned around to the supply container that was on the table next to the machine and searched for a bandage. Finding one, she slapped it quickly on the hole and then pushed the button to receive her money. Eight crisp one-hundred-dollar bills ejected.

Corrynne stared at the money. "Blood money," she said bitterly, realizing her symbolic statement was literally true. It made her attitude even worse. She grabbed the money with an angry swipe. "I deserve this money for putting up with him," she muttered. Corrynne then crumpled up the bills and shoved them into her pocket.

Searchings

Call it fanatical. Call it obsessed. But as the night wore on, anger began to bubble under the surface of Corrynne's controlled exterior. She couldn't help but go over and over in her mind her exchange with Dr. Page. The resulting conflict with Dr. Page was more than just rejection; it was somehow deep and intrusive. His flippant attitude about everything sacred and his illogical refusal to help her and her family felt like a betrayal. His words had seemed cold and calculating. He meant to intimidate her out of her request. He had wanted her to know he was in charge and had all the power.

"What an egotistical fool!" Corrynne muttered under her breath as she ruminated enough for a couple of lifetimes. She decided to rededicate herself to protecting her family. She knew what she needed to do, and Dr. Page or no Dr. Page, she was going to insure protection!

Corrynne began to work on the issues at hand. It was time to find the young nurse she had coddled and held in the dark, early hours on Saturday. She would focus on antibiotics later.

Corrynne picked up the handset of the house phone and punched the fifth floor. "Hello, I need to talk to the charge nurse," she told the secretary. There was a moment when music played in her ear, and then someone new answered the phone.

"Hello? This is Sherry," came the voice on the other end of the phone.

"Hi, Sherry, this is Corrynne from down in the ICU."

"Oh, hi. What's up? If you're trying to transfer, there are no beds up here."

Corrynne smiled as she mindlessly picked up a pen and started doodling on some paper. "No. Actually I'm calling you for a favor."

"What can I do for you?"

"Well, I was up there on a code early Saturday with Dr. Quaid. Were you working? I can't remember."

There was a pause and then Sherry said, "Ah, yes, I was working."

"Good. I need your help in identifying one of your nurses."

"Which one?"

"The nurse for the patient who died during the code. Do you remember who it was?" asked Corrynne.

"Let me think…. Ah…I believe the nurse was a float pool nurse. She wasn't a part of my staff. She was only filling in because we were short."

"Do you remember her name? I can't believe I didn't ask."

"No, actually, I had never seen her before she showed up for work," said Sherry, "and so I don't remember even what she looked like."

"She was a small, timid type. If you weren't looking for her, you would have missed her. Obviously I did."

"Was there a problem?" asked Sherry.

"No, I just have to ask her some questions. I'll call the float pool office to see if they know who she was."

"OK, sorry I couldn't help."

"It's fine. No problem. Have a good rest of the night," said Corrynne as she drew a large circle with a line through it.

"Thanks, bye."

"Bye." Corrynne hung up the phone and put down her pen. Thinking for a moment, she swung her leg slightly. She wondered if anyone was in the float pool office in the middle of the night. She dialed the number to connect her but a recording answered stating that everyone was out of the office and to call back in the morning.

"That's great," she said to herself sarcastically as she hung up the phone.

Thinking again a thought came to her. Wouldn't the nurse's name be on the code sheet? It would have to be on the sheet. The sheet had a place where it listed all the nurses involved in the code. Yes, thought Corrynne, happy with herself. All she had to do is remember what the patient's name was…. She thought for a moment…. Frustrated, she realized she didn't know the name of the patient, either. She blamed herself for not being attentive to the details.

"Let's be logical about this," she said to herself. "The patient died only two days ago…." Corrynne looked around as if the answer was somewhere close by. "Hmmm. The census records! His name would be on the census records of the fifth floor!" Corrynne adjusted her weight forward as she punched the fifth-floor button again.

"Fifth floor, may I help you?" answered the secretary.

"Yes, this is the ICU charge nurse again. Can you look in your census record for the name of the patient who died in room 527 on Saturday morning around 0300?"

There was silence on the other end of the line. Then the answer came back, "Leif J. Boswell."

"Perfect! Thank you!" exclaimed Corrynne as she hung up and called the records department.

"Records," answered a nasal voice.

"Hello! I need to check a record in the file under the name Leif J. Boswell. I'm the charge nurse who ran a code for Mr. Boswell, and I need to review the code sheet. All I'm looking for are the people who have signed the sheet. I need to double check that it's complete."

There was a hesitation and then the woman said, "Boswell...Boswell. Do you have a hospital number or a birth date?"

Corrynne shook her head slightly. "No, but I do know the patient was admitted on September 15th and died on the 16th of this year. Does that help?"

"Ahh, let's see. Ah, yes. I believe I've found his record," spoke the metered voice.

Relief hit Corrynne. "Good. Can you look at the code sheet and read me the signatures?"

"No, dear, I do not do that kind of thing. If you want to look at this record, you'll have to come down here and find what you need."

Corrynne clenched her right hand. What was this lady doing? She was asking such a simple thing! "But I can't right now. I have a floor full of very unstable people here."

"I'm sorry, that is all I can do for you," said the unsympathetic woman.

"Can you send the record up here and I'll return it?"

"No, I can't. Not without a doctor's order."

Corrynne kicked the pole under the desk in frustration. "Fine, I'll be there as soon as I make sure everyone's OK." Corrynne hung up the phone without saying goodbye.

ξξξξξξ

Down in records there wasn't anyone at the desk. Corrynne impatiently rang a bell for service. An older, blue-haired woman, with glasses fitted firmly on the end of her nose, rose slowly from an unseen chair somewhere back in the records room. She had an obvious scowl on her face. "Yes?" she said as she peered pointedly over the top of her glasses.

"I'm the one who called for the record of Leif J. Boswell."

"Swipe your ID, please," said the same cold, nasal voice she had heard on the phone.

Corrynne took the ID badge strung around her neck and swiped it.

CORRYNNE R. ROGERS–CLEARANCE appeared on the adjacent computer with her own pale face smiling back.

The older woman looked back and forth between the computerized image and Corrynne repeatedly. Finally, after being satisfied the ID matched the holder, Corrynne was handed the paper chart.

Quickly Corrynne rifled through the familiar color-coded sheets and finally came to the red-bordered code sheet. With her index finger she looked at all the signatures on the bottom. Dr. Quaid's signature was there in its large characteristic pattern. Corrynne stopped for a moment with her finger on the writing and realized it would probably be the last time she would see his signature. A lump rose in her throat, which she quickly swallowed. She didn't have time to become sentimental. She continued through the signatures to find the patient's nurse's signature…. It wasn't there.

"Dang!" Corrynne said out loud.

"Is there something more I can help you with?" asked the blue-haired woman who, by her look, definitely did *not* want to help.

"No, still looking, but thanks," replied Corrynne.

Corrynne continued to look through the chart for any clue that maybe the nurse had left behind. She found the orders the nurse had noted. Her signature was under each of them.

"There it is!" she said with a child-like delight. But as she tried to decipher the handwriting, it was almost impossible to read accurately. She could make out the first letter of her first and last name, which were an A and a C, but then the endings of both her names were just lines.

"Why do people who work here have such terrible handwriting?" Corrynne unthinkingly asked the blue-haired woman.

The woman just shook her head at Corrynne's frustration. "Comes with the territory, sweetie. Makes it harder to place blame."

The little old lady's comment stopped Corrynne. She guessed it could be true. It was probably psychological from the heavy burdens medical personnel bore. Still, it was amazing that, in an environment where precision was paramount to save lives, the written parts of records were always so cryptic.

Corrynne's mind returned to the task at hand. Again she rifled the record. "There has to be a computerized report in here with her name on it," she whispered. She looked under nursing notes section and, bingo! She was rewarded! Under September 15, "Ann Cain RN" appeared under the comprehensive report. "All right! I found it!" said Corrynne to herself.

"Thank you for your help," she said to the woman politely, even though it really wasn't true.

Corrynne put the chart down on the counter and turned to go. When she was half way out the door, she wondered if she could look at Dr. Quaid's chart.

"Oh, ah, I need another record pulled," she said loudly to the record's keeper as she turned back around. "I need the record of Keith Quaid." Corrynne left off the doctor title so the woman wouldn't become suspicious and deny her request.

"Do you have a date of birth or a hospital number?" asked the woman.

"No, but I know he also died on September 16."

The blue-haired woman went over to another terminal and typed in the name and cross-referenced it with the date of death. After a moment the woman said, "I'm sorry, but there is no Keith Quaid who died in this hospital on September 16th of this year."

Corrynne frowned. "What? How can that be? I'm sure he died here. There'd be nowhere else he'd go. Can you please double check?"

The woman again tried the cross-reference then shook her head. "I'm sorry. We don't have that record."

Bewildered, Corrynne thanked the woman and left the room.

Corrynne decided she'd stop by the emergency room on her way back up to the ICU. She was sure Dr. Quaid's staff would know if he had been brought to the ER the night he died. That kind of thing just didn't go unnoticed.

The emergency room was overflowing. It seemed they had the same story the ICU did: too many patients and not enough staff to treat all of them. One nurse she didn't know was hurrying past her with some lab blood draws. Corrynne quickly took the opportunity to throw a question out to her.

"What happened to Dr. Quaid?" Corrynne asked loudly. "Can you tell me how he died?"

The ER nurse stopped, suddenly frozen in her tracks. She slowly turned to face Corrynne and looked at her and then at her ID. Then she looked around her to see if anyone were looking at her. Quickly she grabbed Corrynne and pulled her around the corner.

With a brisk, urgent demeanor the nurse whispered, "What I'm going to tell you I do out of the goodness of my heart because I don't want to see any more people hurt."

"OK," said Corrynne, feeling the heaviness of her words.

"You can't ever tell anyone that I told you, and you must forget what I look like. I don't normally work here, so it won't be hard for you." The nurse automatically grabbed her own identification tag and hid it.

"Fine," Corrynne agreed, with a concerned look.

"Dr. Quaid died because of his involvement with a dangerous group of people. If you were smart, you'd steer clear of anything that had to do with him or what he was doing. Three other nurses have died the same death, because they asked too many questions, so stop asking questions."

"Are you saying someone is killing them?" asked Corrynne.

"I'm not saying anything other than there are good people who have died needless deaths. Yes, they all died the same way and, yes, I personally think there is a link, but of course there's nothing anyone can prove."

"Did Dr. Quaid come here when he was infected?" asked Corrynne.

The nurse put a finger up to her mouth and looked around. In a low, hushed voice she said, "No. He died in his own bed. His wife and children came home from visiting Grandma to find him already gone."

"Oh no!" said Corrynne as her hand covered her mouth. She could imagine the horror of the family and had to shut up her thoughts to contain her growing emotion. She blinked hard and shook her head. "I am so sorry!

Why didn't he come here when he felt the initial pain? I mean, he knew all the signs. He would have taken antibiotics or something."

"Shhh!" warned the nurse again.

"OK," said Corrynne, whispering even quieter.

"No one knows. Nothing makes sense."

"How do you know all this?" asked Corrynne.

The nurse looked around again and then pursed her lips together obviously.

Corrynne studied the ER nurse for a moment and then nodded. That's all she was going to be told. "OK, thank you. I'll take your advice. I'll stay out of the way."

The ER nurse nodded and patted Corrynne's arm and then hurried away without another word.

Abruptly, Corrynne's pager went off with a piercing scream that made her jump. She covered it with her hand. A voice followed the alarm.

"Corrynne, we need you in room W209, stat."

Corrynne ran to the elevators and used the code blue override to get to her floor.

As the elevator lifted quickly, Corrynne had the sickly feeling telling her that her world was being strangled by unseen hands.

Relief

The call came from the room of the little girl who was on the edge of death due to resistant bacteria in her blood. She knew that there was little she could do and that a doctor would not be present. The nature of the night shift called for Corrynne to put into play protocols set up for the absence of doctors at night. She would call the doctor only if additional orders were needed or if the protocols failed. That knowledge gave Corrynne a foreboding feeling. She was actually afraid for the first time about what she would find in room W209.

Corrynne felt overwhelmed. She didn't want to deal with another tragedy tonight. She was unaccustomed to losing patients. Lately it seemed all her medical knowledge wasn't helping her. She wondered what her real role was in the large scheme of things. Did she really have any control or influence over death or was it all a charade?

As she moved closer to the room a scripture came to mind. She couldn't remember the exact wording but it said that whoever had faith in God's power to heal would be healed as long as they weren't appointed to die.[3] She thought about that scripture as she ran toward the room. Wasn't she showing proper faith in trying to save the sick? She believed that she was; otherwise, she wouldn't try. She knew the hospital's technology was adequate. She knew that her knowledge was real. She knew that her efforts were complete. It should be clear that if the patient died, it was the Lord's will....

Again the scripture began in her head, only in scriptural words this time. ..."he that hath *faith* in me to be *healed*...and is *not* appointed to death...." Suddenly she understood with a new understanding. It freed her immensely! The matter of whether a person lived or died did not depend solely on her efforts, desire, *or* knowledge, something she hadn't considered before. The patient and the Lord were involved in the transaction, too. The patient's survival from the ravages of disease and accident depended on medical science to a certain degree, but it was also directly related to the patient's faith, combined with the Lord's will for that person. It was when science, faith and heavenly will came into alignment that the patient recovered. Suddenly she understood why some patients who seemed like they should live died, and those who seemed like they had no hope of living recovered.

Feeling strengthened and relieved, Corrynne put away her insecurities. Approaching W209 and empowered with knowledge, she headed into the room wanting to help, but knowing she was limited by the other forces at work. She quietly gave the situation into the Lord's hands.

"If it be thy will," Corrynne prayed, "let me help. Show me what to do...."

As Corrynne came into the room, the young girl's mother cried in desperation. "Please, do something for my daughter! I don't want to lose her. She's all I have left in this world."

Corrynne quickly assessed the situation as she gloved and gowned. As her eyes lay on the small form, she saw that the little girl was in the middle of a grand mal seizure. She checked the monitor for a temperature. It was 106 degrees Fahrenheit. Corrynne knew the seizure could be induced by a high temperature. "Get me some Ativan. I need 5 milligrams." Corrynne quietly told a tech who had been watching from outside the room.

The girl disappeared down the hall to find the drug for Corrynne.

"What's been done?" Corrynne asked her staff nurse.

The ICU nurse quickly responded. "We have given acetaminophen around the clock. She has a cooling blanket underneath her and ice bags around her."

"Do you have any ibuprofen?"

"No."

"Send someone to get some from stock." The ICU nurse turned and motioned to her patient care technician, and he immediately responded.

The Ativan arrived, and Corrynne gave a trial dose intravenously. Immediately the seizure lessened in intensity. She gave another small dose. Then she looked at the maintenance IV. It was dripping way too slowly for a temperature that high. The little girl needed to be rehydrated. Corrynne turned up the rate.

"Check her blood sugar. She's using everything she has to fight this infection, and the fever is using up all her energy."

"Blood sugar is fifty. We just checked," answered the nurse.

"I need some D50. Someone get me an ampule."

The tech disappeared again for the errand. The ibuprofen arrived, and Corrynne ordered ten milliliters to be administered through the small bowel feeding tube that provided nourishment to the unconscious girl. The nurse who had retrieved it measured it out and administered it down the tube.

The D50 was handed to Corrynne, and she promptly gave half of it in the IV. Soon the tremoring little girl began to relax.

"I need some water in a basin with alcohol," Corrynne continued to order. "Fever is good to kill the bacteria, but too high will cause brain damage. We have to get this fever down into safe levels." In moments the alcohol mixture was there on a bedside table, and Corrynne was removing the gown of the little girl and covering her midsection with a folded sheet. Then she proceeded to take washcloths full of alcohol and water and wet her skin all over her body. Immediately her temperature began to drop from 106 F to 104 F.

The mother watched silently until she saw the temperature drop and the seizure stop. Suddenly she broke down into uncontrollable sobs.

Corrynne got up from her place and went over to the mother. She put her hand gently on her gowned shoulder. "This is your job," she said as she handed the crying woman the washcloth. "This is something you can do that will help us care for your daughter."

"Oh, thank you. Thank you," the mother muttered through her tears. "I'll do anything, anything you want."

"It's not that we want it. It is your rightful place. We don't want to displace you in this hour," Corrynne said gently.

The woman looked up at her though her tears and stopped crying. Then she took the cloth and began to lovingly wet her daughter's skin.

Corrynne watched for a moment. It was important that the mother have these moments to love her daughter. It was good for both of them.

Corrynne then turned to the team and whispered to them so as not to interrupt the new quiet that blanketed the room. "Be sure she doesn't begin to shiver. If she does, then stop the alcohol bath and cover her. When she stops shivering, start again, but take it slower. Only bring her down to about 102. Don't push further. Fever may be the only thing that can save her life. The ibuprofen will help make the fever not so intense, but it will take about twenty to forty minutes to kick in."

Corrynne continued, "Watch to see if it brings the fever down. If it does, eliminate the baths; otherwise, keep them going. Give the ibuprofen to her consistently as well as the acetaminophen. I'll call the doc and get seizure orders."

"All right," said the ICU nurse in charge of the little girl's care. The others nodded their agreement.

"Corrynne?" asked the ICU nurse, whose name was Sandy.

"Yes?"

"Why are you doubling up on the antipyretics? Does it really help?"

"Yes, the acetaminophen works on the prostaglandins in the bloodstream, while the ibuprofen stops the production. You often see it used in this way in the ER. It's quite effective on stubborn fevers."

"Wow, I didn't know..." said Sandy thoughtfully.

"I'll get the orders for you," said Corrynne with a smile.

"Thanks."

Corrynne walked out into the nurse's station and paged the doctor. "Finally!" she said to herself. "Finally I made a difference. It felt good...*very, very good....*" Corrynne smiled. She knew she had been helped and silently she whispered a thank you to a Heavenly Father that listens.

Notes to "Strange Whisperings"

Inquiry

[1] "And the mists of darkness are the temptations of the devil, which blindeth the eyes, and hardeneth the hearts of the children of men, and leadeth them away into broad roads, that they perish and are lost" (1 Nephi 12:17).

[2] Confidentiality is of the highest priority in the current hospital environment.

Relief

[3] "...And again, it shall come to pass that he that hath faith in me to be healed, and is not appointed unto death, shall be healed" (D&C 42:48).

CHAPTER ELEVEN

BURDENS OF THE FUTURE

"And it shall come to pass afterward, that I will pour out my spirit upon all flesh; and your sons and your daughters shall prophesy, your old men shall dream dreams, your young men shall see visions" (Joel 2:28).

Wednesday
September 20th
7:30 a.m.
Provo, Utah

Black and Blue

There was blue all around, an azure blue that filled the expanse of forever. Braun searched above, to the sides, and below him to find something, anything in the deep environment to figure out where he was as he floated. Despite his efforts, there was nothing else. The blue went on infinitely like a deep, deep ocean of pure blue.

Without reason, the source of the soft, surrounding light faltered and the temperature of the air around Braun dropped. Indescribable cold filtered through him like the creep of a winter fog. It seeped clear down to his bones.

Braun shivered, clenching his jaw. With a great effort, he attempted to pull his arms into his torso to warm himself, but he found all his limbs were extremely heavy and almost impossible to move. An immense force pulled on him until it had claim on every cell of his body, terrifying him.

The clear blue hue that enveloped Braun moments before began to change. He was falling. A gravitational field was claiming his body. The blue was deepening by shades the deeper he fell, until there was only unrelenting blackness. Surprisingly, it wasn't the falling feeling, the heaviness, nor the cold that tortured him the most; it was the darkness. For some reason, it began to claw at his soul as if it were a circling ravenous beast ready to consume him! He waited with all the endurance he could muster, hoping something would yield, but he received no relief. The darkness continued to drain him, demanding all of his life's energy. He began to hunger for light, as if he needed it for sustenance. Never in his life did he want...no, need...anything more. The absence of it was excruciating. It was as if his very essence, his spirit, was being extinguished.

Braun could not stand the void any longer. In an attempt to find help, he summoned his last ounces of energy to separate his jaws and yell through the small space between his teeth. He felt his lungs fill painfully and then contract and his throat vibrate, but even sound was swallowed by the gravity that clutched him. Braun fell deeper into what seemed to be a black hole. His focus became frantic as he mentally searched for heavenly intervention. He pleaded with Heavenly Father for help as tears flowed freely from his eyes. *What was happening to him?*

Suddenly, as quick as it had begun, Braun's body was released from the relentless gravitational force and the control of his limbs was returned to him. He felt light, buoyant, and warm as he floated once again in a weightless space.

A voice spoke to Braun from within the darkness. The words were not identifiable, but the sound of it was fluid and glorious. It filled him up, causing the black to recede. A light appeared that emanated from his own body. It flowed from his chest and filled the space around him. The light was beautiful and sweet, delicious to his starving soul. It made him happy again. The light continued to grow brighter. It restored Braun as he sensed every fiber of his physical body being regenerated into...greatness...if it were possible.

Braun was disoriented. What did all of this mean? Why would the Lord have him experience excruciating darkness, void of warmth, life, and light, and then such brilliant brightness that sprang from within him? Again he turned his attention heavenward. "Why..." was the word that came from his lips but before he could form the next word, he heard the answer. A voice had been speaking to Braun already, but he hadn't understood its message. How long had it been going on? Then in a moment he knew. The message had been repeating forever. It was an eternal message, yet there was more. He needed to understand. With his desire to understand came the keys to a widening perception.

The voice was speaking in a rhythm, almost a chant. It was a soft, clear voice and it spoke not only to Braun's ears, but to his future. Its message was important to him and the Lord's expectations of him. He was meant to understand so he listened carefully.

The voice said, "The darkness is Abaddon[1]...the chains of Apollyon[2]...who has keys to that bottomless pit[3]...from whence there is no light.[4] ...The spirits of the wicked...yea, who are evil...shall be cast out...into outer darkness. ...There shall be weeping, and wailing, and gnashing of teeth.[5] ...And they that dwell on the earth shall wonder...whose names were not written...in the book of life...from the foundation of the world...."[6]

Braun closed his eyes to concentrate. Even though he was hearing the words, what did they mean?

The voice continued, repeating the message as before. "The darkness is Abaddon...the chains of Apollyon...who has keys to that bottomless pit...from whence there is no light...."

What's the meaning of Abaddon? What's the meaning of Apollyon? Braun struggled to remember but he found he was still having difficulty thinking and understanding. Weren't those words, words from another language? He thought they might be Greek or Hebrew, but he couldn't be sure....

As the voice continued to repeat the message, another voice joined the first, just as soft, calm and clear as the first. It said, "Behold...I am the law...and the light. ...Look unto me...endure to the end...and ye shall live...."[7]

The words of the second voice repeated its message as did the first. Both messages, combined with his experience of the frozen, deadly darkness filled his mind. The patterns of the words and his thoughts began to wind in his mind, creating an emerging overall perception...light, dark, creation, destruction, freedom, restriction, law, chaos, life, death...then suddenly—it all stopped!

The effect left Braun breathless. The silence was dramatic. Braun looked around. Was there more? Were the messages and the voices still chanting but he just unable to hear?

After a few moments of nothing, he inquired audibly into the blue expanse, "Is there more?"

Braun waited.

There wasn't an answer.

"What do you want me to do?" Braun asked aloud again. "I am thy servant. I wish only to serve thee!"

Communication then came clearly in his mind, although there was no voice this time, "Yes...I have saved thee because thou hast sought me and thou art a worthy servant. ...Thou art almost ready...."

Braun wondered what was meant by that statement. "For what? What can I do?"

The communication began again, "I have saved others for this purpose...."

Braun waited for the rest of the message, but it never came. Still, he would wait. There had to be more.

After a time that seemed like years, Braun sensed a huge black, solid object above his head. The largeness of it he could not understand. A new darkness came upon him, but it was different from the complete darkness he had experienced before. It seemed more like a shadow.

Braun's eyes searched for the object's dimensions, but he couldn't see the edges because of its enormity. Soon he felt the object encroaching on his space and thrusting its inertia downward. The form of the object pressed heavily against his body, forcing him to come into alignment with it. It thrust Braun's frame down with the great force created from moving through space quickly. He found once again his movement was restrained, but fear did not overtake him.

Again Braun turned his communication towards heaven. "Is this big object symbolic or literal? What should I learn from it?"

The answer came quietly but powerfully. "Literal. In time you will understand."

Braun awoke with a start. His body bounced slightly in the bed. His heart was beating hard in his chest and he felt out of breath as if he had been running. He jumped out of bed, and in a moment he was at the sink. He turned the cold water on full blast.

Throwing water on his face Braun then looked squarely into the mirror into his own dark brown eyes, water dripping down white skin, and open mouth. He noticed his eyes. They were frantic and wide. His square jaw and his tousled brown hair looked foreign to him. He watched the water drip off his nose and chin. With every drip his mind remembered his dream. It had been a true dream; one that meant something. One that he was meant to remember.

Ever since he was fourteen, he had had dreams and seen visions.[8] Strange, overpowering scenes that gave him visions of various events.[9] The best he could do in understanding their meaning was to pray, because often the interpretation came very slowly. He struggled for every ounce of truth they brought to him. On his mission he thought he might be able to understand clearer, but instead he had had more evasive dreams that seemed just beyond his understanding.

Braun let the rushing water swirl in his hands. He noted the pattern and the intensity. His life was like that…not on the outside, but on the inside. On the outside he knew he seemed to have everything organized and planned. Being the firstborn in the Rogers' family of ten children, he had been forced to be responsible and mature at a young age. This early expectation had helped him have success thus far in his life.

Today, at twenty-one years old, he searched himself. Who was he on the inside really? He knew generally he was good, at least what he thought of as good. He followed all the things the Lord had set out for him, and he tried to be consistent. But he wanted to be more than just good. Somewhere inside of him, he knew he wanted to be something different and unique. He wanted to make a real difference, to be someone of consequence. Maybe that was why he was trying to go into the medical field. Being a healer like Christ would be close to fulfilling his yearnings. But then…he didn't feel being a doctor was the exact thing he was looking for. No, it was more. He wanted to…. The thought eluded him again.

Braun hit the edge of the stainless-steel sink with his left palm and shut off the water with his right.

Falling to his knees by his bed, Braun closed his eyes and allowed his vivid dream to return to his thoughts. He reviewed the contrasting perceptions and the intensity. He remembered the answers he received to his questionings in his dream. The answers led him to believe the Lord had something for him to do.

Braun held his breath as he formulated another prayer. After exhaling he began in a whisper, "Dear Father…I am here…. I wish to be all thou desirest me to be, and I pray for direction and understanding. I want to be instrumental in the last days. I'm getting the impression thou needest me to do something, but I don't understand what it is. I pray for the knowledge I need. I pray to know what I need to do to prepare."

Braun hesitated. He wondered if it were prudent to say such things out loud. Was he assuming too much? But then looking inside himself, he felt he needed to continue.

"I believe I am ready to be refined, to be used in thy work of preparation for thy son's second coming. I sense there is something, a mission for me to fulfill, and I wish to begin that task so my soul is quieted.

"Please, Father, Thou dost send visions and doth not fully reveal their nature. Please help me understand the relationship between them, and thee and me."

Braun stopped again and wondered if his zealousness was leftover missionary fanaticism, since he had been off his mission for only six months. But before he had even finished his thought, pure knowledge poured into his mind.

The communication was not in words but in understanding. Braun understood that everything would be revealed in time, and he was to search for his next step. He would know the way to go when he discovered it.

Braun closed his eyes tighter, as his chest constricted with deep gratitude that his Heavenly Father was listening and had been so prompt to answer. Now it was time for him to be patient and satisfied.

Braun was filled with peace. It was enough.

Questions

Corrynne bundled her twins in their winter jackets. It was unusually cold for the end of September. She remembered when the summer seemed to go on for a while and some years, Halloween was so warm the kids didn't even have to wear coats. Not this year. Maybe they wouldn't go.

Deep down, Corrynne knew it wasn't because of the cold weather she was considering skipping Halloween. The truth was she was beginning to be wary of being out anywhere alone. She secretly considered her knowledge about the cult and the man who led them. There was no doubt that what she knew about the group could single her out. The deaths of Dr. Quaid and the ER nurses were hitting too close to home and she was becoming more and more nervous. She couldn't help but feel unsafe. The authorities needed to be alerted to what she thought was happening, but if she went to them would they take her seriously?

With a quick look around, Corrynne loaded up the twins into the little Neon. She struggled to fit the car seats properly in the tiny car. Their Suburban was in the shop and wasn't expected to be repaired for quite a while, considering how many cars had been damaged in the hail storm. She was heading off to the doctor's office. The twins most likely had ear infections.

Corrynne backed out of the driveway and drove down the road. It was comforting to hear her little ones babble to each other. She was grateful they weren't in bad moods right now. As she put the car into drive, her thoughts returned to the cult.

What would she say if she called the police? Corrynne didn't want to sound crazy. She frowned as she contemplated what she knew. After thinking, she realized she really didn't *know* anything. All she knew for a fact was that Dr. Quaid and three other nurses had died from Strep A....Well actually, she didn't even know that. She was assuming that what she was told in the ER was true. She had better find out for sure or leave it alone. At this point, she was sure the police would just look at her and tell her she was paranoid.

"So what do I *know*?" Corrynne spoke out loud to organize her thoughts. She did this often around the twins because they always thought she was talking to them. Predictably, the babies quieted and began to listen to her with wide, innocent eyes.

"Number one," said Corrynne as she turned a corner, "Young people have come to the hospital dying of some terrible disease most likely linked to the tattoos they received at the Raves. Their deaths are a reportable fact. Hospital documents back it up, but that aspect has already been reported to the CDC and world news. So I need something else.

"Number two: The tattoos are being received by young illegal-substance abusers during a religious type of meeting. The meeting is being lead by a spiritual leader who exerts his influence when all the people at the Rave are mentally impaired by illegal drugs. That's an important issue." It was clear to Corrynne and she was sure it would be clear to anyone who investigated the Raves that the population who attend those parties were being taken advantage of. The key would be to get that point documented. The illegal drugs would be great leverage to encourage a law enforcement investigation that would shut the whole organization down. Corrynne was sure of it! Maybe that was what she needed to do.

"So how could I get a Rave documented?" Corrynne stopped at a stop light and tapped her index finger on the steering wheel as she thought. "Video footage would do." She lifted her eyebrows in consideration as she imagined going to the secret party with a camera. But then, she shook her head. "What am I thinking? *That* would be suicide!"

Corrynne licked her lips as the light turned green. Accelerating slowly, she said to herself, "OK, let's try again. There must be something else that would get the police's attention. I can't go about putting my life in jeopardy. A video would be good but impractical to acquire," she said to herself.

"So what else would do? What else do I know?" asked Corrynne as she squinted and racked her brain for something, some tidbit of knowledge that had teeth enough for the law. "I know from a couple of sources that Dr. Quaid died the night after he went to the news about the Raves." Corrynne stopped talking and just thought about things. She remembered that Dr. Page said that Dr. Quaid had died from Strep A. He also said he had an...*umbilical piercing?* Corrynne frowned and shook her head. That bit of information still didn't sit right with her. Sure, umbilical piercings were a new masculine trend in today's society, although she had never thought it would have caught on, but it had; especially in the college bodybuilding crowd. But the question was: would Dr. Quaid be the type to have one?

Struck as if by lightning, a thought dawned on Corrynne. She sat straight up in her seat. With a sly smile she asked aloud, "Just how did Dr. Page know Dr. Quaid had a pierced bellybutton? ...He didn't come to the hospital when he died! He died at home in his sleep!" Corrynne's mind was racing. She started concluding Dr. Page was somehow connected to Dr. Quaid's death. It made a satisfactory kind of sense! "I knew something strange was going on! Dr Page's a snake!" exclaimed Corrynne with a sneer. But then after thinking a few moments, Corrynne relaxed. Disappointment took the place of her gloating. Despite how attractive the thought was to her that Dr. Page might be connected to Dr. Quaid's death, she knew she was getting ahead of herself. What if the piercing was old? Maybe Dr. Page had seen Dr. Quaid without his shirt in the doctor's dressing room. It wasn't unusual for doctors to change scrubs or clothes at the hospital. They practically lived there.

"Hmmm...." Corrynne continued her connections. She shrugged. Even without knowing how Dr. Quaid received his pierced bellybutton, his death was still very suspicious to her. The official story was that Dr. Quaid died from patient contamination, but she didn't agree. For Strep A to cause necrotizing fasciitis, there had to be a point of infection. There had to be a break in the skin somewhere for the Strep A to get in deep enough to start dissolving the tissues and cause death so quickly. For this reason, Corrynne still felt Dr. Quaid was infected with the deadly bacteria on purpose. A new bellybutton piercing would be the perfect way to inoculate someone. No one would suspect foul play. Not even the law.

Corrynne adjusted her weight and ran her fingers through her hair, then planted her hand back on the steering wheel. In frustration, she realized she was getting all excited over nothing. If she was being truthful with herself, she'd admit she was in way over her head. How could one *prove* inoculation of bacteria? The thought was ridiculous! Bacteria would be everywhere in someone who died of infection. It wasn't like a drug the lab could test for in the blood.

But then another thought came to her. Corrynne began to smile. She remembered she had thought of talking to Mrs. Quaid. Was now the time? If she talked to her, she could find out if his piercing was old or new. Then if it was old, she might be able to give herself permission to leave this whole thing alone and just lay low until it all blew over; but if it was new, then…what then? Corrynne didn't know. Maybe it would come to her.

Corrynne reached into the diaper bag and grabbed her phone. She spoke into the receiver and requested directory assistance. The phone dialed the number automatically. After the number dialed, she was connected to Dr. Quaid's home phone. Predictably, an answering service picked up the call. Corrynne left a message for his wife to call her. She was afraid if she said it was in connection with Dr. Quaid's death, her call wouldn't be returned, so she just asked to be called back on her cell. She added that it was urgent, and as far as she was concerned, it was urgent—for the safety of her family and for her own safety, she needed to know details that only Dr. Quaid's wife could tell her concerning his illness. Corrynne hoped she'd call back soon.

ξξξξξξ

The pediatrician's office was very busy. Corrynne picked a spot away from the crowd and prepared for a long wait. She placed the babies on the floor in front of her, where they began exploring. Unexpectedly, her cell phone rang. Corrynne fumbled to find it again in the depths of the babies' bag. "Hello?" Corrynne's voice was urgent.

"Hello, I'm looking for a Corrynne Rogers."

"This is she."

"This is Mrs. Quaid. Did you call me?"

"Yes, yes, I did. Ah, I'm a nurse at the hospital. I worked with your husband the night before he died."

"I'm not interested in talking about my husband's work or with anyone who represents his work. I'm sorry…"

"Please, don't hang up!" said Corrynne. "I really don't want to talk to you about that subject, in particular. I guess I just want to ask you a question that is totally unrelated to work." Suddenly Corrynne felt self-conscious. How was she going to ask such a personal question dealing with this poor woman's dead husband? Corrynne just forged ahead before she could change her mind. "I was wondering if your husband had an umbilical piercing before his death."

"What? A what?" asked Mrs. Quaid.

Corrynne fidgeted and searched for words easier to understand and acceptable in this situation. "A navel piercing, you know a bellybutton ring, or a stud?"

"What does this have to do with?"

"I'm asking because it was reported he had one when he died. I'm trying to figure out if it was new or something he had for a while. Believe me, it makes all the difference in the world."

The woman on the other end of the phone was silent…and then she said, "Yes, he had a stud in his bellybutton. It was something he did when he was in college. I never liked it, but he kept it because it was symbolic of his other life before he converted to Christianity. He wanted to keep a reminder of those days. It helped him remember his mistakes, so he wouldn't repeat them."

Corrynne was taken back. If his stud was old then that meant her assumption that the Strep A could have been injected under the skin by the piercing was wrong. She couldn't believe all her assumptions were wrong. Immediately she felt guilty for bothering his wife.

"Thank you very much," said Corrynne. "I won't bother you again."

Corrynne was about to hang up when Mrs. Quaid said, "Now I need to ask you a question."

Surprised, Corrynne said, "Sure, what can I do for you?"

"Did you work with those patients who died like my husband did?"

"I only worked with one. Your husband tried to save his life, but it was an impossible task."

"I have to warn you about something and I want you to listen to me very carefully," said Mrs. Quaid in a very serious tone.

"OK," said Corrynne as she nodded.

"Refuse to treat those patients when they come to the hospital. There is something dreadfully evil that surrounds them. Protect your family and yourself."

"Well, I don't want to treat those patients, but sometimes I don't have a choice."

"Yes, you do," said Mrs. Quaid.

"Those patients don't know what's happening to them, Mrs. Quaid, and I need to help them."

"By the time they get to the hospital, it's too late for them."

Corrynne waited a moment as she digested Mrs. Quaid's words. She remembered Dr. Quaid saying the same thing.

Mrs. Quaid continued, "Let me tell you again…. All being a hero accomplishes in this situation is death. There are people near you who will make sure of it."

Corrynne was confused. She reflected a moment. Was she talking about Dr. Page? "Are you saying someone in the hospital was responsible for your husband's death?"

The woman's voice began to shake. "No, I am not saying a thing." Then there was a dial tone.

Corrynne took the phone from her ear and just looked at it. "That was very odd," she said out loud, "but illuminating."

"Hmmm," said Corrynne as she considered everything she knew. So Dr. Quaid's stud was old and not the origin of the infection. If it wasn't, then what was? She didn't have the answers, and she didn't know where to go to find them. There was something missing from what she knew. Where could she find more answers? Then she knew.

"Hospital," Corrynne said into her phone, and the programmed number dialed instantly. She asked the operator of the hospital for the PRN department and was connected.

"PRN office," came the friendly answer.

"Yes, I am looking for a nurse named Ann Cain. Does she work in your area?"

"I'm sorry, I cannot give out that information," refused the voice.

"Oh, I didn't tell you who I am. I'm sorry. I'm the charge nurse for the ICU, and Ann helped me with a code. It is imperative I find her to clear up some information."

"Your name?"

"Corrynne Rogers."

"One moment, please.... May I have your ID number?"

"45623."

"Thank you, Corrynne. ...I'm sorry to tell you Ann Cain does not work with us any longer."

"What? Where did she go?"

"I'm afraid I don't have that information."

"Was she fired?"

"No, she quit."

"Does it say why?"

"She gave 'religion' as the reason."

Corrynne's stomach dropped. "Religion?"

"Yes, that's correct."

"OK, thank you very much."

"You're welcome." The phone clicked, and they were disconnected.

"What a bugger!" Corrynne said emphatically to her phone. She couldn't believe finding someone could be so hard.

A young female voice called over the speaker, "Strykker and Striynna Rogers, room ten." Corrynne put her phone into her diaper bag, gathered her little ones, and calmly headed for the room.

Beckoning

Braun strolled around the BYU library. He was between classes. He had gone there to find a quiet place to think and to study. He settled down on the floor in an unoccupied corner and pulled out his organic chemistry book and began to read.

Despite his good intentions, Braun couldn't concentrate. The Krebs cycle was the least important item on his mind. Ever since his intense dream that morning, he had been thinking about Imam Mahdi. He didn't choose to think about the mysterious spiritual man but everywhere he looked, he saw the piercing black eyes amidst a bluish-white aura that he had seen on the Internet. He was beginning to think his dream and the man who claimed to be Christ were connected.

Braun's gaze followed the people who were walking around him. He searched for distractions, but none would relieve him.

With a fist, he punched his book. "Those eyes," Braun whispered, "they haunt me." He squeezed his eyes tight and rubbed them with the back of his knuckles attempting to rub the image out of his mind. But even as he opened them, he could see the two black, deep, beckoning orbs staring right at him.

In frustration that was bordering on anger, Braun jumped up from his place on the floor and shoved his book into his backpack. In one smooth movement he zipped up the opening and swung the heavy pack onto his back.

His feet began to walk, slowly at first, but then the pace increased as if he were trying to escape from a pursuing entity. Braun walked and walked, not knowing where he was going, only that he must go.

Without intending to, Braun arrived at a desk. Seated behind it was a beautiful BYU student with long blonde hair flowing down to her waist. She smiled a perfect symmetrical grin and said, "It's Braun, right?"

Braun was caught off guard. "What? Are you talking to me?"

The girl nodded. "Your name is Braun, or is it Brian?"

"Ah…." Braun scratched the back of his head and looked around to get his bearings. "Braun works."

"I thought so." The young woman laughed in a relaxed manner. "You probably don't remember me, but I was in your New Testament class. I have to tell you how impressed I was with some of your comments. You really seem to understand the scriptures better than anyone I know."

Braun, still dazed, looked at her for a moment. He couldn't tell if she was just being friendly or coming on to him.

"Thanks," he said cautiously.

"My name is Chenille." She held out her hand to shake his.

He reached out his hand, and when their hands touched something almost electrical happened that thrust him into a vision.

Braun saw an event that seemed to take place in the future. He could see himself in a large building in a suit with a headset. There were many languages being spoken around him. He was looking at a hand-held computer. He sensed in this brief moment that he would have something very important to accomplish. When the vision ended, Braun regained his perception of the present finding he was still holding this beautiful, yet strange girl's hand. Braun was instantly uncomfortable.

"Oh, I'm sorry," Braun apologized as he dropped Chenille's hand and stuck his hands in his pockets. "I was distracted for a moment. I'm really not trying to hold your hand."

Chenille smiled shyly and said, "No problem, I had a sort of dejà vu when you shook my hand, too."

Braun studied Chenille. Was she making fun of him? "What do you mean?

"It's a gift I have. I see many deep things."

Braun continued to stare at Chenille. It seemed like she was on the level. "You're not joking?"

"No, I'm being honest."

"What do you see?"

Chenille pursed her lips and then smiled. "Well, I don't want to embarrass you any more than I already have."

Braun shook his head. "No, I'm fine. Tell me what you see."

Chenille gave Braun a sideways glance and said, "I can see paths."

"What kind of paths?"

"Sometimes I can see how to accomplish something that seems impossible. The way just opens up in my mind."

"Hmmm," said Braun as he considered Chenille's answer.

"Right now I'm having great clarity."

"About what?"

"Your heart."

"My heart? What does my heart have to do with a path?"

"I don't know," said Chenille. "To be honest, it's kind of strange. There must be a relationship though."

Braun was surprised. Chenille's answer was a little too personal for him. He could not maintain eye contact any longer. "I don't know if I like you looking into my heart. It's a pretty closed off and lonely place."

"Now *you're* lying," said Chenille. "It's not closed off or lonely, just cautious."

Braun changed the subject abruptly. He felt like he was itching all over. "So what is this place?" Braun asked as he looked around.

Chenille played along. "It's the career center. Don't you know where you are?"

"Yes, I do…" said Braun but he wasn't telling the truth.

"No you don't," said Chenille with wide eyes and a snicker.

Braun looked at Chenille. "Did you see that?"

"Yes, I saw it in your face. You're lost!"

Braun shook his head and said, "I'm not lost, just distracted."

"Now I believe you," said Chenille with a knowing glance.

"Good," said Braun as he turned to leave. This conversation was just too strange.

"Wait," said Chenille, "did I offend you?"

"No, I just have a class I have to get to," said Braun looking at his watch.

Chenille reached for a pamphlet and held it out to him. "I know what you're looking for. I know your path. It's right here."

Braun stopped and slowly turned around. He looked at Chenille from a distance, but didn't move.

Chenille smiled timidly and continued to hold out the pamphlet. "Come here. I'll show you."

Braun slowly came back to the desk and took the pamphlet. It read, "UNITED NATIONS—TAKE YOUR WINDOW OF OPPORTUNITY." He opened it and began to read the contents. He scanned the topics, and his eyes fell on internships. Underneath the heading it said,

> *If you are looking to broaden your professional horizons, an internship with the United Nations is the opportunity that cannot be missed. If you qualify, you will spend a semester at the new England-based UN headquarters, receiving a firsthand vision of the workings of the world's economic center.*

Braun felt very drawn to the idea of an internship at the UN, which surprised him. The thought had never even crossed his mind before this moment. Plus, it was totally illogical. He was pre-med, not a political science major. It just didn't add up. Nevertheless, he took the pamphlet and put it into the side zipper pouch on his backpack.

Braun smiled at Chenille. "You're pretty good at that."

"Thank you," said Chenille as she sat down in her chair. "Take care of that heart. It's a nice place."

Braun smiled for the first time. "Thanks."

"You're welcome," said Chenille as she started shuffling papers.

Braun turned and walked away.

Answers

The pediatrician's name was Dr. Greystone. He was a little old man with a shuffling walk and silver hair, who smiled all the time. Corrynne loved him to care for her children. He reminded her of a grandpa. He would tickle them and hold them up and say the most wonderful things.

Despite his advanced age, he was still very sharp and very well-read. She loved to explore his mind over all sorts of medical topics.

"Well, Corrynne! How's the ICU?" was Dr. Greystone's first question.

Corrynne smiled and looked up at the ceiling. "Well, doctor, do the words 'total chaos' mean anything to you?"

"Sure, sure, take a look around here!" He continued to smile.

"Yes, I see you have your hands full, too. At least my patients stay in their beds and do what I ask."

"Yes, and if they don't, you sedate them."

"I guess there is some truth to that. It's best for them and best for us," said Corrynne.

The doctor chuckled a little. "Hey, I agree. Do me a favor when I get in there."

"Are you planning a stay at Hotel ICU?" asked Corrynne.

"No, no one plans it, but inevitably we all get our turn."

"OK, what?"

"If I'm sick enough to be in the ICU, I'm sick enough to cross over into the light," said the doctor with a smile.

"Not necessarily," said Corrynne. "We bring most of our patients back."

"Don't bring me back. If I'm going towards the light, let me go."

"Well, I'm sure you'll be around for a very long time yet."

"I hope not. This tired old body is ready for a long rest."

Corrynne put her arm around the dear old man and gave him a squeeze. "I'll keep you around just because you're so cute."

"Don't flatter me—it might go to my head." The doctor turned to the babies and said in a soft rumbling tone, "So, little ones, do you have earaches? Keeping Mommy up at night? Let's look." Dr. Greystone took his otoscope and peered into the tiny ear canals. Both twins started howling. He said over their voices to Corrynne, "Yep, you have yourself double trouble!" he smiled contagiously. "Nothing a little Amoxicillin wouldn't help."

The word "Amoxicillin" set off alarms in Corrynne's head. "You know, doctor, I wish there were a shot you could give babies against Strep."

Dr. Greystone's eyes brightened a little. "Corrynne, don't you know there is one?"

"What?" Corrynne was surprised. She didn't know of any. "There is?"

"Yes! You haven't been paying attention. Your twins here have already had three doses of it."

Corrynne's eyes widened. "They have? Where was I?"

"You, my dear, were standing right where you are, all three times."

"OK, cough it up. Stop with the humiliation already."

"Yes, look here." Dr. Greystone picked up a pamphlet lying on the counter. It had the word "Prevzar" and a child smiling. "This is the brand new shot against Streptococcus A, specifically Streptococcus pneumonia, but it has seven other serotypes targeted, too. They are the eight critters responsible for eighty percent of all the Strep-related illnesses. It was developed to help the populations at risk because of age or compromised immune systems avoid meningitis, sepsis, and respiratory infections from those particular bacteria."[10]

Corrynne had a hard time swallowing. Her mouth was extremely dry. She couldn't get her words out fast enough. "Do you think it would help against cellulitis or even necrotizing fasciitis caused from Strep A getting in a wound?"

"Well," said Dr. Greystone, as he scratched his head. "I guess it would...but it's only indicated for children under two and those with compromised immune systems."

"Couldn't people with normal immune systems receive the shot too? I mean, if it's safe for infants, it should be safe for children and adults."

Dr. Greystone looked at her with narrowing eyes. "Oh, I get it. You're worried about the mysterious deaths at the hospital caused by the flesh-eating disease. I saw it on the news.... Amazing!"

Corrynne nodded vigorously. "I've tried to obtain a course of antibiotics just in case I bring it home or contract it, but I've been flatly refused at every front. To me it's logical I should try to protect myself.... If anyone's at risk, it's me. I don't understand why the hospital isn't just handing out something to its staff."

"Their lack of response could be due to a lack of awareness..." began Dr. Greystone.

"Lack of awareness?" Corrynne spat, interrupting the doctor. "They better become aware quickly, because four of their ER staff has been wiped out in the last week!"

"Noooo," said Dr. Greystone as he studied Corrynne.

"Yes."

"Who?"

"Dr. Quaid, an ER physician, and three ER nurses."

"Oh, that's not good," said Dr. Greystone as he shook his head. "That should have made the top story on the news."

"I agree," said Corrynne. "But it isn't. I can't figure out what's going on."

"Well, I know if anyone contracts that particular strain of Strep, there's no cure," said Dr. Greystone with a grimace.

"Exactly my point," said Corrynne. "So how about those shots for my family. Are you game?"

Dr. Greystone rubbed his hands together and nodded. "Well, it hasn't been approved for that use, but should work in theory. So go ahead and bring your family in. I do have to warn you that your insurance will not pay for it."

"I know," said Corrynne.

"It will cost a pretty penny, in the neighborhood of two hundred dollars per shot."[11]

Corrynne shrugged. "In this case I am more than happy to hand over my money to whoever can give me the shots. I just happen to have a way to spin gold." Corrynne laughed a little at her own joke, reflecting on the serum machine at the hospital and Dr. Page's comment. "Thank you, doctor. You may have just saved our lives."

"Well, I wouldn't go that far."

"I would!" Corrynne couldn't help but hug the little man beside her as he wrote the prescription for the Amoxicillin for her babies' ears. She had found her answer. "Seek and ye shall find," she thought to herself. It was very nice to have the Lord on her side. Inside, she glowed.

As the door closed behind the doctor, she picked up her tear-stained babies and swung them around. "We're going to be OK," she told them.

They smiled wide as if they knew what she was talking about.

Sudden Change

After a hard day at school, Braun flipped off his shoes by the couch and sat down. He was in the main house by the fireplace. His father had made a fire, and flames were licking the dry wood hungrily. The warmth was satisfying after being out in the unseasonably cold weather.

Braun watched the flames through the glass doors. He held his legs out straight to the level of the fire as he attempted to warm his socks. He wiggled his toes to unfold them from the cramped position that they had been in inside his shoes.

Braun decided to do some homework that was due the next day while he sat by the fire. He reached for his backpack and looked through the pockets for a pencil and his work. He unzipped the side zipper pouch and the UN pamphlet fell out onto the floor. Braun looked at the pamphlet for a moment and then leaned over and picked it up.

Unfolding the layers, Braun scanned the whole thing. After a few minutes, he decided he must have been under some sort of spell to have thought going to England was a good idea. Why would he want to leave? He was finally where he wanted to be, doing what he wanted to do. Why would he ever think of changing that?

Braun crumpled up the pamphlet and was bending over to open the glass doors to the fireplace. However, as he moved to toss the wadded paper in, he noticed the word "Requirements" standing out in bright yellow writing against a black background. He stared at it for a moment, contemplating whether he should go ahead and throw the pamphlet in or read what it would take to qualify.

Slowly Braun sat back and straightened out the wrinkled paper. He began to examine the expectations:

> *"To qualify for an internship in the most powerful and influential center of the world, you must be a scholastically centered, mature individual with previous international experience. Applicants must have a GPA 3.7 or above, be a political science major or minor, include two letters of recommendation, include a current résumé, and compose an essay that describes a detailed account of goals and international experience. Please send the above information to the address specified. Final applicants will be notified by e-mail. The finalists will be flown, all expenses paid, to England to be interviewed by the UN Secretary General and other selected delegates from all over the world. Though this is not a paid position, all living expenses will be provided for one semester."*

Braun continued to stare at the pamphlet even though he was finished reading. A shock of memory shot through his mind. He remembered his fleeting premonition when he shook Chenille's hand. Did his vision have anything to do with this pamphlet? Was that why he was lead to the Career

Center? It made sense. After all, it was clear in his vision that he was in another place where people spoke many languages. Could that other place be the UN?

After a few moments of deep contemplation, Braun had to admit that his thoughts and feelings were beginning to fit together like a puzzle. Things were feeling right. This must be the next step he was told he would recognize.

"OK! So I didn't recognize it immediately, but now I do," he spoke out loud, looking up but focusing his energy into the cosmos. He was sure the Lord was watching how he would respond. He didn't want to fail. He figured the pamphlet was to encourage him to proceed with something he wouldn't have picked on his own. Suddenly he felt like Nephi when his father told him to go and retrieve the plates from Jerusalem. He was being sent on an errand, and it seemed like it was the Lord's will.

Braun began an audible prayer, "Father, guide me. I will go and do what thou desirest, even though I don't see the wisdom…. But please reveal it to me soon, so I can buy into it, too."

Immediately Braun had a confirming feeling permeate his being. Finally he understood, and it was right! He was ecstatic. "Now that's what I call a definite answer! Thank you!" Braun realized in that moment, he had a feeling of true happiness inside him despite his own will, and it surprised him. He ended his prayer silently.

On a pad and paper he began to outline what he would have to do to apply for the internship. "First, I need to change my major," he whispered to himself as he scrawled it out on paper. He stopped and looked at his writing. That one was a hard one. He loved medicine. But he knew it was more important to trust in the Lord and do what he asked. He was sure he was being lead in the right direction. With that thought he purposefully put remorse out of his head and forged past it.

"I need a few letters of recommendation," he said as he wrote the second thing on his list.

Braun sat back and considered who he should ask. He was sure his mission president would write a good letter. He would be a good choice, considering his international connections. The bishop would give him a letter if he asked him, too. The bishop served as a mission president in Australia. He would know what to say in Braun's behalf. And as far as his own international experience, his mission to Argentina was more international experience than most Americans his age. It would give him an advantage.

"What else?" he asked himself as he tapped his pencil against his thumb. Braun glanced at the wrinkled pamphlet again. "I need to write an essay outlining my goals and international experience. No problem," he said as he wrote "essay" in the third number's space.

Braun thought about what was left on the list that he needed to fulfill. There was the GPA. He needed to obtain a transcript. So in the number four's line he wrote, "transcript".

"Number five," said Braun as he remembered he needed to include a résumé and added it.

Sitting back and looking at his list he nodded. "I'm a dead ringer!" Braun said quietly to himself and was slightly surprised how the internship was such a good fit. But then he scoffed. "How could I not be?" Inside, he knew the Lord had probably been preparing him for this internship even though he hadn't known it.

Braun stood up and went into the family room where the family computers sat in a line on a large table. Each child in the family had their own.

Quickly, Braun logged in and found BYU's site and changed his major online. Then he requested a transcript with the new major. As he was giving his credit-card number, Ry, his little nine-year-old brother, walked in and looked over his shoulder.

"What are you doing, Braun?"

Braun took a deep breath and said, "I am changing my major from pre-medicine to political science."

"What does that mean?" Ry gave Braun a suspicious scowl.

"It means, instead of trying to be a doctor, I am now trying to learn about politics and world events. You know, that kind of stuff," Braun said, trying to make it easy for his little brother to understand.

"Why? It sounds boring."

Braun began to laugh but then swallowed the urge. "Because I'm trying to get an internship at the United Nations. I will meet powerful people from all over the world. It's a great opportunity." Braun smiled, still trying to convince himself as well as his little brother.

Braun leaned down and began to whisper from behind his hand, "Secretly I still want to be a doctor, and maybe I can change it back when I'm done. What do you think?"

Ry shook his head. "I don't think it's a good idea at all. You'll make a great doctor. Don't change anything...." Ry searched for more words.... "I don't even know what a political whatchamacallit does."

"I don't, either," said Braun.

"Then why are you doing it?"

"I was told to do it by Heavenly Father. I need to do this. Don't ask me why, because I don't know yet."

"Does this mean you have to go away again?" asked Ry with pain in his face.

"Yes, I would move to England for a semester or more if I need to."

"No," said Ry matter-of-factly.

"No?" asked Braun, being amused by his brother's stubborn opinion.

"I don't want you to go! You're such a good brother now that you're back from your mission." Ry's eyes filled with tears. "I really will miss you."

Braun's heart suddenly was filled with compassion. "Ry, I won't be gone for long, only a couple of months. I'll bring you back cool stuff from England."

"No, you'll be gone longer. I know it! I don't want stuff from England. I only want you home!" Ry was crying now.

A pit began to form in Braun's stomach. Ry was speaking from his heart. It was what Braun wanted too, but it wasn't an option. "I know you want me home, and I want to be here. There is no place like this place, let me tell you! So, I will rush home as fast as I can and as soon as I can. OK?" Braun took his brother in his arms and hugged him long and hard. "I love you, and don't ever forget that."

After a time Braun drew Ry away and said, "Hey, how about a game of Dragon Masters? I hear you are one of the best dragon masters on Planet Zenos."

Ry looked up into his big brother's eyes.

Braun could tell by how Ry looked at him that knew he was trying to change the subject. He was a bright kid.

Despite that, Ry let up on Braun as he nodded. "OK, but you have to play a long time with me."

"Alright," agreed Braun, figuring he could finish his homework later. He had the rest of the day.

As they turned to leave the room Ry explained, "Jax says I'm not the best dragon master because he's at a higher level than I am."

Braun patted his back. "That's all right. You're the best in my book."

The two of them settled down for many battles in the living room. They were in search of an age-leveling match in the digital world. Maybe it was a game, but it also was balm for a little boy's soul.

Notes to "Burdens of the Future"

Black and Blue

[1] See Revelation 9:11 or the Bible Dictionary.

[2] See Revelation 9:11 or the Bible Dictionary.

[3] "And the fifth angel sounded, and I saw a star fall from heaven unto the earth: and to him was given the key of the bottomless pit" (Revelation 9:1).

[4] Alma the younger had a similar experience of being caught in the "darkest abyss." The darkness is often correlated to the effects of sin. See Mosiah 27:29.

[5] Alma 40:13.

[6] Revelation 17:8.

[7] 3 Nephi 15:9.

[8] Where there is true faith there are miracles, visions, dreams, healings, and all the gifts of God that he gives to his saints (see Bible Dictionary, "Faith," 669-670).

"And it shall come to pass afterward, *that* I will pour out my spirit upon all flesh; and your sons and your daughters shall prophesy, your old men shall dream dreams, your young men shall see visions" (Joel 2:28).

[9] "By the grace of God—following devotion, faith, and obedience on man's part—certain special spiritual blessings called gifts of the Spirit are bestowed upon men. Their receipt is always predicated upon obedience to law, but because they are freely available to all the obedient, they are called gifts. They are signs and miracles reserved for the faithful and for none else...Their purpose is to enlighten, encourage, and edify the faithful so that they will inherit peace in this life and be guided toward eternal life in the world to come. Their presence is proof of the divinity of the Lord's work; where they are not found, there the Church and kingdom of God is not...Faithful persons are expected to seek the gifts of the Spirit with all their hearts. They are to 'covet earnestly the best gifts' (1 Cor.12:31; D&C 46:8), to 'desire spiritual gifts' (1Cor.14:1), 'to ask of God, who giveth liberally.' (D&C 46:7; Matt. 7:7-8.) To some will be given one gift; to others, another; and 'unto some it may be given to have all those gifts, that there may be a head, in order that every member may be profited thereby' (D&C 46:29)." (Bruce R. McConkie, "Gifts of the Spirit," *Mormon Doctrine*, 314).

Answers

[10] The inoculation referred to in this text is patterned after a factual new vaccine called Prevnar,® which targets Streptococcus pneumoniae and is manufactured by Lederle Laboratories Division of American Cyanamid Company located in New York. It is a vaccination offered with the routine inoculation schedule of infants and toddlers under the age of 2. Meningitis (infection that affects the membranes surrounding the brain and spinal cord) and bacteremia (bacteria in the blood) often causes serious, irreversible physical damage and death in an estimated 18,400 children under the age of 5 in the United States each year. Prevnar,® targets the Streptococcus pneumoniae which infects soft tissue, bone, joint and ear infections in children also (for more information and statistics see http://www.prevnar.com/).

In factual science, Streptococcus pneumoniae is a strep bacteria with a jell covering over the cellular surface meant as a defense against the human immune system. As brought out in Chapter 2, changing Strep A to Strep pneumoniae is a matter of a plasmid transfer between live or dead bacteria (see relevant endnotes containing this topic in Chapter 2).

Slight changes in the facts of the inoculation have been added for storyline benefit.

[11] Currently, a child under 2 will generally be covered by insurance if the shot is given. Insurance might even cover a child up to 5 years old, depending on the insurance. The true cost of Prevnar,® for an older child or an adult is approximately $80.00 per shot, but it may be less or more depending on the clinic or doctor's office administering it.

CHAPTER TWELVE

SOMETHING BLUE

"And our spirits must have become like unto him, and we become devils, angels to a devil, to be shut out from the presence of our God, and to remain with the father of lies, in misery, like unto himself; yea, to that being who beguiled our first parents, who transformeth himself nigh unto an angel of light, and stirreth up the children of men unto secret combinations of murder and all manner of secret works of darkness" (2 Nephi 9:9).

Thursday
September 21st
1:30 p.m.
Provo, Utah

Snakebite

Corrynne's cell phone rang out a Rumba. The song stopped and then started again. The sound caused an annoying vibration deep within her brain, as she was brought out of a satisfying sleep. Finally the sound stopped. Corrynne was happy. She believed if the person on the other line wanted to talk to her, they would leave a message and she would call them back later. She rolled over, being careful to not disturb her sleeping twins in her bed, and fell back to sleep with the fleeting idea that she should put her phone on "silent".

Again, the phone started ringing. In frustration, Corrynne lifted her head and looked at her phone. The hospital was calling her. She had better answer this one. Despite Corrynne's desperate desire not to leave her warm, comfortable place in the bed between Striynna and Strykker, she carefully lifted herself off the bed and crawled out from the covers so as not to disturb the sleeping children. Neither of the babies stirred.

"Hello?" Corrynne said in a quiet voice.

"Hello, Corrynne. It's Shana." Shana was the ICU nurse manager from the hospital.

"Hi, there. Whatcha doing calling me during my nap?" Corrynne stifled a yawn.

"Oh, I'm sorry, didn't know that you were taking one."

"Just thought I'd sleep while my kids were down."

"Oh, I understand that," said Shana. "Afternoon naps are nice. I don't get them anymore and that makes me cranky."

"What's up?" asked Corrynne, wanting to hurry the conversation along.

"Hey, I have a question, if you have a minute."

"I have two. On your mark, get set, go. The clock is ticking," said Corrynne in a voice that was kidding the manager but still meaning every word. Her bed was calling her.

"We're missing some drugs...."

"Well, I didn't take them. Kicked that habit a long time ago, so, goodbye." Corrynne's response was flippant and sarcastic. She couldn't believe she was being called at home for such a thing. She wasn't on duty and therefore didn't care that the narcotic count wasn't on. They would have to solve this one without her.

There was a strange, unexpected pause.

Corrynne frowned. Something was up. Shana didn't joke back. "What's going on?" she asked.

Shana spoke hesitantly. "Ah...you worked on Monday?" She was obviously trying to find the words to say something.

"Right," said Corrynne.

"With some of the temporary staff covering patients, right?"

"Sure. What's wrong?"

"Did you notice if anyone was hanging around the narcotic drawers a little too much?"

Corrynne shook her head as she reflected on that night. She had been so busy she didn't remember much about the narcotics area. "Why? Do you think someone stole some narcotics?"

"I don't know what to think. Two whole boxes of Versed are missing."

Corrynne was taken back. "Two? That's twenty vials! *That's serious.*"

"Yes, that's why I'm going to run some names by you to see what you think. Maybe you can remember something that might give us a clue to what happened that night."

"I'll do my best, but Monday was crazy. I was putting out fires all night. I doubt I'll remember very much unless it has to do with those situations."

"Well, let's try."

"OK," said Corrynne now getting nervous. She could feel the intensity in Shana's voice and she didn't like it.

"Do you remember Dan Olsen?"

"Dan...Dan. What was his position on Monday night?"

"He was a Patient Tech."

"Oh, yes, I remember him. He did a great job. Do you suspect him of something?"

"Not really. I was just told that he asked for the narcotic keys to get some Valium for a patient."

Corrynne nodded to herself. "Oh, yes, that's right. He did that for me. I don't think he's your problem."

"How about Sarah Parker?"

"The nurse, right?"

"Yes, from the fourth floor."

"No. I wouldn't suspect Sarah. She wouldn't take the keys when I asked her to hold them. She was skittish about something that night. She had everyone else get her medications. That was a strange situation."

"How about Ann Cain?"

A cold chill pulsed through Corrynne's body with the mention of that nurse's name. "What name did you say?" she asked pointedly.

"Ann Cain?"

"Was she..." Corrynne stopped. Could it be that Ann was working on her staff on Monday night? Could she have been so busy that she had missed her? "Ann Cain was *working on Monday*?"

"Yes, in Room W211."

"What?" Corrynne put a hand to her forehead as she stepped onto the floor and leaned against the wall. "I can't believe it! I've been looking for her everywhere! If she was a snake, she would've bitten me!"

"Why have you been looking for her?" asked Shana with a flat voice.

"She was the nurse for a patient on the fifth floor who died. I needed to talk to her about the code we ran. At that time she was a PRN nurse."

"For our hospital?"

"Yes, that's what the fifth-floor charge nurse said on Monday night."

"Interesting."

"I called the PRN office to see if I could find her, and they said she quit."

"She's an agency nurse now. We borrowed her...well, paid her to work for us during the crunch."

Corrynne's forehead wrinkled as she made a confused face. "So she quit to become an agency nurse then turned around to work at the same hospital? Aren't there rules against that?"

"There used to be. Now because of the nursing shortage, we'll take anyone we can find."

"That's crazy!"

"Yes, but that's what's happened."

"Don't those agency nurses make almost twice what a floor nurse makes?"

"Sometimes. It depends on the agency," said Shana.

"Well, good for her. I guess I'm envious," said Corrynne. "If I were smart I'd do the same thing. Well, at least now I know where she's working."

"Why?"

"Because I have to talk to her. ...I still can't believe she was working alongside of me a whole shift and I didn't recognize her. She's easy to miss, though."

"What do you mean?"

"I had to go to records and look up the deceased patient's name to find her name on the chart because I couldn't remember it. It was quite an ordeal."

"Sounds like you've spent a lot of energy tracking this girl down. It sounds more complicated than a few questions about a code."

"It's a long story. It's really my fault, because I didn't pay attention to her name in the first place."

"Well, she remembered you," said Shana.

Shana's words cut Corrynne like a knife. "What do you mean, 'she remembered me'?"

"She filed a complaint against you."

"Excuse me?" Corrynne suddenly stood away from the wall. Her body became tense.

"Yes, she said she saw you take the two missing boxes from the drawer. She also said that when she went to sign some Versed out for her patient, she saw that her own name was signed for all twenty vials. To be honest with you, I checked out her story and ran the narcotics record with the signatures through the handwriting-analysis lab. The handwriting matched yours on both the missing issues. I even ran it through again to double check. I received the same result. That's forty times your handwriting came up positive."

"You're kidding, aren't you?" asked Corrynne feeling overwhelmed to the point of nausea.

"No, I'm not kidding."

"Tell me this isn't real."

"There are others who back up her story."

"What are you talking about?"

"There are witnesses who have said similar things about you in relation to that night."

"How, *Shana*? I didn't take a thing! Someone's lying! Who are these people?"

"Corrynne, you know that I can't tell you that."

"Wh...." Corrynne's mind was spinning. She shook her head. "What did they tell you?" Corrynne placed her free hand firmly on her hip as she braced herself for the answer to her question.

"There were three people who sent me e-mails about this problem. All of their accounts matched."

"And what did they say?"

"They said Ann told them Monday night that you had taken medications and set her up for the blame. Some of them said they had seen the signatures themselves."

"But none of them said that they saw *me* sign it. Right?"

"No, but I don't think that is even an issue at this point."

"Are you kidding? Come on—help me out here!"

"One of them told me that they counseled Ann to go to management as soon as possible to avoid blame. Ann came to me with the story the next day. She was very upset that she was being framed. I had to have her lie down for awhile just to recover from our interview. Two of the witnesses even said you ran by their room and stared at her—I'm going to use their words—'as if to intimidate her to stay quiet'."

Corrynne remembered the moment Shana was talking about. It was true the nurses were whispering as she ran to the code, and now she knew why. She also remembered the familiar face she couldn't identify. It all made sense now! It was Ann Cain! Ann had been in blue scrubs. Now she remembered! It sickened her. Why couldn't she have put the pieces together then? The whole scenario was maddening.

"That is stupid!" Corrynne said, a little too emphatically.

"I agree."

"I didn't even know she was on my floor that night. Wh…." Corrynne's words failed her as she searched for a hole in the story. She continued, "I didn't know she was the one I had been looking for. …Come on, Shana, you know me better than that."

"Well, I thought I did. Corrynne, hey, if it weren't such a big amount of Versed that was missing I would be able to dismiss this, but I can't. There are just too many unanswered questions and too many things that point to you."

"What does that mean? Do I go to jail next?"

"It means your charge-nurse responsibilities and privileges, including your narcotics access, have been withdrawn until this is solved. I'm not going to press charges until I know all the facts."

"Wait a minute! What is going on here?"

"It's just a temporary precaution till we can work this out. It's not personal."

"Not personal? *This feels personal!*" exclaimed Corrynne. "It's obvious you don't trust me. What about Ann? Have you considered the possibility that maybe she had something to do with this instead of me?"

"Yes, Corrynne. Isn't it obvious that we've been trying to prove you innocent? I was hoping that somewhere there was just a misunderstanding, but everywhere I searched gave me more evidence to blame you."

"Oh, my goodness. I can't believe this is happening," said Corrynne as she began to pace.

"I want you to know that we have contacted Ann and the temp service. She is not to be assigned here until this is resolved, either."

"Great. But I bet she's not on the hook."

"No, she's not."

"Why? Because she doesn't work for our hospital?" asked Corrynne.

"No, because there's no evidence to say she's guilty."

"So I'm the one who takes the brunt of this?"

"Yes, until we can find another acceptable answer."

"Shana! You know me! You know my standards! You know my work ethic! I'd never do this!"

"I know, Corrynne, but I have no choice in the matter. A large amount of a controlled substance is missing. I have to do something."

Corrynne waited for a moment and then said, "OK, but I want to emphasize that *I am in no way responsible for the missing drugs!*" Corrynne's teeth clenched together, as she tried to manage her anger.

"Well, actually you are. You were the charge nurse on duty, and therefore you are responsible. …One question is very obvious: why didn't you catch this huge disparity on Monday during the narcotic count?"

Corrynne was losing patience; her answer came out slow and rhythmic. "Because I didn't count the narcotics myself. I had my RNs count that night. I was too busy with the double census. Anyway, no one reported any shortages to me. If someone had, I would have investigated it. You know that."

"Yes, I do know that," said Shana.

"Anyway, the sheets are taken out of the narcotics book after all the vials are used. If it's true that two complete boxes were taken, then the associated sheets would have been removed from the book and filed for refill. No one would have seen them unless someone was pointing them out, not even me if I had counted. I don't think even *you* would have known if Ann hadn't come to you with her insane story."

"Be careful, Corrynne, that last statement can be taken many ways."

Corrynne continued, getting more loud and emphatic. "Oh, my goodness. None of this could have happened if the hospital had been with the program and updated their narcotics-use process. Practically everyone else is accounting for narcotics automatically with badges, thumbprints, and Accudoses. What is our problem?"

"You know as well as I do that the thumbprint system has its own short-comings. We lose some of our autonomy in the ICU. Sometimes we need medications fast when there aren't any orders written yet. We don't always have the time to have narcotics approved through pharmacy. With our signature system, we can do what we need to do and then obtain the orders later when everything is under control again. You were there at the meeting when we decided to keep it."

"There is an override system built into the Accudoses for emergency situations, you know."

"I know that, Corrynne," said Shana. "However that's just how it works at our hospital."

"OK," said Corrynne filled with rage, "So let me get this straight. Because we have the most archaic, retro way of checking out narcotics, we're now making ourselves prime targets in the drug community, and I'm going to pay for that!"

"I'm sorry, Corrynne."

"Let me ask you one more question. Has this happened before at our hospital?"

Shana hesitated. "Not that I know of."

"That's the problem. Look back and see. I bet you this has happened before. I bet this is the first time someone has caught the problem, and do you know why we caught the problem?"

"Why?" asked Shana sounding annoyed.

"Because this time, *I am the target*, not the drugs."

Shana let out a sarcastic laugh. "What are you saying? Where did that comment come from?"

"I am saying Ann Cain is involved in a cult. She told me about the secret society after the code the other night. Have you been watching the news lately?"

"Yes."

"Then you've seen the news stories connecting the *Strep* deaths to a new religion and the Raves that are going on up in the mountains."

"Yes, I've seen them. I don't know that I believe them. Media will do anything…."

"They are real! Dr. Quaid is dead because he went to the media!"

"You don't know that, Corrynne. Officially, it was just patient contamination."

"Shana, in order for contamination to occur from a patient to a healthcare worker, the bacteria almost has to be injected under the skin, like AIDS or hepatitis. Dr. Quaid protected himself. He wasn't dumb…. No! I know enough to see that I'm in danger too. After this narcotics frame, I know for sure I'm being targeted."

"*Wow*…." Shana slowed her words down to a crawl. She became very quiet to emphasize the next sentence. "You know what's scary?"

"No, what?" Corrynne sensed impending doom.

"Ann said you would say something about that cult. She said…"

Corrynne's fury was unleashed when she heard Shana's obvious slant. "It's the truth! She's setting me up! Think about it. Why would I sign her name in *my own handwriting*? That would be illogical. If I were honestly trying to set her up, I would sign it out in *her* handwriting. You know as well as I do, it doesn't take much to reproduce a signature. A little pocket copier and, voila, you can make convincing stamps! She had access to my signature a whole morning last Saturday during the code on the code sheet! If not then, she could have obtained it any time. With the number of times we have to sign our names to things, she had access twenty-four–seven. All she had to do was come to the hospital and find it. My name is on everything!"

Corrynne waited for Shana to respond, but she didn't say anything. Finally, Corrynne asked, "Why aren't you backing me up? I have been a nurse at that hospital for years without one infraction!"

Shana's voice returned to normal. "I know. And it pains me to do these things to you, but I have no choice as the nurse manager. All I know is something doesn't make sense." Shana stopped for a moment and then said, "The only thing I can think of is for you to somehow back up what you're telling me. I'd take any tiny bit of evidence. I would even take the return of the Versed, no questions asked."

Corrynne laughed sarcastically. "You're asking me for the impossible. It's not my job to collect evidence. I shouldn't have to, and I have nothing to give back! I don't have the drugs, Shana!"

"Well, until you give us something concrete, her story is more physically plausible than yours. We have her name in your writing over and over again. That is evidence. Her witnesses are also evidence."

"It isn't my writing! I didn't sign out Versed the whole night! Those issues aren't even evidence—it's perception, mirrors, and trapdoors!"

"All I can say is, you had better get a lawyer. Ann already has one. She's suing you."

"For what?"

"Ask her."

"This is so ridiculous!" Corrynne practically yelled into the phone.

"It's life." Shana's response was cold.

"Thanks, you're so understanding."

"Good luck."

Corrynne flipped her phone closed and let out a scream of frustration. The sound startled both her twins. Immediate crying ensued.

Corrynne covered her face and slid slowly down the wall into a fetal position. She knew she had been bitten by a viper, and the wound was deep.

White Roses

The doorbell rang. Brea's heart leapt. She was expecting Matt, her fiancé. He was a tall, dark, and handsome returned missionary who was working on his doctorate in microbiology.

Brea flew to the door and opened it, but to her disappointment, no one was there. Instead, a single white rose adorned an otherwise dull black welcome mat. A smile crept across her face as she picked it up. Her fingers grasped the full blooming rose, and she felt the smoothness of its stem. It was thornless.

A thornless white rose was symbolic in their relationship. It had always meant eternal love without mortal flaws. Matt had given her the first white, thornless rose when he had asked her to marry him. With it came a promise to forgo the normal thorns of mortal weaknesses. He promised that never would pride, lust, or materialism interfere with their future marriage. Brea loved that thought, and because she knew Matt, she believed him.

Attached right below the bloom was a red, tiny bow with a card. There was a message, which read:

I love you now,
I'll love you always,
In my heart
Your love ne'er fades.

In the temple park
By the swings
You'll need to come.
Find what love brings.

Hurry to me,
My love so dear,
I'm impatient
To feel you near.

Love,

Matt

Brea smiled brightly as she closed the card and looked out into the orange, pink, and purple sky of the sunset. She took a deep breath, and without another thought she closed the door and ran down the sidewalk to the junky family pick-up truck, which now had a brand-new windshield that reflected the many hues of the setting sun.

Brea jumped in and headed for the park that was nearest to the temple in Provo. She knew exactly where to go. She and Matt had spent many nights just barely swinging back and forth in the park swings, talking about the future of their lives together.

She drove around the bend and as soon as she could see the swings she noticed another white rose. "Oh, this is fun!" she exclaimed. "A treasure hunt!"

Brea turned off the engine and rushed to the rose. Another message was attached.

Hello, my sweet,
I'm glad you're here.
A few more steps
To make things clear.

In the bush
In front of you
Soon will find
A don of blue.

Put on the silk
And come to me
I'll be waiting
At the Magleby."

Love,

Matt

Brea looked up and studied the bushes that lined the fence. She noticed a large box. She knew that's where her next present lay.

Brea quickly retrieved the box and opened it on the spot. A gorgeous, solid azure blue, floor-length silk dress unfolded in her hands. It was a straight, stylish cut that was fitted around the bodice. She noticed another small box in the corner of the big box. Brea tore into it impatiently. There were earrings and a choker necklace that were filled with sparkling bright diamonds. She was sure they were costume jewelry, but it still would be fun to wear them. A squeal of excitement escaped her throat as she held the dress up to her and swung around on the grass. Matt was so perceptive. He was always in tune with her. She loved that about him and constantly thanked the Lord for finding such a worthy, loving, and conscientious future husband.

Brea suddenly stopped. Off in the distance a child was watching her. She thought she must look like a fool! Self-consciously she wrapped the dress around her arm, picked up the boxes, and headed for her truck.

Brea didn't want to take a lot of time, but she needed to go back home to get ready. She wanted everything to be perfect for the dinner at Magleby's restaurant with Matt. She had an inkling of what he was up to since she hadn't received her ring yet for their engagement. She didn't want to expect it, but she hoped this would be the day she would have something to show for their relationship. It was really past time for the ring.

Brea pulled alongside her home and rushed up the sidewalk, leaping over the porch stairs. She was in her room in another instant ripping off her jeans and T-shirt and slipping the soft silky material over her slim body. She reached back to zip up the long zipper, and with unnatural contortions she successfully brought the zipper all the way up to her neck. The fit was perfect. She looked into the mirror and was amazed by what she saw. It had been a long time since she had felt this beautiful.

Next, Brea pulled open the small box that she had set on her dresser and removed the necklace and earrings. Slowly, she fastened the necklace around her neck and put the earrings in her ears. Their brilliance was breathtaking, causing her excitement to intensify even further.

With a feeling of urgency, Brea wrapped her shoulder-length chocolate hair up in a stylish roll and applied a crystal barrette to hold it in place, allowing some hair to fall into her face from the front and sides. After lightly applying heat to give the hair a slight curl, she touched up her makeup with some mascara, eyeliner, and lip-gloss.

When she was finished, Brea looked thoughtfully into the mirror. The glass revealed a young girl becoming a woman. Suddenly, the thought struck her that she would never be little again. With the step of eternal marriage, she would then be grown up. She could never return to little-girl ways but must become responsible, practical, and selfless. The learning times were over, and the teaching times were beginning. She felt pain for the loss of her family and their constant companionship, but the promise of the future was so glorious she had to swallow the pain. Then the thought occurred to her that she wasn't losing her childhood; she was gaining the growth of another era. She realized that there was nothing to be sad about! With those thoughts she slipped on a pair of nice heels, grabbed the long dress coat she shared with her mother and whipped open the door as she rushed back to the truck.

Brea drove up to the Magleby restaurant but didn't see Matt's car. It made her worry. Despite her misgivings, she parked the truck and got out.

Brea entered the door of the restaurant and was greeted by the host. "Brea Rogers, I presume?" he said without hesitation.

"Yes." It surprised her that he knew her name…but of course he would know what she would be wearing so she would be easily identifiable.

"This way, please." The host led her down the hall into a private eating area surrounded by sheer maroon drapes, with lace overlay pulled up at the edges to expose the color beneath. The host pulled out a chair at a table for two with a tall candle burning in the center. As she sat she eyed the third thornless white rose of the night that was set across her dinner plate. With it was another message.

Brea removed her coat, and picked up the rose. Before she read the note, she smelled the symmetrical white flower and held the scent in her mind for just a moment. Its aroma was sweet and pure. It directly symbolized her feelings at the moment. She slowly opened the card attached.

Brea Nicole Rogers,
With this ring, I thee wed….

That was the end of the note. With shaking hands she closed the card and looked through her glistening eyes to see Matt standing tall and in a tuxedo with a ring box in his hand.

Without words, Matt approached. Leaning forward and with an inviting sweep of his arms, his lips brushed hers. In the next moment a kiss was gently placed on her lips. His breath was sweet, and his touch was tender.

With a dramatic flair, Matt knelt in front of Brea. He opened the ring box to reveal a gorgeous, large, princess-cut solitaire with a thick gold band. He took her trembling, petite hand and easily slipped the ring on her finger.

The intensity of the moment was too much, and Brea broke down and sobbed.

Matt gently lifted her out of her chair to stand, wrapping his strong, sure arms around her. As if on cue, soft music drifted into their private world. Slowly Matt began to sway, holding her close. Brea laid her head on his shoulder, and they rocked back and forth to the soft luxurious sounds of French horns. They continued to dance slowly without words. Words were not needed. Everything was perfect.

The Plan

Corrynne stewed all day as she sat on the floor with the twins. They would climb all over her as she stared at the wall for long spans of time. She felt emotionally crippled, unable to function normally. All her thoughts centered on her conversation with Shana.

The door opened and Carea and Dane came in from school. "Hi, Mom!" said Carea.

Corrynne automatically turned her head. "Hi," she said without emotion. "How was your day?"

"Fine," said Corrynne with an insincere smile.

"You're sure?" asked Carea.

Corrynne nodded weakly.

Carea looked at Dane who shrugged, and then back at her mother. "You look like you're sick or something."

Corrynne was distracted at that moment by little Striynna who was in her lap and was pulling on her lower lip.

"Mom?" asked Carea.

"Huh?" said Corrynne as she pulled Striynna's hand from her mouth and looked back up with a glassy stare.

"I asked you if you were sick."

Corrynne lifted her eyebrows and shook her head. "I don't think I am."

Carea shook her head and said to Dane, "Something's wrong. I know it."

Dane looked at his sister and said, "Wow. How'd you guess?"

Carea frowned. With a hand on her hip she said, "Don't be a smart alec, Dane. Why don't you figure out what's going on. I'm going to go do my homework." Carea then turned and bounded up the stairs.

Dane looked back down at his mother sitting on the floor. He thought he'd try again. "Hi, Mom!" he said in a cheery voice.

Corrynne looked up at him and smiled again. "I said, 'Hi'."

"Yeah, but your heart wasn't in it."

Corrynne hugged Dane's bulky calf that stood like a tree trunk from hours of lifting weights. "Thank you for worrying about me," she said. "I'll be fine."

"What's wrong? Can I help?" Dane asked as he squatted down to be eye-level with his mother.

"No, sweetheart. There is nothing anyone can do. I'm caught."

"Come on, Mom, there is always something you can do. You taught me that!" said Dane with an enthusiastic smile.

"The only thing that could be done would put us all in danger." Corrynne's eyes teared and then that was it. She couldn't stop the flow. Silently Corrynne suffered as she slowly touched the tears with the tips of her fingers, wiping them away one by one.

"I bet not. Just tell me, and I'll help you. What's the use of having a strong son like me if I can't help?" Dane hit a pose, flexing both biceps.

Corrynne slowly looked up to see his Hercules imitation, with a silly "Dudley Do-Right" smile. He would always pose like that to try to make her smile.

Despite her sadness, her mouth changed slightly, hiding a developing smile.

"I see that smile, Mom. It's somewhere in there begging to get out. Here, let's try again." Dane hit another pose, bringing his arms in front of him, curling his arms in and making his fists almost touch.

This time Corrynne couldn't help but begin to laugh silently. Dane was just too funny to resist. A feeling of peaceful warmth came over her, dispelling the horrible ache from moments before. "Oh, Dane. Have you looked at yourself in the mirror when you do that?"

"Sure, Mom," said Dane as he hit a third pose. "Every time I'm near one. Never miss a chance!"

Corrynne stood up as she laughed some more. With hands up in the air she said, "OK, OK. Stop!"

"I won't until you tell me what's wrong," said Dane as he hit a fourth pose.

"Fine!" said Corrynne. "I'll tell you," she said feeling like a large wall had fallen. Somehow just laughing and being given the ability to voice her concerns made her feel like her burdens were lighter.

Dane lost his goofy expressions but instead put on a sickly-sweet pseudo-empathetic air as he batted his eyes.

Corrynne stared at him. "How do you expect me to talk to you when you look like that?"

"Sorry." Dane's face went blank. "Is this better?"

Corrynne snickered a little as she shook her head. "Now it's like talking to a stone, but I'll take it."

"Good," said Dane as he folded his arms.

"Do you know anyone at your school who goes to parties called Raves?"

Dane nodded. "Yes."

"You do?" Corrynne was surprised. She didn't know what she was expecting but she knew she didn't want her children to be exposed to the parties or anything in them. "How?"

"The Bats go to them every weekend. They're really into them."

"Bats?" Corrynne's concern escalated. Dane knew the cult's name! It bothered her that he sounded so casual about the group. She became interested in how much he actually knew. How far had this group infiltrated the high school? "Tell me about the Bats, Dane."

"The Bats are a group of kids who claim they feel God at the Raves. I think they are confusing the effects of drugs with spirituality. I don't know how they can talk themselves into thinking what they're doing is right."[1]

Corrynne's face drained as she considered his answer. She couldn't help but realize that not only did her son know of the group, he also knew specific details about them. His obvious familiarity caused her to shiver in horror. Her heart fell as she realized her efforts to keep her family safe had already failed. Their lives were infiltrated with the presence of the cult whether she liked it or not.

Dane, recognizing the look of despair growing on his mother's face, asked, "What, Mom? What's wrong?"

"Are there really a lot of those people at your school?" Corrynne was afraid to hear her son's answer.

"Yes, tons. Remember? Kessa became a Bat."

"No, I don't remember the word 'Bat' coming up when I talked to Carea about Kessa. I knew that she had found another religion, but I didn't know she had joined the Bats!" Corrynne kicked herself for not asking more questions about Kessa. She wondered if Bo knew, because he certainly had not told her about it.

"More and more kids are 'converting' every day." Dane held up both hands and made the quotations sign.

"Why? What do they see in it that makes them want to join?"

"I don't really know, since I haven't been up there, but according to the talk at school it's the free drugs and the popularity of the party. But the people I worry about the most are those who really believe the stuff being told to them.[2] There are some who claim that belonging to the group will save the members' lives during the 'cleansing of the earth.' A lot of people have warned me that I will die if I don't join...."[3]

"Hmmm," Corrynne said as she listened. She continued to hide the extent of her own knowledge until she knew what Dane was exposed to. "Do you know anything else?"

"Yes, another strange thing that attracts new people is the appearance of a great spiritual man. I guess it's like David Copperfield. Poof! He just appears."

Corrynne suddenly felt goose bumps on her arms. The memory of Imam Mahdi's picture from the Internet site appeared unsolicited in her mind as she listened to Dane. She remembered the unbelief she, Bo, Braun, and Brea shared as they learned about him. "What do they say about the spiritual man?"

"Every so often, but not every time, a man in white appears who claims that he is the foretold Messiah from the scriptures. There have been fights at school over whether he's real or not. I guess he can even do miracles. But I

call it magic, because I'm sure they're all just being tricked."[4] Dane
continued, "There are even some kids you know who go."

Corrynne's eyes widened. "Has anyone from our ward gone?"

"Oh, yeah. But it's a secret.[5] No one in organized society can know, or
the members will supposedly be burned."

"Oh, that makes sense from what I know at the hospital. Do you know
who they are?"

"Yes, some of them. I've already talked over that issue with the bishop.
He pulled me aside on Sunday and asked me if I knew who was going to the
parties. He seemed really worried."[6]

"Good." Corrynne returned to the previous subject. "So the members of
the group can tell their friends about the meetings, but they can't tell their
parents. Am I getting this right? So there aren't any adults at these
meetings?"

"Oh, no. There're tons of adults."

"There are?"

"Yep, at least that's my understanding. Anyone can belong, but mostly
those who are not accepted by organized society join. I guess the man in
white calls those who feel they have been rejected by society to join and be a
part of his family. You wouldn't qualify, since you're accepted into society's
ranks. You're an employed nurse at a hospital, a mom, on the PTA—get the
picture? You fulfill productive roles within society's framework. Society is
enemy number one."

"Why?"

"Society brainwashes people. People who belong to it couldn't possibly
understand what goes on at those parties, because their ideas are too formed
by the laws and perceptions that surround them."

"Oh." Corrynne let everything her son said soak in. "So you're telling me
there are different kinds of people who belong to the cult, all ages and races,
and it is not restricted to the youth."[7]

"Right." Dane nodded.

"That might explain why the parents of the victims we've had at the
hospital are trying to protect their privacy. They won't talk to the police, and
they aren't demanding compensation. Everyone is just being quiet. At first it
didn't make sense to me why the parents weren't angry about their family
members' deaths, but if the families are involved in the cult, or at least
understand the risks and consequences, maybe they were protecting someone
else. Wow, the roots of this group may run deeper than it first appeared."

"Or the group could scare the family into not pressing charges. Terror is
the group's motto, and they're anxious to spread it around to keep control."

"How do you know all these things?" Corrynne could not keep back her
amazement at his knowledge, which had gone undetected until now.

"Because everyone keeps trying to convince me to come and check out
the parties. They've tried everything to get me to go."[8]

"What do you say when they ask you to go?"

"I just say, 'No, thank you. I have my own beliefs'."

"Does that make them leave you alone?"

"Maybe for ten minutes. Then some other 'Bat missionaries' come along, and I have to fight them off, too. They're really annoying. It's a big deal to them."

"I'm glad that you're so strong. I am so proud of you," said Corrynne, feeling so thankful for her son's courage. "Continue to make right choices."[9]

Dane nodded.

Thoughtfully, Corrynne began to have a plan form in her mind. "Let's see, I need to tell the hospital I won't be coming in tomorrow."

"Are you talking to me, Mom?" Dane asked.

Corrynne lowered her voice and looked around. No one was listening, so she proceeded. "I'm going to ask you something I never thought I would." She looked into her son's eyes.

"What, Mom?"

"The next time someone invites you to one of those parties, act interested. Find out where it is, and then I'm going to go."

"Why, Mom?"

"I have to. I need to find out what's going on at those Raves."

Dane shook his head with a touch of worry on his face. "I don't think that's a very good idea."

Corrynne nodded as she looked down at her hands. "I know, but my choices are limited. I believe someone at the hospital has stolen some drugs, and I think they're using them in that cult. I need to find out what they're doing with them and get some pictures if I can." Corrynne took a deep breath and suddenly said, "Dane, they've framed me for some stolen drugs at the hospital. They've given me no choice but to prove I didn't do it. I'll lose everything if I can't fix this problem."

"Oh, no!" Dane's face paled.

"I know this may be dangerous, but if I can prove my innocence, they'll give back all my privileges at the hospital and not prosecute me for the loss."

"How are you going to take pictures? They'll kill you if they figure out what you're doing. I hear they kill people all the time."

Corrynne bit her lip. "I don't know yet, but there has to be a way."

"Not for you."

"What?" Corrynne frowned as she looked at her son. "What do you mean?"

"I'll go," said Dane.

Corrynne shook her head. "No, I couldn't have you go. You've made it very clear where you stand. People would wonder. Plus, this is my problem. I should fix it."

"Mom, be real. You wouldn't fit in. Come on, accept your limits."

Corrynne's look became distant. "I have to do something. I'm afraid if I don't, this could threaten my family after they're done ruining me."

"That's why you need to let me go. I can talk the talk and walk the walk. No one would know I was carrying a secret surveillance device. It'll be a challenge. It'll be cool."

Corrynne studied Dane's sincere face. She marveled at his willingness to help her. His sacrifice touched her. She conceded, "Fine, I admit that you're probably a better undercover agent than I would be in this case."

"Good," said Dane, "I want to keep my mom far from danger. It's my job!" Once again Dane hit his Hercules pose with his associated goofy face.

Corrynne laughed without restraint this time and then hugged her son. "Thank you, Dane, you're my hero!"

"OK, Mom, let's plan our mission."

Still smiling, Corrynne said, "I've been thinking about this, and I think we could use Brea's recording device to transmit to the police station. If I can at least show the illegal drug use up on the mountain, I think they'll pay attention. Do you think they would be interested in anything else you could find at those parties?"

"Oh, yeah, Mom. There's so much stuff that goes on up there that's illegal! We could prove tons if I could take in a camera."

"Maybe we could hide the camera in a hat or something."

"A hat? What, a top hat?"

"All right, maybe a hat isn't such a good idea. I'll have to think of what to do. I'll come up with something."

"OK, that sounds cool, Mom. Keep going—you're on a roll."

"I do know one thing. Before we do anything, we all need to go to the doctor and get some shots."

"Shots?!" Dane cowered dramatically.

"Yes, shots to protect you in case you somehow catch the *Strep* A that eats your skin and muscle. So gather everyone up. We'll go now."

"Now?" Dane grabbed his arm as if to protect it.

"Yes, now, the sooner the better. Let's go! The evening clinic is open now."

"Not everyone is home, though."

"I know, but we can't wait. Brea, Braun, and your dad can go themselves, or maybe I can bring the shots home. Don't worry—they'll get their shot. I'll make sure!"

Legacy

"Matt, it's gorgeous!" Brea held out her hand in front of her, over her still half-filled plate of food, and admired how her new diamond glittered in the candlelight.

Matt grinned and reached around their dishware, resting his elbow on the table to take Brea's hand in his. "Not half as gorgeous as you." Then he kissed her hand.

"I have always wanted a simple solitaire. This one's so elegant!"

Matt put down his fork in his right and pointed. "There's a beautiful story behind that ring."

"Really?" Brea looked up at Matt.

"Yes, a love story that will live out the ages."

"Tell me," Brea coaxed softly.

Matt leaned back in his chair and wiped his mouth with his napkin. Then he said, "That ring was brought into existence by my grandfather. It was one of the first mined out of Africa and was made into an engagement ring for my grandmother."

"This was your grandmother's ring?"

"Yes."

"I love it! Tell me the whole story."

"My grandfather was a jeweler by trade. He made beautiful pieces of artwork for the rich in England and Germany and other countries all over the world. He met my grandmother when he was here in America. She was a sassy, beautiful college girl, just like you. In fact, she looked quite a bit like you. They were married only three months after they met. It was a whirlwind relationship that calmed down into stable, true love and yielded beautiful twin girls. One had curly hair and turquoise eyes, and the other had straight hair and deep, chocolate-brown eyes like you. They were a handful, but they were the very heart of my grandfather. Soon my grandmother and grandfather learned they were expecting another child. My grandmother had premonitions that it would be a boy, handsome and intelligent. But before my grandfather could see her impressions fulfilled, he was called away to war. When she was five months pregnant with my father, her true love was killed. His plane crashed, ripping him away from his little family when they were young and tender."

"That is so sad."

"It was sad."

"I think I would just dissolve into nothing if that happened to me."

Matt shook his head and kissed Brea's hand again. "No, you wouldn't. You're strong. You would pick yourself up and raise our children the best you could and live well."

Brea shook her head slightly. "I don't know..."

"This life is just a moment," continued Matt. "It's very important to keep a clear perspective. Eternity goes on forever."

"You talk like you know you're going to die young. You're not, are you?"

Matt laughed and said, "Of course not. I'm just saying you can't guarantee anything here on the earth. There are too many people's choices colliding into each other. That causes unpredictable chaos. The only stable thing is the atonement and eternal life.[10] Everything else is really nothing in the long-term view. The lesson we learn then is that nothing on earth lasts forever. Youth fades, riches dwindle, children grow, and people die."

"What about love?" Brea looked deeply into Matt's deep blue eyes.

"I believe love is an extension of our Savior and the light of Christ. Thus, it has eternal properties and does exist forever if we're worthy."[11]

"Good, will you love me when I'm old and wrinkly?" asked Brea tipping her head so her lips were closer to Matt's.

Matt studied Brea's face and then said, "I will always love you. I want to grow old with you, have children with you, and balance the checkbook with you. I want to share eternity with you."

Brea smiled in an alluring way and said, "Good—that's very, very good."

"Looks are inconsequential, because we all lose our luster"—Matt picked up the white rose that had been laid on the side of the table—"just like this beautiful rose. Tomorrow it will wilt and lose its petals and return to the earth. The memory, however, stays with us in its timeless perfection."

Brea moved even closer so her lips were almost touching Matt's. "I love it when you talk like that! It makes you irresistible!"

Matt smiled but did not advance. Instead he said, "That's good to hear, because I'm full of more of where that came from." Then he moved to kiss Brea's inviting lips, but she pulled back unexpectedly.

In response, Brea lowered her lashes and said, "Not yet, my love, there is something we need to talk about."

"What? Now you're being cruel."

"Yes, that's true, but for a good reason. You are the most vulnerable at this moment and will yield to my every command."

"Ahhh, beautiful *and* manipulative. My mother warned me about women like you. Maybe I should rethink this marriage thing."

"Right on the money!" exclaimed Brea.

Matt looked confused. "Were we talking about money?"

"No, marriage, you said marriage. You're on the right track. I want to talk about *our* marriage. I want to marry you soon, very soon."

"How soon?"

"Like...now! Let's go!" Brea got up from the table and acted as if she were leaving.

Matt caught her arm and sat her back down in his lap. "Be serious, because, to be honest, I was thinking the same thing."

"Yes, right now. Under the blue moon!" said Brea almost laughing. "I think it's shining tonight."

"Please, be serious about this," said Matt.

"I am. I want to get married right now."

Matt ignored Brea's statement and suggested, "What about three months? That should give us time to get ready for a wedding."

Brea stopped smiling and said, "What is there to get ready for? A temple wedding takes no preparation. I've got my temple recommend. Do you have yours?"

"Sure, but don't you want a big reception, flowers, lots of guests, etc.?"

Brea shook her head and hugged Matt. "Nope! I just want you."

Matt pulled back so he could see Brea's face. "Come on, we have to include our families. They would be crushed if we didn't have them as part of our wedding."

Brea thought for a moment. "You're right. OK—a week."

"Two months."

"One month," countered Brea.

"You've got a deal, Mrs. Garrett."

Brea smiled and clapped her hands together. "Sounds wonderful!"

"Can I have that kiss now?"

Brea cocked her head and smiled wistfully. "Maybe a little one, I don't want you getting tired of my kisses."

"I could never do that. Not in a million years!"

Brea leaned down and kissed Matt hard. As Brea pulled away, she said, "One month, huh?" A knowing smile played on her face. "I hope you can wait that long for another one of those." She got up from the table and luxuriously walked out of the room.

Matt jumped out of his chair and knocked it over in his haste to follow Brea. Picking up the chair with one hand, he fumbled in his pocket for the payment for the dinner with his other. After finding the adequate cash from his pocket, he tossed the money on the table.

Brea stuck her head back into the room and said, "Aren't you coming?"

Matt gave her a smirk and rushed after her.

Brea just smiled as Matt caught up with her. She knew she had her Matt hooked. It felt good.

Notes to "Something Blue"

The Plan

[1] To judge whether a claim of truth is right or wrong from any source is to ask the question "does it edify? Does it uplift and build? Is it in alignment with the counsels of the scriptures and the prophet of the church?" President Joseph Fielding Smith stated: "There is no saying of greater truth than 'that which doth not edify is not of God.' And that which is not of God is darkness, it matters not whether it comes in the guise of religion, ethics, philosophy or revelation. No revelation from God will fail to edify" *(Doctrine and Covenants and Church History: Gospel Doctrine Teacher's Manual,* 139).

[2] "One of [Satan's] insidious strategies is to progressively soften our senses regarding what is right and wrong…Satan constantly bombards us with deceptive propaganda desirably packaged and carefully disguised" (Bishop H. David Burton, "Heroes," *Ensign,* May 1993, 46).

[3] "It is outrageous to believe that the devil can hurt or injure an innocent man or woman, especially if they are members of the Church of Christ—[unless] that man or woman has faith that he or she can be harmed by such an influence and by such means. If they entertain such an idea, then they are liable to succumb to their own superstitions" (Joseph F. Smith, *Teachings of Presidents of the Church: Joseph F. Smith,* 117-118).

[4] Despite the performance of 'miracles,' it is not proof of divinity. Joseph F. Smith addressed this subject when he said: "When visions, dreams, tongues, prophecy, impressions or any extraordinary gift or inspiration conveys something out of harmony with the accepted

revelations of the Church or contrary to the decisions of its constituted authorities, Latter-day Saints may know that it is not of God, no matter how plausible it may appear" (*Teachings of the Presidents of the Church: Joseph F. Smith*, 117).

[5] Secret combinations were the major cause of the destruction of two Book of Mormon groups, the Nephites and the Jaredites (see Helaman 6:10-41 and Ether 8). Moroni warns modern-day saints of similar dangers in our days. Following is a list of the major characteristics of secret combinations: 1) Satan is the source and foundation of all such organizations; 2) The Lord considers these organizations "above all wickedness of the whole earth" (3 Nephi 9:9 and Ether 8:18); 3) One of the basic tenets of these organizations is secrecy; 4) their main objective is to get power and/or gain (*Book of Mormon Student Manuel*, 359-340).

"Secret combinations are parasites that live off the spiritually dead of a society. They may not be the immediate cause of a nation's downfall, but they are the symptoms of its loathsome condition. Secret societies are formed to implement the ambitions of those who seek for power and gain. History has shown that these groups thrive in an atmosphere of conflict and social immorality. Efforts to police them or exterminate them through legislation have only forced the evil underground where it has continued to survive. This disease has proved fatal to at least two civilizations, and the Book of Mormon makes it abundantly clear that the appearance of this awful parasite endangers any society" (*Book of Mormon Student Manuel*, 492).

[6] "....Many are deceived by the voice of false shepherds, and are misled by false influences. They are deceived; they know not the truth; they understand not what they do and, therefore, they are arrayed, as it were, against the truth, against the work of the Lord; so it has been from the beginning" (Joseph F. Smith, *Teachings of Presidents of the Church: Joseph F. Smith*, 114).

[7] Often it is perceived that antisocial behavior is a folly of youth. This discrepancy can be seen in all aspects of our society. It manifests itself in the prison societies, anti-government groups, and gang societies of today. The evolution of a destructive belief system and associated behaviors, which lead to a multi-generational and enduring source, can be witnessed by studying the gang societies in America. Gangs in the United States typically include adult members. These members are usually the veteran gang members who are the gang leaders because of their age and experience. The gang leaders do not participate in illegal activities as much; instead they have the younger gang members participate in the gang crimes, because if the younger gang members are caught, their prison sentences are typically minor compared to if they were tried as adults. Another trend in this country is generations of gang members. Hard core gang members will raise their kids as gang members, and thus the tradition continues (for further information see T. Wiederhold, *Predictive Variables of Gang Membership and the Structure of Gangs in Utah County*, 19-21).

[8] "When people are wrong they are reinforced in their wrong by being part of a like multitude. Perhaps it is the seeming anonymity. Perhaps they somehow feel less responsible...But plain people as well as prophets irritate incorrect majorities. No wonder there is scorn and shame heaped upon those who will not go along with that which is wrong, especially when evildoers become rigidly proud of their patterns of living" (Neal A. Maxwell, *Things as They Really Are*, 14).

[9] "The valiant among us keep moving forward anyway, because they know the Lord loves them, even when they 'do not know the meaning of all things' (1 Nephi 11:17). As you and I observe the valiant cope successfully with severe and relentless trials, we applaud and celebrate their emerging strength and goodness. Yet the rest of us tremble at the tuition required for the shaping of such sterling character, while hoping we would not falter should similar circumstances come to us!" (Neal A. Maxwell, "Plow in Hope," *Ensign*, May 2001, 59).

Legacy

[10] "Ultimate hope, of course, is tied to Jesus and the great Atonement, with its free gift of the universal Resurrection and the proffer of God's greatest gift, eternal life (see Moroni 7:40-41; Alma 27:28; D&C 6:13; 14:7)" (Neal A. Maxwell, "Plow in Hope," *Ensign,* May 2001, 60).

[11] "At the end, what really matters is who you loved and who loved you. That circle of love is everything, and is a great measure of a past life. It is the gift of greatest worth. Our Lord and Savior's message was one of love. It can be as a light to our personal pathway to exaltation (Thomas S. Monson, "Dedication Day," *Ensign,* Nov. 2000, 66).

CHAPTER THIRTEEN

WHERE HAS MY LITTLE DOG GONE?

"Verily, verily, I say unto thee, blessed art thou for what thou hast done; for thou hast inquired of me, and behold, as often as thou hast inquired thou hast received instruction of my Spirit. If it had not been so, thou wouldst not have come to the place where thou art at this time" (D&C 6:14).

Friday
September 22nd
4:30 p.m.
Provo, Utah

Pepper

"Here, Pepper!" Ry threw a ball onto the grass from the cement porch. The little jet-black poodle took off after it and tackled it as if it were a small rodent, tossing the ball playfully into the air before he brought it back to Ry.

"Good, Pepper!" exclaimed Ry as he took the slimy ball from his dog's mouth. Ry aimed once again and threw it in another direction. The ball flew in an arch and then bounced wildly into a group of bushes. "Darn!" Ry said emphatically, as he stood on his tiptoes to locate it. Unable to see the missing toy, he trudged toward the bushes to try to find the little ball.

As he approached the bushes, a hidden person dressed in black bolted out of the bushes and ran down the sidewalk.[1] The sudden movement startled Ry.

Pepper took off, barking loudly at the stranger's heels.

Ry stood still as he watched his dog and the stranger run farther and farther away until both disappeared around the street corner. "Pepper!" he yelled fiercely. "Pepper! Why do you have to chase everyone? Come back here!" he yelled, but Pepper did not return. Ry continued to mutter angrily to himself as he trudged down the sidewalk. Now he would have to go find him.

At the end of the sidewalk, Ry looked down the street for his dog and the stranger. There wasn't a sign of either. Ry decided to go back to the porch and wait for Pepper. He would come home sooner or later. Ry was sure of it.

To pass the time, Ry sat on the cement porch and traced some small cracks with his finger as his chin rested on his knee. He saw an ant and followed it with his eyes until he lost it in the grass. Sitting up and wrapping an arm around a post, he stood up. Next he swung around and around the pole, all the time keeping an eye out for Pepper. Finally, Ry decided to go inside and ask someone to come out and help him look for his dog. He found Braun on the computer.

"Hey, Braun."

"What, Bud?" asked Braun automatically.

"I think Pepper scared some guy and ran off after him. Will you help me find him?"

Braun was studying the screen when he said, without looking back, "He'll come home when he's hungry. Don't worry."

"But, Braun, what if the dog catcher caught him? He's never been gone this long."

"He has tags on. They'll bring him back. They like the revenues from the ticket they'll give us for not having him on a leash." Braun snickered.

Ry didn't find his big brother's joke funny. He walked away deciding to try someone else.

Brea was painting her nails in her room, admiring her new ring in the light.

"Brea, please help me find Pepper. I can't find him," said Ry.

"I can't, Ry-guy, I have wet nails. It'll be awhile before they dry. Go ask Carea to help you."

Ry trudged down the hall and then up the stairs to Carea's bedroom. He knocked on the door but there wasn't an answer. He turned the knob and found Carea talking on the phone. "Carea, will you help me...."

Carea shook her hand at him and pointed to the door, obviously meaning for him to leave, so Ry did.[2]

Down the stairs, one by one, Ry slid lazily, taking his time getting down. Dane wasn't home, or else he would ask him. Who else should he ask? As he came around the corner of the living room he could see Jax and Roc outside jumping on the trampoline. It looked like they were playing a game. Ry walked outside and watched them string tricks together with only one bounce in between. Jax was obviously better than Roc.

Ry listened as Jax bragged, "When you're my age, you'll be as good as me, but then I'll be better than you still, because I'm older."

Only meaning to forget about Pepper momentarily, he jumped and lifted himself onto the side of the trampoline. "It's my turn next," he said. "I could beat you, Jax."

Jax looked at Ry with a dull, but irritated glare. "No you couldn't. I'm still way better than you, too."

"Na uhh," said Ry as he jumped onto the trampoline uninvited. "I'll show you..."

Soon all three of them were competing. It was a boy's world where boys always won. It was enough to distract anyone.

Hassle

Carea was sitting on the floor next to her bed with her knees drawn up to her chest. It was her favorite way to talk on the phone. "Sorry, that was my little brother barging in here to ask me something. I told him to leave. Now, what did you say?"

"I said Jack really likes you. Why don't you give him the time of day?" came the young female voice over the phone. It was Kessa.

"What do you care? He isn't even from our school. Why are you fighting his case?"

"Because he found out we're friends, and he asked me for a favor. I know him from the Raves."

"No offense," said Carea, "but most of the Bats give me the creeps. Their perception of reality is twisted. I wish you would re-think your association with them."

"Carea, do you know how awful you sound?"

"I'm not being awful, just honest. Didn't you want more honesty in your life? I'm giving it to you. It's true the Bat group is different. Many of them have been on an alternate sphere too long. It's left them permanently confused. Don't get me wrong, Kessa, you're not like that. In fact, at least you're doing what you're doing because you're looking for a higher meaning in life rather than just going to get plastered. I know you. I get you—that 's why we still get along."

"Carea, we're all children of God. We're no different from each other. We should just stop segregating and give in to peace, or terror and war will force us to."

"Whoa, why did you just say that?" asked Carea.

"It's what I believe and also what Imam Mahdi teaches. It will happen, you know."

"Kessa, now *you* are giving me the creeps. You know I believe in world peace. I just don't want to date a Bat. Sometimes rifts are just too big. He'll expect too much. Dating is different from friendship."[3]

"I think you're just intolerant. What happened to all the patience and love you said you believed in?"

"I still believe in it."

"Oh really?"

"Bats just think differently, they act differently, they have strange priorities," explained Carea.

"Well, so do you."

"Maybe to some it might seem that way, but my religion is at least normal."

"How's that?"

"We don't sneak around with secrets, mark up our bodies, take drugs, and worship voodoo men."

"I don't know. The Mormons seem to have a lot of weird things they do, too."[4]

"No, we don't, and we're not called 'Mormons' anymore."[5]

"Sorry, Latter-day Saints."

"I don't know what you're referring to. We don't do anything weird! Everything we do is good and true. Our religion teaches us to be upstanding citizens, to be kind to everyone, to be honest, to love your spouse and your children. I could go on and on. What's so weird about that?"

"I guess it's your point of view. You're just setting yourself up to be labeled 'prejudiced,' but we've been over this before. Even though your religion says it accepts everyone, it tells you to push away everyone who's not like you."

"Prejudiced? I don't think so! Kessa, you've gone over the line, and you know it."[6]

"So, then, why don't you marry outside your religion?[7] Why do you date only guys who believe what you do?[8] I'm surprised you let me be your friend, since I'm not like you. Maybe you'll stop."

"That was a low blow and I wish you'd grow up. I don't want to date a non-member, because I don't want to marry one.[9] I don't want to marry one, because I want my husband and me to have the same belief set.[10] I want us to have the same belief set so our children will have peace and unity at home.[11] I want my children to believe what I believe. It's good. It will give them solid footing. It will teach them all the things that will give them direction.[12] And as far as you being my friend, you are my friend, because I sincerely like you and, no, I won't stop, even though you're being obnoxious right now."

"OK, I'm sorry. I didn't mean to push you into a corner. I guess you have your reasons. I just think you should give the Bats a break. At least they're living their religion, which is more than I can say for most people…except you, of course."

Carea shook her head. "I'm just tired of all of this. So many of the Bats have been hassling me to come to their parties. They say, 'Come see for yourself.' Well, I have no interest to see for myself. I have my own way of thinking. I have my whole life mapped out, and it doesn't include wild parties woven with a pseudo-religion."

There was silence on the other side of the line. Then Kessa said, "Your brother's going to a party tonight."

"Dane?"

"Yes."

"He's not. He would never do that. He's one of the most straight-arrow guys I know," said Carea, getting a little angry.

"It's true. I heard it from tons of people. Everyone in school is talking about it. For being a close family, you sure don't know what's going on with one another."

"Why are you being so mean?" asked Carea.

"I'm not. I'm just telling you the truth."

"I don't care what you say. I'm sure you're wrong."

"Why do you always think I'm wrong? Why can't you be wrong?" asked Kessa. "In fact, why don't you ask your brother, and we'll see who's wrong?"

"Well, I will, as soon as he comes home from football practice."

"Good."

"It was a pleasure talking with you," said Carea.

"That was a snide remark from Little Miss Perfect."

"Just drop it."

"Dropped."

"Bye."

"Bye."

Carea was mad. She got up from her position on the floor and began to pace in her room. She threw the phone on the bed and turned around and stared out the second-story window of their home. There was no way her brother would even think of going to a Rave. She was sure either he was playing a joke or telling them he was going to get them off his back. There had to be a logical explanation, and she would find out.

Looking out the window, Carea noticed Dane drive up in the truck and pull around the house into the garage. By the time he came into the house, Carea was already waiting for him at the door.

"Dane, there's talk you're going to a Bat party tonight. It's not true, is it?"

Dane stood there, half in the house and half out. He quickly put his finger up to his lips and closed the garage door as he stepped inside. He tiptoed through the kitchen and up the stairs as he motioned for her to follow him.

Carea followed, frowning. Dane was acting strange. This was not a good sign. Secrecy always meant trouble.

At the top of the stairs, Dane went into Carea's room and closed the door after him and his sister. "Carea, this cannot be broadcast all over the house."

Carea was really bothered. Now she knew the answer. He *was* going! She couldn't believe it! In an angry voice she said, "So tell me what's going on!"

"I can't tell you right now."

"Is it a dare from your football buddies? Because if it is, it can get you killed. Those Bats are serious about their religion and will kill anyone who makes a fool out of them. I've heard terrible horror stories of people being burned alive."

"Carea, no one is going to get killed. I just have to go there for maybe an hour or so tonight and check things out."

"Why? What happened to avoiding the appearance of evil?[13] What kind of example will you be if people see you at a Rave?"

Dane scratched his head in irritation. "I'm not going to *do* anything. I'm just looking around. No one will really remember me, anyway. They'll all be too busy partying."

"Mom says she sees people come to the ER with a Strep infection that eats your flesh. She says people get it at the parties."

"I know, but we got the shot, remember? That's what the shot was for."

"So you're serious," said Carea, not believing what she was hearing.

"Yep. Got to go, don't have a choice."

Carea made a questioning face. "I'm confused. Have you made a pact with someone? Are you in trouble?"

Dane closed one eye and looked up at the ceiling. "No...and no. Any other questions, *nosey*?"

That was her signal to stop asking questions. She was only trying to make sure he was safe and he was being rude in return. She opened the door and shoved him out, slamming the door in his face.

"You can rot for all I care!" Carea yelled through the door.

Dane stood for a moment beyond the door. He was tempted to yell something back at his sister, but then had second thoughts. It wasn't fair to make Carea this mad. It wasn't her battle. He didn't want to tell her about the situation because he wanted to keep her safe. He knew her doting ways and knew she would try to protect him. But this time she couldn't. He didn't want her anywhere close to the party. No, he would have to do this by himself. It was best if she knew nothing, even if she was angry.

Incognito

It was getting late. Darkness had covered the neighborhood. Corrynne stared out her upper bedroom window as she obsessed about how they were going to document the Rave without putting Dane in danger. She had originally thought it would be perfect to use the camera Brea used at college that videotaped and recorded audio, then transmitted the recording to a TV at the police station by setting up a receiver there. It had seemed like a perfect plan. It would be real-time footage exposing everything. There would be no question of tampering or falsifying, since the police would be witnesses to its making. Plus, they would be able to guarantee the safety of the record themselves. The difficult task was figuring out how to get a camera into the party without being seen. It was this aspect that put her at a loss. No matter how she considered mounting the camera, she was sure it would be obvious they were trying to record the party.

Corrynne almost gave up the plan and decided to use a digital camera instead of video when she had a brainstorm. Dane's winter coat was a ski coat. It was big, bulky and black. She could cut out the lining under the arm and hide Brea's tiny video recorder's form in the batting of the coat. She could then cut a small hole where the lens and the microphone would be and glue the material to the plastic surrounding those pieces. That would make the material secure, ensuring it wouldn't slip and obstruct the view of the party. She quickly went to work accumulating and constructing the incognito video setup when Dane walked into her bedroom.

"Hi, Mom, ready to go?"

Corrynne looked up. She didn't think she was going to the party with Dane, but his question made her realize that he should have someone backing him up just in case something went wrong. If she just dropped off the TV at the police station, she could go with Dane.

Corrynne hesitated for a second to wonder how she could get the police to watch the TV if she didn't stay and convince them they needed to watch. Maybe she should ask for the police chief and get his permission, then let him explain about the TV to the other officers. After making sure they were watching, she could feel good about leaving with Dane to protect him. But then, what protection could she be? Maybe she could talk on the cell phone with the police as they watched the video feed…. She was tempted to tell Bo about the situation and ask him to go with Dane. He'd be more protection than she could be, but then again, she was afraid he would veto the whole thing. So she decided she would have to back up her son without her husband.

"Almost, Dane. Try this on." Corrynne handed him his jacket and took off his glasses.

"Hey, why did you do that? I need my glasses"—then Dane looked at the bulky coat with disdain—"and, Mom, I don't need a coat."

Corrynne looked at him with a perplexed look and said, "Go put your contacts in. I have a feeling this is going to be a rough crowd tonight. If you get pushed around you don't want to worry about glasses flying off your nose."

A look of understanding came into Dane's face, then determination. "If anyone pushes me around, they'll get a pounding!"

Corrynne frowned. "Be careful, Dane, you don't want to get beat up by being overconfident. You have to be strategic in your thinking, not physical. Remember, there will be many, many of them and only one of you. Plus, you're going to have a camera embedded in your coat. You don't want them touching you and finding it. So even though you don't normally wear a coat because 'real men' are never supposed to get cold for some reason, this time you need to. It's our eye into their world. We'll be watching everything that happens. So try it on, Macho Man."

Dane nodded once. "Oh, cool, got ya, Mom." Dane put on the coat. Corrynne stepped back to look and see how naturally the camera fit in his armpit. For some reason, it hung in an odd way. It looked very *un*natural. However, she could not see the lens or the microphone. It was nicely camouflaged in the black nylon.

Corrynne turned and ran down the stairs into Brea's room to get the strap that came with the camera and ran back up the stairs. "Dane, take off your shirt."

"Why?" Dane's eyes were wide. He was very modest.

"Because I need to secure the camera to your body somehow so it doesn't hang in your coat." Dane removed his coat and then his shirt. Corrynne took the strap and adjusted it to fit around his chest. Then she took her scissors and attempted to cut a hole into his shirt at the armpit to allow the strap to be threaded through.

"Whoaaa!" yelled Dane

"What's wrong?!" asked Corrynne, surprised at his unexpected outburst.

"That's my favorite shirt! Don't cut it!"

"Well, go get one I can cut into," said Corrynne.

Dane grabbed his shirt and threw it on over his bare chest then trudged down the stairs to retrieve a less favorable shirt. He mumbled as he left, "Everybody is going to know something's up because I'm going to look like a dweeb."

Corrynne called after him, "Oh, Dane! It's only a shirt! Look, I'll buy you a new one when this is over, so wear something you would normally wear!"

Dane soon appeared in his football jersey. Corrynne stood frozen with the scissors in the air. "Dane! What are you thinking? I can't cut into a school jersey!"

"Why? This is something I would normally wear. Plus these tear-away shirts are supposed to get ripped when we play football. They just throw them away after the season. Just rip it instead of cut it. It will add character for the game."

"Well, I did pay three hundred dollars for you to play this year. With those fees, I'm sure I should own this shirt," said Corrynne.

Dane took off his jersey, and Corrynne poked a hole in the armpit and then ripped it until the hole was big enough for the strap to fit through. She attached the camera strap through the armpit of the coat, around the body of the camera inside the lining, through the strap loops on the camera in the material of the coat, then back out the same way. After that, Dane put his jersey on and then his coat. Corrynne took the straps that were hanging from the inside of the coat and threaded them through the new hole in the armpit of the jersey. Then she adjusted the Velcro that was already sewn into the strap around Dane's chest to fit skintight.

Corrynne stepped back and looked at the setup. Dane was standing with his arms out straight to allow her to adjust the apparatus. "Put your arms down."

Dane complied.

Corrynne was pleased. Her plan had worked perfectly. The camera fit snugly under Dane's arm and didn't move. She was sure no one would notice it.

"Wonderful!" she said as she clapped her hands and did a little hop of excitement. "I think this is going to work!"

Dane went over to the mirror and inspected it himself. He nodded in agreement. "Yep, I think you're right. Looks good. But how is the camera going to see from under my arm?"

Corrynne approached Dane and pointed at the mirror. "Look, the lens points out from your armpit with the body of the camera under your arm. Look, your arms don't get in the way. See?" asked Corrynne as she moved Dane's arms for him.

Dane nodded. "That will stink."

"What will?" asked Corrynne.

"The camera will after I'm done with it."

Corrynne shook her head. "I hope you used deodorant today."

"I did," said Dane. "But I can't guarantee it hasn't worn off."

"It will be fine," said Corrynne letting her mind move on to the next topic. "OK, what comes next? Let's see, do we still have those mini walkie-talkies we bought for Disney World?"

"Yeah, but I can't talk to you through one. That would be too obvious."

Corrynne nodded. "I know, but if you have one in your pocket, you could beep me once for 'I'm OK' and twice for 'help.' If it's in your pocket, no one will notice you're hitting the button. We can even say three times for 'call 9-1-1!'"

Dane laughed. "Right, Mom."

"You never know. You might need to call for help."

Dane smirked and said, "OK, Mom, I'll go get them if it will make you feel better."

"Yes, I would like that. Now, I'll get my cell phone, and we'll be off. You go get those walkie-talkies and make sure they have new batteries in them."

Both Dane and Corrynne went down the stairs. They were in the process of gathering their things when Corrynne poked her head in the family room to see her husband at the computer. "Bo, I'm going out for a little while."

"Oh, hi, Corrynne, I thought you were at work. Why aren't you going tonight?"

"I'm taking a vacation day. I decided to do something with Dane. It's our night out."

"Oh, yeah? I didn't hear about this. What are you doing?" asked Bo.

"I'll call you with the details—we're late. The twins are sleeping in the boy's room. I love you."

"Love you, too."

Corrynne turned to go, but was startled by Carea standing right in her way. With a hand on her chest, Corrynne exclaimed, "Carea! You startled me! What are you doing sneaking up on me like that?"

"What are you doing, Mom?" Carea's eyes narrowed and pierced Corrynne's heart.

Feeling uneasy, Corrynne calmly said, "I'm going somewhere with Dane. I'll tell you all about it later. I've got to go."

"Could you be going to a *Rave?*" Carea raised her voice just enough so that Bo could hear.

Corrynne was instantly alarmed. She frowned dramatically and brought her finger up to her lips. "Shhh! Please don't do this. Carea, I need to set things right. I don't want your dad to worry."

Carea, not inhibited by her mother's efforts to quiet her, said, "Sorry, Mom, won't cover for you." Carea then raised her voice to an obvious level. "You always taught me secrets destroy relationships, and I don't think now is a good time to start keeping them."[14]

Suddenly, Bo was looking over Corrynne's shoulder at Carea. "What's going on here? What about a Rave and Mom?" Bo had a very distinct frown on his face that matched Corrynne's, who turned to look at him. "What are you really going to do, Corrynne?" He was flexing his jaw muscles, which meant he was exhibiting extreme restraint.

Corrynne's voice and presence softened. She looked up at her husband and said, "Bo, I've been framed at the hospital for stolen narcotics. They pulled all my privileges. They told me the only way I could have them back was to bring them the drugs or give them evidence of my innocence or someone else's guilt."

"That's ridiculous!" Bo's face was reddening.

"I know. I said the same thing. Since the drugs were stolen on my shift, I was responsible whether I took them or not. No matter what I said to the nurse manager, the end was still the same. I was responsible and until it was solved, I would not be able to have any charge or narcotic privileges until further notice. I'm sure this will mushroom to include my practicing license, too."

"Do you have any idea about what happened?" asked Bo.

"Yes, Ann Cain, who was the nurse who helped me during the code when I found out about the Raves, was working that night with me on the floor. She somehow signed out twenty vials of Versed in my handwriting and then told everyone that she saw me steal the drugs to frame her. It's a huge mess!"

"Did you tell the nurse manager that Ann was probably involved with the Raves and most likely took the drugs for them?"

"I tried, but she acted like I was crazy. I guess Ann told her I had concocted a wild story having to do with her and the cult. Believe me, it didn't help my side of the story."

"This Ann girl really thought things out, didn't she?" asked Bo.

Corrynne's face contorted into a twisted, frustrated look. "Well, whether she thought of it or someone else did, it seemed to work…and that really bothers me! I don't know why the manager would believe Ann over me. I've worked in that unit for thirteen years! You'd think that'd count for something!"

Then Dane came around the corner with the two walkie-talkies in his hands. "Come on, let's go! I'm boiling in this coat!"

Bo, Corrynne, and Carea all turned and looked at him together. Dane looked funny with his flushed face and beads of sweat beginning to form. Everyone knew Dane wouldn't be caught dead in a coat for longer than he absolutely had to. He had always been hot-blooded. There had to be some sort of coercion involved in this scenario.

"What are you doing wearing a coat in the house?" Bo asked.

Dane looked nervous and said, "Well, I'm kind of hooked on this coat.... It's real cool." He nodded his head at his half-truth. "Yeah...." Still nodding his head, with wide eyes, it looked like he didn't know what else to say. Quickly, he turned to exit.

"Or really hot?" Bo smiled a sarcastic grin.

"Yeah, that's right." Dane turned back, smiled, and pointed at his dad. He began to back up with a controlled saunter then turned suddenly, once again to head for the garage. "I'll be leaving now. Bye!" He quickly left.

"OK, what did you do?" Bo asked Corrynne, a grin still plastered on his face.

"Well, I hid Brea's camera in the lining of his coat and strapped it to his body. I'm going to take a TV to the police station and have the police watch real-time video of the Rave."

"So he really is 'hooked' on the coat?" Carea asked, beginning to smile.

"Yep, afraid so," Corrynne answered, nodding her head. All three of them began to laugh. It was a nice relief from the building tension.

Bo took a deep breath and looked down at the floor. "Corrynne, let it go. You don't need to work any more. You've put in your time." Bo then searched his wife's eyes. "Let them take away your license. Who cares? It's not worth it! Quit. Get normal sleep. Be free. What's most important is our family. These kids need you to be safe and alive. Why would you put all this at risk for something that isn't even true?"

"It's not that, don't you see?" asked Corrynne. "It's not my license, or my charge privileges; it *is* my family I'm fighting for. At some point in time we're all going to have to stand up for what we believe.[15] We can't lie down and allow Satan to take our freedoms away because we aren't willing to take risks. He's depending on our complacence. He wants us to sit back and let someone else take care of it."

For a moment, Corrynne and Bo's eyes locked. There was a long silent pause.

Corrynne began again in a softer voice. "I've prayed about this over and over, Bo. Every way I look at it, I feel it's time that I do something. I feel like the Lord is leading me. I've tried to ignore the situation, and that was fine until it was time to do something else. You know, the Lord knows everything from the beginning to the end, and he understands timing much better than I do."[16]

Corrynne continued, "This plan is the only thing I can think of that is semi-safe. ...You know I'm normally against getting involved or fighting, but this is one time it's worth fighting. I think you can feel the truth. You also know we're fighting, literally, for the souls and the futures of our children."[17]

Bo looked at Corrynne without blinking. He seemed to be softening to her agenda. "Well, what are your goals tonight?"

"First of all, I want to document the illegal use of drugs. Second, I want to demonstrate the potential of the Strep originating from the ceremonies. Third, I need to find Ann and the drugs she took to set the record straight at the hospital. Dane can accomplish all of these objectives by walking around tonight, allowing the camera to record what happens during the Rave. Once we have something to take to the public"—Corrynne touched Bo's hand—"this will not be a personal battle. The theory is, if we can successfully show the authorities there is something to worry about, then we won't be alone in our efforts."[18]

Bo thought for a moment, reviewing and weighing Corrynne's plan. Finally he took her in his arms and held her. "I love you, Corrynne. I don't want you in any more trouble than you already are."

Bo pulled away and then walked to the coat closet. "Corrynne, you go to the police station," he said with a sudden stern look. "I'll go and watch out for Dane. This is a job for a father."[19]

"Why? Because you're a man?" asked Corrynne.

"Well, frankly, yes. It's my divine duty. Plus, I have more life insurance on me than you do." Bo smiled and winked at his wife and headed for the garage. "I'll keep in touch with the cell." At the last minute, Bo looked back and said, "Having me involved was your original plan, wasn't it?"

Corrynne smiled and then looked down at the floor. "Yes, I just wasn't sure if you would buy into it."

"Well, I guess you got me." Bo said as he walked out the door.

"Thank you, Bo. You are my knight in shining armor," Corrynne said with a smile. Even though he didn't hear with his ears, she knew he could feel in his heart what she thought.

Warning

Carea, after witnessing her parents' planning together to single handedly bring down the Raves, turned and started for the stairs to her room. Things in her house were very confusing lately. She needed to call Kessa again and let her know what was happening. She wondered if it would change Kessa's mind about her newfound religion.

As Carea climbed the stairs, she reflected on the past few hours. Now her earlier conversation with Dane made sense. Suddenly she had greater respect for her brother. He wasn't just a big brainless football player; he was self-sacrificing, brave, and obedient. A feeling of pride welled up inside of her.

From somewhere, Carea heard a muffled whining. It was hard to identify where it was coming from. She heard it only once, and then it was silent. It sounded to her like their dog. Was he caught in some closet? Sometimes that would happen as the little boys played. She ran up the stairs to see if that were the case.

"Pepper," Carea called in a soft, high voice. "Pepper, where are you?" Carea listened intently, but there was no response. She continued to look, opening the doors of all the closets. When her search was unsuccessful, she went downstairs to find the little guys. They almost always knew where Pepper was.

Carea found Ry looking in the refrigerator with a blank stare. "What are you looking for?"

"I'm hungry."

"Again?"

Ry nodded.

"Sorry, I don't think anyone is going to make anything more for you tonight. Why don't you make yourself some Ramen or something?"

His eyes brightened. "OK." He opened the pantry door to retrieve his favorite snack food. "I'm starving! I'm always starving."

"You're growing." Carea changed the subject. "Hey, Ry, do you know where Pepper is?"

Ry looked at Carea as he pulled on the soup packaging. "He's not home yet?" he asked, looking troubled.

"No, I know he's home. I just heard him crying somewhere. I just can't find him."

"Where did you hear him?" Ry put his food down on the counter.

"I was going up the stairs when I thought I heard him in a closet, but I looked in all the closets. He isn't anywhere."

Immediately Ry went to the front door and opened it. "Pepper!" he yelled into the night air. His breath made a cloud in front of his face. He walked out onto the porch. "Pepper!"

A whining sounded somewhere near. "Carea! I hear him! He's out here."

Carea moved with Ry out onto the porch and stooped down, looking around the perimeter of the house.

Another whine helped them zero in on the sound.

Carea found their dog behind the bushes in front of the porch. He was a shivering, glistening mass.

Ry went down to pick him up when Carea yelled, "Stop, don't touch him!"

Ry jumped back suddenly as Pepper snapped at him.

"He's hurt, Carea," said Ry.

"I know. Let me go get Mom. Don't touch him or he'll bite you."

Ry complied, frozen, as he blinked to try and see Pepper clearer in the dark.

Carea ran into the house. "Mom! Pepper's hurt!" Carea continued to search the rooms until she found her mother and the twins in one of the back bedrooms. She had been on the phone with the police station.

Corrynne clicked the off button on the phone and said, "Carea, what's wrong?"

Carea was becoming very upset. "Mom, I don't know what's wrong, but Pepper is hurt really bad. He's bleeding everywhere! He's hiding in the bushes outside and won't let us touch him."

Seeing that Carea was on the verge of crying, Corrynne immediately held out her arms, and Carea flung herself into her mother's embrace. Corrynne held her tight for a second. "These things are always shocking at first," she said to her daughter. "It'll be fine."

"I just hate blood. I don't know why it bothers me so much." Carea was trying to hold back the tears.

"It's just because it's something you don't deal with very much. It will be fine."

"Come quick, Mom!" Ry yelled from down the hall.

The babies took off through the opened door, down the hall, crawling toward Ry's panicked voice. Corrynne followed.

"I bet Pepper's frozen!" said Carea, who was becoming more controlled now. "Who knows how long he's been out there in the cold."

"Let me get a towel or something. That way I can pick him up without being bitten." Corrynne went into the bathroom and emerged with a dark towel.

The twins peered out the front door and were attempting to crawl down the step onto the porch. "Ry, take the babies back into the house and close the door. I'll get Pepper and bring him in."

Ry quickly obeyed.

Corrynne walked along the porch until she saw Pepper. He had crawled farther under a bush to try and hide.

"OK, Carea, you pull the bush back, and I'll throw this towel over Pepper and pick him up." Carea pulled, and the towel landed perfectly over Pepper. Corrynne carefully reached around Pepper's shaking body and supported all his limbs, while covering his face to avoid being bitten.

Pepper was silent and didn't struggle but continued to shiver.

Corrynne took Pepper inside the house and put him in the bathtub. By this time, Roc and Jax had heard Pepper was hurt, and all seven people who were in the house were crammed in the tiny bathroom to see what had happened to their little dog.

Striynna and Strykker stood at the side of the tub and reached in to try to touch the water as Corrynne leaned over the opposite end with Pepper. She kept the towel over his head and slowly uncovered his back end. With the warm water she rinsed the blood from his body. As the blood was removed, the sight continued to be shocking. His full, black, curly poodle hair had been shaved off. His pale skin shined white as the water poured over him. He looked like a rodent with a stubby tail.

"Where's his hair, Mommy?" Roc asked.

"It looks like someone shaved him bald. Maybe he was having a bad hair day, and someone was merciful," Corrynne replied, trying to keep the feeling light in the bathroom.

Ry laughed nervously, and the others just looked on.

Corrynne continued to unwrap the dog to expose some bleeding wounds on his back. "Here's where the blood is coming from. It doesn't look bad, just some surface flesh wounds. Those bleed a lot, but they're really not serious."

"Oh, good," breathed Carea.

Corrynne continued to inspect the dog but found no broken bones. He had large scrapes of some kind on his back. When Corrynne looked at his left paw, there was something embedded deep into the padding on his foot. She removed the silver sliver with tweezers. Corrynne held up the thin, sticklike piece of metal in the light to see it better.

"That looks like a broken needle or something," stated Jax, looking intently at the long, slim steel.

"It sure does," agreed Corrynne as she looked at the end of the piece. It did come to a point just exactly like a needle from a hospital.

"I wonder where he would step on something like that," continued Jax, acting very adult.

"I don't know. It's a good question."

Finally, with the towel completely off and the blood washed from his body, Pepper looked up at the gawking family and continued to shiver and lick his lips repeatedly.

"He looks like a rat!" said Ry, laughing.

Laughter of relief echoed off the bathroom walls as the other children recognized the similarity, too.

"Yeah, I didn't know Pepper looked like that under his hair!" laughed Roc.

Ry suddenly became serious. "Mom, don't you think it's odd someone would shave our dog?"

"Yes, I think it is very strange."

Roc looked closely at Pepper's wounds. "T-A-B," he said out loud.

Corrynne's interest suddenly turned. "What did you say?" she asked Roc.

"His hurts look like upside-down letters," Roc said, pointing at the still-oozing wounds.

Corrynne quickly turned the dog around and for the first time saw what her little son had seen. It definitely looked like letters scraped into Pepper's skin. It looked like someone had taken a potato peeler and just peeled away the first layers of skin to write the letters B-A-T. Unmistakably, this was a warning.

"Ry, when was the last time you saw Pepper?"

"We were playing ball, and he ran after a stranger. I tried to catch him, but they ran too fast. He's been gone all day."

Corrynne turned to Carea. "Find my phone. I have to call Dad right now."

Carea left and returned with the phone.

After one ring Bo's voice was on the other end. "Hello?"

"Bo, we found Pepper with the letters B-A-T carved in his skin. I think this is a warning that they know who we are and where we live. I'm sure it's a warning to stay away."

"Corrynne, go to the police station now."

"I don't want to leave the children, especially with this threat. Those people may still be outside."

"Take them all with you."

"How do I do that?"

"Take the Suburban, some sleeping bags, popcorn, and a movie or two. Let them watch movies on the DVD player with the car TV right outside the police station's front door. That's the safest place I can think of for you guys right now."

"OK," said Corrynne. "Yes, that's a good idea. That way I can still take the receiver to the station, while making sure the kids are safe."

"Go now. This is getting out of control. Those Raves have to be stopped."

Notes to "Where Has My Little Dog Gone"

Pepper

[1] We must always be aware of our environment to recognize evil for evil despite a harmless front. "For among my people are found wicked *men:* they lay wait, as he that setteth snares; they set a trap, they catch men" (Jeremiah 5:26).

[2] Little children easily feel the presence of danger or evil. Although they may not understand nor convey the intricacies of their perceptions, their words of warning are wise beyond their years. Their innocence makes them vessels of the Spirit. "And now, he imparteth his word by angels unto men, yea, not only men but women also. Now this is not all; little children do have words given unto them many times, which confound the wise and the learned" (Alma 32:23).

Hassle

[3] "Remember, young women, the importance of proper dating. …Our Heavenly Father wants you to date young men who are faithful members of the Church, who will be worthy to take you to the temple and be married the Lord's way…My young sisters, we have such hope for you. We have such great expectations for you. Don't settle for less than what the Lord wants you to be" (Ezra Taft Benson, "To the Young Women of the Church," *Ensign,* Nov. 1986, 84).

[4] The Lord has said in multiple places in the scriptures the world would perceive the church and its beliefs as "strange." But in its foreign nature, men will discern truth.

"What I have said unto you must needs be, that all men may be left without excuse; That wise men and rulers may hear and know that which they have never considered; That I may proceed to bring to pass my act, my strange act, and perform my work, my strange work, that men may discern between the righteous and the wicked, saith your God" (D&C 101:93-95; see also Isaiah 28: 21, and D&C 95:4).

[5] This change was announced from the pulpit to 25,000 congregations around the world, during March 2001. The message came from a letter from the First Presidency of the Church

of Jesus Christ of Latter-day Saints. Members were asked to "use the full name whenever possible" in referring to the church, thus eliminating the terms "Mormon" or "LDS church." This came as a response to the member's growing responsibility to "proclaim the name of the Savior throughout all the world" ("Church Emphasizes its Official Name," *Ensign,* May 2001, 110*).*

[6] "The Lord has given us some important guidelines for relationships—and they apply to *all* relationships, including dating. We're counseled to treat all people charitably and kindly, to forgive, and to love not only God and others but also ourselves" (M. Gawain Wells, "Breaking Up without Going to Pieces: When Dating Doesn't End in Marriage," *Ensign,* June 1982, 58).

[7] Be ye not unequally yoked together with unbelievers: for what fellowship hath righteousness with unrighteousness? and what communion hath light with darkness?" (2 Corinthians 6:14).

"The most important things that any member of The Church of Jesus Christ of Latter-day Saints ever does in this world are: 1. To marry the right person, in the right place, by the right authority and 2. To keep the covenant made in connection with this holy and perfect order of matrimony—thus assuring the obedient persons of an inheritance of exaltation in the celestial kingdom" (Bruce R. McConkie, "Celestial Marriage," *Mormon Doctrine,* 118).

[8] "Because dating is a preparation for marriage, date only those who have high standards, who respect your standards, and in whose company you can maintain the standards of the gospel of Jesus Christ" (*For the Strength of Youth,* Pamphlet published by The Church of Jesus Christ of Latter-day Saints, 7).

[9] "As members of the Church, we are counseled to marry in a temple of the Lord. And we marry those we date" ("They've Turned Sixteen—Now What?" *Ensign,* Aug. 1985, 30).

President Harold B. Lee said, "The purpose for dating which leads to courtship and ultimately to marriage is a social process by which young people ultimately find their mates in marriage. It is a truism that we find our husband or wife among that company we frequent the most" (*Ye Are the Light of the World,* 72).

[10]"Every successful marriage requires much selfless effort and adjustment on the part of both partners. The more ideals and fundamental purposes in life that are held in common by the husband and wife, the more likelihood of success in their marriage. When differences exist, they can become a source of constant or recurring stress and contention" (Dean L. Larsen, "Marriage and the Patriarchal Order," *Ensign,* Sept. 1982, 6).

[11]"And he commanded them that there should be no contention one with another, but that they should look forward with one eye, having one faith and one baptism, having their hearts knit together in unity and in love one towards another" (Mosiah 18:21).

[12] "And ye will not suffer your children that they go hungry, or naked; neither will ye suffer that they transgress the laws of God, and fight and quarrel one with another, and serve the devil, who is the master of sin, or who is the evil spirit which hath been spoken of by our fathers, he being an enemy to all righteousness. But ye will teach them to walk in the ways of truth and soberness; ye will teach them to love one another, and to serve one another" (Mosiah 4:14-15).

[13] "Prove all things; hold fast that which is good. Abstain from all appearance of evil" (1 Thessalonians 5:21-22).

Incognito

[14] In difficulties within marriages, it is always wise to solve problems together and not keep secrets from each other. Secrets cause contention and promote hasty behaviors, and erroneous conclusions. Although the following scripture is focused on relationships between neighbors, it also applies to any relationship, including marriage. "Go not forth hastily to strive, lest *thou know not* what to do in the end thereof, when thy neighbour hath put thee to shame. Debate thy

cause with thy neighbour *himself;* and discover not a secret to another: Lest he that heareth *it* put thee to shame, and thine infamy turn not away" (Proverbs 25:8-10).

[15] "And again, the Lord has said that: Ye shall defend your families even unto bloodshed. Therefore for this cause were the Nephites contending with the Lamanites, to defend themselves, and their families, and their lands, their country, and their rights, and their religion" (Alma 43:47).

[16] "But the Lord knoweth all things from the beginning; wherefore, he prepareth a way to accomplish all his works among the children of men; for behold, he hath all power unto the fulfilling of all his words. And thus it is. Amen" (1 Nephi 9:6).

[17] "In a very real sense it is a war—a hot war—a war between right and wrong, between the powers of heaven and the forces of Lucifer…This is not a war for territory or wealth; it is a contest for the eternal souls of men and women, boys and girls, the literal offspring of God, our Heavenly Father…If we *do* know what is right, have we the courage to stand up for it, to defend virtue, to declare the validity of our faith, to oppose false teachings, and to fight the unpopular battle?" (Mark E. Peterson, "Where Do We Stand?" *Ensign*, May 1980, 68).

[18] "We believe that men should appeal to the civil law for redress of all wrongs and grievances, where personal abuse is inflicted or the right of property or character infringed, where such laws exist as will protect the same; but we believe that all men are justified in defending themselves, their friends, and property, and the government, from the unlawful assaults and encroachments of all persons in times of exigency, where immediate appeal cannot be made to the laws, and relief afforded" (D&C 134:11).

[19] "…The family is ordained of God. Parents have specific duties and responsibilities—fathers preside, provide, and *protect*…" ("The Family: A Proclamation to the World," *Ensign,* November 1995, 102).

CHAPTER FOURTEEN

TASTE OF EVIL

"For ye see your calling, brethren, how that not many wise men after the flesh, not many mighty, not many noble, are called: But God hath chosen the foolish things of the world to confound the wise; and God hath chosen the weak things of the world to confound the things which are mighty" (1 Corinthians 1:26-27).

Friday
September 22nd
10:20 p.m.
Provo, Utah

Father's Words

Bo drove the Neon into Provo Canyon. He was anxious to get this night over with, but at the same time, the escalating stress awakened something primal inside of him. The phone call from his wife detailing Pepper's wounds pushed his buttons and started his juices flowing. He could feel his pulse from his head all the way down to his toes. Suddenly he was eager to be the tool that could bring some kind of consequences to the people who would be up in the mountains that night. His wife was right; the safety of his family was *worth* fighting for.

Bo and Dane followed the winding road up the mountain in silence except for the intermittent directions given by Dane at the few forks in the narrow road. While they drove along the dark twisting path, Bo's intense emotions began to turn to thankfulness for his large son sitting next to him. He was impressed with Dane's willingness to put himself second for the benefit of his mother. How often would you be able to find that in a seventeen-year-old?

He thought about how he and Corrynne had tried to weave the gospel into the family's daily lives and to be at the crossroads during the moments when their children needed counsel and direction. It seemed that so far the wise and inspired advice from the Brethren of the Church had helped create human beings who were ready and willing to contribute to society. Bo's thankfulness became deep and poignant. He felt the sharpness of it like a pain in his chest.

An impression fell heavily on Bo to talk to Dane and tell him that he loved him. Often he felt this way, but rarely was he able to act on these feelings the way he knew he should. His two oldest sons had passed this way before, and he had regrets that he hadn't had the resolve to tell them enough how much they meant to him. Sure, he had informally interacted with them in recreational settings, but for some reason, verbalizing the deep feelings he bore seemed nearly impossible. He knew it was his weakness. He wished to change things. The future seemed to be closing in on their family, and who knew what would be around the next corner? He decided that he would begin the discussion playfully, to cover up his hesitancy.

Bo took a deep breath and grabbed his son's knee hard, right above the knee cap.

Dane jumped and reflexively pushed his dad's hand away. While laughing, he said, "Hey! That tickles. Don't you think I'm too old for that?"

Bo looked at Dane innocently and said, "Not my fault you're ticklish. You've really got to get over that."

"Right, Dad," said Dane as he shook his head.

"Ah, Dane?" started Bo.

"Yes?"

"I want to tell you how proud I am of you."

There was a pause for Dane to respond, but no response came.

"Seriously, I don't tell you enough," continued Bo. "Your mom has always given me a bad time about not being able to say how much you kids mean to me, but that doesn't change the fact that you're the reason I do what I do. Every day I get up in the morning to go to work for my family, and every night I come home eager to be surrounded by this familiarity. It's my expression of love. I worry that I've waited too long to tell you...." Bo continued in a thoughtful voice, "It's strange how time just passes, and suddenly my tiny sons are big. I used to think I had so much time to get to know you, but now I look at you and realize I allowed life to get in the way."

"It's OK, Dad." Dane shifted his weight in his seat. It was obvious he didn't think this confession was necessary. "You're a great dad. You have nothing to apologize for."

"Well, you've made me proud, and I love you. Don't ever forget that I do."

Silence again filled the car.

Dane seemed to struggle with his father's words but then said, "I'll remember," he said as he patted his dad strongly on the shoulder. Somehow that gesture was enough.

Both Bo and Dane knew the rest of the words and excused each other from the physical chore of saying them. They understood with one heart and one mind, and it was fine.

"Dad?" asked Dane, after a few minutes of driving.

"Hmmm?" answered Bo as the car rolled around another mountain curve.

"Do you mind if I change the subject?"

"No, go ahead. I'm done."

"OK, so, I know that we've talked about not drinking and smoking millions of times, but I want to ask you a question from another perspective."

"Shoot," said Bo, keeping his eyes on the road.

"What's so big about partying? There must be something I'm missing, because it's happening everywhere. My friends say it's the only way to have a 'good time'. What's a *good time*? Personally, I don't see what's so fun about drinking urine-tasting, throat-singeing liquid, not remembering anything, vomiting, and waking up with a hangover."

Bo couldn't help but laugh at his son's description. Then he began, "I believe people *think* they're having fun. Otherwise, they wouldn't do it."

"That's the thing I don't get. How can people think they're having a good time when they really aren't? Don't you know when you're having fun?"

"It's the false, chemically induced sense of happiness achieved with drugs and alcohol that people are after."

"Why? It seems like a lot of torture to go through for some moments of happiness that doesn't really exist."

"I know, son, but that's how it is."

"I just like clean living. Only good side effects," said Dane. "No apologies, no surprises, total control and an accurate memory, not to mention a clear conscience. I don't know how some people live with themselves the day after."

Bo nodded. "Said like someone who wants to know in which direction he's going."

"That's exactly right," said Dane. "I'm doing something with my life. I'm going to be someone. I don't ever want to look back with regret."

"Great plan, son. Your way is also the Lord's way. I think deep down others believe the way you do but then they come to believe it's too difficult. They would rather deal with the side effects of drinking and obtain satisfaction from a bottle. It's easier than doing all the work necessary for true happiness."

"Still, it doesn't make sense to me."

"That's because you don't do it. Those who use substances must subconsciously believe the side effects are an acceptable price to pay for the end result. It's like football. Do you like to play football?"

Dane's face twisted into a confused look. "Sure," he said hesitantly, wondering where his Dad was going with this.

"Well, in football you get hurt and have long practices and limited free time, but still the end result must be worth it because so many kids play the game, or games like it, all over the world. Now, don't get me wrong—I'm not saying partying has the same ethical value as football, but the comparison is still the same."

Bo went on. "Science has looked at substance abuse for a long time. They say that turning to drugs and alcohol for the physical satisfaction that it offers evolves into a faulty coping mechanism.[1] It allows people to escape their responsibilities and other negative feelings.[2] Normal behavior changes during these times, and inhibitions are quieted.[3] Often it's in this impaired state that teen pregnancy occurs, car accidents happen, or violence takes a life."

"That's what I'm talking about! That's so stupid!"

"I know. But everyone has their own reasons for doing things."

"If drinking is so dangerous, why aren't police at all these parties, breaking them up?"

"Police can't control everything," said Bo. "They respond when they know where to respond. But the secrecy of these parties allows the illicit behavior within them to continue. For all the history of the earth, evil has used secrets to protect its ways."[4]

"That's why the place of the party is never written down, only told by mouth," said Dane nodding.

"Exactly, so there's no paper trail."

Dane was quiet for a moment. Finally he said, "Satan is smart."

"You bet he is. He was one of the sons of our Heavenly Father who had authority in the pre-existence and was likened unto Christ himself.[5] He knows us intimately. He knows what we naturally desire. You see, it's a natural tendency for us to want to be happy and protect ourselves from threatening situations. Satan knows this and uses it to entice people to run to substances to help them achieve a false sense of security. Eventually they learn to hide from life's stresses rather than deal with them."[6]

Dane interjected, "That just makes the problems bigger."

"Yes, and as we know, the results can be devastating." Bo shook his head. "Satan tells people they don't have control over their actions, especially when they're under the influence. This leads them to believe that they harbor no responsibility for bad things that happen to them.[7] We have been told that our minds are open to evil suggestions when we're under the influence of substances. In some cases, they've said it takes away our freedom to choose, which is why we're here in the first place. It's another way Satan can destroy our agency. It's a terrible circle to become caught in."[8]

"I can see that."

"I have friends that I grew up with whose lives became so crazy because of alcoholism that they made all the wrong choices, like abandoning their children and wives, breaking the law and ending up in jail, or even killing themselves. The consequences were harsh for those people."[9]

"That's sad," said Dane.

"Yes, it is. However, all of it could have been avoided. Scientists, teachers, the government, and religious leaders have long warned of the detrimental and lifelong effects of substance abuse. Satan laughs when we're caught with limited options. Elder Ballard once said, 'Satan wants your destruction. It's that simple. Your defense is equally simple—live basic gospel principles.'"[10]

Dane nodded as he contemplated Elder Ballard's statement. "You know, it *is* that simple. If you don't taste it, you don't want it. …I don't want it. I never have."

"Right, and you have a good head on your shoulders." Bo smiled. His son was one in a million.

"Still," began Dane, "my friends are very persuasive. I used to worry that I was missing out on something. Now I don't."

"That's the work of Old Scratch. He's a liar. He wants you to worry about what you're not experiencing. He wants to tempt you with the perception of loss. That's the great lie.[11] The truth is that you are *gaining* by not partaking. Like you said before, you have your whole life under your control. You can create any outcome you choose. You are free."

Dane's face became wistful. "It's sad that everyone doesn't have that freedom. Everyone should."

"Everyone can. They just need to see the downfalls of choices and choose to change. That's why there are missionaries and good examples of the gospel like you—to lead people to the light and give them life."

"Why don't parents stop their kids from going to these things? I mean, all of them know their kids are gone somewhere.[12] What do they think they're doing, eating cake and ice cream? I mean, if I were a parent, I would force my kid to stay home."

"I'm sure many parents have tried, but I don't think force is the answer."

"What's the answer then?"

"The answer begins many years before children or teens are faced with temptations in society. The recipe for successful children includes consistent instruction in the home involving the teachings of Christ, parental involvement, helping children decide early how to deal with temptations, and consistent discipline and consequences.[13] Trying to control all their actions when they're teens, without the proper foundation, will fail miserably."[14]

Dane nodded slowly, as he considered what his father was teaching him.

Bo continued, "In the ideal situation, when kids become teens, parents' roles change. Parents continue to be an integral part of their children's lives, not to exhibit force over them, but to fortify and direct them. They're to be consultants and confidants at that stage.[15] Involved parents can help their children resist evil, but they can't force them to."

"I can see that."

"This life is difficult. Satan designs temptations to be difficult to resist. Teens need to have a tremendous amount of self-control. Having their parents' strength can help fortify them in the midst of the winds of evil.

Friends, church,[16] and individual spirituality are also needed to make them strong enough to make correct choices."

"Well, some of my friends say their parents know they're partying. What's with that? Are their parents stupid?"

"All parents have a tough job and, in the process of trying to keep a good relationship with their children during their teen years, some parents try to prove that they're 'fun.' But I think there's something else going on here, too. Partying sometimes is like a rite of passage, in many cases. Their parents did it, and it's perceived as normal teen behavior.[17] Despite the dangers, it's excused as acceptable."

"Yeah, but some of the best people I know will have kids at the party tonight. That really bothers me. They sit in the same church meetings I do. They've been taught the same things I have. Why do they still do this?"

"Only those families could really answer that one. Maybe some families go to church but don't live the gospel principles at home.[18] Then there are those who would rather not know what their children are doing. Denial is safe for them."

"What do you mean?"

"Well, imagine a situation where reality is so hard to accept, you're unwilling to see the danger. It's an escape mechanism and stems from the belief that 'If you can't see it, it doesn't exist.' A little of that 'All is well in Zion'[19] syndrome. This is another avenue Satan takes to ruin families."

"Do you think that by showing our video to people, they'll change?"

"I think it would be a very good idea, but you understand it might make a lot of people mad at you."

"Well, if it saves my friends, it's something I'm willing to deal with."

"That's a very brave viewpoint."

"Yep, that's my job tonight. To cause a ruckus! This is going to be fun! I want our community to wake up and realize the danger that's out here. It's only right."

"I'm with you there, son."

Finally, they came to the top of the mountain. Bo saw floodlights from somewhere over the crest. They were almost to their destination. A lump formed in his throat. Despite both his and his son's vigilance, he couldn't help but worry he was sending his son into the lion's den without proper preparation. He wanted to make Dane's job simple to help him avoid danger.

"So, review with me the plans," Bo said, as he turned the last corner and parked.

"Mom and I decided I would put this walkie-talkie in my pocket and push the page button once for 'I'm OK,' twice for 'I'm in trouble,' and three times for 'call 9-1-1.'" Dane laughed, but this time it wasn't as funny. His chuckle hung in the air. "You're supposed to keep in contact with Mom with the cell."

"Do you know what things you're supposed to do out there?"

"I think so."

"OK, let's go over it. This is very important. We have to do this right, because this is probably the only chance you'll get to document what's going on up here."

Dane nodded. "First, I have to video people being smashed and stupid."

Bo had to laugh. "That's an interesting way to put it, I guess."

"So I'll just walk around and try to have the camera see everything."

"OK, what next?"

"Next, I have to ask if anyone knows a girl named Ann Cain."

"Right," said Bo. "We need to find her. Hopefully she's there with the drugs that are missing from the hospital. If she is, Mom's off the hook."

"Got it."

Bo pivoted in his seat so his back was against the door. "Now, let's talk about some precautions...."

"I knew this was coming," said Dane. "What?"

Bo clasped his hands together and looked down at them. "Do not under any circumstances eat or drink anything."

Dane shrugged. "Well that's a no-brainer. Probably everything's spiked."

Bo held up a finger. "Also, don't let anyone touch you with sharp objects."

That comment made Dane laugh out loud. "Yeah, Dad, as if!"

"You know Mom can trace those deaths from Strep to this place, don't you?"

"That's what I hear," said Dane.

"So that's why I say what I say. They might try to make you a part of their group. That entails tattooing and piercing. Get out of there if it seems like you're being cornered."

"Fine."

"The last thing I want to talk to you about is the man who claims he is the Messiah."

Dane squirmed uncomfortably. "Dad, I'm sure all the talk about some spiritual man coming to the parties is just some sort of parlor trick. I don't believe he, or his power, is real. It's probably someone somewhere with a cable and a sheet up on a mountain or something."

"Well, despite what's really going on verses what seems to be going on, I have to tell you that Satan is real."

"I know that, Dad."

"I think this party is an extension of his designs."

Dane nodded. "I can see that."

"Satan wishes to sift you as wheat.[20] He will do whatever it takes to steal you away from your eternal rewards and your family that loves you. Take my word for it. You are one of the noble and great ones talked about in the scriptures.[21] I feel it when I'm around you. You have missions to accomplish on this earth. So take care. *Do not* put yourself in any compromising positions. If you feel you're in danger, run back here. Get out. If you can't get out of danger, then page me. I'll be here if you need me. Remember, prayer is a real tool. The Lord will give you direction. Be listening for it."

"I will."

Rave

Dane slowly climbed the rocky ridge surrounding the Rave. He could hear the music blaring into the cool night air. As he reached the pinnacle of the rock he was on, he felt the massive beat of the bass competing with his own heart.

The view of the party and the city unfolded before him. He took a moment to study the layout. The gathering was situated on a flat area extending out from the summit of Squaw Peak, lying north and south, parallel to the city below. From Dane's vantage point, elevated above the group on the ridge east of the party, he could see that beyond the group was a sheer cliff that dropped dramatically hundreds of feet seemingly into the pocket of lights that twinkled below. All around the gathering, except for where he stood, were more steep cliffs, which encapsulated them. He took mental note that if he needed to escape quickly, the only way out was the way he came in.

Dane returned his vision to the sights below him. He allowed his eyes to drift beyond the party down over the cliff to the lights of Provo. It surprised him how many lights burned brightly in the night. He knew Utah had been the one of the fastest growing States in America for quite some time now,[22] but this was the first time he had really noticed the difference in his hometown. He hadn't been up on this mountainside since a campout when he was fourteen. He remembered the scattered lights of the city below then, but now they were crowded together, filling the land below him completely like a sequined blanket.

Subconsciously, he searched for a landmark that he could identify. Quickly he picked out a brightly lit oval, which marked the huge stadium for Brigham Young University. Just northeast of that landmark, he saw a golden spire reaching like a column of fire into the night. Its familiar glow comforted him. It was the temple. He hoped its nearness would act as a defense for him that night.

Dane looked back to his right, to the north, searching for the Timpanogos temple. His eyes followed the line of cars along Interstate 15. Then he saw it, almost out of sight around the bend of the mountain he was standing on. There it was. Suddenly, Dane couldn't help but let out a deep laugh as he wondered at the choice of location by the party planners for the Rave that night. They couldn't have picked a worse place for their meeting. It was right smack in the Lord's country, on a mountaintop, in between two temples. It sure wouldn't be his choice if he were an Antichrist who wanted to win a battle. Smiling, Dane felt his confidence growing. "But we all know how this story ends anyway, don't we?"

Next, Dane studied the gathering. He watched the people moving together in a rhythmic fashion under the neon flashing lights. Any white and pastel material glowed brightly, as they danced, unaware of his gaze. He still didn't understand why the police hadn't been able to find these Raves. Although its location was secret, they certainly weren't being secret about their presence.

That thought made Dane remember to turn on the camera. With a feeling of urgency, he traced the form of the camera under his right arm with his left hand. He blindly found the switch to turn it on. He flicked it and listened for the mechanisms to make its characteristic purring sound. Hearing it, he smiled as he imagined all the police watching the video at that moment. Quietly he said down into the microphone, "This is where the party is." Then he laughed to himself.

Cautiously, Dane began his descent into the party. Looking around, Dane noticed he was out of place in his big black jacket. Most of the guys were clad in black leather and blue jeans, with different-colored bandanas around their heads. Others were in normal leisure clothing. The girls, however, dressed lightly in summer shorts and midriff shirts despite the cold, almost frosty air. He looked down at himself. He unzipped his jacket to reveal his white football jersey. He would pose as someone just checking the party out. He was sure there were others like him there.

Soon he was among the party goers. Most of the people were strangers to him, but he recognized the characteristic "B.A.T." tattoos. "Yep, I'm in the right place," he said quietly, knowing the camera could hear him. "Bats everywhere with no cave to hide in. Too bad." The police would be coming soon. He knew it. He had to hurry.

"Hey, dude!" A voice drawled deeply behind him. He turned to see one of his acquaintances from school. He wouldn't really call him a friend. He didn't even know his name, but he had talked to him a couple times about the Raves.

"Glad you're here. Whatcha doing, buddy?" The young man held out his right hand that was free of his drink. Dane grasped it firmly for a brief moment.

"Just checking things out. You've told me so much about these parties I decided to come up here myself."

"Isn't it past your bedtime? I thought you church boys were 'early to bed'-ers," the superficially friendly young man taunted.

"Maybe…but it's cool." Dane nodded his head while looking around. His hands felt obviously idle. He slid them into the pockets of his jeans.

"Hey, you guys," the boy suddenly yelled to some other people standing just down the hill close by.

Dane was startled and he turned to see who the guy was yelling at.

"Everyone, Dane, the big man football player, came up here to check us out!" The rough young man held up the drink he was holding, took a drink, and then motioned to his friends. Soon a small crowd began to form around

Dane, as more people from his school came to chide him. "Why do you think he's really here?"

"Oh, yeah, he's one of the cute ones," said one of the girls, as she nestled in the arms of another guy who was obviously drunk. "He's probably a spy."

Dane cringed inside. Was the girl really suspecting him of being a spy, or was she just joking? He hoped she and her friends were too plastered to put two and two together so early in his spying career.

"This doesn't make sense," said yet another guy who had multiple graduated earrings in both ears and a stud in his nose. "I thought you were too good for us. Are you slumming it? Or have you come up here to try and save our souls?" The crowd burst out laughing. The second guy, also a little-known acquaintance from school, continued, "Are you a missionary today?"

"Yeah, preach to us, Mormon boy!" called out another girl beside him.

Dane attempted to ignore all of them and tried to push through them, but he was thrust back into the center of the circle by many arms. He began to get angry but remained silent and controlled himself.

The young man with the nose piercing, who seemed to be the ringleader of the bunch said, "You know, guys, I wonder if he's on the level. What about a test to see what his intentions are?"

The crowd yelled its chaotic agreement.

"You're our prisoner," said the leader. "It's your job to prove to us you're not here to mock us, then we'll give you freedom."

Dane shook his head. "I'm not mocking anyone."

"Sure you're not," said the guy with the piercings. "We all mock each other, that's how come we know you're mocking us too."

The crowd laughed again.

With a strong pat on his shoulder, the leader said, "No, really, we're actually a little bored and you will give us some entertainment."

"How can you be bored here?" asked Dane.

The leader looked around and said, "OK, we're not bored, just curious. We all think it would be fun to see someone like you do something reeeeally bad."

"Yeah, come on!" The group laughed boisterously as he was shoved from one side to the other of the gathered circle.

Although Dane remained stoic outside, inside, his blood was beginning to boil. Dane consciously rolled his shoulders to try to cool down. He knew a hot head would not solve anything. If he became physical, these guys would love to trounce him. There were way too many of them, drunk or not. He knew he would be minced meat.

"Oooh, look at him, Mr. Control. I think Mr. Control needs a lesson."

"Hey, Kyle, bring over some booze!" yelled the first kid to a guy who was in another circle.

Dane saw Kyle take off. Dane wondered to himself what he should do in this situation. Suddenly he remembered his father's advice to pray. Silently he began to inquire of the Lord which direction he should take, fiercely thrusting his energy to heaven. Struck with an idea, Dane began a ploy.

"Don't choose booze. That's an easy one," Dane spoke coolly and calmly. His words caught the crowd off guard. They looked at him suspiciously, suddenly quieting.

"Oh, the big football star speaks! Tell us, 'Oh Mighty One,' what bad thing do you wish to perform to prove yourself and gain your freedom." The small crowd rolled in riotous laughter.

"Choose something with blood." The words slid out of his mouth. Inside, he was shocked. Why would he say something like that? His parents specifically told him not to let anyone touch him. Plus, he couldn't take off his jacket—everyone would see the camera.

"Blood, huh?" said the leader with a questioning look. "The tough guy here wants to prove himself with blood."

"Yeah," yelled the first guy he had seen that night with doubled up fists.

The leader nodded. "That's cool. Blood's something we can do."

Then Dane was lead out of the circle of people to an area where he could tell tattoos and piercings were being given. There were chairs and cots spread out.

"Here we draw blood," said the group leader.

The crowd chuckled.

"Tell me more," Dane said as he looked around. "Where do I go first?" He talked generically to the crowd. He couldn't believe his opportunity for video footage. This was exactly what he had come here to record. He couldn't have planned this better if he had tried.

"Go to the first table to choose the sugar of your choice."

"What's 'the sugar'?" asked Dane.

"Something to sweeten the experience," said the leader.

"You mean drugs?"

"Duhh, you're really stupid, aren't you?" asked a nearby girl.

Dane ignored the slur and asked, "So, the drugs are free?"

"Yep, all the candy you would want," said the leader

"How can this group afford that?" asked Dane.

"The big guy just creates it out of thin air. Manna from heaven." Another roll of laughter peeled around the circle.

"Who's the 'big guy'?" asked Dane.

"He comes after awhile," said the same girl. "He's why we're here."

"So what's going on around here?" asked Dane pointing to the cots, even though he already knew.

"Here's where you join our group man. You want to join us, don't you?" asked the leader, laughing and looking back at his cronies.

The group laughed and nodded. "Yeah, don't you?" asked a couple people sarcastically.

Dane shrugged. "I don't know. Tell me what you have to do."

"You have to go through this line and receive your mark and your ring and then give your blood in return."

Dane cringed. "And why would I want to do that?"

"It's solidarity, man. Solidarity. We become your family," said the first boy that introduced him to the crowd. "And you get all the drugs and girls you want."

Dane's eyebrows lifted as if he was interested. "How?" asked Dane.

"Tell them, Christy," said the leader.

Christy was the outspoken girl that had been throwing comments out at him. With a sigh she began. "The tattoo is the mark all of us carry that says we belong together and will die together, which means being loyal to the cause of creating a New World. There are great benefits to that one you'll find out later. The piercing is your own identification. Then after that, you'll cut yourself with the ceremonial knife with the other new members. You'll share your blood in the ceremony, and thus we'll become one."

"Now do you want to become a part of us?" asked another skimpily clad girl in a whisper, as she traced Dane's shoulders with her finger.

Dane shivered. He felt like running back up the mountain and getting out of there but instead he nodded. "Why not? What else am I going to do tonight?"

The crowd erupted in a loud and bawdy cheer.

"But I have a question," said Dane.

"Shoot," said the leader.

"What's the purpose of getting a rush?"

"Because it's fun."

"OK," said Dane, "But if you really believe this stuff, being high while you do it takes away all the significance of the rituals. It would seem like the pain and remembering the experience should be a part of the whole thing."

"Do you like pain or something?" asked the leader.

Dane shook his head. "No, not really, but if you really believe in something you should be willing to suffer for it. Doesn't that make sense?"

The girl behind him leaned over his shoulder and in a sultry voice said, "When you're high, you still feel the pain, but you don't care."

Dane held out his hands and said, "But, I want to care. To me it's important. If I'm going to do something, I want to comprehend fully what happens to me."

The people in the crowd just looked at each other with blank stares.

"Show me how this is done," said Dane.

The leader looked around. Spying a couple about ten yards away, he motioned toward them. "OK, Lisa over there is doing a tattoo on that guy...whoever he is."

Dane was lead to the cot. When he got there, he was shocked to see that Lisa was his next-door neighbor. "Lisa!" he exclaimed.

Lisa turned around when she heard her name. Terror struck her eyes as she realized who Dane was. "What are *you* doing here?"

"Scoping things out, huh, guys?" Dane said to the gathering.

The crowd began to play with Dane now that he seemed willing to participate. "Sure, this big guy wants the whole enchilada," said the leader.

"He's going to become a Bat." said another.

"No!" Lisa got up from her seat and stood toe to toe with Dane. "*Go home! This is not a place for you.*" She stared coldly into his eyes to emphasis her message.

Dane felt sickened inside. He hated that Lisa was here. She was not someone he wanted to hurt. "Who are you with?" Dane stood on his toes to see around her. Lisa tried to block his view, but suddenly he realized it was one of his football buddies whose dad was a U.S. congressman for Utah. "Hey, Steve! Can't believe you're here!" Steve was not in a condition to talk coherently. He opened an eye and quickly closed it. It was obvious he had had his fair share of some substance.

"*Get out of here! Now!*" yelled Lisa, pointing the way out.

"Well, I would like to go, but my new friends here are set on showing me the ropes. I don't think they'll let me go anytime soon."

"Not without being marked for life!" said one person in the crowd.

The group laughed.

Fear grew in Lisa's eyes. She was speechless. She broke out in tears and left her position next to Steve. Quickly, she walked away.

"Wow. Something's bothering her!" Dane tried to sound callous.

"She's not a true Bat. You could see it from the very first time she came. She only comes because of her boyfriend."

"I didn't even know they were dating!" Dane returned, looking down at his football teammate. Changing the subject, Dane rubbed his hands together and said, "OK, now I need you guys to help me out with something."

"What is it, man?" asked the leader.

"I'm looking for a cute little nurse who comes here. Her name is Ann. I want her to do my tattooing. I know she's up here somewhere. I actually came looking for her."

Immediately the ringleader knew who he was talking about. "You want her?" He scrunched up his face.

"Yeah, isn't she fine?" asked Dane, using every ounce of his acting skills.

"No, I think she's a mouse, but, if that's what you like, she's over there." He pointed his thick finger to a small hunched-over girl with wispy, straight hair and glasses. She was bent over someone, doing something Dane couldn't see.

"What's she doing? Is she already hooked up?" asked Dane.

"No, don't think so. Here, I'll take you over there." The leader led Dane across the short distance to where Ann was working.

"Ann, this guy says he has the hots for you. *You lucky lady, you.* He's quite the jock!" Ann didn't look up. It seemed she had been teased a lot and was ignoring the comment.

"You can be next," she said in a small voice.

"Next for what?" Dane asked.

"She pulls back a flap in your hand and implants a computer chip," said Christy.

"Why?" This was something Dane hadn't heard of before.

"Because when the world goes to 'heck in a hand basket,' it's the thing that will feed you. If you have one of these"—she held up her hand to show fresh black stitches sticking out of her white palm—"you have the key to the kingdom. It's one of those benefits I was telling you about. You get to survive."

Dane nodded. "I see. Well, I want one of those first."

"You can't. That comes after the first ceremony," said Christy.

"I don't care. I'll do it right now, without the drugs. Just bring it on!" said Dane flexing his muscles in one of his poses, beginning to get into his rambunctious role.

"Yeah!" yelled a couple in the crowd, seeming to feed off his energy.

The leader's eyes grew wide with interest. Turning back to his friends he said, "I think we're going to sit here and watch the show."

For the first time, Ann looked up. "That's dumb. Why would you want to have pain? I have this medication here that will not only help you with the pain but make you forget the whole ordeal."

"I don't care," said Dane. "I promised my friends they could watch you draw some blood and give me some pain. A deal is a deal."

The crowd erupted in a vulgar response.

Ann shook her head. "OK, come lie on the cot. I don't want you to faint. …Stupid boys," she muttered under her breath.

Dane moved to the cot and prayed for the fortitude to follow through. Secretly he was shaking in his boots, but outwardly he was controlled. This might be a questionable move and totally against what he said he would do, but it didn't involve amateur people putting holes in his skin. He also felt good about avoiding all the drugs. It was the only thing he could think of to fulfill what everyone wanted and bring back a trophy to boot. He thought bringing back the chip might help the police track more Raves down, especially if it happened to be technologically linked somehow. Now, if he could just endure the pain….

Ann cleansed the area with a brown liquid. It made his hand feel frozen in the cold air. Then Dane felt a horrid sting as she began to cut through the thick skin of his palm. Dane closed his eyes, gritted his teeth and held his breath to blunt the pain. A couple times during the procedure, he cried out in pain, which the audience loved as they laughed and joked at Dane's expense.

"I bet that tickles!" yelled one of them. Dane didn't know which one, and he didn't care.

"OK, the show's over," said the leader as Ann tied the last knot. "This boy's proved himself. I didn't think he'd really follow through." Taking a few steps forward he leaned over Dane and said, "It's good to see you have guts. See ya around." He patted him on the shoulder, and then turned around to speak to his friends. "It's almost time for the appearing. Let's go."

The group staggered after the leader and left Dane and Ann alone.

After the bandage was applied, Ann stood and began cleaning up the area. She threw away the blood-soaked pad she had placed under his hand and all the packaging from the equipment she used. She then waved a machine of some sort over his hand. "OK, you're activated. As soon as you feel like you can stand, you can get up and go."

Dane lay on the cot a few minutes. He was extremely lightheaded from the stress of the pain. His hand throbbed. He looked at his bulky dressing and noted that blood was already beginning to soak through.

"Put pressure on it," Ann said as she saw him stare at the dressing. "It will be fine in a few minutes."

"What if I get an infection?" asked Dane.

"The chip is dipped in a substance that won't let you get one."

"When you waved that machine over my hand, what were you doing?"

"That activated the chip so our satellites can see you now."[23]

"Satellites?"

"Yes, now, no matter where you are, you're among the fold. All your needs are taken care of. Imam Mahdi will know of you. You are one of the firstlings of his flock."

"What do you mean?"

"I mean eventually everyone in the whole world will have a chip implanted in their hand and seek the help of Imam Mahdi. You will never know hunger, because you were one of the first."

"I see," said Dane, dazed. He had second thoughts about this chip thing. "What if I don't want it anymore?"

"If you try to remove it, you will die."

"What?" Dane's heart jumped. "How will I die?"

"You will die by fire. That's all I know." Suddenly, Ann began again, "I have seen people die by fire, and it isn't something you want to mess with."

Dane sat up, but then he had to lie back down again. Ann continued to busy herself with her supplies. He wondered if the threat were real or just an attempt to control him.

"The appearing will be happening soon. You should go." Ann was beginning to close up shop. Dane got up slowly and tried to position himself so the camera could look at her materials. He couldn't identify anything in particular, but he hoped his mother could.

"Your name again?" Dane asked.

"That's not anyone's business."

"It is Ann, isn't it? Ann Cain?"

The small nurse stopped what she was doing and froze. After a second she replied, "No, I don't have a name anymore."

Dane thought he could see a tear fall down her cheek. "Is there something I can do for you?"

"No, I'm of no consequence."

Dane got up to go when he saw out of the corner of his eye a book lying on the ground. On the outside it had the words "Ann Cain" embossed on the cover. It looked like a journal of some sort. Without letting Ann know he had seen it, he hobbled shakily away.

Dane reached into his pocket to feel the walkie-talkie. For the first time, he pushed the page button once to let his father know he was fine. "Whew," he thought to himself. That experience had been way too intense.

Police Station

Bo dialed Corrynne's cell phone. It rang once, and Corrynne answered the phone quickly.

"Hello?"

"Hi, sweetheart! What's going on? Are you watching the monitor?"

Corrynne was quiet. She was at the police station. He could hear police dispatch in the background. Then, almost with a gurgle, she began to speak and had to clear her voice. "Ah, yeah, we're watching everything. Bo, it's been very nerve-racking being here while he's there. He's been doing some pretty fast talking. I was very proud of him."

"Can you tell if he's safe?"

"I think so. Some of the sound cut out on us for a while so we couldn't make out some of the dialogue. They were talking something about computer chips and satellite dishes; I didn't quite understand what they were saying. Plus, we couldn't see what was going on because the camera was pointed at the sky. That means Dane was lying down. I don't quite understand what that was about, but everything seems to be working now, and he seems to be fine. That's the important part."

"Yes, he paged me once. I was hoping he was telling me he was fine."

"Well, as far as I can tell, everything's great."

"So tell me, were the police interested in watching the monitor when you got there?"

"At first they weren't. They thought I was pretty strange, but I asked for the police chief. After I hooked everything up and turned the TV on, the first image it showed was the drugs displayed on a table. That got their attention very fast. Now I have a whole crew watching the monitor. It's become more popular than a soap opera in a beauty parlor!"

"Great!"

"They're amassing a large group to go up there and bust the whole thing right now. Where did you say it was located?"

"Squaw Peak. They need to go as high as they can go. Before they start descending, there's a turnoff in the brush. The party is beyond that and over a ridge." Bo heard Corrynne's voice grow dim as she took the phone away from her ear to give directions to someone nearby. When Corrynne came back to the phone, he asked, "Has Dane been able to do everything we needed him to do?"

"Oh, yes, it's beautiful! He's doing such a great job. He found Ann, and I think I saw the Versed among all of her medications. He has also shown that the piercings and tattooing are originating at the parties. The media should have a heyday with all that information before the night is over."

"That's great."

"But one bad thing is that Lisa, our next-door neighbor, is at the party with a football player from Dane's team at school."

"Oh, no!" Bo said.

"That's not the worst of it. The boy is Congressman Seal's son."

"Oh, boy! That's not good," said Bo.

"The politicians won't like that one."

"No, I'm afraid they won't. Well, I'll call you later."

"Fine, take care of our son," said Corrynne.

"Sure thing. Call me if you see something that I should help with, just in case he doesn't push the page button."

"OK."

"Love ya."

"Bye."

"Bye." Bo pushed the end button and looked toward the lights out his side windows. It was taking every ounce of self-control to stay in the car.

Imam Mahdi

The crowd congregated around the south end of the party, where an empty, glittering golden pedestal stood. Mammoth spotlights were focused on the space, creating a feeling of anticipation. Suddenly the music stopped. A hush came over the crowd.

Somewhere one voice began to chant. Another joined the first, then another and another, until the whole crowd was chanting an odd, rhythmic, repeating message. From his removed place up on the hill and to the left of the crowd, Dane strained to hear the words. After a few moments, he realized that they were in another language. It sounded like an Eastern religious chanting he had seen on one of the satellite channels at home, but he couldn't remember which religion.

Soon the crowd was swaying with hands held high in the air. The chant began to pick up the pace, and so did the sound level. It continued to gather speed and volume until suddenly it ended in an ecstatic fervor and the people dropped to their knees on the ground. It looked like they were bowing.

There was a great explosion of fire, sparks, and smoke above the pedestal directly in front of the crowd. The crowd remained on their knees with heads down, but Dane continued to stand, refusing to follow the rituals of the crowd. Suddenly, what looked like a man appeared from seemingly nowhere.

Dane was astonished. His jaw dropped, as he shielded his eyes to see clearer. The man on the pedestal was wearing a white shimmering robe that reflected the bright lights. It made the sight of him almost unbearably bright. As Dane refocused and became used to the lighted figure he noticed the mysterious man had dark, long, straight hair that draped his shoulders and a thick dark beard. He had his hands outspread as if to accept the worship of the members of the crowd. It was obvious the impression was meant to reflect deity.

Through the loudspeaker system, the man began to speak. His voice rumbled with deep intonation. Some of the sounds caused Dane's body to quake from the sheer volume.

"I am he that has been foretold for centuries. I am Krishna. I am Miatrya. I am Imam Mahdi. I am the Messiah. Come to me, ye who are cast out, and I will make you whole."

Dane felt like his breath was knocked out of him. "What is this?" He tried to form thoughts in his head to understand what was happening around him, but confusion overtook him.

The voice continued in a mesmerizing rumble, "Take upon you my mark and ye shall be saved in the last day. For fire shall come down from heaven and consume the unbelievers. Through me ye shall find shelter, protection, and manna. Come near unto me, and I will come near unto you. Pray unto me often for purity so as not to be burned yourselves, for, in that day, your heart shall surely fail."

Dane's knees became weak, and his head began to become light. He looked down at his hand, and the bandage was soaked with blood. Large drops began to fall into the dust and rocks at his feet. It seemed the world was slowing down, and every second elongated into another unidentifiable timeframe. Dane ripped the bandage from his hand and began to hold pressure on the wound. He could feel the foreign object under the surface of the skin, and the pressure caused excruciating pain, but he knew he had to stop the bleeding or he would soon faint.

"I come to unify the world, to feed the hungry, to clothe the naked," the amplified voice continued. "I come to bring the prideful low and raise up the obedient. In me ye will be blessed, for in division ye will find unity. In pain ye will find joy. Through war ye will obtain peace. Through death ye will find life. Through exclusion ye will find inclusion. Give all, and you will receive the world."

Dane's knees began to buckle. Despite his effort to try to continue to stand, he fell to his knees. He knew he would soon black out, and it was unavoidable. He reached into his pocket and pushed the page button twice on his walkie-talkie, hoping his father had not fallen asleep. He repeated this action to clarify his meaning. He was calling for help.

"I bring terror to the unbelievers, and in this we will establish our world, the perfect society."

Dane's face fell hard onto the sharp rocks and gravel that he had been standing on, but he was unaware of the pain. He had lost consciousness.

Ageless Battle

The double page went off, loud in the quiet car. The sound caused all of Bo's muscles to tighten and his mind to become alert. He stopped himself from opening the door, contemplating whether he should act on the page or wait for a confirmation, just in case Dane had accidentally hit the button. The double page came again, giving Bo the clear communication that Dane was calling his father. Sudden fear mixed with determination in Bo's mind. So many scenarios played instantaneously in his head as to why his son would be calling. He knew it had to be serious, because Dane wouldn't call for help if he didn't really need it. Right then, the cell phone rang.

Bo hit a button and said, "I'm going to help Dane right now, so stay on the line," knowing it was Corrynne telling him to go. Without another second's hesitation, Bo put the cell phone in his pocket and bolted outside in the moonlight. Dodging branches and skidding among rocks he rushed down the slope. Bo lost his footing as he rounded the corner leading to the gathering but quickly gained his balance after holding his hand out to steady himself on a boulder. In another few steps, he was on the slope looking down on the mass of people who were now kneeling attentively before a bright white figure.

Bo pulled the phone out of his pocket with one swift motion. "Where's Dane?" Bo asked urgently, searching the crowd for his son.

Corrynne answered quickly, "Dane was standing behind and to the left of the crowd. He was wearing a black coat, so it might be hard to see him in the dark. It looked like he either fell down or took off his coat, because the camera is now dark. We know it's still recording because we can hear that man, Imam Mahdi talking."

The reflected light from the figure created huge, deceptive shadows on the hillside from various rocks and sparse vegetation, making it nearly impossible to see anything accurately. Farther down the hill, Bo saw more dark shadows and wondered if one could be his son's form on the ground.

"Why didn't we think of bringing a flashlight?" Bo said angrily as he searched the rocky ground in the approximate area Corrynne described. Quickly he skidded down the hill, causing gravel and rocks to fly around him. Suddenly his feet hit something soft and solid, and Bo flew over it with excess momentum. He landed painfully on his palms and knees on the sharp rocks that cut into his skin, ripping his pants at the knees. The cell phone went flying out of his grasp and skidded further down the hill. He did not chase it. Instead, he turned around and crawled back to the soft mass, which was so dark he didn't see its borders.

As he moved closer, he realized what he had thought might be, was. He had tripped over his son, Dane. He was face down and unresponsive.

"Dane!"

Still no response.

Bo turned his son over carefully to expose his face and his white football jersey. With the light from the stage area and the partial moonlight, he was able to see that Dane had some bleeding cuts on his face from falling on the rocks but Bo couldn't make out any other injuries.

Bo gently laid Dane face up on the ground while he skidded down the hill to find his cell phone. Luckily the light was still on, casting a green hue on the surrounding rocks.

"Bo! Bo! Can you hear me?" came Corrynne's frantic call.

Bo picked up the phone and hurried back to his son's side. "Hi, Corrynne, I'm here. I've found Dane. He's fainted. I don't see anything obvious that would cause it. Maybe he's been hit over the head. His face is cut, but it looks minor."

"Well, keep checking. There might be something you're missing. We didn't see any indication of a violent attack from here." Corrynne was getting impatient.

"Hey, I'm doing the best I can. It's dark out here." With the phone caught between his chin and shoulder, Bo continued to search Dane as they talked. Feeling down his arms systematically he eventually grasped Dane's right hand to feel a familiar wet, sticky feeling. Bo withdrew his hands unconsciously at the discovery. Instantly, a wave of dizziness hit him. Bo realized Dane was bleeding.

"I think I've found the problem. Dane has a large cut somewhere on his hand. By the amount of blood that's present, it looks like it's been bleeding for awhile…." Bo gathered courage to try to look closer at Dane's hand, but it was nearly impossible to tell any details due to the darkness and the amount of blood that continued to seep out of the wound.

"Put pressure on the wound and just above the wound, Bo. Stop that bleeding."

Bo began to feel nauseated, but he was determined to help his son. Bo ripped off some of Dane's jersey and balled it up and pressed it on the wound. Bo then took his shoes and socks off and tied one sock around Dane's hand and the other around the wrist. Quickly, he replaced his shoes on his bare feet.

"I did it, Corrynne. It should stop bleeding soon."

Corrynne said in a worried voice, "Why is his hand bleeding so much?"

"I don't know," said Bo.

"He must've broken a blood vessel or something."

"Maybe."

"Do you think Ann could've done something to him?"

"I don't know, but I'm beginning to get queasy," feeling his head pounding along with the nausea, Bo looked around for a soft place to lie down. He didn't want to faint, too. He would lie down and let the lightheadedness pass.

"Bo! Be careful. We need you alert to help with Dane. The police are on their way—hang on!"

"I'll be fine in a moment," Bo said into the phone as he lay down on the cold ground. Against his will, he began to sweat and shiver. He knew his blood pressure was dropping. It always did when there was blood anywhere.

Beside him, Dane stirred.

"Dane! Are you OK?"

Dane moved his head from the right to the left, moaning something about his hand.

Bo crawled closer to be able to hear him better, but Dane was silent once again as he seemed to lapse back into unconsciousness.

Suddenly, without warning, a powerful spotlight was focused on them.

Bo covered his eyes. He had been oblivious to the loud voice and its rumbling message as he had attended his son, but now he understood the man in white was using them as an example.

"Look and take note. These are they who are not of us." The deep voice escalated, filled the ridge, and echoed off surrounding mountains. "They come to our mountain to mock us. But God will not be mocked!"[24] After a dramatic pause the man continued, pointing his finger, "See how they have been struck down. Their weakness overcomes them. Our enemies all over the world will fall in their own blood in a like manner. See and be a witness!"

The crowd mumbled recognition and bowed low once again.

Bo looked down at himself and his son in the light and noticed that both of them looked as if some wild animal had attacked them. Blood was everywhere and their clothes were ripped. Despite this, Bo, feeling stronger, stood up defiantly. In response to the threat, his lightheadedness decreased and his nausea diminished.

"What you see here is not a symptom of weakness!" he yelled into the night, his voice small in comparison to the amplified, deep tones of Imam Mahdi. But Bo continued, gaining vital strength. "It is a sign of love, unity, and humility. These things make us strong. I sacrifice my own will, as does my son, to the will of the Father. We are on his errand."

Imam Mahdi turned again to the couple on the hill. "To what Father do you refer? There is no Father. I am the Father and the Son. There is no other."

"Then you lie to these people," Bo yelled. "I refer to the Father of our spirits[25] and his son, the Creator of heaven and earth. One who has power to make us clean from our mistakes and give us eternal life."[26]

Imam Mahdi walked down the steps of his platform toward Bo and Dane. "Oh, ye are bound under a foolish and a vain hope, with frenzied minds. Why do ye bind yourselves with such foolish things?[27] There is not a creator of this earth or heaven. They have existed always. There is not one who has power to cleanse you from your sins, because there are no sins. Man fares in this life according to the management of the creature; therefore every man prospers according to his genius."[28]

In response, Bo spoke boldly, as the white robed figure came closer. "The laws of justice and mercy demand that there is a Christ who suffered for our sins,[29] who died so we could live, who lives now in a body of flesh and bone, which is in similitude but separate from the Father."[30]

"This is an unknown being, who you say is God—a being who never has been seen or known, who never was nor ever will be.[31] Here I am. See me now. I have a body of flesh and bone. I exist. Feel me. Touch me. My power is real. I have the power to call down fire from heaven.[32] I have the power to strike you dead with the words of my mouth.[33] Do not cross me, or you will feel my wrath." Imam Mahdi came closer. Then awful and impossible words came out of the spiritual man's mouth. *"Bo Rogers, worship me."*[34]

The shock of hearing his name from the lips of the man he would label an Antichrist filled Bo with cankered blackness despite the white, glowing illumination. The fact that this person knew his name made his knees weak again. However, praying, Bo received strength and continued to stand strong in front of his son's unconscious body.

Bo filled his lungs with night air and, growing stronger, began, "I say as Moses said to Satan on a high mountain like this one, 'Who art thou? For behold, I am a son of God, in the similitude of his Only Begotten; and where is thy glory, that I should worship thee?'[35] For it says in the scriptures that man cannot look upon God in his natural form. He must be transfigured,[36] but I look upon you with my natural eyes and yet I do not burn.[37] So I say to you, get thee hence; deceive me not!"[38]

A growl came from the glowing figure. He continued to advance in slow, steady, strong steps. *"Bo Rogers, fall down and worship me!"*

Bo's voice grew louder from his spot on the hill. "In this moment, I call upon God for deliverance. I will not cease to call upon God. I know him, wherefore I can judge between him and thee. *Depart hence!*"[39]

The crowd stood motionless. Imam Mahdi was now only ten to fifteen feet from Bo. His black eyes pierced Bo's heart, turning it cold with its darkness. The earth began to shake under Bo's feet, and dark clouds filled with lightning began to thicken overhead. Again Imam Mahdi commanded Bo, saying, ***"I am the Only Begotten! Worship me!"***[40]

Bo shook his head defiantly. *"Depart from me! I will worship only the true and everlasting God, who is the God of great glory!"*[41]

Imam Mahdi, close enough to grab Bo, reached out a shaking, clawed hand as if to touch Bo to send him to his death, but Bo stood strong and calm. With a strong, confident voice he said, ***"In the name of the Only Begotten, Jesus Christ, depart hence, Imam Mahdi!"***[42]

Imam Mahdi began to tremble. The look on his face turned from evil wrath to horror. He cried with a loud voice and let out a bloodcurdling scream that caused his podium to split in two and the lights to burst, and then suddenly he was gone.

The crowd looked on in disbelief. Amidst the dark and the silence, someone suddenly yelled, "That man killed Imam Mahdi! Kill him!" The crowd erupted from its frozen state.

Bo turned to arouse Dane. He had to get him to stand so they could escape. Dane was just too heavy to carry.

Dane was partially aroused and opened his eyes slightly, but then closed them again.

Bo turned and with both hands around Dane's arms, dragged his limp body up the hill toward the car. They had gone only a foot or two when Bo realized that he heard sirens somewhere in front of him. In the next moment, dozens of blue-clad officers came over the ridge, rushing like wolves down the hill to round up their prey.

The rushing crowd turned immediately and ran away from the police, but they could only run as far as the cliff. Pushed against the sheer edge, the group members had no choice but to give up and allow themselves to be taken into custody.

Over the top of the ridge rushed Corrynne, beaming from ear to ear. She wrapped her arms around Bo and kissed him, then knelt down to look at Dane, kissing his head and hugging his chest after finding the bleeding was under control.

After a few moments, Corrynne gazed up at Bo. "Tell me what happened up here."

Bo looked at his wife numbly. He didn't know what to say.

Corrynne continued, "I jumped in the nearest police car when I saw how Imam Mahdi was treating you. I was afraid something terrible was going to happen!"

Bo continued to stand still with his feet seemingly stuck to the ground. "The power of the priesthood is real, Corrynne. All I can say is that the Lord definitely protected us! It's on him we should focus our gratitude."

Corrynne stood and buried her face in her husband's neck. As she did, her heart overflowed with immense joy and relief. All she could think of were the words, "Thank you, Father! Thank you!"

Notes to "A Taste of Evil"

Father's Words

[1] "The increasing problem of substance abuse and dependence in our society has drawn both public and scientific attention. Although our present knowledge is far from complete, investigating these problems as maladaptive patterns of adjustment to life's demands, with no social stigma involved, has led to clear progress in understanding and treatment" (James Butcher & Robert Carson, "Alcohol Abuse and Dependence," *Abnormal Psychology and Modern Life*, Ninth Edition, 296).

[2] "Typically the drinker experiences a sense of warmth, expansiveness, and well-being. In such a mood, unpleasant realities are screened out and the drinker's feelings of self-esteem and adequacy rise" (James Butcher & Robert Carson, "Alcohol Abuse and Dependence," *Abnormal Psychology and Modern Life*, Ninth Edition, 299).

3 "Alcohol is a depressant that affects the higher brain centers, impairing judgment and other rational processes and lowering self-control. As behavioral restraints decline, a drinker may indulge in the satisfaction of impulses ordinarily held in check" (James Butcher & Robert Carson, "Alcohol Abuse and Dependence," *Abnormal Psychology and Modern Life*, Ninth Edition, 299).

4 Secrecy is the foundation of many evil practices. It has been the cause of the demise of whole societies. Secret combinations are difficult to police due to their subversive culture. "Secret combinations are parasites that live off the spiritually dead of a society. They may not be the immediate cause of a nation's downfall, but they are the symptoms of its loathsome condition. Secret societies are formed to implement the ambitions of those who seek for power and gain. History has shown that these groups thrive in an atmosphere of conflict and social immorality. Efforts to police them or exterminate them through legislation have only forced the evil underground where it has continued to survive. This disease has proved fatal to at least two civilizations, and the Book of Mormon makes it abundantly clear that the appearance of this awful parasite endangers any society" (*Book of Mormon Student Manual*, 492).

5 The name Lucifer means *the Shining One*; also *Lightbringer* or *Son of the Morning* in Hebrew (see Bible Dictionary, "Lucifer," 726). It was Satan's name before he fell from his place of authority in the pre-existence (D&C 76:25). He has been described in the scriptures as "like unto the son of man," meaning Christ (Abraham 3:27). His fall from heaven was great, causing the whole heavens to weep over him (D&C 76:26).

6 "...the drinker enters a generally pleasant world of unreality in which worries are temporarily left behind" (James Butcher & Robert Carson, *Abnormal Psychology and Modern Life*, Ninth Edition, 299).

7 "A susceptibility to alcoholism impairs its victim's freedom to partake without addiction, but his free agency allows him to abstain and thus escape the physical debilitation of alcohol and the spiritual deterioration of addiction....Beware the argument that because a person has strong drives toward a particular act, he has no power of choice and therefore no responsibility for his actions. This contention runs counter to the most fundamental premises of the gospel of Jesus Christ...Satan would like us to believe that we are not responsible in this life. That is the result he tried to achieve by his contest in the pre-existence. A person who insists that he is not responsible for the exercise of his free agency because he was 'born that way' is trying to ignore the outcome of the War in Heaven. We *are* responsible, and if we argue otherwise, our efforts become part of the propaganda effort of the Adversary" (Dallin H. Oaks, "Same-Gender Attraction," *Ensign*, Oct. 1995, 7).

8 "Agency, or the power to choose, was ours as spirit children of our Creator before the world was. (See Alma 13:3; Moses 4:4.) It is a gift from God, nearly as precious as life itself. Often, however, agency is misunderstood. While we are free to choose, once we have made those choices, we are tied to the consequences of those choices. We are free to take drugs or not. But once we choose to use a habit-forming drug, we are bound to the consequences of that choice. Addiction surrenders later freedom to choose. Through chemical means, one can literally become disconnected from his or her own will!" (Russell M. Nelson, "Addiction or Freedom," *Ensign*, Nov. 1988, 6).

9 "Alcohol is the most widely used and abused drug in America. According to the 1993 National Household Survey, 103 million people in the United States are current drinkers and 11 million are heavy drinkers. Alcohol-related crimes in the United States account for 54 percent of murders and attempted murders, 68 percent of manslaughters, 52 percent of rape/sexual assaults, and 48 percent of robberies. Because their mothers drink during pregnancy, 40,000 babies are born each year with birth defects from alcohol abuse. In families with one alcoholic parent, the child is 34 percent more likely to be alcoholic than children of non-alcoholics. Social costs of alcohol addiction amount to $100 billion per year in lost productivity and related health costs. Alcoholism is one of the most preventable illnesses; yet 7 out of 10 adults drink alcohol. Of these, one out of seven is an alcoholic" ("Just the Facts:

Alcohol," *Florida   Alcohol   and   Drugs   Association,*   available   online: www.fadaa.org/index.html).

[10] "How to Find Safety and Peace," *New Era*, Nov. 1997, 4.

[11] "Lucifer and his followers are committed in their evil direction. But we must never forget this about Lucifer: he is a liar. He is the father of all lies and has been from the beginning. He was cast out of Heavenly Father's premortal kingdom because of his disobedience, and now he has one goal, one eternal commitment that has never changed from the time of the war in heaven until the present day. His sole purpose is to make you and me as miserable as he is, and the best way for him to accomplish that is to entice us into disobedience" (M. Russell Ballard, "How to Find Safety and Peace," *New Era*, November 1997, 4).

[12] Despite the difficult task of directing teenagers, it has been shown parental involvement has proven to be a main determining factor in drug abstinence. "Few parents appreciate the enormous influence they exercise over the attitudes and actions of their teens about smoking, drinking and using drugs. Teens who have never used marijuana overwhelmingly credit their parents as the determining influence on their decision" (Joseph A. Califano Jr., "It's All in the Family," *America,* 15 Jan. 2000, 1, available online: www.findarticles.com, search "drugs+teens").

[13] "Daily scripture study, daily prayer, regular family home evening, obedience to priesthood authority in the home and in the Church constitute a great insurance policy against spiritual deterioration" (James E. Faust, "Search Me, O God, and Know My Heart," *Ensign*, May 1998, 17).

[14] "Teach your children when they are very young and small, and never quit. As long as they are in your home, let them be your primary interest" (Pres. Gordon B. Hinckley, "Your Greatest Challenge, Mother," *Ensign*, Nov. 2000, 98).

[15] "Our youth find this tempting stuff all about them. They need the help of their parents in resisting it. They need a tremendous amount of self-control. They need the strength of good friends. They need prayer to fortify them against this flood tide of filth. The problem of parental direction of sons and daughters is not new. It is perhaps more acute than it has ever been, but every generation has faced some aspect of it...My heart reaches out to our youth, who in many cases must walk a very lonely road. They find themselves in the midst of these evils. I hope they can share their burden with you, their fathers and mothers. I hope that you will listen, that you will be patient and understanding, that you will draw them to you and comfort and sustain them in their loneliness. Pray for direction. Pray for patience. Pray for the strength to love even though the offense may have been serious. Pray for understanding and kindness and, above all, for wisdom and inspiration...So lead your sons and daughters, so guide and direct them from the time they are very small, so teach them in the ways of the Lord, that peace will be their companion throughout life" (Pres. Gordon B. Hinckley, "Great Shall Be the Peace of Thy Children," *Ensign*, Nov. 2000, 51-52).

[16] "Teens who consider religion an important part of their lives are much less likely to abuse substances. Those who attend religious services at least four times a month are less likely to smoke, drink or use drugs than those who attend such services less than once a month. Fifty-six percent of teens who attend religious services at least four times a month say they will never use an illegal drug in the future, compared with only 15 percent of those who attend such services less than once a month. Teens who attend services less than once a month are more than twice as likely to smoke marijuana as are those who attend such services at least four times a month" (Joseph A. Califano, "It's All in the Family," *America*, 15 Jan. 2000, 4).

[17] "Experimentation with alcohol and other drugs is no longer characteristic of only a small proportion of youth; rather, it has become the norm among the current generation of American adolescents (Schinke, Botvin, & Orlandi, 1991). It appears that adolescents may even perceive drug experimentation as a "transition" to maturity (Jessor & Jessor, 1980)" (Lisa Lisnov,

"Adolescents' Perceptions Of Substance Abuse Prevention Strategies," *Adolescence Magazine,* 1, available online: www.findarticles.com, search "Teenagers Drug Use").

[18] "Private religious behaviors, such as personal prayer, personal scripture reading, and fasting, were even more influential in preventing delinquency than public religious behaviors, such as attendance at meetings, family prayer, and family home evening" (Brent L. Top & Bruce A. Chadwick, "Helping Teens Stay Strong," *Ensign,* Mar. 1999, 27).

[19] "And others will he pacify, and lull them away into carnal security, that they will say: All is well in Zion; yea, Zion prospereth, all is well—and thus the devil cheateth their souls, and leadeth them away carefully down to hell" (2 Nephi 28:21).

[20] "Behold, verily, verily, I say unto you, ye must watch and pray always lest ye enter into temptation; for Satan desireth to have you, that he may sift you as wheat" (3 Nephi 18:18).

[21] "Now the Lord had shown unto me, Abraham, the intelligences that were organized before the world was; and among all these there were many of the noble and great ones;" (Abraham 3:22).

Rave

[22] The 2000 census shows that Utah was the fourth fastest growing state in America by percentage change since 1990. The rankings of the first five are Nevada 66.3%, Arizona, 40.0, Colorado, 30.6%, Utah, 29.6%, and Idaho, 26.4%. (*U.S Census Bureau,* [Internet release date, 2 April 2001], available online: http://www.census.gov/population/cen2000/phc-t2/tab03.xls).

[23] A global tracking device using satellites is not a new idea. It exists for the world's elite to combat kidnapping and is produced by a company known as Gen-Etics, known as "Sky-Eyes" (http://www.telegraph.co.uk:80/et?ac=000118613908976&rtmo=aw3wHaxL&atmo=rrrrrYs &pg=/et/98/10/6/wchip06.html). In this report, a 4mm X 4mm chip is embedded in the hand or the forehead, which acts as a beacon to find missing persons.

Ageless Battle

[24] See Thessalonians 2:4. The Antichrist will claim to be God.

[25] "When one speaks of God, it is generally the Father who is referred to; that is, Elohim. All mankind are his children" (see Bible Dictionary, "God," 681).

[26] "…apply the atoning blood of Christ that we may receive forgiveness of our sins, and our hearts may be purified; for we believe in Jesus Christ, the Son of God, who created heaven and earth, and all things; who shall come down among the children of men" (Mosiah 4:2).

[27] This conversation is reminiscent of the teachings and beliefs of an identified Antichrist, Korihor in the Book of Mormon (Alma 30:13, 16).

[28] Korihor's teachings: Alma 30:17.

[29] "And thus mercy can satisfy the demands of justice, and encircles them in the arms of safety, while he that exercises no faith unto repentance is exposed to the whole law of the demands of justice; therefore only unto him that has faith unto repentance is brought about the great and eternal plan of redemption" (Alma 34:16).

[30] "Jesus, who is called Christ, is the firstborn of the Father in the spirit and the Only Begotten of the Father in the flesh. He is Jehovah, and was foreordained to his great calling in the Grand Councils before the world was. He was born of Mary at Bethlehem, lived a sinless life, and wrought out a perfect atonement for all mankind by the shedding of his blood and his death on the cross. He rose from the grave and brought to pass the bodily resurrection of every living thing and the salvation and exaltation of the faithful" (see Bible Dictionary, "Christ," 633).

[31] Alma 30:28: these sayings are a continuation of the teachings of Korihor.

[32] In Revelation 13:13 it indicates the Antichrist will have the power to call down fire from heaven.

[33] This is a lie, told by the Antichrist, meant to intimidate the character. It is conceivable that the Antichrist will tell many false things to achieve his goals against the saints.

Although the Antichrist will be able to do miracles (Revelation 13:14), he will not have the power to hurt righteous saints with that power. (See endnote in chapter 3, "Something Borrowed Something Blue.") However, in Revelation chapter 13 and in the times of the early church, Saints were martyrs by the hands of the wicked. Wicked choices can be made by wicked people to kill Saints, but their deaths cannot be brought about by evil miracles.

[34] In a confrontation between Satan and Moses, Satan called Moses by name (see Moses 1:12).

[35] See Moses 1:13. This confrontation is very similar to the one found in the first chapter of Moses where Satan comes to Moses as Christ and demands that Moses worship him.

[36] "For behold, I could not look upon God, except his glory should come upon me, and I were transfigured before him. But I can look upon thee in the natural man. Is it not so, surely?" (Moses 1:14).

[37] "But now mine own eyes have beheld God; but not my natural, but my spiritual eyes, for my natural eyes could not have beheld; for I should have withered and died in his presence; but his glory was upon me; and I beheld his face, for I was transfigured before him" (Moses 1:11).

[38] Moses 1:16.

[39] Moses 1:18.

[40] Moses 1:19.

[41] Moses 1:20.

[42] See Moses 1:21.

CHAPTER FIFTEEN

PIECES

"A good man out of the good treasure of the heart bringeth forth good things: and an evil man out of the evil treasure bringeth forth evil things" (Matthew 12:34).

Privileges

"Corrynne…Corrynne." A fluttering whisper filled and echoed through Corrynne's mind. In another realm someone was calling her. As if in a deep pool, she could feel herself rising to the surface, going toward the entity that called her name. Suddenly, she was aware. With effort she opened her eyes, only to be met with a shocking ache in her neck. As she put her hand to her neck to cradle the stiff muscles, another part of her recognized who had called her name. Shana, the ICU nursing manager, was standing over her in her son's hospital room.

An exquisite scent blanketed her surroundings, like a mist of dew on a spring morning. She recognized the smell. Shana's style was unmatched, and she always presented herself in impossible perfection; the expensive perfume was just one element of that. Corrynne blinked twice to focus on Shana's flawless face. Instantly she was keenly aware of her own disheveled appearance from sleeping in the recliner next to the hospital bed. She covered her mouth immediately to spare Shana from the potential morning halitosis.

Shana smiled broadly, pretending not to notice. "Hi, Corrynne. I'm so glad that you're here. I want to speak with you. Would this be a good time?"

Corrynne looked around quickly to survey the scene. She straightened the blanket that was hanging half off her body and squared herself in the recliner. Pulling on the lever on the side of the chair, she sat up suddenly as hidden springs catapulted her forward. Her hair fell forward into her face from the sudden movement. Corrynne couldn't help but feel disadvantaged. Appearance was everything in the world of silent feminine power, especially with Shana.

"Ah, I guess we can talk a little. I don't want to wake Dane. He needs his rest." Corrynne really did not feel like talking, but Shana was very busy. It was obvious that she was taking a moment out of her time to come and talk with her.

"I'll talk quietly, unless you would rather step out into the hall?"

Corrynne cringed as she imagined how she looked. She couldn't be seen like this in the place where she worked. It would take away part of her edge as medical mentor and accepted leader among some of her colleagues. "No, I would rather talk here. We'll just be quiet."

"OK." Shana knelt down beside the recliner, to reduce her height and become equal with Corrynne, a movement that surprised Corrynne. It was a gesture that communicated Shana's desire to eliminate the rank between them. Women often did this to create an atmosphere of acceptance. Corrynne suspected that an apology was coming.

Shana began, "I was watching the news last night when I saw the amazing things that you and your family were able to do. You were very brave."

"Thank you, but we just did what we felt we had to do."

"I could never have done anything like that. I'm a wimp at heart."

"I doubt that. I have never seen you be even slightly wimpy."

Shana smiled and then took a deep breath. "I was unfair to you, Corrynne. I put you in a difficult position. I'm afraid that I was influenced by outside sources and pressures instead of listening to my conscience. I knew that you were innocent, but you were a quick fix to a threatening problem."

Corrynne looked down at the hospital linen that she had made beds with for years. She nodded. "I knew that was the case."

"I am sincerely sorry."

Corrynne looked up again at Shana's face. "I know it must be difficult to have to make all the ends meet to satisfy administrative demands all the time. I'm sure that sometimes the burden is overwhelming and the easy way out looks attractive."

"Yes, that's exactly how it is. Sometimes I am so tired that I decide whatever seems logical must be the answer. It's been too long since I've been down in the trenches and been a true advocate. I cheated you in that service. I should have supported you and represented you rather than caved into expectations for my own appearance."

Corrynne was impressed with Shana's candor. Her honesty was refreshing. Corrynne replied, "It's really not an issue any longer. Everything's solved now. I'm happy that we found the Versed and documented that Ann was using them for the cult." She cocked her head and continued in a soft, wistful tone, "I just feel sorry for Ann. She's the one who really lost today."

"Why?" Shana's eyebrows lifted as she waited for Corrynne's answer.

"Did you see how sad she was on the news?"

"No, I didn't notice."

"Well, my heart broke when I was watching the video and Dane asked Ann her name. She answered him by saying she didn't have a name. She looked so lost at that moment, and I thought I even saw her crying as she turned away from the camera. This kind of thing always makes me realize that even if the worst happened to me professionally, I would still have my family, my beliefs, and my identity. Those things are so precious to me that losing my job or my privileges is insignificant compared with them."

"I envy your priorities. I envy *you*," said Shana.

Corrynne was taken aback. "What? You're so beautiful and talented. Look at what you've become. You're a picture of perfection. Don't envy me. See your own value."

Shana looked down at the floor. "It's the picture part that bothers me. I may look like I have control on the outside, but on the inside I'm an insecure little girl, struggling to play the game and losing more than I win."

Corrynne reached her hand out and placed it on Shana's shoulder. "We all play games. It's the society that we live in. It demands that we dance the dance of life. Some of us do the steps differently, but still we all feel the beat and move as it moves us. The secret is to know when we're playing the games and when the games are playing us. We need to know which beat is the true beat for us and be loyal to it. In that, we find harmony. We find our center. Then we won't be caught without a place when the music stops."

Shana stared at Corrynne for a long time. "You are wise. Thank you." Shana smiled and stood up. "I guess it goes without saying that your privileges and your position have been restored."

"Thanks, Shana." Corrynne winked. "Have a good day."

Restored

Corrynne looked out the second-story ICU window, contemplating her conversation with Shana. She smiled as she felt the warmth of the sun shining through the window. In that fleeting moment, she was whole. No distractions, no failings, no problems—just the window, the sun, and Corrynne. She studied the light as it came through the window. She realized, of all the strange illusions in the world, the sun was not one of them. It was real. It was what it seemed. The energy that came from it was the source of all life on earth. It had to be straightforward to fulfill its potential. She loved that thought and wished she could live her life like that: true, bold, and without agendas that interfered with the straight nature of her desires.

Corrynne peeked back over her shoulder at the hospital bed where her son was sleeping. A flood of reality reminded her that, although she worked in this facility and in this unit, her role as a mother was different from her role as a nurse. It was strange to have Dane in bed in the room. She noted that even she, with all her experience, still felt vulnerable as the patient's mother. She was unaccustomed to that feeling within those walls. She didn't like having to depend on others for her son's welfare but knew that under the circumstances, there were no other choices. Because of her son's blood loss, he needed new blood—something he had to be admitted to receive. She took note of her feelings and filed them away to be remembered the next time she was on shift. It would be good to remember what it was like in that position to add empathy for the family side of the equation.

She watched out the window as a bird searched for worms in the wet grass. Even from the second floor, Corrynne could see that it was a beautiful robin. It would search and then lift up its head abruptly to watch its environment for danger. After it eyed the surroundings, it would peck at the grass again. Finally, the robin found a worm. It grabbed it with its beak and pulled hard, the worm stretching with the tension. The robin would let go and eye its prey, look around for danger, and then resume the difficult task of extricating the worm from its home. Pulling on the worm repeatedly, the robin would not give up. Each time it pulled, it achieved a little more headway. Eventually the bird was able to pull the worm free, or it had ripped in half from the struggle—Corrynne couldn't tell. The robin flew from the ground into a tree and looked around again, the worm wiggling wildly in its beak. After a moment, the robin flew away, apparently satisfied it had accomplished its goal.

The robin scenario made Corrynne think of the previous night when her husband stood face to face with an Antichrist. Thankfully, they had been successful in their task of extricating their own worm. Sadly, she didn't believe that the worm had been eliminated. Maybe his organization had been stopped temporarily in Provo, Utah, and maybe all of Utah, but since the group seemed to be worldwide, she was sure the worm was only wounded rather than eliminated. Just like the robin's prey, she wondered how much of the worm actually still was underground.

Corrynne gazed at her sleeping son and couldn't help but touch his hair lovingly. To hear him breathe and have him alive was such a gift. She had been so afraid of losing him or her husband the night before. Again, she whispered a thankful communication toward heaven.

The curtain separating the beds in the room rattled as it was pulled aside from the other side. Corrynne looked up to see the police chief she had met the night before.

"Hello!" came his friendly, low voice.

"Hello, Chief Morgan."

"How is our hero doing this morning?" the chief asked as he removed his hat. He approached the hospital bed to look at Dane.

"I believe everything is almost back to normal. He received two units of blood. His blood is still a little low, but because he's young, he'll make more. He is completely stable at this point. I think he'll even go home tomorrow."

"That's great." The chief was fingering his hat.

"How's your battle?" asked Corrynne, smiling.

"Great. Because of your footage, we were able to break up that cult. For now, we have everyone who was on that ridge contained. I think we have excellent cases that will be prosecuted. I just wish we got the leaders. All of them got away."

Corrynne shook her head. "That's too bad. Did you arrest an Ann Cain?"

The police chief pulled out his digital assistant and plugged in the name. "Ann Cain," he muttered. He shook his head. "No, I don't believe so. How do you know her?"

"She was a nurse I worked with once."

"That name sounds familiar. Tell me who she is."

"She was the person who implanted the computer chip in Dane's hand."

"Oh, yes," said the chief thoughtfully. "I remember her." He shook his head. "I don't know why we didn't catch her. We corralled all the people up there. There shouldn't have been any way anyone could've gotten away."

Corrynne shrugged. "She probably disappeared with the others down some secret door."

"Maybe."

"I just hope this doesn't mean my family's still in danger."

Chief Morgan shook his head. "I don't believe that'll be a problem. But if you see anything suspicious, just know that you have friends in the legal system." The chief winked. There was a pause, and then suddenly the chief laughed out loud.

"What?" asked Corrynne, startled by his sudden change in demeanor.

"I was just thinking of what a circus that place was last night. Did you know that everyone we pulled in thought that they were invincible? I'm sure it was partially the drugs speaking. However, they thought that they were on the side that couldn't be beaten. Even today, some of our guests are telling us that we're going to be burned for offending the 'chosen generation'." Chief Morgan shook his head. "As long as I've been in this business, I still am amazed at the things that people get away with. Using religion is an underhanded way to trick people. I actually feel bad for most of those chumps."

"I agree. I'm just glad in this area the group was stopped. The drug abuse and trickery was inexcusable, but I couldn't stand back and watch the Strep, which they were responsible for, kill any more people."

"What Strep?"

"You didn't hear?" asked Corrynne, shocked.

"I—I," said the chief as he tried to remember. "I think I heard of it, but tell me what you're talking about."

"Well, supposedly if the members disobeyed their leader, they would be attacked by a bacteria that was able to digest their tissues and paralyze the conduction of their heart from microbial toxins. It's a wicked way to die, pardon the pun. I still don't know how the cult controlled who lived and who died."

"OK, yes, I saw a report like that on the news. So this was the group responsible for those deaths?"

"Yes."

"Wow, double bingo!" said the chief, seeming very happy.

"I thought you knew."

"I guess I was distracted by all the other strange facts about this group. Maybe I did know but had forgotten." The chief was quiet for a moment. "Ah…Mrs. Rogers, I need to ask you a question."

"Go ahead."

"Now I'm worried about something."

"What?"

"Some of the people we took into custody last night are complaining of pain in various parts of their bodies."

"Really?" Corrynne was instantly concerned. "Have you had anyone look at them?"

"Sure, our doctors have looked them over but none of them have been able to figure out why so many are describing such horrible pain in the same way."

"Oh, Chief Morgan, I would pay attention to those people."

"At first the docs thought their pain was contrived to try and obtain more drugs, but now we've noticed that some of them have developed small purple patches on their skin. All of them who are complaining have the same blotchy appearance, and some have even developed sores."

Corrynne considered what the chief was saying. With strength she said, "Chief Morgan, those people need antibiotics immediately or they will die. This is the Strep manifestation I was talking about. They needed the medication yesterday! It takes only six hours for someone to die of this particular bacterium."

The chief fumbled for his phone. "What kind of antibiotics?"

"A Penicillin type."

The chief called the station and asked to talk to the doctor. As he was talking, Corrynne leaned over the side rail of Dane's bed with her head down. She knew what was coming next. She had lived through it in her waking hours and many times in her dreams. Death was coming, and it was coming to many. But why? What had these people done wrong? Why were they being punished? Anger was welling up inside of her. This wasn't fair! It wasn't the people in the cult's fault that they were caught by the police. It was hers…or was that the real reason? Was the mass deaths that were about to occur meant to be a message to her? Was someone punishing her through the death of others?

Corrynne shook her head and forced the thought from her mind. She couldn't think like that. She couldn't allow something that could never be proven give her guilt. It wasn't her fault people were dying. She hadn't marked anyone. She hadn't abused people's trust and hope. No, that was someone else and she would not carry any burden of human suffering. She did what needed to be done and that's all she would consider.

The police chief pulled the phone away from his ear and asked, "Should we give everyone antibiotics, or only those with the sores?"

Corrynne breathed controlled breath and shook her head. "Give it to all of them."

The chief gave the order and hung up the phone. "Good thing I came in here when I did. Thank you, Mrs. Rogers."

Corrynne looked at the chief and said, "It might be too late for those people who have the purple spots."

"Why?" asked the chief.

"Because the bacteria has been allowed to begin dissolving the tissue. Those with the sores, if they can be saved, will be grossly deformed. They'll have to amputate the dead tissue to save their lives."

The police chief's eyes narrowed. "I understand. At least we may be able to save most of them. I've got to get back to the station to assess the situation."

Corrynne nodded as a pit formed in her stomach. "Goodbye and good luck," she said, trying to shake off the dread she was feeling.

"I'm sure I'll be back here soon," said Chief Morgan with a small salute. "Sounds like it's going to be a long day. I'll let you know what happens."

"Thanks," said Corrynne, not knowing if she really wanted that to happen, but still wanting to be polite.

The police chief quickly exited the room and Corrynne sat down in the recliner. She was beginning to feel sick.

Exposure

Corrynne strolled to the back of the room to gaze out the window, just as she had earlier in the day. Looking out the window helped her focus her thoughts. She didn't want to think about anything negative. She tried to clear her mind.

Someone came into the room. Corrynne assumed that it was Dane's nurse. She heard rummaging in his bedside supply cart. Peeking around the center power column to see what was going on, she was surprised to see a strange person in the room. The woman was dressed as a nurse but Corrynne didn't know her. She thought maybe she was just more temporary help.

Corrynne watched from the back of the room as the nurse drew up a rare vial of potassium. First of all, Corrynne wondered where she found a vial, since they were removed from the hospital setting a long time ago, but secondly, why she was doing it in Dane's room.

After the nurse was finished drawing up a ten-milliliter syringe, she drew up another. When she was finished, she approached Dane's bed with the two syringes in her hand and took out an alcohol swab.

Corrynne frowned. It looked like the woman was going to push the potassium into Dane's IV! That would kill him! Corrynne rushed to the bed. "*Stop! What are you doing?*" she demanded angrily as she stepped between the nurse and her son.

The unfamiliar nurse jumped and looked at Corrynne in confusion. "Oh, you scared me! Why did you yell at me like that?"

"*Because you were just about to kill my son!*" Corrynne said in the boldest voice she could muster.

"Excuse me?" said the nurse taking a couple steps backward as she looked at her syringes. She acted like she didn't know what Corrynne was talking about.

"If you pushed that potassium into my son's IV, you would have stopped his heart!"

"No, I wouldn't have!" said the nurse defensively.

"Absolutely you would've! Don't you know that potassium is one way they kill death-row inmates? A bolus of potassium stops the heart!"

"*What?*" asked the nurse, looking terrified.

"Where'd you get this potassium anyway?" asked Corrynne as she snatched the empty vial from the countertop. "We can't get vials of potassium anymore for that reason. It kills! Potassium is always mixed in a drip. Always!"

The nurse looked down at the syringes and dropped them as if they were suddenly hot. They landed on the bedside table that stood next to the head of the bed. "I'm so sorry! I just was following the doctor's orders. I just didn't think…."

"What orders?" demanded Corrynne.

The nurse answered quickly, "Dr. Page just came by and told me that your son's potassium was low because we gave him blood. He told me to give him forty milli-equivalents IV."

Corrynne studied the nurse. "But you can't push it! You have to give it slowly over hours."

"I'm so sorry! I'm not used to giving potassium. I normally work on the sixth floor."

"Well then you should ask someone what you should do," said Corrynne, losing her patience with this nurse.

"I did," said the nurse.

"You did?" asked Corrynne. "Who did you ask?"

"I asked Dr. Page."

"And what did he say?"

"He said to 'just push it through the IV.'"

"He said to 'just push it?" asked Corrynne frowning. "That doesn't make sense."

The nurse's eyes were wide and unblinking. "Yes, he told me to push it and that it was 'as easy as eating a banana in your sleep.'"

Corrynne shook her head. "I'm sure you misunderstood him. He would never tell you to push it. Anyway, the order doesn't even make sense. A person's potassium doesn't fall when you give blood."

"It doesn't?"

"No, it's calcium that falls after a patient receives blood, not potassium. Potassium actually rises, not falls."

The nurse just looked at Corrynne with a blank stare.

"Didn't you learn this in nursing school?" asked Corrynne. A pit was growing in her stomach. It was becoming obvious this nurse was her worst nightmare.

Thoughtfully, the nurse said, "I'm sure I did, but I don't remember those details. Can you tell me why the calcium would be low in a patient that received blood?"

Corrynne was astonished! How could someone like this be allowed to work in the ICU? Despite her growing alarm, she answered, "I'm sure you remember that calcium is used in the clotting process in the human body."

"Yes, I remember that. But why would that deplete your son's calcium? Did he bleed that much? Is he still bleeding somewhere?" The nurse looked down at Dane as if to find blood on the sheets.

"No, he's not bleeding," said Corrynne. "A substance known as 'citrate' is added to donated blood that binds with the free calcium in it to stop the clotting process. This has to be done since it's impossible to give clotted blood through an IV."

"Oh, OK. That makes sense," said the nurse nodding.

"Then, when donated blood is given to a patient, the citrate binds with the patient's calcium in his or her blood, too, only it's greatly diluted and doesn't affect the patient's clotting ability. It does, however, lower the free calcium level. This lower level is detected by the ionized calcium blood draw."

"OK, now I understand."

"The patient's potassium is untouched by blood infusion unless a certain amount of the blood cells delivered have been lysed. Older units of blood have higher amounts of potassium in them because as blood cells age, some rupture. This causes the potassium level to rise in the blood and thus in the patient, because there are large amounts of potassium inside red blood cells."

The young nurse looked ashamed, but she nodded, trying to show her willingness to learn. "I'm sorry. I guess I just trusted Dr. Page's instructions."

The mention of Dr. Page made Corrynne frown again. "Go get the chart. Let's look at it. I want to see these orders."

The nurse nodded and then scurried out of the room and returned with the large, long, blue, hard-covered notebook. The spine read ROGERS. It was Dane's medical chart. Corrynne flipped to the "physician's orders" section and looked at the first page of orders where she would find an order that had been written last. There in Dr. Page's unreadable scrawl was an order dated that day.

She studied it for a few seconds and said, "I believe this says 'give 1 amp of CaCl now,' but his writing is so bad that anyone could look at the 'c' and the 'a' together and interpret it to be a 'K', making KCl, or potassium chloride. However, potassium usually comes in mini-equivalents rather than amps, so potassium wouldn't have made sense anyway. One other thing is that one can push calcium chloride but not potassium chloride. I bet you just got everything confused."

"It looks like it," said the nurse with a defeated tone. "I'm just glad you were there to stop me."

"Me too," said Corrynne. "When the writing is this bad, you need either to ask someone else to try to interpret it or call the doctor himself. Normally the doctors tell you what they write just so they don't get a needless call later."

The nurse looked doe-eyed at Corrynne. "I did ask him, remember? He really made it sound like it was potassium that he was talking about."

"Fine." Corrynne continued to try to be patient with the naive nurse. "Then the next thing you should do is try to think out the logic of the order." Corrynne went to the computer and pressed her thumb to the identification plate. She pulled up Dane's labs and looked at his chemistry. "Look here." She motioned to the nurse to come look at the screen. The nurse complied. "See, his potassium is 4.4, which is within normal limits, but his ionized calcium is 1.0, which isn't too bad, but it is low enough to be replaced."

"Yes, I see. I guess I needed to look at those labs. I just thought that the doctor already had…."

Corrynne cut off the nurse. She wasn't seeing the danger her actions could have caused. "Well, even if Dane needed potassium, you must have a central line to the heart to administer it, and it must be diluted and run over a long period of time. If given quickly in a small IV in the arm, it is very painful, not to mention deadly."

The nurse slowly looked from the screen on the computer and back to the chart. She seemed to be overwhelmed with all the information. "I didn't even think to question the doctor. I didn't even check the chart. I just did as he told me. I don't think I could even decipher what that writing said without your telling me."

"Well, if you did understand Dr. Page correctly, there is something very wrong. Where is Dane's regular nurse?"

"She suddenly got sick. That's why I was called down from the other floor. Dr. Page asked for me himself."

"That's not how it normally happens. Normally the charge nurses work out nursing staff."

"I know, but Dr. Page said that he had been watching me and felt I was a perfect match for this particular patient. I was flattered that he would think highly enough of me that he would bring me down here to work in the ICU.

So I came...." The nurse looked at Corrynne closely. "I'm sorry, but I didn't get your name. It is obvious that you work here."

"Yes, I'm the charge nurse in this unit at night."

"Well, I'm very glad to meet you...a little embarrassed, but very thankful that you caught my mistake."

"Next time, always check the orders, labs, and patient's ID. Despite what the doctor says, always, always find out for yourself if his orders are appropriate. It's true that doctors don't often make mistakes, but they are human. We need to be double checking everything that happens, especially here in the ICU where life hangs by a thread most of the time."

"I understand. Again, I am sorry."

"So what do you think was going on when Dr. Page asked you to push potassium? Did he seem like he was serious?"

"Very serious."

"Hmmm." Corrynne considered the possibilities. She could not avoid the conclusion that hit her in the face. There was something ominous surrounding Dr. Page. Maybe her original thoughts about his being connected with the cult were right. She just couldn't find the connection yet. She wondered if Dr. Page had really been trying to hurt Dane. What would he achieve from hurting him? She decided the only way to find out was to ask him. Corrynne walked over to the power column in the room and reached out for the 'code blue' button. Her hand hovered for a moment as she considered her options.

"What are you doing?" asked the nurse, looking like a scared rabbit as she cowered, backing up against the sink behind her.

Corrynne turned back to the nurse, raising her finger in thought. "If you would have given potassium as Dr. Page had ordered you to, a code would have been going on right now. If you are correct about what he said to you, I think we can surprise him with a theatrical performance. Don't you think we should fulfill his expectations and see what happens?"

The nurse shook her head vigorously, bringing her hands up to her ears as if to shield them from Corrynne's plan. "Oh, no. I don't like that."

"Why?"

"I don't know. You just don't hit that button unless someone is dying," the nurse tried to reason.

"It's fine. Just watch," Corrynne said as she fumbled in her bag for her Blackberry. "In fact, I think I want to record what Dr. Page says when he finds out that there is no code and that Dane is fine. I think it could be quite revealing." Corrynne pushed the record button and walked around the bed to set the device on the counter by the sink. She strategically placed it behind some cards that had come earlier that day. "Next, I need to get our patient to cooperate." Corrynne reached down and pushed Dane hard into the bed. Dane opened his eyes. "Hi, Dane." She gave him a big smile and reached down and kissed him on the cheek.

"Hi, Mom, what are you doing?" Dane stretched his arm attached to his IV and yawned.

"We're going to fake a code with you."

"Why?"

"Because something strange is going on, and I need to know who our friends are. Are you game?"

"Whatever, Mom, you know me. Always ready for an adventure."

"OK, just lie there and pretend to be out cold. Don't worry—I won't let them intubate you."

"Good, I wasn't in the mood for that, anyway." Dane smiled his famous goofy superman smile and then closed his eyes.

Corrynne smiled too, but then became serious. She reached up to the monitor and pushed control buttons until the EKG screen appeared. She decreased the gain of the waveform until the "asystole" alarm began to ring. Red lights lit the monitor both in the patient's room and out on the main screen at the nurses' desk as the alarm rang loudly. Next, she confidently hit the code button on the power column behind the monitor.

All over the ICU, the familiar code blue voice came across the sound system, and suddenly the room filled with medical personnel. In came the crash cart. Corrynne pressed in on Dane's chest, as if doing CPR, but because she did not place the hard backboard behind his back, she was able to press his whole body into the bed rather than depress his chest wall. Dane continued to play along and be unresponsive.

Dr. Page came running into the room. "What happened?"

Corrynne innocently began to give him information in between compressions. "He was fine...then suddenly...his heart stopped...for no reason!"

"What rhythm do we have?" asked Dr. Page as the leads from the crash cart were applied.

The staff nurse studied her monitor. Then hesitantly she said, "Normal sinus rhythm?"

"Normal sinus?" asked Dr. Page as he came and studied the monitor himself.

"Yep, it looks like it to me," the staff nurse returned, now more confident.

"Oh, I'm so glad! I like normal sinus. It does a body good!" said Corrynne as she stopped compressions. She looked up at the monitor that was still displaying a flatline pattern for the EKG. "There must be something wrong with the monitor," she said casually. "It's not sensing his rhythm." She reached up and readjusted the gain. A normal sinus rhythm began to be displayed once again. "There, all better." Corrynne smiled, gaining eye contact with Dr. Page.

Dr Page suddenly developed a suspicious look. "What did you do, Corrynne?"

"Nothing, he just came back on his own," she said innocently.

Dr. Page looked around the room for the nurse he had sent in to treat Dane. After locating her, he said, "Code over," without removing his eyes from her. The staff filed out, and the doctor closed the door after them. "So what's really going on?" Dr. Page's look was deadly.

The newly assigned nurse looked down to avoid his stare.

"That was my question," returned Corrynne.

"...And mine." Dane opened his eyes, sat up, and smiled as if someone were taking a picture.

"So you give potassium 'as easy as eating a banana'? 'Just push it'? Interesting words, Dr. Page," taunted Corrynne. "So why was this nurse perfect for my son? Was it because she knew nothing about ICU medicine? She trusted you? She was a good fall guy? I noticed in your orders you covered your tracks, but your writing is just bad enough that the calcium chloride might look like potassium chloride to someone who was not familiar with your chicken scratch. Bad patient to choose to kill. Did you think that I wasn't in here? Or did you care?"

"Yeah, did you care?" Dane echoed, still smiling.

"Those are serious accusations, Corrynne. I heard you were losing it, but this is really bad. You seem to think everyone is after you. A little paranoia, maybe? I guess your son has bought into it, too. That makes you both delusional."

"Tell me, doctor, you weren't surprised when that code alarm rang through these halls, were you?" Corrynne continued, ignoring his reference. "In fact, you were more surprised that Dane wasn't dead. We all saw it. You couldn't put all the pieces together for a few moments. Boy, we sure had you going."

"I should have told the team to shock him! That would have been a perfect ending to your ruse." Dr. Page was starting to turn a deep red. Corrynne was beginning to get to him.

Dr. Page lifted his hand and pointed a finger at the young nurse from the sixth floor. "That nurse misunderstood my orders. If she told you that I told her to push potassium, she probably just heard me wrong."

"Did the whole ICU core hear you wrong?"

"What ICU core? There was no one around when I was talking to her."

"How convenient! Interesting that you should notice. Did you plan that? I'm sure now that you did. Just like you made sure that she had *as little experience as possible*."

"What are you talking about? I didn't do anything of the sort. I don't know what you are insinuating. I don't even know this nurse or what she knows or doesn't know."

"You didn't hand pick her from the sixth floor?"

"Well, I knew the sixth floor had an extra nurse because I had just discharged a few patients. I was only trying to help because Dane's nurse was so sick. It seemed like a perfect solution."

"That was so nice of you. Did you do that so the charge nurses didn't have to hassle with it? Because this is the first time that I've known you to get personally involved in staffing."

"Corrynne, no offense, but you have flipped your lid. You need a psych consult. Too bad you're not one of my patients, or I would get one for you."

"So you wouldn't mind if I call my friend, the police chief, right now, would you? He told me to call him if anything suspicious happened. This is definitely suspicious." Corrynne pulled her phone from her pocket and dialed 9-1-1.

Suddenly, the doctor leapt in Corrynne's direction before she could push the connect button. His sudden movement startled her and she dropped the phone on the floor and then the doctor kicked it under the bed.

Dr. Page's face twisted into a hideous grin. He laughed wickedly. "You're a bluffer, Corrynne. You really aren't as tough as you seem. You're just as scared as everyone out there." Dr. Page took a step toward Corrynne.

The sixth-floor nurse ran immediately around the power column and to the far corner of the room.

"All of you are chickens! Bawk, bawk, bawk." The doctor began to cluck and move around the room like a chicken, taunting all of them.

"I see only one example of poultry in here," Dane said defiantly from his bed.

Dr. Page stopped suddenly and looked Dane square in the face. His gaze moved to Corrynne and then to the floor nurse. "I know what you're trying to do. I know that you're trying to make me confess something sinister." Dr. Page came close to Corrynne and spoke into her face in a loud whisper. "But the fact of the matter is that you have *nothing*!"

Corrynne continued to back up as Dr. Page advanced, until her back was against the bedside table next to Dane's bed.

"As far as this nurse goes,"—he pointed to the back corner of the room— "she's a nothing. No one will believe her over me. I have written orders to back me up. Nurses misunderstand orders all the time. It's not my fault that she can't listen."

"*You're a liar!*" spoke the nurse energetically from the back, a response that surprised all of them, including Dr. Page.

"Face it!" Dr. Page looked around the power column to see the nurse. "It was only a matter of time before you killed somebody. You have more medication errors than anyone else in this hospital. ...Isn't that true?"

"I thought you didn't know anything about this nurse. ...Sounds to me like you've done your homework!" Corrynne growled.

The doctor whipped his head around to look at Corrynne again. They stood and stared at each other for a few long moments. Then, slowly and deliberately, the doctor walked to the front of the room and drew the drapes to shield them visually from the hall. Corrynne began to worry about what would come next.

The doctor continued, suddenly calm, "Corrynne, no one will believe you, either. In your personal file I've written a note saying that you have shown clinical symptoms of being mentally unbalanced, that you have episodes of paranoia alternating with beliefs of grandeur. This nonsense about my being after you will only help my case." Again the doctor laughed deeply.

Corrynne responded boldly, despite the feeling of dread that was beginning to fill her. "Doctor, you forget that there are three of us here. All of us are listening to your strategies. You're overestimating your influence and credibility. Now who is having delusions of grandeur?"

In response to Corrynne, the doctor reached deep into his pocket and pulled out some kind of instrument. Corrynne could not tell what it was because it fit perfectly in Dr. Page's hand.

Dr Page approached Corrynne until they were nose to nose. This made her feel very uncomfortable and arch back over the bedside table to get away from him. The edge of the table dug into her back. She pulled her hands behind her to blunt the sharpness of it. It was then she felt an object roll slightly and hit her hand on the table.

The doctor spoke into Corrynne's face. "I believe that you are again mistaken. I do not reveal myself at all."

Corrynne cringed inside as she could feel his hot breath fall on her own lips.

Then Dr. Page stepped back to speak to Dane. He continued, "In fact, I reveal only what I wish to reveal. You see, I tell you these things of my free will, not because you were clever or manipulative."

Finally, the doctor moved so he could see the sixth-floor nurse from around the power column. "Why do I do that? Because soon you will not be a threat any longer."

With those words, Corrynne knew without a doubt that they were in danger. She frantically searched her mind for the next thing to do. Like lightning striking, she remembered with clarity what was on the bedside tray behind her without looking.

"You see, my initial plan was to allow you and your family to live," continued Dr. Page. "You would have lived in terror and sadness. I think that's good for the soul, don't you?"

"What do you mean, let us live? Are you going to kill us now?" asked Corrynne.

"Ding, ding, ding! You win the prize! Ladies and gentlemen, see what the smart charge nurse has won today!" Dr. Page put his hand to his ear and changed his voice to a low announcer's voice. "Yes, Corrynne Rogers has earned one life experience of the flesh-eating disease! Yes, that's right, you, that poor excuse of a nurse and your loved ones will soon be experiencing painful death the nano-chip way."

Dr. Page's threat was too much for the sixth-floor nurse, and she began to cry quietly in the corner, only allowing small sobs to escape periodically.

Dane continued to sit in his bed without emotion, watching everything that was happening around him, his muscles tensing as his levels of adrenalin rose. For a fleeting moment, Corrynne's and Dane's eyes met. She sent a silent message with a simple look that Dane would take cues from his mother if things got too dangerous.

Dr. Page continued, "Since you people are not going to be a threat any longer, I want to tell you a story that will set me free and be good entertainment for you...." He took a wide stance. "You see, I know I'm a genius, but I found that being a genius isn't any fun unless others think so, too. The lure of exposing myself has been intoxicating but to have to keep it secret has been excruciating. So, let me share with you my marvelous plan. Even though this discussion will not change your destiny, I want to see the look in your eyes when you hear everything. Aren't I benevolent? I knew that you would be appreciative." Dr. Page smiled wickedly again.

While the doctor eerily continued, Corrynne felt around blindly for the syringes full of potassium that the nurse had dropped earlier on the bedside table. Finding the two cylindrical shapes, she traced their form to identify the size of needle they had on the end. She could tell by feel that it was a 1.5-inch needle with an 18-gauge bore hole in the end. This was a very large needle used for drawing up medications quickly.

Dr. Page started to pace between the sink and the bed. His voice turned musical as he entertained himself. "Once upon a time, I had published some amazing research I had done on nanotechnology[1] and placed it on the Web. My original plan was to drum up interest and venture capital, something I thought would take a long time."

What would she do with syringes full of concentrated potassium? Corrynne didn't think that they would be deadly unless she infused the solution into a vessel that led directly to the heart. If it were pushed into tissue, it would burn like fire. ...That acknowledgement was ironic.... She flicked the protective caps off both the needles with her thumbs. She allowed the sheaths to slide silently to the tabletop. Yes, burn like fire. It seemed appropriate.

"I had found that it was possible to select a virus or a bacteria to be encapsulated, injected into the body, and held in stasis without harm to the host or the microorganism. Then, with a trigger, which could be certain chemicals or defined physical movements, I could cause the capsule to break apart and allow the virus or bacteria into the tissue," continued Dr. Page. "This precise control is achieved by a tiny computer chip so small that we called it a nano-chip. In actuality it's a nanocomputer,[2] similar to a nanobot, that receives its energy from the body itself."[3]

Dr. Page continued speaking rapidly. "One day a gentleman from the Middle East called me with an offer I couldn't refuse. He was a very wealthy man who had worldwide goals. He had a political agenda that I was not interested in, but he promised me that I would become one of the richest men in the world if I would work with him. I checked him out and found what he said was true. We teamed up. It was a perfect partnership."

"Was this Imam Mahdi?" asked Corrynne, acting interested to gain time to think things over.

"He had many names that he would call himself. I call him Al."

"Al?" The simplicity of the name caught Corrynne off guard. "Is that his real name?"

"I don't know. All I know is that he introduced himself as Al Mahdi.[4] His name doesn't matter to me anyway, as long as his money is real. Believe me, he has given me a taste of it, and it is as reeeeal and sweet as honey." Dr. Page rubbed his hands together greedily.

Corrynne looked away to hide her distaste for his attitude. She continued to ask questions in a more subdued manner to maintain control of her emotions, which were beginning to boil. "But he's the one who led that cult, right?" she said as she still looked away from him.

"Yes, but I'm not involved with his religion or his beliefs. I just gave him the tool to make it seem as if he could control people." Dr. Page began to pace again.

"How did you do that?"

Dr. Page turned back to look at Corrynne and smiled. "See? You're interested. I knew you would be."

Corrynne looked up quickly. "Of course I'm interested." Corrynne played to his desire to be acknowledged for his work. "You have always been amazing to me. Your knowledge is unmatched by anyone I know." She didn't smile but allowed her face to be pleasant and as sincere as she could manage.

Dr. Page hesitated for a second. "Boy, you seem almost nice. What's wrong?"

"Nothing. I've been trying to figure out how that flesh-eating disease was controlled by that man. It's been driving me crazy." Corrynne shook her head as she fingered the syringes.

Dr. Page smiled like a proud papa. "There is more than one way to skin a cat. You couldn't figure it out, because no one else out there can do what I can do. That was the whole idea. No one else would know how it happened. It would seem like a miracle."

"Well, you accomplished your goal. That's exactly how it seemed," said Corrynne.

"So stop teasing us and tell us how you do it," said Dane with a serious voice.

Both Corrynne and Dr. Page looked at Dane. Corrynne was surprised, but he really seemed interested. The added audience caused Dr. Page to become even more self-absorbed.

Dr. Page continued. "Al wanted the highest level of compliance from those he would eventually control. He theorized that if he could inspire fear as well as worship, he would have the perfect mixture which would encourage ultimate leverage among his followers. Part of his plan was to incorporate a deadly consequence to defection or dissident behavior without having to police his followers. With my technology, that would be easy."

"So you programmed the chips to do what?"

"Slow down, I'm getting there.... Anyway, Al...or Imam Mahdi, whatever you want to call him...is obsessed with fire. He wanted people to burst into flames if they ever went against him, but I couldn't deliver that kind of response. The best I could do was have people *feel* like they were burning, using a virulent form of Streptococcus A."

Corrynne's stomach turned as Dr. Page exposed his actions without any sort of remorse. A look of satisfaction covered his face as he continued to expound his own genius. Corrynne bet he had never seen the people actually suffering from his discovery...but she had.

"We theorized that if we did our jobs right and led the followers to believe that we knew what they were doing and saying at all times, they would truly believe they could die by fire if they were the least bit disrespectful. The emotions they would feel in the face of the threat of death during such times would cause them to have a catecholamine rush."

"You mean they would be afraid."

"Yes. High levels of adrenaline would course through their veins. We made the chips sensitive to the level shown by research to be associated with humans during extremely stressful events, so that when the programmed level of adrenaline was achieved, the capsule would dissolve and the bacteria would be unleashed to do the punishing. Voila! Instant plague brought about by disobedience toward the prophesied Imam Mahdi. Isn't that godlike? Little did they know that it was their own body that betrayed them. Al was extremely pleased."

Corrynne's eyebrows furrowed as she considered the possibilities of such a weapon. "What about the adrenaline levels of other stressful events? What if the followers had a bad dream, saw a scary movie, or broke up with their boyfriend? Even the drugs that are offered at the parties can cause people to have terrible hallucinations that can cause the same fear response."

"Good point," said the doctor. "I have to admit, that was one problem that we experienced."

"Problem?" Corrynne laughed sarcastically. "Killing innocent people, because they were trusting and believed things they were told, is a *'problem'*?"

"Whoa, girl. Down. We fixed that situation. There were more deaths than we expected or wanted, so we had to up the trigger level to preserve the faithful. There has been a dramatic drop in infections since...." Dr. Page stopped in the middle of the room and thought for a moment, then continued, "But I'll tell you, the whole scenario worked like a well-oiled engine. We caught many who thought they were being sneaky and were trying to leave us. But we got them, even though we were miles and miles away. Ingenious, huh?"

Corrynne refrained from responding. She was beginning to feel nauseated. "Did you inject the bacteria into the tissue during the tattooing and piercings?" She already knew the answer.

"Absolutely. The group did it to each other." Dr. Page suddenly laughed uproariously, slapping his knee. "I never dreamed it would be so easy to gain total control over a mass of people.... And that's not the end. You should see what comes next! We have a computer chip that we embed into the palms of people that will act as their homing devices. With that device we can track our followers! However, the technology goes so much further than that. I don't have time to go into it now, but the whole world will sell their souls for our chip."

"What if they remove the chip?" Dane asked stoically.

Corrynne knew he was referring to the chip in his own hand.

"The only way to do that is to cut off the hand. If anyone tries to take it out, there are thousands of capsules that will break down and eat their hand."

"I'd cut off my hand to get rid of it. I could live with only one hand," said Dane.

Dr. Page looked at Dane thoughtfully. "Good point. Maybe we should start putting it in the forehead. There's a lot of the body's energy available there to run the chip. That would solve that problem. People couldn't cut off their heads and live.... I'll mention that idea to Al."

There was silence in the room. Then Corrynne asked, "What were the secrets that people were not supposed to divulge? There were a couple of patients who died who said they were being punished for telling secrets."

Dr. Page smiled. "There weren't any."

"What?" Corrynne's grip tightened around the syringes.

"No, we wanted them to go out and get followers, but we told them not to tell the enemy."

"Who was the enemy?"

"We didn't tell them anyone, really. We let them come to their own conclusions. We did say that organized society wouldn't understand our way of thinking, so many of them thought the enemy was the working class or the religious, sometimes the parents or the government. It's amazing how you plant a little seed and the information grows into a thorny, gnarled bush."

"I see...."

"The whole plan worked like a charm. The teachings were supposed to be ambiguous. In not defining ourselves, we allowed the people to come to their own conclusions, which gave the illusion that we had more control than we really did."

Corrynne's eyes narrowed as she gathered up her courage to ask the question that had been haunting her. "Did you kill Dr. Quaid?"

Dr. Page turned to look at Corrynne, with a menacing smile. "It was necessary."

"I knew it! I knew it!" Corrynne said in a loud whisper. She could feel her face getting hot. She swallowed hard to keep back her tears.

"He was the one person who was nosing around that we couldn't scare away. You see, our power is great only if people believe us. It's kind of like magic. If the real answers are found, then it takes all the power away. He was a necessary expenditure."

Despite Corrynne's heightened emotions, she couldn't help but ask the obvious question. "How'd you do it?"

Dr. Page began to laugh. "You want all the dirt, don't you?"

"No, I just don't know how you tricked a doctor. He knew too much."

"Oh, it was easier than you'd think. Everyone thought Dr. Quaid was so brilliant, but what you didn't know was Dr. Quaid was a slob. He always left his clothes crumpled in the locker room floor instead of putting them in his locker. He constantly left notes, books and belongings all over the hospital."

Corrynne nodded. "That's true. I've found his stethoscope in my patient's rooms on more than one occasion."

"See? You even saw it too. It was disgusting!"

"Yes, but how does that fit in?"

"Well, the thing that made him such an easy target was his sloppy habit of leaving cans of pop out on the counters in between seeing patients."

Corrynne took in a breath as she began to understand. "Did you put something in his drink?"

"Wow, you are smart! Rohypnol, a drug that's the cousin of Valium, dissolves easily in drinks and causes the victim to lose their memory for 8 hours.[5] I gave Dr. Quaid a large dose so it knocked him unconscious. …He never knew what hit him."

"How did you get him home, because I heard that's where he died."

"I took him there."

"You did?"

"Of course. I did what any caring doctor would for a friend." Dr. Page smiled wickedly.

Corrynne had to look away. "Didn't his wife think anything was strange?" she asked looking at the floor.

"No, she wasn't home. I didn't know where she was, but she didn't find her husband until it was too late. It was perfect."

Corrynne thought for a minute. She knew Dr. Page wanted her to be impressed with his plans, but she couldn't muster another ounce of false support. She felt cornered. She didn't know what else to say and sensed that the conclusion of their conversation was approaching. She decided to honestly confess her feelings. "Dr. Page, you make me sad."

"Why?" Dr. Page frowned. Suddenly he became very defensive.

"You could have been so much with all your talent. You could have changed the world," said Corrynne.

"Could have? I've already changed the world. The world will *never* be the same."

"No, I mean for good."

"Where's the fun in that?" Dr. Page shook his head. "No, too many rules and committees. I like to be free."

"I'm afraid if you think this is freedom, you're trapped just like I am. Your accountability will catch up with you and cut your victory party short."

Dr. Page looked at Corrynne stone faced. Suddenly, a resolved expression filled his countenance. "Corrynne, can I tell you that you have been a thorn in my side? I will be relieved when I don't have to worry about you anymore."

Corrynne stood, silently looking at the doctor.

Dr. Page continued, "...You have enough knowledge and guts, mixed with sheer stupidity, to threaten what I'm doing. I can't let you do that. You're like a dog that smells meat. We tried scaring you, taking away your privileges, interfering with your family, affecting your friends—nothing worked!"

"What did you expect?"

"I expected you to back off!"

"I couldn't."

"You couldn't, or you wouldn't?"

"Both. I had to protect that which I love. I still have to protect it. I don't care what cost my actions require, I am willing to pay it. Whatever it takes to shut your organization down, I will do it. I might die doing it, but it will be worth it."

Dr. Page stood looking at her with moistened eyes, seeming to be affected by her resolution. "That is my frustration. You're a 'do-gooder,' a real one. Earlier in my life, I would have enjoyed being associated with you. This world is full of imitation friends, especially if you're anyone of consequence. But I think you would have been a real friend. I would have liked to experience a true friendship. I don't believe I have ever had that pleasure."

Dr. Page looked down at Dane, who was still sitting emotionless. "You are lucky that this woman's your mother. She's a good mom. I'm jealous that she would risk her life for you and your family." Then Dr. Page turned back to Corrynne. "You see, Corrynne, there was a time when I really liked you. In fact, as I contemplate finally stopping you, I find it difficult. That's the reason I have to eliminate you. You're my weakness. As long as you have any influence over me, I'm weak. Your friendship makes me weak. I look back and see that because of your friendship, I didn't just infect you last week and be done with you."

Corrynne's features softened. "You know that you don't have to follow through, John," she said gently, trying to influence Dr. Page to spare them.

The use of Dr. Page's first name made the doctor stiffen. His face turned almost purple, and a vein bulged obviously down the middle of his forehead. His voice sounded strangled as he said through his clenched teeth, *"Now you lie! You are like the rest.... Manipulation...."* He didn't finish his sentence.

The sudden change in the doctor's demeanor caused Corrynne's senses to become alert. She studied his movements, trying to understand his intentions.

Dr. Page immediately flicked something in his right hand with his thumb and reached into Dane's bed. He touched Dane's bare leg with the unknown instrument, and there was a loud escape of air. Dane yelled in sudden pain.

With Dane's loud outburst, Corrynne stabbed the syringe in her right hand into Dr. Page's right shoulder blade. Contacting bone with the needle, the whole needle length did not go into his skin. Still, she pushed hard on the plunger. Although very little fluid escaped the syringe, it caused the doctor to throw his head, arch back and scream, trying to reach back to remove the large needle.

With Dr. Page's quick rotation to the right, the syringe with the needle intact was ripped out of Corrynne's hand, and it fell with the heavy liquid to the floor.

Dr. Page whipped around to face Corrynne as she changed the second syringe from her left hand to her right. But quicker than he could respond, she sank the second needle deep into his upper left chest, just below the collarbone. Again he reeled back, but the syringe with the long needle stayed embedded. Dr. Page was falling. His feet were caught in Dane's IV tubing. Frantically, he tried to catch his fall by turning his body over. His chest hit the floor, deploying the plunger with his body weight. Within seconds, his body was still.

Relief

Corrynne stood over the doctor, frozen.

The sixth-floor nurse moved from her corner and slowly approached. "Is he unconscious? Is he OK?"

Corrynne just shook her head with her mouth open.

Dane knelt in his bed and looked over the rail at the lifeless form.

Suddenly, the door opened behind the drape and the police chief poked his head around it. His face changed from pleasant to confused as he saw Dr. Page laying on the floor. Looking back up to Corrynne, he asked, "What happened?"

Corrynne tried to speak but she couldn't. Not yet.

"He tripped," said the sixth-floor nurse who must not have seen what had happened.

Blood was seeping though the doctor's white jacket over the right shoulder blade.

The police chief squatted and pushed on the doctor's shoulders. "Hey! Doctor, are you OK?" There wasn't a response. "How long has he been like this?" the police chief asked, looking back up at the three.

"Only a few seconds," said Dane. "He got his feet caught in my IV and face-planted on the floor."

The police chief carefully rolled Dr. Page over to expose the vacant face that a moment before had been full of rage and the telltale empty syringe that was still embedded in his chest.

The sixth-floor nurse gasped and then dissolved into tears, leaning on the bed rail for support. It was obvious she had no idea Corrynne had stabbed him.

Corrynne felt her own tears well up and drop from her eyes as the relief of the moment gave way to pent-up emotion.

Dane, seeing his mother was unable to function, climbed out of his bed, pulled off the leads to the monitor, and knelt down next to the doctor's body. His IV had been ripped from his arm when the doctor had become entangled in it. Now it was bleeding. Dane was oblivious to the small trickle of his own blood that was advancing down his arm from the torn IV site.

Both Dane and the police chief felt for a pulse on opposite sides of the doctor's neck. Dane shook his head as he looked at his mother.

"No pulse," said the police chief, finishing Dane's thoughts for him. "This man is dead."

Corrynne couldn't help but weep openly with the police chief's words. Her shoulders convulsed violently, as large gasps escaped her. Dane left his place beside the doctor and took his mother into his arms. She continued to cry relentlessly, her chest giving in to great heavings and her face buried in her son's chest.

Dane rocked her gently, patting his mother as he consoled her.

The police chief closed the door to the gathering crowd to block the view of the body from the other patrons and hospital staff. Then he escorted the sixth-floor nurse to a chair, offering her a tissue from inside his jacket.

The nurse accepted it readily and pressed it to her face with both hands.

Next, the police chief pulled a phone from his inner pocket. Before dialing, he looked at Corrynne and asked, "Can I use this phone in here?"

Corrynne looked at the monitor that demonstrated that Dane was not hooked to it and then she nodded. Cell phones normally couldn't be used in the patient's rooms, but this obviously was an exception.

After Chief Morgan hung up, he faced the distraught group. In a quiet voice he asked, "Does anyone want to tell me what happened in here?"

Corrynne lifted her face from her son's chest and pointed to her Blackberry on the counter. It was still in the recording mode. "It's all on there. I hope the volume is loud enough for you to hear everything."

Chief Morgan looked behind the cards and carefully picked up the device. "Has anyone in here touched this since you started it?"

Dane shook his head, and Corrynne answered shakily, "No. We turned it on because this young nurse," Corrynne pointed to the young, recovering, sixth-floor nurse who was still sitting in the chair across the room, "was given orders by Dr. Page that were life threatening for my son. The orders were very inappropriate and would have instantly killed him. I caught the discrepancy and turned on the Blackberry without Dr. Page's knowledge. I

questioned him, wanting to record his answers so I could analyze them later."
Corrynne reached for a tissue herself from a box on the counter next to her
and dabbed at her nose. "I've caught him being dishonest in the past and so I
didn't trust him. I hoped I could figure out what was really going on. It was a
very scary situation."

"Hmmm." The chief looked down at the Blackberry. "So all of you were
witness to what happened in here, right?"

All three of them nodded.

Corrynne gestured to the still form on the floor. "We never thought that
the conversation would turn into this!"

"He told us that he was going to infect us with the Strep A disease to kill
us," said Dane. "He's still holding something in his hand that he touched me
with. I think he was trying to kill me first." Dane turned his right leg to show
the large, raised, red welt. "That's where he got me."

The police chief pulled gloves out of his pocket and put them on. Then
carefully, he opened the doctor's right hand. There he found a metal
cylinder-like object. There was a button on one side and a round opening on
the other side.

The chief studied the instrument. "This looks similar to a needle-less
syringe. I've seen similar ones in the military. It uses air to force liquid into
the skin." Then he slid it into a baggie that he pulled from his other pocket.

Corrynne commented, "I believe that three nurses and Dr. Quaid may
have been infected by that very instrument, or one like it. I don't know if it's
too late to look at their bodies, but I believe that if you did, you would find
that they would have a spot somewhere on them like Dane's, unless all the
skin was destroyed."

Chief Morgan stood up and said, "Dane, we better get you some
antibiotics fast so you don't get sick with that wicked bug." He turned to
Corrynne. "Don't you think so?"

Corrynne smiled slightly despite her obvious sad countenance. She was
deeply thankful that she had listened to the quiet warning that had told her to
prepare for something like this event. "We have all received shots that make
us immune to the most common strains of Strep A. It's a new inoculation
given only to immuno-compromised groups and children under two, but I
was able to obtain some for my family. I think it will work, but there are
many serotypes. We should put him on antibiotics just in case there are slight
differences."

"Good thinking." The chief turned to Dane again. "Do you mind if I take
a picture of your leg?"

"Go ahead, I have always wanted to be in entertainment. A picture of my
white leg should be very entertaining."

The chief laughed and pulled a tiny camera out of his pocket. He took a
couple pictures of Dane's leg and more of the doctor on the floor. Finally he
asked, "What was in that syringe?"

Corrynne looked around on the floor until she found the other one that had rolled under the bed. "The same stuff that's in this syringe. It's IV potassium. We give it in the ICU. It's safe if given slowly and diluted. This was full strength. This was what the doctor wanted to give Dane—it was verbally prescribed incorrectly. He would have died the same way the doctor did."

The chief opened another baggie, and Corrynne slid the syringe in. "Whose prints are on this syringe?"

"Mine and hers." Corrynne gestured to the silent sixth-floor nurse. "We both handled it." Corrynne hesitated and then added, "I wasn't trying to kill Dr. Page, just get him away from Dane. I didn't even have time to push the medication. He fell on the plunger when his feet became tangled in Dane's IV line. Normally, the fluid doesn't cause death if not given in a vein. I don't understand why it killed him. The only thing I can think of is that maybe it was injected into the subclavian vein. I was trying to miss his heart—that's why I aimed high."

Chief Morgan smiled. "All of you need to know that you shouldn't have anything to worry about here. I believe that all the evidence tells the story. You really didn't have a choice but to try to protect yourselves. I believe that you acted appropriately. There will not be any charges as long as what is on this recorder is what you told me."

The little sixth-floor nurse spoke up. "It's as they say. ...I, for one, am glad it's over. ...I think I'll have second thoughts next time someone asks me to help in the ICU. ...It's too dangerous down here."

Suddenly, Dane let out a loud, "Amen to that!"

Notes to "Pieces"

Exposure

[1] "Nanotechnology, or what could more specifically be termed *molecular nanotechnology* or *molecular manufacturing*, is the anticipated ability to inexpensively fabricate complex devices, both large and small, with precise control over the arrangement of the individual atoms that constitute the device. Educated guesses are that this technology will arrive sometime in the next 15 to 30 years" (Jim Lewis, "What is Nanotechnology?" *Jim's Molecular Nanotechnology Web.*, Oct. 1998, available online: http://www.halcyon.com/nanojbl/#anchor602495). For more information search the Web for "nanotechnology."

[2] Nanocomputers are factual, in development, and on the horizon in the scientific realm, if not available in research markets today. Their functions are multifaceted and do in fact include biological manipulation.

"Building on the atomic scale, mechanical computers with the power of a mainframe could be manufactured so small, that several hundred would fit inside the space of a biological cell

(http://www.asiapac.com/EnginesOfCreation/). If you combined microscopic motors, gears, levers, bearing, plates, sensors, power and communication cables, etc. with powerful microscopic computers, you have the makings of a new class of materials. Programmable microscopic smart materials one could use in medicine" (Bill Spence, "Super Medicine,"

NanoTechnology   Magazine,   May   2001,   available   online: http://nanozine.com/NANOMED.HTM).

[3] Small computer chips are in existence that can be embedded into the body and use the body's energy source to function. (See Bruce Johnston, "Microchip implants to foil VIP kidnaps" *Electronic Telegraph*, Issue 1229, 6 October 1998, available online: http://www.telegraph.co.uk:80/et?ac=000118613908976&rtmo=aw3wHaxL&atmo=rrrrrrYs& pg=/et/98/10/6/wchip06.html).

[4] Al-Mahdi and Imam Mahdi are both titles for the promised Messiah for the followers of Islam (see http://www.al-islam.org/mahdi/nontl/Chap-3.htm#two for more information).

[5] This is a factual drug used illegally in America in predator crimes. See U.S. Department of Justice Drug Enforcement Administration, "Flunitrazepam (Rohypnol) 'roofies,'" available online: http://www.usdoj.gov/dea/pubs/rohypnol/rohypnol.htm.

CHAPTER SIXTEEN

SIXTH SEAL

"And I beheld when he had opened the sixth seal, and, lo, there was a great earthquake; and the sun became black as sackcloth of hair, and the moon became as blood" (Revelation 6:12).

Sunday
September 24th
10:30 a.m.
Provo, Utah

Beautiful Annoyances

Carrying the twins, Bo wrestled Striynna as he walked down the hall toward Gospel Doctrine class. Kicking wildly, her little chubby body slipped in his arm. She hung with her elbows and arms above her head as she kicked Bo's upper thigh. It was obvious she wanted to get down onto the floor to crawl. Strykker, however, sat quietly on Bo's right side, watching his sister flail about.

Sacrament meeting had been very difficult. Bo had been left alone with the twins and his three younger sons. Usually, Corrynne and his older children would help control the wild ones, but today his wife was still at the hospital with Dane. Brea, Braun, and Carea were attending another ward for a missionary that had just returned from a mission in China. However, Braun had said to him that morning that he would return to teach the Gospel Doctrine class. Bo looked around hopefully as he struggled to reclaim his grip on Striynna. He held up his knee to push her little body back into his arm as he wished Braun would show up. He didn't know how long he could wrestle her before she'd win.

Sister Hoskins, an elderly ward member, stopped in the hall and said, "I saw your family on the news this morning. You're a hero now, you know."

Bo nodded politely and smiled back as he held tight on Striynna's now arching body.

"Yes, I saw you, too," said Brother Hoskins, "and I just want to tell you that I'm impressed with your willingness to get involved in our societal problems." Brother Hoskins held out his hand to shake Bo's hand.

Bo looked at Brother Hoskins' hand as he wondered how he was going to manage a handshake. In an effort to be polite, despite Striynna's continued kicking, he jostled Strykker's body deeper into his elbow on his right side and pinned him. This freed his right hand from the wrist down, allowing him to hold out his hand momentarily in a precarious balancing act.

Brother Hoskins, oblivious to his tussle, shook the free hand vigorously, smiling widely, placing his other hand on Bo's shoulder behind Strykker.

The shaking motion, despite Brother Hoskins' good intentions, loosened Bo's grasp on his baby son. With a quick grab, Bo caught Strykker's sliding body on his upper thigh. Striynna, by that time, had wiggled so much that she hung with only her head and face caught by Bo's forearm. He had no choice but to squat down in a crooked manner to let Striynna down to the floor. She had won.

"Oops! You lost one!" said Sister Hoskins.

Bo stifled the urge to give the woman a glare. As if he wasn't aware! Instead he said, "Yeah, funny how that happens. I'm outnumbered, I guess." He pulled Strykker back up onto his waist and then took off after Striynna, dodging feet and running children to try to grab hold of her once again before she was trampled during the break before Sunday School.

"Good job, Brother Rogers! You should receive the 'Good Citizen of the Year Award,'" said a voice behind him, probably referring to the news broadcasts that littered the media. Bo continued his pursuit of Striynna, holding up a hand to the unknown voice to acknowledge the compliment.

"Yes, bravo!" said another. This time Bo nodded; he almost had his daughter.

"Bo Rogers! Your family's gutsy! Way to fight the bad guys!"

Bo, now having Striynna in his grasp, flipped her back to his left side and stood but now a dull ache was starting in his lumbar area. Securing Strykker on his right side once again, he squared his shoulders and walked back to the Gospel Doctrine class.

"I'm getting old," Bo said under his breath.

"Daddy?" asked a small child's voice from behind him.

He turned to see Roc. "Why aren't you in your class?"

With the sound of her brother's voice, Striynna stopped struggling and stared at her brother unblinkingly. Bo looked at her with surprise. He hadn't realized before how taken Striynna was with Roc. She was studying him intently.

"Because I forgot my scriptures in the car," said Roc. He was wincing.

Bo frowned. Every day at home, Corrynne would read out of children's books that summarized the scriptures and had pictures of gospel characters. Roc called them his 'scriptures.' He had smuggled them into the car at the last moment today to take them to church. "Roc, those aren't real scriptures. Go to class."

"No, I want my scriptures!"

"No, you can't have them right now. You're going to be late. Please turn around and go to class."

"Noooooo!" Roc began to jerk up and down quickly and bounce backwards against the wall. His injured arm hung heavily in its cast as he threw his fit.

"I'm sorry, but look around you—there's no one left in this hall. Your teacher is probably starting her lesson by now. You had better hurry, or you'll miss it."

Roc looked at his dad with anger. Then his eyes brightened. "Hey, I have an idea."

"What's that?" asked Bo, already feeling like he needed a nap.

"Can I take yours to class?"

"My what?"

"Your scriptures?"

Bo nodded. He was tired of struggling. "Sure, you can have my scriptures."

Roc held out his hands.

Realizing that his arms were full of the twins, he wondered where his scriptures were. After thinking for a moment, he realized that he had left them in the chapel.

"They're in the chapel. Do you remember where we were sitting? If you can find them, you can have them."

Roc smiled and took off running down the hall.

"And don't run in the church," said Bo, shaking his head but grateful that he didn't have to go back into the chapel himself.

Bo looked at his twins. They were staring down the hall, both still watching Roc. In that moment it struck him how cute their little chubby faces and innocent eyes were. He gave them both a little squeeze that caused a burst of energy to ignite in his chest, making him very grateful. Despite momentary frustrations, he had to admit his children were worth the hassle. After all, it was the hassles that made the good times that much sweeter!

Transition of Time

Bo entered his class through a door that had been propped open. As he entered, the class became obviously silent. One by one, the members in the room began to stand up with their eyes focused on Bo.

Bo stopped as he began to comprehend that the class was standing in reference to him. An expression of confusion came over his face, which was met with a confirming smile and nod from Brother Anderson, standing in the front of the classroom. Bo realized this treatment was in response to the arrests from the night before. He hadn't imagined it would've caused this much attention.

Bo slowly advanced, looking for an inconspicuous seat in the back, but all the seats were taken. He continued row by row until he found two seats near the side aisle in the front. Not wanting to make a greater spectacle of himself, he sat, placing both of the babies on the floor in front of him.

As Bo sat down, the class members also took their seats. Then, without a cue, elderly Brother Jess stood up with the help of his cane and gave the opening prayer.

After the prayer, Brother Anderson took his place in front of the room and planted his feet squarely on the floor with his arms still folded. He looked down and then up, appearing to be having a difficult time finding words. Finally he began, "I am thankful for the gospel. ...I know you hear it from me often, but this week I am especially grateful because of the direction we receive in the face of adversity. I bear witness that we are not alone in a mad world. It's a truth that is very comforting to me.

"The world was left in spiritual ignorance for almost two thousand years; then suddenly a light burst forth upon those that sat in darkness.[1] The gospel was restored to a world that is described as 'ever learning, and never able to come to the knowledge of the truth.'[2] Today we live in an era when it is possible to be bathed in the glow of rich, glorious, spiritual light.

"In the pre-existence, we lived as beings of light with the Father.[3] Because of this truth, we are naturally born on earth with the light of Christ.[4] Beginning as children we search here on earth for the truth and light from whence we came. We hunger for it. However, evil influences take advantage of that need, imitating the appearance of light to lead us away from the true light.[5] As we grow, the evil influences cause our memory to become darkened.[6] When we are tricked or persuaded to follow the imitation, the true light becomes a hidden light. It continues to exist but is blocked by darkness like a solar eclipse."[7]

Brother Anderson continued. "In Moroni 7:15-17, the prophet Mormon, who lived in a time of great wickedness, reminded us to weigh all the influences in our lives as good or evil. To do this, he gives us a standard by which to judge. He teaches us to analyze the direction in which an influence leads us. If we are led to the true Christ, then it's of God. If it leads us away from him or his teachings, then it's of the evil one. It is my prayer and testimony that if we hold this to be our standard, we will never be misled."

Brother Anderson turned to Bo. Bo did not look up but continued to focus his gaze steadily on the floor, where his twins were sitting.

The teacher began to speak pointedly. "Without further delay, I want to say 'thank you' to Bo and his family for exposing a dark imitation that existed in our own community. Because of their example, coupled with the generous media coverage, potentially thousands or even tens of thousands may be saved from dangerous influences."

With that statement, Bo looked up and smiled, nodding his acceptance of the teacher's compliment.

"Now," said Brother Anderson as he clapped his hands and rubbed them together. Smiling broadly, he said, "Not to change the subject, but is everyone ready for our concluding lesson about the sixth and seventh seals of Revelation?" Brother Anderson searched the group for faces that reflected his same excitement.

The class responded favorably with individual smiles, nods, and quiet chuckles.

"Last week I invited Braun Rogers to speak to us concerning the sixth and seventh seals. I thought this would be a great addition to what we have already learned. This subject deserves special attention since we are approaching the time of its complete fulfillment. And since Brother Rogers is standing in the back of the class…"

The class members, including Bo turned to look for Braun who indeed was standing, leaning against the doorframe of the door in the back.

Bo nodded a hello and Braun returned the gesture.

"Bear with me as I review a little from our last lesson so anyone who may have missed last week's meeting can catch up." Brother Anderson continued, "We were talking about the meaning of the seven seals introduced in Revelation 5:1, which reads, 'And I saw in the right hand of him that sat on the throne a book written within and on the backside, sealed with seven seals.' We find in D&C 77:6-7 Joseph Smith asking for the meaning of the book that was sealed with seven seals. He was told that the book contained the 'will, mysteries and the works of God,' and each of the seals represented one dispensation of man's time on the earth, or approximately one thousand years…." Brother Anderson looked back to where Braun was standing. "Am I right so far?"

Braun raised his eyebrows, smirked and nodded slowly.

"We covered the first five seals last week. Today we continue with the next two," Brother Anderson said to the class, then back to Braun. "OK, Brother Rogers, I have this group primed and on the edges of their seats, waiting for you to fill them in on the rest."

Braun moved slowly to the front of the classroom as Brother Anderson took a seat next to Bo on the front row.

Braun opened his scriptures to a marked spot. In a quiet voice, he began, "I have been searching this topic diligently lately. The appearance of Imam Mahdi and my family's involvement with him has brought home the reality of the scriptures and their practical applications.

"From my study, I have developed a fervent testimony of the Lord's wishes to save us from the endless torment that awaits those who are wicked.[8] He holds out glorious gifts[9] to us if only we reach out and take them. In this spirit, I want to discuss the potential meanings of the scriptures concerning the seals and the Second Coming.

"Now." Braun's eyes quickly scanned the room, not really looking at anything. "With those thoughts in mind, let's make the transition into the sixth seal, or approximately the time period of 1000 AD to 2000 AD. What are the things that we know of that happened during that time?"

Multiple hands went up. "Brother Jess?" said Braun.

With narrowed eyes, Brother Jess said, "The gospel was restored," nodding emphatically.

"Yes, it was. Thank you, Brother Jess. What else?" Braun looked for another hand. "Sister Stand?"

"Ah...we built temples and performed temple work?" asked a small middle-aged woman in a high pitched voice.

"Of course, excellent. Anything else?" Braun's eyes fell on his own father. "Brother Rogers, can you think of anything?"

"Sure." Bo adjusted his weight in his chair then said, "The Jews have gained their homeland in Jerusalem and have begun to gather there."

"Right. Who else has gathered during that time? Brother Anderson?"

"The tribes of Israel are being gathered from the corners of the world."

"Good, very good." Braun looked around the room. He could feel the energy picking up. "I'm sure it doesn't surprise you that these events are identified in the scriptures as happening during the time covered by the sixth seal. We find it in Revelation, chapter 7:1-3 and in Doctrine and Covenants 77:10. Elias is described as coming to the earth to restore all things and gather the twelve tribes of Israel. He also cries to angels not to hurt the earth until the elect have been gathered and sealed to God. Joseph himself wondered when those events were to happen, and he asked, 'What time are the things spoken of in this chapter to be accomplished?' The Lord answered clearly, 'They are to be accomplished in the sixth thousand years, or the opening of the sixth seal....'"

Braun stopped suddenly. "Repeat to me what I just said...Sister Anderson?"

The teacher's wife, who was sitting among her friends in the middle of the room, looked surprised. "Which part?"

"The very last phrase."

"Ummm, I believe you said, 'They are to be accomplished in the sixth thousand years, or the opening of the sixth seal.'"

"Very good memory. Yes, the Lord reveals something about his thought processes concerning the definition of the 'opening' of a seal. Did all those events happen at the beginning of the year 1000 AD?"

A couple of people shook their heads confidently.

Braun responded, "No, in fact, most of them happened at the very end of that era, after the 1800s. Since we know that the book the seals are attached to represent the 'mysteries, will and work of God,'[10] maybe the term 'opening' does not always refer to the beginning of the time designated by each seal. Maybe 'opening' has a dual nature. The phrase 'in the sixth thousand years' obviously refers to time, but the statement 'opening of the sixth seal' could be reflective of the Roman tradition concerning contracts representing fulfillment of the writing within the book.

"If we look at the tradition of John's day, we find that important documents were often sealed with the symbol of the owner. This was done to prove the document was authentic and then to close it, protecting it from any changes by other parties.[11] Only one who had authority could open the seals. In the case of an agreement, once the document was opened, the contents were to be disclosed and executed.[12] So we return to the word 'opened.' It implies that one of authority opens the seal and fulfills the contents of the book, leading us not only to a time definition, but task orientation. Thus a seal can be opened at any time and the contents carried out, whether at the beginning, middle or end of that era."

The people in the room nodded as they began to understand.

"Now let's turn our attention to another scripture about the sixth seal. Please turn to Revelation 6:12-14. Sister Cox? Would you read that, please?"

Sister Cox found her place and began to read. "And I beheld when he had opened the sixth seal, and, lo, there was a great earthquake; and the sun became black as sackcloth of hair, and the moon became as blood; And the stars of heaven fell unto the earth, even as a fig tree casteth her untimely figs, when she is shaken of a mighty wind. And the heaven departed as a scroll when it is rolled together; and every mountain and island were moved out of their places.'"

"Thank you. ...Now, Sister Cox, can you tell me if those things have happened yet?"

Sister Cox got a worried look in her eye. "I don't think so, but I don't know.... Maybe it has."

"I know that was a confusing question, forgive me. It's a confusing question to everyone. But because we have recorded world history since 1000 AD, we know that those events have not happened. Many people suppose that we have opened the seventh seal, after the year 2000, and still those events have not occurred. Are the scriptures wrong?"

Brother Jess pointed his cane at Braun as he quoted a scripture loudly, "'*For as I, the Lord God, liveth, even so my words cannot return void, for as they go forth out of my mouth they must be fulfilled*'! You'll find that scripture in Moses, chapter 4, verse 30!" Brother Jess maintained pointing his cane at Braun, as if to warn him against further heretical words.

"OK, OK, Brother Jess, don't strike me down just yet. I was asking the question to promote thought."

Sister Anderson raised her hand as Brother Jess slowly placed his cane back on the floor.

"Yes, Sister Anderson?"

"I'm not a great scriptorian, but my husband and I often talk about the Bible and compare its passages to the Book of Mormon or the Doctrine and Covenants. We know by revealed knowledge that some meanings in the Bible have been changed from their original form because of translation differences and misinterpretations. Maybe this is one of those mistranslations."[13]

Braun nodded and then shrugged. "That's a logical theory, but I'm not sure if it is or isn't true. ...I do know that you are correct about the mistranslations in the scriptures. Nephi stated that when the Bible was first written it was 'easy to understand of all men.'[14] In fact, Joseph Smith said that Revelation was 'an easy book to understand.'[15] So we must have lost something somewhere, because it seems to be very difficult reading now. Not surprisingly, Elder McConkie disagrees with me. He says there are 'clear and plain' parts that the 'Lord's people should understand.' He also goes on to say that certain parts are not clear and are not understood by us—which, however, does not mean that we could not understand them if we would grow in faith as we should. The Lord expects us to seek wisdom, to ponder his revealed truths, and to gain a knowledge of them by the power of his Spirit."[16]

Braun peered at the class to assess how much everyone was absorbing; it seemed everyone was ready to continue. Braun returned to his previous subject. "So let's grow in faith and seek and ponder further. ...Getting back to my previous question, I ask, if the earthquake removing all the mountains and islands and the moon turning to blood and sun to darkness, etc., has not happened yet, when will it?"

Silence continued in the room with no one challenging it.

Braun continued, "Take a look once again at those verses in Revelation 6:12-14. Read them to yourself. Don't the descriptions give the impression of major destruction? Ask yourself, how many times can the world have an earthquake of that magnitude?"

Whispers rolled around the room as the class members tried to solve the mystery.

Braun waited for a moment until the whispering died down. "I want to draw your attention to a similar event that is outlined to happen in the seventh seal.

"In Revelation 16:18-20, after the seventh seal has been opened, again we read of an earthquake so great that 'every island fled away and mountains were not found.' Isn't that phrase reminiscent of the wording in Revelation 6:14? Didn't we just say that every mountain and island would be moved out of its place in relation to the sixth seal?"

The room quietly acknowledged Braun's point with renewed whispering. Some members looked intently in their scriptures.

"This isn't the only time this event is described. It is predicted in multiple places in the scriptures: Joel, chapter 2; Matthew, chapter 24; Joseph Smith Matthew, chapter 1; Doctrine and Covenants, sections 29, 34, 45 and 88. With so many places in the scriptures describing the same event with very similar words in similar order, from different prophets, surely they refer to one cataclysmic event occurring at a time of great importance. In the *Millennial Messiah*, Elder McConkie says, 'These signs and wonders of which we speak are indeed the crowning and culminating signs of the times, and their occurrence will be *almost or actually concurrent with the great and dreadful day of the Lord.*'

"He continues, clarifying his meaning by saying, 'Various passages of scripture tie these signs together.... The signs of which we speak are:'"— Braun turned around, walked around the table behind him, and quickly began to write on the dry-erase board. As he spoke the words, he wrote—

-Manifestations of blood, and fire, and vapors of smoke.
-The sun shall be darkened and the moon turn into blood.
-The stars shall hurl themselves from heaven.
-The rainbow shall cease to appear in the mists and rains of heaven.
-The sign of the Son of Man shall make its appearance.
-A mighty earthquake, beyond anything of the past, shall shake the very foundations of the earth.[17]

Braun turned back around to face the class and twirled the dry-erase pen in his right hand. "If it's true what Elder McConkie says, then we are looking at a repeated account of the same event, written in two different places, referring to two different times. How could that be?"

Silence again permeated the classroom.

Braun walked back around the table centered in front of the dry-erase board. He leaned against it as he waited for some ideas from the class. When nothing was offered, Braun continued, "To be honest, I don't think anyone knows the answer to that question. The truth of it has not been revealed. However, we can look at what we know and come up with theories.[18] What could be a possible theory?"

Brother Jess began to speak out, "What about repetition?"

"What do you mean? I'm not sure what you are talking about. Could you repeat yourself?" Braun teased old Brother Jess and then winked.

The class laughed at the joke.

Brother Jess, refusing to laugh, narrowed his look. He pretended to be offended and looked around the classroom. Finally he clarified himself in a sarcastic tone, "Whenever anything is important, the Lord repeats his message so thick-headed people will figure it out."

Braun smiled at Brother Jess, putting up with his sarcasm. "You're right, Brother Jess, Moroni did appear to Joseph Smith four times with the same message."

Brother Jess continued, "Exactly. You made the point yourself that all the rattling and shaking, ripping out mountains and causing general chaos, was reviewed in other places in our good books. I'm telling ya it's like telling a young whippersnapper something over and over again until he gets it."

"That's true, and I'm sure we seem like a world of 'whippersnappers' to the Lord sometimes." Braun tossed the dry-erase pen in the air and caught it again. "We are very slow to hear and even slower to obey.[19]

"Any other ideas?"

Brother Anderson's hand slowly came up as he spoke out, "What about symbolism?"

Braun began to pace a little. "Yes, symbolism is always something we should consider when we are reading John the Beloved's writing." Braun stopped pacing at the far end of the room as he turned back and faced the class again. "We know that the numbers he uses, the descriptions, and the personifications are often allusions to other impressions or states of reality. So what could be the symbolic meanings attached to the sixth and seventh seals?"

Brother Jess raised his cane and waved it in the air to get Braun's attention again, making it impossible to be missed.

Braun smiled and slowly began to walk back to the center of the room. "Yes, Brother Jess? It looks like you have another idea."

Brother Jess put his cane on the floor and took his time answering; taking advantage of the attention Braun had given him. Finally, his answer came, drawling out of his mouth thickly in a condescending manner. "As long as I can remember, which is almost five times the amount of years you have been on this earth, the sixth seal has been called 'Saturday'."[20]

Braun laughed and turned to the class. "OK, I believe that, but explain what you mean."

Brother Jess scowled, as if Braun were an idiot. "Saturday is reserved to get ready for Sunday, of course."

"Oh, yes, of course! I believe this line of thought is leading to something. Don't we see this theme repeatedly in the scriptures? For example...take note of these scriptures as I read them." Braun found a marked place in his scriptures and began to read, "'Wherefore, if God so clothe the grass of the field, which *today* is, and *tomorrow is cast into the oven*, even so will he clothe you, if ye are not of little faith.' That scripture is found in 3 Nephi 13:30. Here is another one." Braun turned his scriptures to another place. "'For after *today cometh the burning*...for verily I say, *tomorrow all the proud and they that do wickedly shall be as stubble*; and I will burn them up, for I am the Lord of Hosts; and I will not spare any that remain in Babylon.' That scripture is found in D&C 64:24. Both of these scriptures are talking about the last days, and both use the terms '*today*' for the time to prepare and '*tomorrow*' as the time of burning."

Braun continued. "From what we know about the prophesied events of the sixth and seventh seals, those scriptures correlate '*today*' with the sixth seal and '*tomorrow*' with the seventh. These statements could therefore meet the 'Saturday' and 'Sunday' analogy quite easily.

"I also want to draw your attention to the footnotes when you have a moment. You'll find that the words 'sixth seal' in Revelation 6:12 is footnoted as the 'last days,' which means 'the days that come before....' I think it's obvious what it's referring to. These topics insinuate what Brother Jess was saying, that Saturday is the day for preparation. When we look up the footnotes to the 'seventh seal' in Revelation 8:1, we're directed to look up the topics 'Jesus Christ, Second Coming' and 'Sabbath,' which shouldn't be surprising. I believe everyone will agree that 'Sabbath' translates directly to Sunday. Thus, we have our Saturday and Sunday allusion."

Various people in the class nodded again as they continued to listen and look at their scriptures.

Braun took a deep breath and smiled. "I believe we have connected enough dots to be comfortable with our interpretation, but what does this have to do with the destruction mentioned in Revelation 6 happening in the sixth thousand years instead of the seventh?"

Bo raised his hand.

"Dad?" Braun caught himself and turned a shade of pink. "Excuse me, Brother Rogers?"

"How about this idea…?"

"Yes?"

"Every day has a night. In that night is the midnight hour. It is the moment between day and night in which there is a transition between both days, and one could say that it is shared by both. Maybe the destruction and cleansing is at the midnight hour and shared by both Saturday and Sunday. This kind of thinking corresponds to the parable of the ten virgins. We find in Matthew, chapter 25, that it is at the darkest hour, the 'midnight hour,'[21] that the bridegroom comes to the wedding, catching half of the virgins unprepared."[22]

Braun seemed genuinely caught off guard. "Wow, you're right…. I wonder why I haven't thought of that passage as being a transition between the two days before…." Braun smiled and pointed at his father. "But we all know that dads are always right."

Bo's right eyebrow elevated slightly as a smirk threatened to expose itself. Bo continued, ignoring his son's insinuations. "Another impression we receive from that parable is that the bridegroom's coming happens suddenly, not allowing the unprepared virgins to find oil for the wedding. That feeling of rapidity blurs the transition between the ending of the sixth and the beginning of the seventh seals."

Braun nodded as he turned down his bottom lip for a moment in contemplation. "Yes, there are indications in the scriptures of that possibility also. The scriptures say, '*this generation, in which these things shall be shown forth, shall not pass away until all I have told you shall be fulfilled.*'[23] To me, that scripture means that the signs of the times, the ripening of the world, the rise of the beast, and the great calamities will all be witnessed by the same people on earth, limiting the amount of time they can encompass. The Lord also says 'I cometh quickly,'[24] meaning that the suddenness will surprise the world, catching many as a 'thief in the night.'"[25]

Braun looked down at the floor and then continued. "Whatever the interpretation, I promise that no matter how confusing the Book of Revelation is to us now, we can be sure that if we study it and the other scriptures, listen to our prophet, and pray for understanding, all things will become clear to us.

"In summary," Braun continued, "the sixth seal is the time of spiritual preparation, gathering of the elect, building of temples, and the sealing of God's chosen to him. It is known as the Saturday before the Sabbath, the 'today' before the 'tomorrow,' and it should be filled with the signs of the times. The seventh seal is to be a time of cleansing and purification at first, but then it will become a time of restoration of all things: Sunday, the Sabbath, the Millennium, the 'tomorrow' after 'today,' the day the Lord shows his face to the world and gives us a new heaven and earth."

Braun looked down at his scriptures and thought for a moment, fingering the thin, gold-lined pages. He looked up at the class and smiled. "So let it be obvious that we should all continue to ponder and wonder after truth, using prayer and the Spirit to guide us to receive such revelation, so we might not be deceived...."

Suddenly Braun's head began to swim. A poignant, dark memory filled him and wrapped itself around him. The word "deceived" started to ring loudly in his mind. He began to feel bound, losing strength in his legs, feeling like a captive in chains. A familiar deep voice began to sound loudly in his head in a monotone chant, pushing out any other thoughts. "For this is Abaddon...the chains of Apollyon...who has keys to that bottomless pit...from whence there is no light...." Braun shook his head. His hand came up to his forehead. "...the spirits of the wicked...yea, who are evil...shall be cast out...into outer darkness...." Braun's knees buckled slightly, and his scriptures fell to the floor.

Bo rushed forward and held out a hand to Braun. "What's wrong, Braun?" he asked in a quiet but persistent voice. "Are you OK?"

Other class members stood to come forward to offer support if needed.

With every ounce of strength, Braun sought freedom from the unseen chains that were squeezing him from the inside out. All at once, he remembered the origin of the voice and the memory. It was his dream. Braun shook his head, and then suddenly the voice was gone.

Braun straightened back up, gaining strength in his legs. He smoothed his suit jacket and bent down to pick up his scriptures.

The other people, seeing him gaining his awareness, began to sit down. The last to leave him was his father, who hugged him sharply.

"I'll be fine," Braun assured his father.

"OK." Bo was still reluctant to leave his side, but slowly inched his way back to his chair. Both Striynna and Strykker, frightened by the sudden movements of the people around them, stood up along Bo's legs, reaching for him. He picked them both up in reassurance as they continued to whimper softly.

Braun leaned against the podium in front of him.

Brother Anderson approached Braun and said, "Do you want me to take over?" he said in a whisper.

"In a moment. I have something else to say."

"Fine, I'll just stand here." Brother Anderson stood as solidly beside Braun as a soldier, with his hands clasped in front of him, as if to protect.

Braun smiled and then took a breath meant to clear his mind and organize his thoughts. "I am sorry about that dramatic display. Without too much explanation, let me say that I feel very impressed to say something. Since we are at that transition between today and tomorrow, darkness and light, danger and safety, I wish to leave with a warning. Satan wishes to destroy every one of us. He wishes to drag everyone he can into the bottomless pit with chains from which there is no escape. Abaddon,[26] or Apollyon,[27] both words meaning 'the destroyer,' has established a powerful realm on this earth. Although his kingdom will be short-lived, it will be strong and very dangerous. It is up to us to stand tall and strong, teach our children, find the truth our souls are hungry for, and fall in line with the Lord's hosts to prepare for the Lord's Second Coming.

"I say these things in the name of Jesus Christ, amen," concluded Braun.

"Amen," echoed the class.

"Thank you again, Brother Rogers," began Brother Anderson. "It's always a pleasure to hear from you." He paused and took a breath. Then he slowly and deliberately concluded his remarks. "Thus, today is the day of our summer to prepare for the coming winter. It is time to lay up stores for our welfare for a tumultuous time. Spiritually, our storehouse is our knowledge, testimony, faith, and hope. We obtain these through study, fasting and prayer. There has never been a more appropriate time than now to identify these hallmark testimonies from our scriptures.

"In the name of Jesus Christ, amen."

Notes to "Sixth Seal"

Transition of time

[1] "And when the times of the Gentiles is come in, a light shall break forth among them that sit in darkness, and it shall be the fullness of my gospel" (D&C 45:28).

[2] 2 Timothy 3:7.

[3] "Man was also in the beginning with God. Intelligence, or the light of truth, was not created or made, neither indeed can be" (D&C 93:29).

[4] "And the Spirit giveth light to every man that cometh into the world; and the Spirit enlighteneth every man through the world, that hearkeneth to the voice of the Spirit. And every one that hearkeneth to the voice of the Spirit cometh unto God, even the Father" (D&C 84:46-47).

[5] "...for, behold, priestcrafts are that men preach and set themselves up for a light unto the world, that they may get gain and praise of the world; but they seek not the welfare of Zion" (2 Nephi 26:29).

[6] "Yea, the light of the wicked shall be put out, and the spark of his fire shall not shine The light shall be dark in his tabernacle, and his candle shall be put out with him" (Job 18:5-6).

[7] "And no marvel; for Satan himself is transformed into an angel of light" (2 Corinthians 11:14).

[8] "LISTEN to the voice of Jesus Christ, your Redeemer, the Great I AM, whose arm of mercy hath atoned for your sins; Who will gather his people even as a hen gathereth her chickens under her wings, even as many as will hearken to my voice and humble themselves before me, and call upon me in mighty prayer" (D&C 29:1-2).

[9] "And, if you keep my commandments and endure to the end you shall have eternal life, which gift is the greatest of all the gifts of God" (D&C 14:7).

[10] D&C 77:6-7.

[11] Richard D. Draper, *Opening the Seven Seals*, 53.

[12] Richard D. Draper, *Opening the Seven Seals*, 54.

[13] "And after these plain and precious things were taken away it goeth forth unto all the nations of the Gentiles; and after it goeth forth unto all the nations of the Gentiles, yea, even across the many waters which thou hast seen with the Gentiles which have gone forth out of captivity, thou seest—because of the many plain and precious things which have been taken out of the book, which were plain unto the understanding of the children of men, according to the plainness which is in the Lamb of God—because of these things which are taken away out of the gospel of the Lamb, an exceedingly great many do stumble, yea, insomuch that Satan hath great power over them" (1 Nephi 13:29).

[14] "Wherefore, the things which he shall write are just and true; and behold they are written in the book which thou beheld proceeding out of the mouth of the Jew; and at the time they proceeded out of the mouth of the Jew, or, at the time the book proceeded out of the mouth of the Jew, the things which were written were plain and pure, and most precious and easy to the understanding of all men" (1 Nephi 14:23).

[15] Revelation is "one of the plainest books God ever caused to be written" (Joseph Smith, *History of the Church,* Vol. 5, April 1843, 342).

[16] "Understanding the Book of Revelation," *Ensign*, September 1975, 87.

[17] "The Promised Signs and Wonders", Bruce R. McConkie, *Millennial Messiah*, 406-07.

[18] "We are left to speculate relative to some of these matters, which is not all bad as long as any expressed views are clearly identified for what they are. In fact, in our present state of spiritual enlightenment the Lord deliberately leaves us to ponder and wonder about many things connected with his coming; in this way our hearts are centered upon him so that we will qualify in due course to receive absolute and clear revelation on many things" (Bruce R. McConkie, *Millennial Messiah*, 413-14).

[19] "O how foolish, and how vain, and how evil, and devilish, and how quick to do iniquity, and how slow to do good, are the children of men; yea, how quick to hearken unto the words of the evil one, and to set their hearts upon the vain things of the world!" (Helaman 12:4).

[20] "We are now living during the final years of the sixth seal, that thousand year period which began in 1000 A.D. and will continue through the Saturday night of time and until just before the Sabbatical era when Christ shall reign personally on earth, when all of the blessings of the Great Millennium shall be poured out upon this planet. This accordingly is the era when the signs of the times shall be shown forth and they are in fact everywhere to be seen" (Bruce R. McConkie, *Doctrinal New Testament Commentary*, Vol. 3, 485-86).

[21] Matthew 25:6.

[22] See Matthew 25:1-13.

[23] Joseph Smith Matthew 1:34.

[24] This phrase is included in the scriptures 19 times. For example, see D&C 51:20: "Verily, I say unto you, I am Jesus Christ, who cometh quickly, in an hour you think not. Even so. Amen." This scripture insinuates that his coming will not necessarily be soon, but abrupt, not leaving time to prepare.

[25] See 1 Thessalonians 5:2; 2 Peter 3:10; D&C 45:19; D&C 106:4; JST Luke 12:41-45 (Appendix); JST 2 Peter 3:3-13 (Appendix).

[26]Apollyon: *"Destroyer,* a Greek translation of the Hebrew word Abaddon, or destruction; in Rev. 9: 11 it is the name of the Angel of the Abyss (bottomless pit) made familiar to English readers by Bunyan's *Pilgrim's Progress"* (Bible Dictionary, "Apollyon," 611-612).

[27] "And they had a king over them, *which is* the angel of the bottomless pit, whose name in the Hebrew tongue *is* Abaddon, but in the Greek tongue hath *his* name Apollyon" (Revelation 9:11).

CHAPTER SEVENTEEN

THIS TOO SHALL PASS AWAY

"Watch ye therefore, and pray always, that ye may be accounted worthy to escape all these things that shall come to pass, and to stand before the Son of man" (Luke 21:36).

Monday
September 25th
3:07 p.m.
Provo, Utah

Countdown

Carea slammed the front door.

Corrynne, who was unloading the dishwasher, poked her head around the corner into the entry. When she saw it was Carea, she put her dishes down and went into the living room to meet her.

Striynna and Strykker, who were fingering the silverware in the silverware tray, decided to follow their mother.

"Hello, sweetheart," Corrynne said in a singsong manner.

Carea stood in the entry and dropped everything in the middle of the floor, with a dejected look on her face.

"What's wrong? Did you have a hard day? Did people give you trouble at school?"

Carea didn't even answer but went directly to her mother.

Corrynne wrapped her arms around Carea and stroked her hair. "Let me guess, Prince Charming passed you up today?"

"Mooom," Carea said, irritated.

"OK, that's not it, let's see. …The Wicked Witch of the West stole your ruby slippers?"

Carea pulled back to look at her mom, who was slightly shorter than she was. "No," she said.

"Then what? What could make my sweet girl so sad?"

"Mom, some of my friends were awful about the arrests," said Carea as she sat on the arm of the couch.

"Why do you call those people friends?"

"I don't know," said Carea as she shook her head. "I don't let them bother me. Let them think what they want."

"That's a good attitude. So then, what's bothering you?"

"I'm worried about Kessa."

"What's wrong with Kessa?" asked Corrynne.

"She wasn't at school today."

"Was she sick?"

"I don't know. I called her house on my cell, but no one answered."

"That's strange. Maybe the family went out of town for some reason."

"No, Mom, I think she was up on the mountain on Friday night. I was on the phone with her earlier that day and she said she was going to that party that Dane went to."

Corrynne's hand covered her mouth. She stared wide-eyed at Carea, and for a few moments she considered the possibility that Kessa could be suffering from the flesh-eating disease at that very moment. "Oh, no, Carea! Didn't you tell her how dangerous it was up there?"

"Yes, but that doesn't do anything. I've told her over and over that she's been messing with danger, but she was convinced that she was being protected by her association with the Bats."

"Oh, I am so sorry."

"Do you think she's at the prison waiting for trial with the rest of the Bats?"

"She could be," Corrynne said as she bit her lip.

"I'm going to call and see," said Carea as she pulled her cell phone from the back pocket from her jeans.

"The prison won't tell you if she's there. They're not releasing the names of the party members to anyone yet."

"Well, then, how do I find out?"

"The only way's to call her family."

Carea looked at the floor. "I've tried to call her brother but he doesn't answer. I guess I can keep trying."

"Maybe you can knock at their door."

"That's a good idea," said Carea as she returned her phone to her jean pocket.

"I would be so sad if Kessa were arrested," Corrynne said in a faraway voice. "The reports on the prisoners' health hasn't been favorable."

"Oh, no! Mom, don't tell me that!"

Corrynne shrugged, "I'm sorry, Carea. I'm just trying to prepare you."

"Tell me anything but something bad. I don't want to let my thoughts run wild until I know for sure what's happened. I'm going upstairs to start calling everyone I know. Maybe someone else knows something."

"All right, good luck."

Carea picked up her things and ran up to her bedroom, taking two stairs at a time.

As Corrynne watched Carea go, she felt sick to her stomach. Strykker crawled up to her leg and pulled himself up, hanging on with a shaky stance as he tried to stand. He looked up at her, turning his chin as high as it could go, and squeaked a high-pitched note. It was obvious he wanted her to pick him up. Corrynne picked her little guy up. She pulled him close and hugged him a long time. This world was such a scary place; hugging him somehow made it easier to bear.

Corrynne turned to go into the kitchen when she heard someone tapping on a computer keyboard in the family room. Corrynne was perplexed. She didn't remember anyone else coming home from school yet.

"Striynna, come with Mama," Corrynne said as she went through the dining room into the family room. She didn't wait for her crawling baby because she knew she would follow. She always did.

Braun was on the Internet. "Oh, hi, Mom," Braun said without looking up. "Got an e-mail from Conrad. He says his bike was stolen."

"Oh no!"

"It's OK. Another missionary who was going home gave him his."

"Oh good," said Corrynne as she set Strykker down on the floor just as Striynna was tugging on her pants.

"I printed it for you. It's in the printer."

"Thank you, sweetheart." Corrynne carefully broke away from her twins and moved behind Braun, leaving them on the dining room floor to navigate the single stair down into the family room. "What are you doing?"

"Well…." Braun paused for a moment. "I'm seeing if I've been accepted as an intern at the UN."[1]

"What? I'm sorry, did you say the UN?"

"Ah…yes, that's what I said." Braun's voice remained monotone.

"Do you mean the United Nations?" Corrynne's heart sped up.

"Yes, I believe that's the one."

"When did this happen? I didn't even know that you applied." Corrynne felt a pit in her stomach. She began to comprehend that she was losing her son to his adult life. She had been dreading this moment.

"A little while ago. I wanted to keep it secret, because I wasn't sure if I really wanted to go."

His statement gave her satisfaction that he wanted to stay home. After a moment, she realized holding on to her son was selfish. She resolved to be supportive and not make this decision more difficult. She noticed the muscles were tense in her back and shoulders. She consciously relaxed them, as she tried to smile. "So do you?"

Braun nodded and continued his gaze at the computer screen. "I've had some time to think about my options. I think I know now that it'll be best for me."

"Wow, it's amazing what a mom can miss if she blinks." Corrynne laughed nervously, still trying to be positive. She went closer to the screen to take a better look at what Braun was reading. It was an official form with the UN letterhead at the top. It was inviting Braun to fly to England for an interview. Despite her initial feelings, the letter was very persuasive. She had to admit, of all the decisions he could make, this one was a very good one.

"I'm impressed! This seems really great!" It was becoming easier for her to be supportive. Corrynne waited for a response from Braun, but nothing came. She leaned sideways to look at his expression. "Isn't it great?"

"Yes, it's just a big change. I'm thinking about how much I'll miss it here. I feel like I'm leaving on another mission, and I just got used to being home!"

Corrynne smiled. She felt guilty, but those words out of his mouth were like music to her ears. She swallowed her emotions and returned to her supportive role. "I'm sure this is right, Braun. If you felt good enough about applying, I trust your intuition. You'll learn so much with an internship to the UN. It's time that you spread your wings and see what happens."

"I know, Mom. That's one reason why I applied. It's really an honor to be picked. I guess they had thousands who applied from all over the world."

"Thousands?"

"That's what it says here." Braun pointed to another line down farther in the letter.

"Congratulations. That's excellent. Boy, this can be a great springboard for you. Think of the experience and references you'll have."

"I know! I think for the first time I'm feeling happy about this. I guess it will be great."[2]

Corrynne bent over and hugged her son from the back, placing her cheek against his. Then she whispered, "You'd better e-mail me every day, or I'll haunt you in your sleep!"

Braun laughed. "Oh, I can't afford my mom haunting me. I have enough strange dreams as it is!" He hit the close button. "I'll see you later, Mom. I've got to go to the library to do some research."

Corrynne called after her son as he walked toward the door. "OK. I love you, son, and I'm really impressed with your initiative. You surprised me this time."

Braun turned back as he was turning the knob. "I surprised myself!" he yelled back. Then the door slammed.

Smiling, Corrynne took a seat behind the computer screen as her twins finally managed the step and began searching the floor for interesting fuzz balls.

As she gazed at the screen, Corrynne grew serious. She had been wondering if the Internet site had changed since Imam Mahdi's organization had been broken up in their area. She opened the Internet once more and went to his site. Almost afraid to see the images that would remind her of the last few days, she sat back in her chair as if to distance herself.

The morphing religious symbols met her eyes and involuntarily, she flinched. "Well, that hasn't changed," she murmured to herself. She hit the page-down button to scan the rest of the site. "Nope, no change. I guess he's still operating out there somewhere." Corrynne knew he would be.

The memories of that emotional weekend streamed through her consciousness. She paused as she considered Dane and the chip that was implanted in his hand. It made her angry that he was going to have to leave it in until they found out more information about what Dr. Page had programmed the micro-computer to do if someone tried to remove it.

Corrynne scanned the pages of the Internet site. She came to the one that had the numbers Braun, Brea, Bo and she had previously thought might be a clock. But the numbers were different today. Today the display read 01:03:05, 02:27:20. She looked at her watch. It was 2:30 p.m. Her eyes narrowed as she tried to make connections between her watch and the numbers on the screen. What did they refer to?

Corrynne sat still as she studied the second set of numbers' last digits as they continued to count down as if counting seconds. Since they were moving backwards and not forwards, she felt confident they weren't telling time, at least not like her watch would.

Corrynne continued to watch the last set of digits. She mentally counted with them. "18, 17, 16…those have to be seconds," she reaffirmed. "Or have something to do with seconds." Her eyes turned to the clock that was displayed in the right-hand corner of her computer screen. It said 2:32 p.m. Corrynne thought for a moment, and looked at her watch once more. "My watch's two minutes different from the computer's clock. I wonder…" she said, but didn't finish. Her thoughts were way beyond words now. Corrynne wrote down on a piece of paper the numbers that were ticking down with a nearby pencil that had been left on the desk. Then she Googled the words "world time." Up popped a screen that showed thousands of Internet choices having to do with time. She remembered that there was a world center that counted time somewhere. She racked her brain to remember where it was. After a few moments of trying, she decided to scan the choices to jog her memory.

One of the choices on the screen said "Greenwich Mean Time." Somehow that seemed familiar, so she clicked on it. Up came the title "World Time."[3] "That's it!" she said under her breath as she read, "Pick the city for current time." She clicked on the link. Up came a screen that allowed her to scroll through major cities of the world. She clicked on Salt Lake City, since it was listed among them and the current time was displayed. Now the current time was 2:36 PM. She glanced back at her watch and realized that her watch was three minutes slow. She quickly reprogrammed her watch to the correct time.

Next she indulged herself and looked for the current time in England, since Braun would be there soon. In England it was now 9:37 p.m., so it was seven hours ahead of Provo. She wondered what time it was in Jerusalem, where Conrad was on his mission. The screen said that it was 11:37 p.m., so Jerusalem was two hours later than England and nine hours different from Provo. Only two hours different. Braun and Conrad would be relatively close to each other then. That was good.

Corrynne's mind wandered as she imagined her son sleeping. It was near midnight where he was. She had just finished lunch and he was dead asleep. The comparison amused her. Although they were doing completely different things in their own little worlds, it was comforting to imagine his activities. It made him seem closer.

Corrynne, involved in her thoughts, haphazardly continued to search the time site. But then her eye caught sight of the word "Zulu." It struck a strong chord in her memory. Wasn't that the word used on Imam Mahdi's site? That, along with other words like blood, fire, and death. Strange how he had put those words together, but she still remembered distinctly that Zulu was one of the words he had used. She clicked on the words "Zulu time."

A screen came up that had big numbers that said, "Current Zulu time is 9:39 p.m." Corrynne was confused. Wasn't that England's time? After thinking a second, she knew that it was. It was 9:37 in England and 11:37 in Jerusalem two minutes ago. That's what made her think about her son sleeping and how close Braun and Conrad would be. So how was it the same time in Zulu *and* in England? Were they near each other? Where's Zulu anyway? Wasn't it in Africa?

Quickly, Corrynne searched for the country of Zulu on the time site. There wasn't such a place. Next she Googled the word. Suddenly she realized Zulu wasn't a country, it was the name of an African ethnic group. Feeling silly at her ignorance, she knew that the term "Zulu" must apply to something else rather than a place.

Returning to the previous Internet site, she searched how the word "Zulu" was being used. She saw a link that said, "What is Zulu?" She clicked on it. A script appeared that told her that Zulu[4] represented the zero meridian of the world, which passed through Greenwich London. It was the place in which all other time on the earth was calculated by time zones. Other time zones were identified by a reverse-order alphabet and words that represented each letter. She wasn't sure, but it looked like Utah was in the "T zone," or the "Tango Zone." She continued to read that Greenwich Mean Time and Zulu time were synonymous, as was UTC, which stood for "Universal Time Coordinated."

Corrynne stopped and thought. It was confusing that England, Zulu, UTC, and GMT were all different names for the same thing. But one subject was becoming clearer. England seemed like the center of many things. She reviewed quickly how often Europe had come up in her thoughts over the last couple weeks. Not only was it the time center of the world, but Europe was going to be the center for many of the things that would take place in the last days. It would eventually dominate the world, create a one-world economy, and combine with the Antichrist. She wondered if it were an accident that the UN was now located in Europe, too. She had a feeling that it wasn't.

A new comprehension came over her. There was only two hours difference between England to Jerusalem, bringing Braun and Conrad close to each other but it also meant that since they were geographically close to each other, it wouldn't be difficult for a UN ground army to attack Jerusalem. It was a thought she hadn't considered before. In Corrynne's mind's eye, she imagined the armies of the earth gathering against Jerusalem just as the scriptures prophesied.[5] Would the UN be the instigator of that invasion? It had already used its power to make Israel give in to the Palestinians, and she knew that if the contention continued, there would be more acts of force from the UN. That would definitely fulfill the scriptural account of the future stating that all the nations of the earth would fight against Jerusalem.[6]

Corrynne's mind was whirling with thoughts as she picked up the piece of paper on which she had written the numbers from Imam Mahdi's site. She whispered rapidly to herself as she began to put the pieces together, "Zulu...fire...blood...seven hours difference...Europe as the center...." It was beginning to make sense! "If Imam Mahdi's organization was worldwide, it would make sense that he would use Zulu time to communicate with his followers. Quickly she hit the back button a couple times to take her to Imam Mahdi's Internet site. She found the clock now read 01:03:05, 02:10:30. Quickly she did the math. Now she *knew* it was a count down! If it was 2:50 p.m. now in Utah, then in England or Zulu time, it was 9:50. In 10 minutes and 30 seconds it would be 10:00 p.m.! 2 hours past that it would be 12:00 midnight! The fire and blood, whatever is meant by that, would happen at midnight Zulu time! The clock on the Internet site was counting down to some event!

A vision of Imam Mahdi filled her thoughts, reminding her of his angry predictions. She remembered him telling Bo at the Rave that he could call fire down from heaven and that society would fall in its own blood so that he could rebuild a perfect society. She understood plainly that he was planning to somehow cause an attack somewhere involving fire and blood. She remembered Dane telling her that Bat members were supposed to be protected from such a strike.

"Oh, this is big!" Corrynne said out loud as she stood up from her seat and then sat down again. She felt like she needed to do something but didn't know what. After looking around, she focused on the screen again. "Now I need to calm down and find out what the first set of numbers stands for. They might refer to a date. I can figure this out," she told herself.

With a concerted effort to focus, Corrynne stared at the unmoving first set of numbers reading 01:03:05. She wondered if they were also a countdown. She tried to remember the Saturday date when she first saw the numbers on Imam Mahdi's site. She counted back and realized that nine days had passed. Since today was Monday, September 25th, that would have made that day September 16th. Yes, and that matched what she remembered. The clock had read 01:03:14. She had stared at them that day too. With that confirmation, Corrynne knew that the last digits of the sequence represented the days, because fourteen minus nine was five. Excitedly, Corrynne continued her line of reasoning, realizing that if her theory was correct, she would know for sure in two hours, because in two hours England time would reflect the next day, and the number in the last section should change.

Next she focused on the second set of digits in the first sequence. She realized that, since it was the end of September, a new month would begin in five days. If her logic were true, then the numbers in the middle would change also. Once they did, that would leave the numbers in the beginning of the sequence to represent years. She was sure of it and she would look for it.

Corrynne firmly planted her elbow on the desk in front of her and rested her chin on her palm. She looked up at the wall, as if it held the answers to her questions. She contemplated waiting five days. In this situation, she wasn't sure that she wanted to. Instead, she decided to continue to search the Internet. Maybe there was something about how dates were written in England that might help her.

Corrynne hit the back button on her Internet browser a couple of times, which took her to the world time site that she had originally selected. Her eyes quickly scanned the information on the first page. She pushed the page-down button until she saw a frame that showed her the current Greenwich time again; only this time she noticed that it had the date as well as the time. Underneath the date and time there was a subscript. In tiny letters it said, "The international standard (ISO 8601) date notation is YY:MM:DD."[7] Corrynne stared at it for a moment. She knew in an instant that the clock was displaying the countdown in the very same format. The days matched the days place, and since the time was being expressed according to Zulu time, why wouldn't the countdown also be expressed in international format? ...Now it seemed all too obvious.

Corrynne could feel her heart beating fast. She swallowed. She was almost afraid now to calculate the date the clock referred to. Slowly, as if her hands were swimming in molasses, she picked up her scratch paper again. She held it frozen in front of her. Her eyes focused and refocused as she gathered her courage.... "One year...three months...and five days...." She began to calculate the months. "October, November, December...that would take us to...midnight on New Year's Eve next year." Understanding was filling her mind. "Midnight, take away seven hours for the time zone difference, would be 5:00 p.m. here on New Year's Eve." Corrynne sat numb, still holding the piece of paper in her hand, not knowing what to do next.

"Fire, blood, destruction, terror...beasts acting together...break down to build up...." The knowledge she had learned over the last few weeks rippled through her mind.

Corrynne closed her eyes. It was too much.

Notes to "This Too Shall Pass Away"

Countdown

[1] An internship at the United Nations is a factual position. For more information, you can retrieve eligibility criteria at http://www.un.org/Depts/OHRM/examin/internsh/intern.htm .

[2] The details provided in this text are fictional and point to future expectations of the UN. For current detail, see the above Web site.

[3] Greenwich Mean Time is the actual time clock of the world out of England. For all factual information about universal time, or time zones of different places on the earth, see http://greenwichmeantime.com. See http://www.cl.cam.ac.uk/~mgk25/iso-time.html#time for universal time notation.

[4] Zulu does in fact represent the zero meridian of the earth. For more information and definitions of time acronyms, see http://www.cl.cam.ac.uk/~mgk25/iso-time.html#zone.

[5] "And thou shalt come up against my people of Israel, as a cloud to cover the land; it shall be in the latter days, and I will bring thee against my land, that the heathen may know me, when I shall be sanctified in thee, O Gog, before their eyes" (Ezekiel 38:16).

[6] "For I will gather all nations against Jerusalem to battle; and the city shall be taken, and the houses rifled, and the women ravished; and half of the city shall go forth into captivity, and the residue of the people shall not be cut off from the city" (Zechariah 14:2).

[7] International standard date notation can be found at this Internet address: http://www.cl.cam.ac.uk/~mgk25/iso-time.html#date.

MILLENNIAL GLORY VI

The AFFLICTION

of

JUSTICE

Look for it!

WWW.MILLENNIALGLORY.COM

MEDICAL TERMS GLOSSARY

Acetaminophen   Medication that reduces pain and fever. Tylenol is a brand name.

Adrenaline   A hormone that stimulates the body increasing heart rate and blood pressure.

Amoxicillin Antibiotic   Kills bacteria. Often used for ear infections.

Amp, Ampule   Medication contained in one glass container.

Antibiotics   Medicine that kills bacteria.

Antibodies   Products of the immune system, which target foreign substances in the body such as bacteria, fungus, and viruses.

Antipyretics   Medicines that lower fevers. Aspirin, Ibuprofen, and Acetaminophen are examples.

Arrhythmia   Irregular beat of the heart.

Asystole   Absence of heartbeat.

Atrial flutter   When the upper chambers of the heart beat more often than the ventricles.

Atrium   Upper chambers of the heart.

Atropine   Drug used to speed up the heart rate, increase blood pressure, and normalize heart rhythm. Used in Code situations.

Bolus   Concentrated substance given at one time.

Cardiac   Having to do with the heart.

Cardiopulmonary arrest Heart lung failure.

Catecholamine   Chemicals the body uses in stressful situations, like adrenaline.

Cath lab   A specialty procedural room in which the heart vessels are opened to stop evolving heart attacks or avoid future heart damage.

CDC   Center for Disease Control.

Central line   Large IV that is inserted in a main vessel that leads to the heart. Used for strong drugs that can irritate smaller vessels.

Claforan   Antibiotic, drug that kills bacteria.

Code blue   Code word to indicate a patient whose heart or lungs have stopped functioning normally and need medical support.

Coma	Unconscious state.
Compromised patients	A patient that has many physical problems, including low immunity.
CPR	Cardiopulmonary resuscitation. Procedure that consists of forcing the heart to beat and the lungs to inflate.
Cranial	Having to do with the head.
Crash cart	Slang medical word to indicate a cart that holds all the supplies and electrical equipment needed to perform life saving procedures due to a stopped or erratic heartbeat.
D50	A sugar solution compatible for blood infusion. Used in situations of low blood sugar.
Diaphoretic	Sweating.
Dilated pupils	Pupils dilate to the absence of light, stress, and brain damage.
DNA	Deoxyribonucleic acid. The cell center that controls the functions of the cell.
Dopamine	Drug used to treat shock due to difficulties with the heart, kidneys or infections.
EKG	Electrocardiogram. An electrical tracing that senses the heart pattern.
Endotracheal tube	A tube placed in the trachea to help the patient breathe.
Enterococci	Types of bacteria found in the intestines. There are strains that are becoming resistant to antibiotics.
Epinephrine	Drug that restores cardiac rhythm in cardiac arrest.
ER	Emergency Room.
Fentanyl	Extremely strong pain medication.
Gentamicin	Strong antibiotic drug that kills bacteria.
Grand mal seizure	Major seizure characterized by loss of consciousness and convulsions.
Gurney	Wheeled cot used in hospitals.
Hematocrit	A percentage of red blood cells in whole blood.
Ibuprophen	Medication that reduces pain and fever. Longer-acting than acetaminophen. Brand names are Advil and Motrin.
ICU	Intensive Care Unit. The unit in the hospital that cares for the most physiologically fragile patients.
Infusion	The act of dripping a fluid into the veins of a patient.

Intensivist	A doctor whose specialty is intensive medicine found in the ICU.
Intubate	The action of inserting a breathing tube down the throat to help a person breathe.
IV	Intravenous, referring to administration of fluids or medications into a vein through a plastic catheter.
Joules	Unit of electrical energy.
Levophed	Drug used to restore a falling blood pressure to normal levels.
LPN	Licensed Practical Nurse, a nurse who can practice under the direction of a registered nurse or doctor.
Methicillin	Antibiotic, kills bacteria. Related to penicillin. Bacteria are becoming resistant to its effects.
Milliequivilants	One thousandth strength of a chemical. Often electrolytes like potassium are expressed in this measurement.
Necrosis, necrotic	Dead or dying tissue.
Nitroglycerin	Drug used for chest pain, heart attacks, and high blood pressure.
Op site	Clear dressing placed over a wound or IV.
Pacer pads	Pads applied to the body that deliver electrical shocks to control the beat of the heart.
Passive immunity	Antibodies made by one person and then given to another to combat a bacteria or virus.
Pathophysiology	Study of diseased states of the body.
Penicillin	One of the first antibiotics created to kill bacteria.
Pericardium	Protective layer that surrounds the heart.
Plasma	The fluid part of blood in which the red and white blood cells are suspended.
Pneumothorax	Collapsed lung.
PRN	Medical term that stands for "as needed." Medicines, nursing staff, treatments are ordered "PRN" or "as needed" depending on the situation.
Prophylactic	Preventive treatment against diseases.
Prostaglandins	Substances within the body responsible for fevers.
Pseudomonas	Bacteria found in the soil and on fresh fruits and vegetables. Physiologically threatening to people with low immunity. There are strains that are becoming resistant to antibiotics.

Resistant bacteria	Bacteria that has developed ways to counteract antibiotics.
RN	Registered Nurse. Licensed professional practitioner who can function independently or under the direction of a doctor.
Rohypnol	Drug used illegally to cause memory loss or unconsciousness.
Saline	Salt water that is compatible with the blood.
Sepsis	A system-wide infection with bacteria, fungus, or viruses in the blood.
Serum	Pink tinged fluid originating from blood, void of red blood cells and clotting factors.
Sinus rhythm	A normal heartbeat.
ST elevation	A pattern on the EKG which tells medical personnel the heart is not getting enough oxygen. A sign of a heart attack.
Staph aureus	Bacteria found on the skin becoming resistant to antibiotics.
Stat	A medical word meaning "immediately."
Transducer	A device that translates a measurement of blood pressure or another pressure to the monitor and computer systems.
Triage	The transfer of a patient from one unit in the hospital to another.
Valium	Drug used to relieve anxiety. Used to treat seizures.
Vasoactive drips	Medications given in the veins that control the diameter of the vessels to raise or lower blood pressure.
Ventilator	Machine that pushes air into lungs of those who are too sick to breathe on their own.
Ventricles	Bottom chambers of the heart.
Versed	Drug used to relax and sedate patients. The effect of the drug causes amnesia.
Vital signs	Measurements of heart rate, respirations, blood pressure, and oxygenation.